The Solomon Curse

ALSO BY CLIVE CUSSLER

The Solomon Curse

CLIVE CUSSLER
and RUSSELL BLAKE

MICHAEL JOSEPH
an imprint of
PENGUIN BOOKS

MICHAEL JOSEPH

UK | USA | Canada | Ireland | Australia
India | New Zealand | South Africa

Michael Joseph is part of the Penguin Random House group of companies
whose addresses can be found at global.penguinrandomhouse.com.

First published in the USA by G. P. Putnam's Sons 2015
First published in Great Britain by Michael Joseph 2015
001

Text copyright © Sandecker, RLLLP, 2015

The moral right of the author has been asserted

Printed in Great Britain by Clays Ltd, St Ives plc

A CIP catalogue record for this book is available from the British Library

HARDBACK ISBN: 978–0–718–17989–2
TPB ISBN: 978–0–718–17990–8

www.greenpenguin.co.uk

MIX
Paper from
responsible sources
FSC® C018179

Penguin Random House is committed to a
sustainable future for our business, our readers
and our planet. This book is made from Forest
Stewardship Council® certified paper.

The Solomon Curse

PROLOGUE

Guadalcanal, Solomon Islands, one week ago

Aldo pounded through the brush, crashing through the jungle, as he ran for his life. His breathing rasped as he pushed vines from his path, sweat coursing down his face, eyes searching for a hint of a trail. Branches scratched him, drawing blood. Ignoring the pain, he drove himself harder, listening for sounds of pursuit.

He stopped at the edge of a winding stream, a tangerine moonglow on its rippling surface, and debated crossing it to continue deeper into the rain forest or following it to the sea.

Then he heard them.

Dogs.

They weren't far behind.

He needed to keep moving. If his pursuers caught him, he was worse than dead.

Aldo's bare feet splashed in the stream as he chose to follow the water. A jagged stone tore his foot open. Ignoring the spike of pain, he continued along the far bank, veering in and out of the water to throw off the dogs.

His moves were driven purely by instinct. Aldo was just seventeen, but tonight he'd die like a man if he was caught.

The thought fueled him: lose them or die. There was no third option.

He picked up his pace when he heard the snap of twigs behind him. Only a heartbeat away. Urging himself forward, caution abandoned, he fought to put enough distance between himself and his trackers to buy a slim chance at survival.

A native of Guadalcanal, Aldo never came to this part of the island—nobody did—so he had no special knowledge of the area, no sly tricks that would gain him an advantage. All he had was panic-fueled energy and the desperation of a cornered rat.

He heard them closing in on him.

How had he gotten sucked into this nightmare? It seemed impossible, yet he was racing for his life in the dark of night. A thicket of bamboo rose out of the darkness on his right and for a moment he considered trying to hide, his exhaustion arguing for it with every ragged gasp.

Aldo's side hurt, a sharp lance of pain below his rib cage, but he didn't allow himself to think about it. He had to keep going.

But where? Assuming he evaded his pursuers, where could he go that he would be safe? It was a small island. He could just return home, hoping that it was all a bad dream. But they would come for him before he could tell anyone and he'd just disappear.

Like the others.

Thunder roared overhead. The heavens let loose a deluge of warm rain, and Aldo smiled even as his gaze roved over the brush. The rain might throw the dogs off his trail.

A bolt of lightning streaked across the sky and for a second his surroundings lit up in the bright flash. He spotted a faint game track in the heavy foliage to his left and made a snap decision. The ground was spongy and slick from the cloudburst as he climbed the bank and followed the route parallel to the waterline. Now Aldo could clearly hear the dogs on his trail, all pretense of stealth discarded as they sensed his proximity.

Any hope he'd lost them evaporated as claws scrabbled on the ground behind him, followed by clomping boots. Aldo willed himself to move even faster, now running blind, the skin of his feet shredded and bleeding.

And then he tumbled and slipped onto his back and down a slope on a blanket of wet leaves, gravity pulling him inexorably to the bottom of the gulch the trail skirted. He thudded to a stop, stunned, his momentum halted by a tree trunk. When he reached up and felt his skull, his fingers came away slick with blood. Gulping for air like a drowning man, he tried to orient himself as he fought the dizziness.

Aldo forced himself up. His ribs and left arm radiated pain and immediately he knew he'd broken bones. Thankfully, not the ones he needed to run, but the agony was enough to hobble him in the harsh environment. He looked around in the near-total darkness, his vision blurry from the fall, and spotted a promising opening between the vines. He moved into the gap and found himself on another track.

His pulse thudded in his ears as he drove himself to the limits of his endurance. His cracked ribs sent searing spasms through his chest with each breath. The sound of his trackers faded as he pushed himself to the brink, and for the first time since he'd bolted for freedom he dared hope he might make it.

Aldo's foot snagged under a vine and he went down. He uttered an involuntary cry as he hit the ground and his ankle gave way with a sickening snap. Tears of rage welled in his eyes, and then the world faded as he passed out.

When he regained consciousness a few minutes later, Aldo found himself staring into a snarling canine's muzzle. His heart sank even before the hated voice of his pursuer drifted to him through a fog—the last words he'd ever hear, he was sure.

"Don't you know you can never escape on an island?"

A boot slammed into his temple before he could get his mouth to cooperate with his brain, to protest or plead or curse or beg for mercy. A starburst exploded in his head; the agony was excruciating. He tried to muster a defense, but his arms and legs were leaden.

Aldo's last thought was that this was some kind of mistake, a misunderstanding, and then the boot landed again, harder. His neck snapped with a crack, and Aldo's final living sensation was the tingle of the warm rain splattering on his face, and then he silently slipped into another world.

CHAPTER 1

Guadalcanal, Solomon Islands, 1170 A.D.

Dawn's glow shimmered off the flat ocean as a column of islanders marched along a jungle trail, their voices hushed as they neared the coast and their destination, the new city said to have been built on the very surface of the sea.

At the head of the group was the chief holy man, decked out in a colorful robe in defiance of the ever-present heat. His skin was the color of jerky, and a sheen of sweat coated his face. One of the few to have already made the pilgrimage to the just completed palace near the western tip of Guadalcanal, he was now leading his flock to the site. He gazed back at the procession with satisfaction—he'd collected the most important men in the kingdom for the journey, many of whom were newly arrived from the surrounding islands, for the ceremony and festivities that were to last the remainder of the week.

Slivers of light filtered through the overhead canopy of tropical trees as the group moved along the faint game trail, surrounded on all sides by dense jungle. The islands were untamed, and the majority of the Guadalcanal tribes lived within a hundred yards of the shore, avoiding the inland areas that abounded with predators both real and imagined. Legends of giants, ferocious creatures more than twice the size of a man, that traversed the island through a series of underground caves and satisfied their thirst for human blood by attacking the unwary or the careless. Besides, there was no reason to brave the unknown in the interior of the island when a generous bounty from the sea could be had for the asking.

The shaman halted at the top of a rise. The miracle beyond now jutted from the bay—buildings rising from the waves where before had only been water. He pointed at the impossible spectacle with his staff, ornately carved with reliefs of deities, and murmured the king's name in a tone reserved for prayer to the gods. Indeed, the king seemed like he'd descended from heaven, so unlike ordinary men that he had become a legend in his own lifetime.

This—King Loc's greatest achievement—made all his others pale in comparison. Loc's vision of a series of man-made islets had been realized using local rock in the relatively shallow half-moon-shaped harbor. After the celebration, the buildings would be used as the royal residence.

The island's holy men considered the compound sacred, evidence of Loc's divine superiority. His builders had spent a decade creating it, with thousands of men quarrying and transporting the rock to the shore. Nothing like it had ever been seen, and the king had assured his counselors that its completion signaled the beginning of a new era.

Nobody doubted his word—Loc was a ruler who had transformed his island from a humble trading collective to a wealthy kingdom, an empire with untold riches legendary among his people. By organizing a primitive mining effort focused on locating gemstones and gold, he'd made the island's fortunes. What had been just another stop on a lackluster trade route had become a hub of wealth whispered about on distant shores.

Over the years, the islanders had grown to appreciate the value of their legacy. Traders from other islands and as far away as Japan came to exchange goods for the treasures the natives amassed. Gold was especially prized, and now there were whole tribes devoted to mining the precious metal in the mountains. Their existence had evolved into one of relative prosperity, all under the encouragement and watchful eye of their benevolent ruler.

The shaman and his followers shuffled forward and filled the clearing at the top of the hill, surrounding the holy man with murmurs of awe and disbelief. A stocky chieftain from the large island to the south moved to the shaman's side and pointed at a platform on the nearest islet, where a group of figures emerged slowly from an ornately crafted stone temple.

"Is that Loc?" he asked, squinting at the tallest of the men, whose tunic's gemstones and gold adornments glinted in the sunlight.

The holy man answered, "Yes. It is he."

"The temple is magnificent," the chieftain said. "It symbolizes the beginning of our thousand-year ascension as foretold in the prophecy."

It was widely held that Loc's reign symbolized the start of a golden era for the islands, a time when the kingdom would become the region's power center, revered by all, and prophesied to last twenty lifetimes. The oral traditions spoke of a powerful magic that would accompany the appearance of the "chosen one," the earthly embodiment of celestial power. It was believed that Loc was that being. The massive treasure he had accumulated only solidified his position, as if the earth were validating his dominance by offering its riches to its new master.

The chieftain nodded. Who could doubt that this was no ordinary man, given the strides he had made since taking the throne? Any skepticism the chieftain might have harbored vanished at the spectacle before him. When he returned to his island, he would bring with him miraculous news.

A flock of birds flapped noisily into the sky, sharp cries piercing the morning stillness and reverberating through the rain forest. The shaman looked around at the assembly, a puzzled expression on his face, and then the ground began to tremble. The shaking was accompanied by a dull roar. His breath caught in his throat as the vibrations intensified, and then the earth began pitching like the deck of a ship in a storm as he groped for a nearby vine to steady himself.

A man screamed as the ground split beneath him and he disappeared into a steaming fissure. His companions scattered as more rents in the earth's crust tore open. The world tilted, and the shaman dropped to his knees, a prayer frozen on his lips, as he gazed out at where the new city had stood.

The temple and islet where Loc had been moments before were gone. The water had pulled back from the shore as though sucking out to sea any trace of the impudent king's puny attempts to conquer nature. What had taken ten years to build was erased in a moment as the earthquake intensified, and the entire coastline dropped into nothingness as the bottom of the bay collapsed.

The holy man's eyes widened in terror as the ocean rushed to fill the chasm that had been the shallow bay, and then as suddenly as the nightmare had started, it was over. The island lay still. The hiss of vapor from the new cracks in the earth's crust was the only sound besides the moans of injured and terrified tribesmen. The survivors were on their knees, looking to the holy man for guidance. His panicked gaze roamed over the sea, and then he forced himself to his feet.

"Run. Get to higher ground. Now," he cried, clambering up the trail as fast as his shaky legs would carry him. He had heard stories of moving walls of water from the elders of the dim past, when the gods of earth and sea had fought for dominance, and some primitive part of his brain understood that when the ocean returned, sucked into the new trench that was even now filling, it would do so with a vengeance.

The men ran in confused flight to a safe elevation, but only a few made it. When the tsunami attacked the island, the wave was a hundred feet high. The surge as it crashed against the unyielding rock carried half a mile inland, wiping the ground clean like the swipe of the sea god's hand.

That night, the shaman and a handful of the survivors huddled around a campfire, well away from the shore, the ocean no longer their benevolent provider.

"It is the end of days," the holy man said with the conviction of a true believer. "Our ruler has angered the giant gods. There is no other explanation for what we endured. We have been cursed for our arrogance and all we can do is pray for forgiveness and return to lives of humility."

The men nodded. Their king had put himself on the same level as the giant gods and had been punished for his insufferable sin of pride. His temples and palace were gone, and he with them, erased as though he'd never existed.

In the following days, the survivors gathered and spoke in hushed tones of the day the gods' harsh justice had been meted out. The holy men gathered for a summit, and after three nights emerged from their sacred grove to counsel the islanders. The king's name must never be spoken again, and any reference to his kingdom, his temples to his own glory, would be erased from their collective memory. The only hope was that by banishing his existence from the island's lore, the giants would be appeased and forgive the islanders for his actions.

The stretch of coast where the city had once stood was considered cursed by those who lived through the disaster. Over time, the precise reason was forgotten, as were the events of the dark times that ended the island's prosperity. Eventually, the cove that looked out over the placid bay became an encampment of the diseased and the dying, a place of suffering colored by a reputation for misfortune that grew hazier over the years.

Occasionally the king's name could be heard as a muttered curse, but, beyond that, his thousand-year legacy faded into obscurity, and within a few lifetimes Loc was only remembered in forbidden stories told in whispers by the rebellious. The legend of his divine palace and its riches diminished with each successive generation until finally it was considered to be folklore, ignored by the young, who had no time for the fearful stories of the past.

CHAPTER 2

Solomon Sea, February 8, 1943

Gale-force winds churned the heavy seas into white foam as the Japanese destroyer *Konami* plowed southeast of Bougainville Island. The ship was running without lights in the predawn gloom as it bucked through the massive waves. Engines strained as forty- and fifty-foot breaking cliffs of black water slammed into the bow.

Conditions aboard were miserable. The vessel rolled ominously as it pursued a course well away from the calm straits to the west, where the naval force evacuating the last of the soldiers stationed on Guadalcanal was steaming through flat ocean.

The Yūgumo-class destroyer, with a long waterline and sleek engineering, was capable of over thirty-five knots wide open. But tonight it was crawling along at less than a third of that speed, and the power plants throbbed steadily belowdecks as the weather slowed its progress to a crawl.

The sudden squall had hit unexpectedly, and the exhausted and emaciated soldiers being transported home were hard-pressed to keep their rations of rice down. Even the seasoned faces of the sailors were strained at the pounding they were receiving. One of the seamen moved along the cots, dispensing water to the soldiers, offering what limited comfort he could. Their uniforms were little more than rags now, their bodies in the final throes of starvation.

On the bridge, Captain Hashimoto watched as the helmsman tried to meet the chaotic swells to soften the worst of them. There seemed to be no rhythm or direction to the confused seas, and the ship was battling to stay on course. He'd briefly considered deviating to flatter water but had chosen to keep forging north toward Japan. His schedule allowed no time for detours whatever the reason.

The destroyer had been conscripted on a top secret mission under cover of darkness, capitalizing on the confusion caused by the Japanese's final evacuation of the island. The officer they had taken aboard had been deemed too important to the war effort to be risked in the main evacuation, so he and his elite staff had been spirited away aboard the *Konami*, which had veered east while the rest of the force proceeded on a more westerly tack, running the customary gauntlet from Guadalcanal to Bougainville Island.

Hashimoto didn't know what was so special about the army officer who required the dispatch of a destroyer for his transport. He didn't care. He was accustomed to following orders, often seemingly in conflict with common sense. His role as a Japanese destroyer commander wasn't to second-guess the high command—if the powers in Tokyo wanted him to take his crew to hell and back, his only question would be how soon they wanted him to leave.

A monster of a wave appeared from out of nowhere on the port side and slammed into the ship with such force that the entire vessel shuddered, jarring Hashimoto from his position. He grabbed the console for support, and the helmsman glanced at him with a worried look. Hashimoto's scowl matched the storm's ferocity as he debated giving the order he hated. He sighed and grunted as another mammoth roller approached.

"Back off to ten knots," he grumbled, the lines in his face deepening with the words.

"Aye, aye, sir," the helmsman acknowledged.

Both men watched as the next cliff of water rose out of the night and blasted over the bow, for a moment submerging it before passing over the ship's length. The vessel keeled dangerously to starboard but then righted itself as it continued its assault on the angry seas.

Captain Hashimoto was no stranger to rough weather, having guided his vessel through some of the worst the oceans could throw at the ship since her christening a year earlier. He'd been through two typhoons, survived every type of adversity, and come out alive. But tonight's freak storm was pushing the limits of the ship's handling and he knew it.

When morning came, he'd be faced with an even greater danger— the possibility of being hit by a carrier-launched Allied plane equipped with a torpedo. Night was his cloak, and usually his friend—with light came vulnerability and the ever-present threat of breaking the streak of good fortune that had marked his short wartime career.

Hashimoto understood that at some point his number would be up, but not tonight—and not from a little wind and a few waves. Could it be that the war was lost now that their occupation of Guadalcanal was over? If so, he would do his duty to the end and die a courageous death that would do justice to his rank and family name—that was a given— and he would follow the course of so many of his fellow combatants in the best samurai tradition.

The army officer they'd rescued from the island entered the bridge from below. His face was sallow and drawn but his bearing ramrod stiff. He nodded to Hashimoto with a curt economy of motion and eyed the frothing sea through the windshield.

"We've slowed?" he asked, his sandpaper voice hushed.

"Yes. Better to proceed with caution in this weather than race to the bottom."

The man grunted as though disagreeing and studied the glowing instruments. "Anything on radar?"

Hashimoto shook his head and then braced himself for another jolt as a big wave reared out of the darkness and broke against the bow with startling ferocity. He stole a glance at the army officer's face and saw nothing but determination and fatigue—and something else, in the depth of his eyes. Something dark that caused Hashimoto a flutter of anxiety, an unfamiliar sensation for the battle-hardened veteran. The man's eyes looked like one of the classical illustrations of an *oni*, a demon, from his childhood. The thought sprang to mind unbidden and he shrugged it off. He was no longer seven years old and had seen real-world devils since the war had started; he had no need for belief in the mythical past.

He was turning to ask the officer what he could do for him when the ship shuddered like it had run aground, and then everyone on the bridge was yelling as alarms sounded.

"What's going on?" the officer demanded.

"I don't know." The captain didn't want to speak his darkest fear out loud.

"Did we hit something?"

Hashimoto hesitated. "There's nothing to hit. We're in nine thousand feet of water." He paused as a junior officer approached with a pallid face and gave a grim report. Hashimoto nodded and issued a terse instruction, then turned back to the army man. "I'm afraid we must prepare for an unpleasant possibility. I need to ask you to go below and follow the emergency instructions that are issued."

"What?"

Hashimoto sighed. "It appears that a repaired area of the hull has split open. We're going to do everything we can, but it's uncertain whether the pumps can keep up. If not, we may have to abandon ship."

The officer's face went deathly white. "In this?" He stared through the glass at the storm.

"We'll know soon enough. Hopefully, we can control the damage." He looked away. "Please. Leave me to my duty."

The army officer nodded grimly. He turned and moved to the stairs and barely kept his feet when another big wave crashed into the port bow, causing the ship to list alarmingly.

Hashimoto went through the motions, directing his crew to take all possible measures as the helmsman struggled to keep the ship right, but in the end the fury of the sea proved too much. As the dark waves continued their assault and the last of the bridge lights flickered off, the vessel's heavy steel hull now an anchor as it sank, his thoughts drifted to his wife, Yuki, and his one-year-old son—the son with whom he'd only spent a few short hours while on leave and who he'd never see grow into a man.

But even that vision couldn't erase the shame he felt at having failed in his mission. He vowed that he would die with dignity, going down with his ship, rather than struggling to survive like a coward.

Three hours later, the seas flattened as the storm moved north. The depths had swallowed the four-hundred-foot-long ship without a trace. With no record of its journey and no escort or other vessels within hailing distance, its demise would go unremarked, its existence scrubbed from the official record, taking its final secret to the bottom with it.

Only four survivors were eventually rescued by an Allied ship; heavy weather and sharks killed the rest. The Allied command showed no interest in what a Japanese ship was doing so far off the beaten path, and the men pulled from the ocean had nothing to offer but stoic silence. Their part in the war was over, their disgrace a fate worse than death.

CHAPTER 3

Guadalcanal, Solomon Islands, present day

Three fiberglass skiffs tugged at the lines that secured their bows to palm trees as the cobalt blue water surrounding them sparkled in the afternoon sun. Sam and Remi Fargo sat in the shade of one of the palms, the fronds stirring in the light breeze. Remi shielded her eyes from the glare with a manicured hand and watched the heads of divers bob to the surface near a fourth boat ninety yards offshore.

Sam shifted and brushed his fingers through his medium brown hair and glanced at his wife and partner for life. Refined features bereft of makeup were framed by long auburn hair, and her smooth skin glowed from the sun's caress. His gaze traced down her athletic form, and he reached out a hand to her. She took it with a smile and sighed. Even after countless globe-trotting adventures in search of archaeological treasures, they were still inseparable, a testimony to the strength of their bond.

"I could get used to lying on this beach, Sam," she said, closing her eyes.

"It's gorgeous, I'll give you that," he agreed.

"If only they had a Bloomingdale's . . ."

"Or a decent dive shop."

"To each their own." Remi slipped a Valentino flip-flop off her heel and dangled it from her toe.

They hadn't been sure what to expect when they'd agreed to fly to Guadalcanal and were relieved to find themselves in a tropical paradise of warm water and blue sky.

A tall, lanky man in his fifties approached from down the spit of sand, with a face that was red from sunburn, a pair of battered steel-rimmed spectacles perched on his hawklike nose. His scuffed hiking boots threw up a cloud of white with each step. A group of islanders lounged nearby, watching the divers, laughing among themselves at some private joke. The man's shadow stretched long on the shore as he neared them. Sam looked up at the new arrival and a grin lit his ruggedly handsome face.

"Well, Leonid, what do you make of all this?" Sam asked.

"It's definitely unlike anything else on the island," Leonid said in his slight Russian accent. "Looks man-made. But as I said on the phone, that's impossible. It's in eighty feet of water."

"Maybe you found Atlantis," Remi offered brightly, teasing Sam's longtime friend. "Although you're about five thousand miles off the mark, if the traditional accounts are to be believed."

Leonid frowned, his expression conveying nothing but his usual disapproval of anything and everything. An academic on a three-year sabbatical from Moscow, Leonid Vasyev was an unhappy man even when freed from the Russian winter to roam the globe in search of lost civilizations—his passion—made possible by a grant from the Fargo Foundation.

When Sam and Remi had gotten his call about reports of a sunken find in the Solomon Islands, they hadn't hesitated to travel halfway around the world to join him on his quest. They'd landed that morning, arriving too late to secure diving gear until the following day, and had contented themselves with reading the background matter he supplied while enjoying the tranquillity of the beach.

Two weeks earlier, a baffled teacher on Guadalcanal had called her former professor in Australia with an odd story. Her husband and son had registered unusual readings on their new fish finder and had turned to her for help. The Australian had been too busy with classes to do anything besides refer her to Leonid, a colleague she knew was footloose and fully funded.

After a series of long-distance discussions, the reluctant Russian had flown in to see for himself what the teacher was describing. Over the past few days, he'd grown increasingly puzzled by the formations his divers reported. The fishermen had thought that the irregularities might have been war wreckage, but they were mistaken. Their fish finder, one of the first on the island, had spotted something unexplainable—what appeared to be man-made structures jutting up from the bottom of the sea.

That was when Leonid decided to seek out reinforcements. He was an academic, not a deep-water diver, and he knew that he needed help. Since the Fargos were his benefactors and friends, he decided to go straight to the top, and after a long-distance conference call they'd agreed to come join him on Guadalcanal.

"Your underwater camera system could use some fine-tuning," Sam said, eyeing a blurry photograph taken the prior day. "And couldn't you get some photo paper? This looks like someone spilled wine on a newspaper."

"You're lucky I found a place with a color printer. In case you haven't noticed, Guadalcanal isn't La Jolla," Leonid said drily. He considered the image Sam was studying. "Come on. What do you think?"

"It could be just about anything. We'll have to wait until I suit up and dive. This might as well be a Rorschach test, for all the detail it's showing."

"Do you see your mother's angry face?" Remi asked innocently.

Leonid eyed them like they were insects in a jar. "I see the infamous Fargo sense of humor hasn't melted in the heat. That's quite a relief."

"Lighten up, Leonid. We're in paradise, and this seems like it might be exactly the kind of mystery we love. We'll get to the bottom of it," Sam said. "Although Mom did look kind of annoyed in that last snapshot." He looked over at the divers. "You sure I can't borrow some gear from one of the locals?"

Leonid shook his head. "I already asked. They're fiercely protective of their stuff. Sorry. We'll reserve some for tomorrow once we're back in town." Because of the limited amount of equipment, during high season most of the island's reliable gear was already claimed by the local dive tour companies.

"That'll work," Sam said.

"I'm going to check on what the divers found this time around," Leonid said, wiping his brow with the back of his hand.

They watched him trudge down the beach, ungainly as a stork in his long khaki pants and tropical-weight long-sleeved shirt. Remi leaned in to Sam. "What do you make of this?"

Sam shook his head. "I have no clue. I'll reserve judgment until we know more. But it's definitely intriguing."

"What baffles me is how anything could remain undiscovered this close to shore."

Sam looked around the desolate bay. "Well, there isn't a lot going on here, is there?"

Remi nodded. "I think we agreed on that a few minutes ago." She shook out her auburn hair, and Sam noted that she was already getting tanned. He eyed her reclining form and slid closer.

They watched Leonid bark at the lounging islanders, who reluctantly rose and pulled one of the skiffs to the beach so he could board.

A small wiry man wearing cutoffs and a dark brown T-shirt splashed to the stern and hoisted himself over the side. After three energetic pulls on the starter cord, the old motor roared to life, and they backed away from shore and cut a beeline to the dive boat.

Remi glanced down the beach to where several of the islanders were dozing in the shade near the water's edge and sighed.

"You have to admit the place is idyllic. I mean, blue sky, warm water, trade winds . . . What more could you ask for?"

Sam grinned. "Cold beer?"

"The one-track Fargo mind surfaces again."

"Not entirely one-track," Sam said.

Remi laughed. "We'll have to try out a track or two tonight."

Leonid's boat returned several minutes later, and when he disembarked, the frown lines on his face were etched deeper than ever. He glared at the loafing natives and stomped back to where the Fargos were sitting. "They confirmed that there are a number of mounds covered with marine growth. They think they're structures."

Remi's eyes narrowed. "Structures? What kind of structures?"

"They aren't sure, but they appear to be the ruins of buildings."

Sam gazed off at a line of storm clouds on the horizon. "Curiouser and curiouser."

"They have to be ancient," Leonid said, and then glared at the boat. "Damned locals and their superstitions . . ."

Remi's brow furrowed. "Why do you say that?"

"Oh, the head of the local team's giving me problems. Says after this he doesn't want to dive on the site any longer. That he remembers his great-grandfather saying something about this bay being bad juju or some such idiocy." Leonid snorted, and wiped his brow with a soiled red bandanna. "Trying to get more money out of me, the crook. Old gods indeed."

"What did you tell him?"

"That if he wants to get paid at all, he'll finish out today's dives, and then based on what he's able to find, I'll decide whether to hire him again. I won't be extorted. I'm already paying well over top dollar. That shut him up."

Sam studied the Russian. "Leonid, while it warms my heart to see you so tightfisted with our budget, from what you've described, these guys are the only game in town, right? If you don't use them, what's plan B?"

"I'll get my own people to fly in."

"With all their own gear?" Sam asked skeptically.

"Sure," Leonid said, but his look conveyed less confidence than his words.

"If there are really ruins down there, maybe we should try to locate an expedition ship? Something self-contained that can go the long haul?" Remi suggested. "Who do we know in this part of the world?"

Sam thought for a moment. "Nobody springs to mind . . . Leonid?"

The Russian shook his head. "I can ask around."

"We'll give Selma a call. She'll find someone."

Remi nodded. "Too bad there's no handy cell tower nearby."

Sam smiled. "Not a problem. I packed the sat phone," he said, and rooted around in his backpack. He retrieved an old but reliable Iridium Extreme satellite phone, powered it on, and then checked the time. "She should be around."

Leonid shifted from foot to foot, obviously antsy. Sam wandered to the waterline while he listened to the warbling ring, and Leonid returned to the nearest group of natives. After several seconds Selma picked up and her perky voice drifted over the line.

"Selma! Guess who?" Sam said.

"Collection agency?"

"Very funny. How are things in San Diego?"

"Same as they were two days ago when you left. Except Zoltán's eaten another hundred pounds of steak. And Lazlo's loitering around here, driving me nuts."

"Sounds like you've got your hands full. Listen, we've identified something on preliminary dives and want to get a mother ship here. A vessel with all the bells and whistles. Sonar, dive gear, magnometer, the works. Think you can find something suitable?"

"Of course. It's just a question of time and money. When do you need it and for how long?"

"Open-ended on duration, yesterday for how soon."

"So the typical leisurely schedule."

"Never a dull moment, Selma."

"Indeed. I'll get right on it. Probably out of Australia or New Zealand, I'd think."

Sam nodded to himself. "That sounds about right. And could you also pull up anything you have on ancient civilizations in the region?"

"Of course. I'll send whatever I find to your e-mail?"

"That would be perfect, Selma. Good luck on locating a ship."

"Budget constraints?"

"The usual." Meaning none, within reason. The Fargo Foundation had more money than it could spend in ten lifetimes, with additional cash coming in every day from Sam's portfolio of intellectual property relating to his inventions, so expense wasn't an issue on their own expeditions.

"I'll call when I have someone qualified."

"Very well, Selma. Thanks, and pet the bear for us." Zoltán was a massive German shepherd Remi had adopted during an adventure in Hungary who resembled nothing so much as a grizzly walking on all fours.

"Sounds like a good way to lose some fingers, but anything for the cause," Selma teased. Zoltán adored her and glued himself to Selma's side whenever the Fargos were out of town. For her part, she doted on the dog like the child she'd never had, coddling him at every opportunity and spoiling him worse than rotten.

Sam hung up and examined the battery indicator. Plenty of charge.

He returned to Remi and plopped down next to her. "Selma's on the hunt," he reported.

"Good. No offense to Leonid, but a couple of questionable wet suits and a rowboat's probably not the right way to handle this," Remi said.

"True, but I can see his logic. Why call in the cavalry before he knows whether he's found anything? For all he knows, it could have been a downed plane or a sunken landing craft. Don't forget that Guadalcanal was hotly contested during the war. A lot of junk's strewn around the islands."

She nodded. "Some of it still explosive even after all these years."

"Just like you."

Remi ignored him and glanced at the dive boat. "What do you think this is?"

"Man-made structure at eighty feet? You got me." He stretched his arms over his head and eyed Remi. "But we'll know soon enough."

Remi ran her fingers through her hair and was about to reply when the stillness was shattered by a bloodcurdling scream.

CHAPTER 4

Sam leapt to his feet, followed closely by Remi, and they raced to the grove of trees by the water, where the screams were now shrieks of pain. Sam stopped her with an outstretched arm as they neared the thicket and pointed to a long green reptilian tail thrashing out of the brush.

A gurgle and several wet thwacks sounded from the grove. The tail stiffened and lay still. Leonid's boots thumped on the sand behind them as he arrived with other islanders, two of whom were carrying machetes and one a fire axe.

Another agonized scream split the air. Sam stepped through the vegetation and moved next to the massive body of a male saltwater crocodile, now dead from three grisly axe wounds to the head. On the ground in front of it was one of the locals, clutching the mangled remains of his right leg. Five feet away, another islander stood with an ancient axe in his trembling hand, his eyes wide with shock and fear.

A bright stream of arterial blood sprayed from the victim's shredded thigh. Sam pulled his belt free as he knelt next to the victim. Remi closed the distance as he wound the makeshift tourniquet around the man's upper leg and pulled it tight.

The injured man moaned and lost consciousness.

"He's not going to make it unless he reaches a hospital fast," Sam said, his voice tight.

Remi looked up at Leonid. "Let's get him onto one of the trucks. Seconds count," she said.

Leonid was staring at the dead crocodile with saucered eyes, frozen in place, all the color drained from his face.

"Leonid. Come on," Remi snapped, her tone hard.

The Russian spun around to the islanders, who were standing in a group several feet behind him, and ordered them to carry their unfortunate companion to the Land Rover. Nobody moved. Sam shook his head and slipped his arm under the bleeding man. "Get out of my way," he said, and lifted the victim upright. Remi rushed to help him, and together they carried him to a vehicle parked near the trail that led from the main road.

They loaded him into the backseat in seconds, and Sam turned to Leonid, who was arguing with one of the locals near the water's edge. "Who's the best driver?" he demanded, but the men shook their heads.

Remi and Sam exchanged a glance, and Sam held out his hand. "Fine. Give me the keys. I don't know what's wrong with you people, but your friend here is dying and needs help. Who can show me where the nearest hospital is?"

Leonid fumbled in his pockets as the islanders muttered among themselves, and then a youth in his late teens stepped forward. "I'll go. That's my uncle Benji," he said, his English thick with a pidgin accent.

"What's your name?" Remi asked as she climbed into the passenger seat.

"Ricky."

Sam slid behind the wheel. Leonid moved to the door and handed him the keys. "I'll be right behind you in the orange truck."

"Fine." Sam looked at Ricky. "Get in the back with your uncle and make sure the belt stays tight. How far are we from the hospital?"

"Maybe forty-five minutes . . ." Ricky said doubtfully.

Sam frowned. "Buckle up. We'll see if we can make it in fifteen."

Remi and Ricky strapped in as Sam cranked the engine. He dropped the transmission into gear and they roared off, bouncing down the track that was little more than a thinning passageway through the encroaching jungle. The big motor labored on the mushy terrain, and it took what seemed like forever to reach the ragged pavement strip of the coastal road that ringed the island. Once on the asphalt, Sam floored the gas, his gaze intent, his concentration absolute, and the SUV surged forward, tires screeching as he took the curves at double any sane speed.

Remi's knuckles whitened as she gripped the armrest. "It won't help him very much if they have to send an ambulance to scrape us off a rock."

"Don't worry. I used to own a Ferrari."

They drifted around a bend, all four tires protesting as they lost traction. Sam gunned the engine and downshifted to regain control. After a glance at Remi, he shrugged and slowed a few miles per hour, still pushing the limit of what the heavy vehicle could manage.

Remi twisted to look at the injured man, who was soaked in blood and laboring for breath. Ricky had his hand clenched on the belt, a frightened expression on his young face. His eyes met Remi's and he swallowed hard.

"You think he'll make it?" he asked.

"We'll do everything we can to see that he does. What's the hospital like? How advanced is it?" she asked.

He shook his head. "I guess it's okay. I've never been anywhere else, so I don't know what others are like."

"Do they deal with a lot of injuries?"

"I think so." He sounded doubtful.

Sam accelerated on a relatively straight stretch and called over his shoulder. "Are there many crocodile attacks here?"

Another shrug. "A few. Mostly, people just disappear, so we don't know for sure the crocs got them." His tone was matter-of-fact, like he was describing the regular rainstorms or the onset of old age.

Remi fixed him with a hard stare. "Why didn't anyone help him?"

Ricky scowled. "They're superstitious. They were so busy talking about how the area is cursed, nobody could decide what to do. It's like that a lot when there's any sort of disagreement."

"Cursed?" Remi repeated.

"One of the older divers was saying there were rumors that it's haunted. Damned. Like I said, superstition." He regarded his uncle. "At least I think so."

"That was a huge crocodile. Weighed at least a couple thousand pounds," Sam said. "No superstition required, just a hungry croc and a couple of guys not watching what they were doing."

"Is Leonid going to have a hard time getting anyone to help him now?" Remi asked.

Ricky looked away. "Not a lot of people want to push their luck in crocodile territory for a few dollars a day," he explained.

Sam caught Remi's expression and dared a glance in the rearview mirror.

"No, I don't suppose they would." It was obvious to everyone that Leonid's exploration had just hit a major obstacle, if not a wall. "I can't believe that nobody had a rifle if there are crocodiles around this area."

Ricky shook his head. "Guns are illegal here. Ever since the Australian peacekeeping force took over."

"That's a big win for the crocs, I suppose," Remi said.

They rounded the westernmost point of the island and headed east toward the capital city of Honiara, where the only real hospital was located, according to Ricky. By the time they pulled up to the emergency entrance, twenty-six minutes had elapsed, and Ricky's uncle was in desperate shape. Ricky darted from the car to get help, and moments later two islanders, accompanied by a handsome woman in a green medical smock, came running out with a gurney.

Remi's eyes locked with the woman's as she approached the car. She looked like an islander, but her hair was styled differently from the other locals they'd seen, and her bearing commanded immediate attention. This was clearly a woman in a position of authority, in spite of her smooth skin and relative youth. When she reached the victim, she glanced at Remi and Sam before focusing on his wounds.

"How long ago did this happen?" she asked, her English colored with a marked Australian accent.

"Half an hour ago. Crocodile on the east side of the island," Remi said.

The woman took in the bleeding man with a glance. She eyed the butchered leg before turning to the orderlies and giving a rapid-fire order in pidgin. The men leaned into the vehicle and dragged out Benji's inert form. They placed him on the gurney, which looked like it had survived the Japanese occupation, and inspected the tourniquet. Seeming to intuit Sam and Remi's doubts about the care he was going to receive, the woman pursed her lips.

"Don't worry. The gear in the OR is in better shape than this relic." She held out her hand. "Dr. Vanya. I'm the chief medical officer here." Remi shook it, followed by Sam.

"Sam and Remi Fargo," Sam said.

Dr. Vanya appraised them for a lingering moment and then turned to where the orderlies were wheeling Benji into the hospital. "If you'll excuse me, duty calls. You can wait in the emergency room. There's a bench and a ten-year-old copy of the *Times*. Oh, and nice work with the tourniquet."

Before either of them could say anything, she disappeared into the building. Sam eyed the smear of blood on the car seat, and his gaze drifted to his clothes, covered with rust-colored stains. They'd only been on the island for a few hours and already they'd helped save a man who was now battling for his life.

A troubling start to what should have been a low-key underwater exploration and an ugly omen for their time in the Solomons.

CHAPTER 5

Leonid's pickup truck rolled into the lot several minutes later and pulled up next to the SUV. Leonid got out and waved to the driver, who gunned the engine and veered back onto the main road in a cloud of exhaust. The Russian approached Sam with a hangdog expression on his face.

"Did he make it?" he asked.

"Barely," Sam said. "It'll be touch and go, that's for sure."

"Poor guy. What a way to go."

"I can't believe they didn't warn you about the crocodiles," Remi said.

"They did. That's why they had the machetes and axes."

Sam eyed Leonid. "Couple of AK-47s would have been a better idea."

"Believe me, my friend, if there were any on the island, I would have had them."

"Where's your crew?" Remi asked.

"Back at the bay. They're packing up and returning by sea with the boats and gear. Nobody wanted to ride with me. I have a feeling they blame me for their friend's misfortune for some reason." He paused. "Did you see the size of that creature? It was longer than the truck."

"And it may have family in the area," Sam said.

Remi nodded. "Yes, and the relatives might hold a grudge. Take your butchering of their friend personally."

Leonid looked alarmed. "I didn't do anything."

Sam gave Remi a sad smile. "You don't need to explain it to us. Save it for the crocs."

They trooped into the building, which was as primitive as the exterior promised. The emergency room lounge was a squalid rectangle with poor ventilation and a dozen sick or injured waiting on a row of shabby benches. Ricky had claimed an empty area on the far end and was staring off into space. They moved to the bench and sat beside him as the overhead fans orbited in a futile attempt to cool the stifling interior. After a few minutes of sweating, Remi stood again. "I'll wait outside."

Sam rose and Leonid followed suit. "We'll keep you company."

Remi turned to Ricky. "Will you come get us when you hear something?"

"Yes." Ricky looked unfazed by the heat. "Dr. Vanya's the best we have, so he's in good hands."

"That's a little bit of luck, at any rate," Remi said, wiping her brow.

An old man sitting nearby coughed with a wet, thick sound, and Sam took Remi's hand and led her to the exit. Outside, the temperature was baking, but, even so, it felt refreshing after the hotbox that was the hospital's waiting room. They found a shaded area near the side of the building, and Sam inspected his shirt.

"Probably not a bad idea to get back to the hotel to change." He looked at Remi, who also had dried blood on her. "Want to make a quick run?"

Remi glanced at the Land Rover. "If we pass a car wash, you've got my vote."

Leonid nodded. "I'll give you a lift. No point standing here cooking."

They piled into the SUV, and Leonid took the wheel. After the breakneck ride from the bay, the Russian's conservative driving felt like they were standing still. Leonid's face looked like he'd been drinking vinegar as he navigated the busy streets, surprisingly clogged with cars.

"We're pretty much shut down now," he said. "There's no way that crew's going to want to return to the bay after this."

"Have you talked to them?"

"Only two indicated any willingness to go back tomorrow."

"What about boats?"

"None of the captains want anything to do with us now. Bad luck, that."

"Especially for the uncle," Remi said, eyeing her shirt. "I can't even imagine what he's going through."

"He's lucky you two were there. If we'd had to wait for the others to do something, he'd be dead," Leonid stated flatly.

"Ricky said that's cultural. Nothing moves fast on the island."

"Except the crocodiles," Leonid said.

They got to the hotel and, ignoring the horrified looks of staff and the few other guests, went directly to their room. After quick showers and a change of clothes, they were ready to return to the hospital. Leonid was waiting for them in the cool lobby, where he was studying the photographs he'd salvaged in the chaos. Sam and Remi took seats on either side of him, enjoying the slight chill of the air-conditioning.

"If you look at this one, you can see another structure in the background. The head of the dive team said he thought there were at least six of these, maybe more," Leonid said, holding up a photo.

"If he's right, it's an incredible find. Not only an ancient ruin but one that's been lost for long enough that nobody remembers it. Never mind that its location presents an intriguing mystery," Remi said.

"Obviously, some sort of natural disaster," Sam speculated. "This area has a history of earthquakes. That's got to be how it wound up underwater."

"Yes, but more interesting to me is the construction. Stone. There's no history of stone building here. This is an important clue to a past we never imagined," Leonid said.

"It is odd that there's no record of it, isn't it?" Remi asked softly.

Leonid put the photos down. "Not to me. This is a fragmented society that relies on oral tradition. There are over seventy languages in the islands. That speaks to separatism. It could be that everyone who knew about it was wiped out. Imagine how big an earthquake would have been required to sink the entire shore to that depth."

An idea occurred to Sam. "Assuming it was built on the shore."

Remi gave him a puzzled look. "Why would you think any differently?"

Sam sat forward. "Have you ever heard of Nan Madol?"

"No."

"The ruling dynasty built islands out of big rocks on top of the coral reefs there—a similar approach to Venice—with a series of interconnected canals," Sam explained. Leonid stared at him thoughtfully. "If it was built in a lagoon or on a reef, that would better explain why it's submerged. If the shelf collapsed in a big earthquake—"

"Exactly. Anyway, without diving the find, that would be my first guess. We'll know more once Selma finds us a research vessel."

They rose and reluctantly traded the comfort of the hotel lobby for the muggy heat outside. The squall line that had been lingering on the horizon was approaching, pushing humid air ahead of it, and as they made their way back to the hospital, the sky was darkening.

Leonid had been on Guadalcanal for a week and was by now used to the schizophrenic weather. He glanced up at the clouds without interest. The interior of the SUV smelled like a slaughterhouse, and he pulled over at a car wash being operated out of an empty field next to a grocery, its water supplied by runners with buckets, the workers shirt-less and shoeless, laughing as they worked on a short line of vehicles.

The good humor abruptly died when the lead youth got a glimpse of the Land Rover's interior. Remi, Sam, and Leonid spent the next half hour beneath a banyan tree, watching the washers work in nervous silence. A police car appeared at the curb halfway through, and two officers approached them and questioned them briefly before radioing the hospital and getting confirmation of their account.

Leonid exhaled a sigh of relief once the police left. His gaze moved to the clouds when distant thunder boomed across the sea.

"Sounds like it's coming on fast," he commented.

"That will stir up the water and decrease visibility if we try to dive tomorrow," Sam said. "Presuming you're still game."

"Did you not see the crocodile the size of a freight car back on the beach?" Remi asked.

"Right. So we know where he is."

"You're serious, aren't you?" she said.

"What's life without a little stimulation?"

She frowned. "The word you're looking for is 'safe.' Or maybe 'long.'"

Sam waved a hand at the sky. "Bah. Let's head over to the hospital and check on the uncle and then see about reserving some gear. I want to get a close-up look, now that we're here. I don't do well sitting on the sidelines. Besides, the attack happened on the beach, so the safest place in that bay is anywhere but where we were."

Leonid nodded. "The hard part will be getting boats. The ones I rented today won't be back."

"Drop us off at the hospital while you nose around for some others. Leave a message for us at the hotel with the details if you're successful," Sam said.

"And see if you can find someone with a nice, lightly used .50 caliber machine gun, while you're at it. In case our reptilian guest wasn't alone," Remi said.

The thunder was nearing when Leonid left them at the hospital and they barely made it inside before the heavens opened and sheets of rain poured down. Drops the size of golf balls hammered a rapid-fire tattoo on the corrugated metal roof of the waiting area, where Ricky was sitting immobile as a statue, his eyes closed. The crowd had thinned and now only the old man with the cough, a laborer with an obviously broken arm, and a fisherman with a gash on his hand remained.

They took seats on the bench next to Ricky. He stirred and cracked an eye open. Remi smiled at him and he returned the favor with a tentative grin of his own.

"Any word?" she asked.

He shook his head. "No. But it's only been a couple of hours. I don't expect anything yet."

Neither had to voice the probability that, at the very least, his uncle would lose the leg. That he was still alive after the savage attack was miracle enough. Hopefully, that questionable luck would hold.

Another hour went by and then Dr. Vanya pushed through the emergency room's double doors, still wearing surgical scrubs. Ricky stood, and Sam and Remi joined him as she approached.

"Well, the good news is, he's stable. We managed to get enough blood into him so his chances look reasonable. But the next twenty-four hours will tell. The biggest risk now is that he succumbs to shock or that infection sets in. He's in decent physical shape and fairly young, but there are no guarantees."

"And the leg?" Ricky asked softly.

"The bones were splintered into a hundred slivers by the jaws, so even if I'd been right there, we'd still have had to amputate. I'm sorry," she said.

"Can we see him?" Ricky asked.

Dr. Vanya shook her head. "Let's give him some time, shall we? Maybe this evening." She turned her attention to Sam and Remi. "How did you happen to be so close when the attack happened? The crocodiles generally stay away from the tourist beaches. Hopefully, that hasn't changed."

"We were on the other side of the island with him. Pretty remote," Sam explained, keeping it vague. It wasn't his place to share the details of Leonid's expedition, even though by now word of the attack had probably spread like wildfire, along with gossip about the buildings beneath the sea.

"What on earth were you doing there?" she asked.

"Helping a friend with a project," Sam said.

"A project?" Vanya pressed.

"Archaeology."

"Ah," Vanya said as though that explained everything. "You're American, aren't you?"

"Our accents give us away?" Remi asked.

"Well, yes. Most of our visitors are from Australia and New Zealand. We don't get nearly as many Americans as we did when I was growing up. Back then, there were still a lot of veterans who came to revisit the old battlegrounds and pay their respect. But no longer," she explained.

"Oh, you're an islander?" Remi said, surprised. There was no trace of the local pidgin accent in her speech.

"Until I was ten. Then my family moved to Sydney, where I went to school. Somewhere in all that I lost my accent." She smiled. "But you know what they say: you can take the islander off the island, but you can't take the island out of the islander. After I graduated and completed my residency, I wanted to give back to my people, so I returned nine years ago."

"That's a wonderful thing to do," Sam said.

"Well, it's where I was born. My current project is raising funds for several rural clinics around the island. It may seem like a small place, but when you cut yourself or have an accident, traversing the roads can take a lifetime. And also for vaccinations and the like. Unfortunately, the government's always been a disaster, so fate leaves it up to the private sector to do what it can."

"That sounds like a noble calling," Sam said. "Maybe you can give us some information about it?"

Vanya appraised him. "Why? Feel like donating?" she asked bluntly.

Remi stepped in. "We oversee a foundation that does charitable work all over the world."

Vanya blinked twice and then smiled, the tiny stress lines around her eyes crinkling. "Well, in that case, you must have dinner with me. How long will you be on Guadalcanal?"

Remi shrugged. "We haven't decided."

Sam chuckled. "Until they throw us off."

Everyone laughed. Vanya nodded. "Given your recent act of heroism, that's unlikely. Seriously. If you're free this evening, I'd love to show you one of the local hideaways. I'm having dinner with a colleague and I'm sure he'd be interested in discussing your project. We don't get a lot of archaeologists nosing around. And of course I want to tell you all about my clinics."

Remi exchanged a glance with Sam. "Are you sure it's not an imposition?"

"Absolutely," Vanya said. "The truth is, I get bored out of my skull around here after a time. I could use some time with fresh faces, hear some new stories. I'm afraid after my time in Sydney, Honiara doesn't have quite the interest it did when I was ten. I assure you my invitation is purely driven by selfishness."

"Well, then, it's a date," Sam said. "Shall we meet you here?"

"If you like." She paused, thinking. "Or I can swing by wherever you're staying. That way, I can go home and freshen up, and, if it's still pouring, you won't have to brave the rain to get here. What hotel?"

Sam gave her their information and they agreed to meet in the lobby at eight. Vanya spent another minute with Ricky, explaining his uncle's condition to him, and then returned to the bowels of the hospital after stopping to briefly examine the man with the broken arm.

CHAPTER 6

When Sam and Remi checked at the front desk for Dr. Vanya, the clerk handed them a message slip.

"Looks like we're in business," Sam said as he read the note. "Leonid's going to be picking us up at nine tomorrow morning."

"I have mixed feelings about diving in a crocodile-infested swamp," Remi said.

"It's not a swamp. And it was only one crocodile."

"What's the exact procedure for fending off an underwater crocodile attack? I wonder if it's like a shark?"

"Not to worry. I have the tactical skills necessary."

"That's very thoughtful. But it does raise the question of what your plan would be if one attacked."

"Oh. Simple," Sam said. "I'm a fast swimmer."

"Not faster than one of those things."

"I don't have to be." He smiled. "I just have to be faster than you."

Remi returned the smile. "Touché."

"Thing about saltwater crocs is they're solitary and territorial, so it's unlikely another will move into the area so soon. We'll keep an eye peeled, but where we're diving we should be safe."

Remi gave him a sidelong glance. "Let's hope someone told the crocs all that."

The doctor pulled up in a silver Mitsubishi SUV that was covered in mud. They piled into the backseat and buckled in. The rain had stopped with the approach of dusk, but the roads were still flooded in many places, and Vanya drove cautiously to the waterfront.

"I hope you like seafood. This is the best place on the island. Very authentic, but not fancy," she said. "It's been here for twenty years, so they're doing something right."

"That's perfect," Remi said. "I love fish."

"Me too," Sam chimed in.

The exterior of the restaurant showed fading blue paint peeling from crooked wooden planks. A simple hand-lettered sign over the door featured a stylized depiction of a crab and the restaurant name: *Eleanor's.*

"She owns the place. A magician with recipes. Whatever the fresh catch is, you can't go wrong with it," Vanya assured them.

The interior matched the outside—simple and run-down, but with heady aromas drifting from the kitchen. The dining area was packed with locals, conversing boisterously over their seafood platters. Vanya waved at a table near the back, where a heavyset man with skin the color of coal grinned at them, his suit and tie out of place in the surroundings. They approached and he stood, hand outstretched in greeting, and he was so tall that his head almost hit the ceiling. Vanya made the introductions.

"Sam and Remi Fargo, meet Orwen Manchester. Orwen is a genuine celebrity here—he's one of the few members of parliament who's survived for more than fifteen minutes in the confusion that's our system."

"Well, that's too kind, Vanya. You really should consider government work with that silver tongue of yours," Manchester said, his voice deep and good-humored. *"Halo olketa,"* he intoned, the traditional island greeting. Remi shook his hand, which was twice as large as hers, and Sam did the same, noting that the man was careful about his grip, given his stature.

"Nonsense, Orwen, your humility doesn't become you. You're a venerated Solomon Islands icon. And that takes some doing, given how often the administrations are booted with votes of no confidence every other week."

"I've been very fortunate," Manchester said with a practiced smile. "And the good doctor exaggerates. I like to say I have one of the jobs nobody sane would want, so the competition for my seat isn't particularly stiff."

Manchester's English was as polished as Vanya's, and his accent marked him as a product of the Australian education system. Everyone took seats around the table, and a server approached, looking harried with the packed house. The man spoke rapidly, his pidgin thick as tar, and then repeated his question more clearly when Sam and Remi looked at each other with puzzled expressions.

Vanya saved them from embarrassment. "If you like beer, the local SolBrew is quite good, and I understand from my friend here that it's kept very cold by the management. They also have a nice selection of sodas."

Remi asked for a cola, and Manchester and Sam ordered beer. Vanya requested a bottle of water, explaining that the caffeine and sugar would keep her awake all night if she went with soda. "Women don't drink alcohol in the islands—or, at least, almost none do. Everyone would be scandalized if they saw me having one with you," she said. "One of many things I miss from my days in Australia. Cold beer and good wine."

"I don't envy you," Sam said as the server returned with their drinks and four laminated, single-page menus.

"Fortunately, that quaint custom doesn't apply to men. Cheers!" Manchester said, and raised his sweating bottle in a toast. Sam clinked his against the big man's beer and took a cautious pull.

"That's quite good. I could see making a habit of this," he said.

"Sam's never met a beer he didn't like," Remi said, studying the menu. "You recommended the catch of the day?"

"Oh, yes. It's always excellent," Vanya assured them, and Manchester nodded in agreement.

Sam's attention was drawn to a nearby table where the islanders were feasting on fish, eating with their fingers. Manchester followed his gaze and smiled. "That's tradition for you. Don't worry. Everyone at this table uses a proper knife and fork."

They ordered four servings of the fresh mahi mahi, and the server took their menus. Once he was gone, Vanya offered the table a smile and sat back. "The Fargos are here doing something archaeology related. Isn't that right?"

Remi nodded. "We're helping a friend."

"When did you arrive in Guadalcanal?" Manchester asked.

"This morning."

"And quite a first day they had, Orwen. I met them when they were bringing a crocodile attack victim to the hospital."

"Good Lord! You're joking!" Manchester said, genuinely shocked.

"I wish she was," Sam said. "Although our man won the fight, he paid for it in blood."

"Shocking. I'm sorry that was your first experience with the islands. We normally try to keep the crocodiles and attorneys away from the tourists, at least in the beginning. It's bad for business." Manchester paused. "You can tell which ones are the crocodiles because they're friendlier."

Everyone laughed, and he continued. "So this is a two-time-loser of a day. First a crocodile and then dinner with a politician."

Vanya grinned. "But you're one of the good ones, right?" She looked at Sam. "Of course Orwen's also an attorney. So you got all three local hazards in one fell swoop." She reached across the table and patted Manchester's hand.

Manchester finished his beer and held up the bottle. "I'll drink to that." He looked over at Sam, who was only halfway done with his, before gesturing to the server with two fingers. "Being the resident evil is a thirsty business." He studied Sam and leaned forward. "How bad was the attack?"

Vanya interjected. "He'll live, minus a leg. His nephew said the creature was twenty feet long, so he's fortunate it didn't bite him in two."

Another round of beer arrived, and Manchester grinned at Sam. "You learn in this heat to drink them fast or they get warm."

Sam smiled back at him. "Maybe we can get a bucket with some ice? I'm a lightweight. Plus, I'm going to be diving tomorrow and even a trace of a hangover can make it a pretty unpleasant experience."

"Diving, you say? Fascinating. What's this all about? Vanya mentioned archaeology?" Manchester asked, and took a mammoth swig of his fresh beer before waving to the waiter, who scurried over. A hushed discussion ensued, and then Manchester returned his gaze to Sam. "What on earth could archaeology have to do with diving? Unless you're talking about a sinkhole . . ."

"Our friend found some anomalies off the coast and asked us to take a look," Remi said.

"Really? Are you archaeologists?"

"That's one of our passions."

"How remarkable. For some reason, I never associate the profession with such . . . vitality," Manchester said, admiring Remi.

"The world's changing. Full of surprises," Sam said, and held his beer aloft in another toast, hoping to distract the politician, who was treading dangerously close to being rude.

"And what are these 'anomalies,' as you put it?" Vanya asked.

"We don't know. We just got here and were sidetracked by the crocodile," Remi said.

"Might it not be leftovers from the war? The place is littered with them," Manchester said.

"Could be," Sam agreed.

A bucket brimming with ice arrived, and Sam positioned his second beer in it. Manchester finished his and signaled for another. Vanya gave Remi a gentle roll of her eyes as if to say "What can you do with the big lug?"

"But enough about our little hobby," Sam continued, then changed the subject. "What's all this about setting up clinics?"

Vanya beamed at him. "It's been a long time in the planning. I've given up on the government doing anything for its people but robbing them blind, so I'm taking matters into my own hands. Children are getting sick and not being treated. People are dying who could be saved. All for want of some remedial care. It doesn't have to be that way, and I'm saying in the twenty-first century it shouldn't be that way. We have the knowledge, all we need are the resources. Which is where our generous donors come in."

"Sounds like a worthwhile cause. Do you already have many contributors?" Remi asked.

Manchester guffawed as the third beer materialized and the empties were whisked away. "I'll say. She's got every pharmaceutical company she can shame into pledging something."

"Would that it were enough, Orwen. It's just scratching the surface. Reality is, nobody much cares about our people, and, at best, I've been able to get them to commit to token charity. Any of these groups could easily write a check and solve most of our infrastructure issues with the stroke of a pen, but they don't. Because we're not high visibility. We're stuck in a corner of the world nobody knows exists. So they commit to some crumbs, which is better than nothing, but not much."

"How much do you still need to raise?"

"My target's half a million U.S. dollars for the first year and then two hundred thousand every year thereafter. The first year will pay for simple buildings and some primitive equipment, but those costs won't recur." Vanya shook her head. "These companies spend more on a slow day advertising tooth whitener. But like I said, we're not a revenue source, so we don't matter. So far, I've marshaled a hundred and fifty of the first year's requirement and a soft fifty for the second."

Remi looked to Sam, who had a small smile on his face. "We'll take it under advisement. Do you have a plan? A budget written out?"

"Of course. An entire presentation."

"Could we get a copy?" Remi asked.

"I'd be delighted. Is it really something you think your foundation might be interested in supporting?" Vanya asked, her tone excited.

Sam finished his beer. "No promises, but let's see what you have. I know the foundation has funded other worthwhile causes."

Steaming platters of fish arrived, and Manchester made a point of studying his silverware for blemishes before digging in. By the size of his bites and the speed with which he ate, it was clear he was a man who didn't miss any meals. Silence reigned at the table until the fish was gone. Sam sat back. "That was wonderful. Like they just caught it."

Vanya nodded. "I'd be surprised if it was more than a few hours old. Thankfully, there's no shortage of marine life here. One of the ways we've been blessed."

"That and the mineral riches we can't seem to get organized enough to pull out of the ground," Manchester chimed in, sounding bitter.

"Really?" Sam asked. "Like what?"

"Good gracious, man. Oil. Tankers full of it. And every kind of rarity you can imagine. Gold by the truckload. Emeralds. Rubies. And on and on. We should be richer than the bloody Saudis, but instead all we do is bicker with each other and chase our own tails."

"Don't get Orwen started. It's one of his pet peeves," Vanya chided as the plates were cleared.

"We've had a history of corruption and of foreigners coming in and taking anything of value. How much do you know about our history?" Manchester asked with a slight slur.

"Not enough, obviously," Sam said.

"We were a British protectorate for years and then the Japs invaded and took over the islands. Then the Yanks fought them off, only to hand us over to the Brits again after the war. We've been passed around like a pack of smokes at a rock concert, and, up until recently, nobody, including ourselves, thought that we might actually be entitled to self-determination rather than being somebody else's possession." He barked a humorless laugh. "Fat lot of good it's done us. We might as well be destitute. We're sitting on a fortune in natural resources and we can't make a go of it. Saddest story you'll ever hear."

Vanya sighed, obviously having heard all this many times before. "Next, he'll be railing about the gold mine."

"So there's still gold?" Remi asked.

"Of course there is. But you wouldn't know it to look at us, would you? And as Vanya alluded to, people get frustrated at all the jockeying and ineptness, so they kick their administration out with regularity, so the mentality of most politicians is to grab what you can while you're in office because chances are you won't be much longer. It's a vicious circle. One I've lived in the last twenty years."

Vanya eyed the big man with a gentle gaze. "Orwen here is one of the last good ones. Don't let him sour you on Guadalcanal. It's got its share of problems, but it's a beautiful place filled with warm-hearted people."

Manchester drained his beer. "And crocodiles. Can't forget them. Maybe we should let them have a turn at running the thing. Can't do much worse than we have."

The conversation stalled, and Vanya did her best to bring it back to center. "It's confession time. I haven't been completely honest with you two," she said in a low voice.

"Really?" Remi said with arched eyebrows.

"Yes. I'm a bit of a research fanatic, and when I went home to change, I googled Sam and Remi Fargo. I suppose you know what I found."

Sam looked sheepish. "Can't believe everything you read on the web."

"Perhaps." She eyed Manchester. "Orwen, I'll have you know you're sitting with celebrities. Sam and Remi are renowned treasure hunters."

Manchester's face could have been carved from granite. "Treasure hunters?"

"A distortion the media loves. They sensationalize everything," Remi explained. "We've been fortunate a few times in locating significant finds. Some of our archaeological projects have turned up some historically valuable items. But it's not like we find treasure and keep it," she said, frowning. "It goes to the rightful owners for charitable work and enrichment."

"That's right. It's a case of man bites dog. Anything to sell papers," Sam echoed.

"And modest as well as famous," Vanya said. "The Fargos have discovered more hidden booty than anyone else on the planet, Orwen. Don't let their humility fool you."

Sam waved a hand. "Most people have better things to do than root around in old temples and the like. That's a meaningless statistic," he said. "It's like having seen more ghosts than anyone. Doesn't say much."

"Where did you say you were diving?" Manchester asked, his tone polite but with a hint of frost to it.

Remi smiled megawatts at him. "We didn't. It's our friend's expedition, so not ours to talk about. But I can assure you there's no treasure involved."

His eyes narrowed. "It's a small island. I'm sure everyone's already talking about the attack. Secrets like that don't stay that way very long around here."

"Probably, but we have to respect our friend's wishes. He's an academic and these kinds of things are important to him. Bragging rights," she said.

Manchester nodded. "I completely understand. I just thought that perhaps I could be of service if you need any help with permits or that sort of thing."

Remi gave a polite yawn behind her hand, and Vanya took the hint and gestured for the check. When it came, Sam snatched it from the waiter's hand before she could reach it. "Please. Let us buy dinner. That was the best fish and some of the most engaging company we've had in ages. It's the least we can do."

Vanya's eyes flashed, but she smiled. "That's very generous. Hopefully, that generosity will extend to helping my people."

"Hell, if I'd known someone else was buying, I'd have drunk more!" Manchester declared with a guffaw.

Vanya dropped Sam and Remi off at the hotel with a promise to e-mail them the clinic plan and they in turn said they'd stop by the hospital soon to check on the injured worker.

"Manchester's a character, isn't he?" Sam said as they shouldered their way through the door under the vigilant gaze of the desk clerk.

"That's an understatement. He seems angry, doesn't he? Not that far below the surface. Resentful."

"I can't blame him. Sounds like he's fighting a thankless battle and losing two steps for every one he gains."

"Assuming he's telling the whole truth. He didn't strike me as suffering too badly."

CHAPTER 7

When Leonid picked Sam and Remi up, two ratty dive suits and well-used rigs lay in the back of the SUV. The Russian looked like he'd had a hard night, his eyes red and two days of salt-and-pepper stubble dusting his jaw.

"Good morning, sunshine," Sam said as he studied his friend's profile. "You lose a round to the local rum?"

Leonid smiled ruefully. "Don't ask."

"Were you able to get another crew?"

"I guess we'll see when we get out to the bay. I had to pay double what it cost yesterday, but I think they'll show up."

Sam checked his watch and pulled the satellite phone from his backpack as they made their way out of town. Selma answered after two rings, her tone businesslike.

"Good morning, Selma," he began.

"Afternoon. Six hours effective time difference. Although technically it's tomorrow there, so it's actually eighteen hours."

"That's right. Good to know." He paused. "Any luck locating a ship?"

"We were fortunate. There's a boat on its way from Australia, although it won't be there for a few days, weather allowing. A hundred-foot expedition yacht that barely makes twelve knots."

"That's wonderful news, Selma."

"It was doing research on the Great Barrier Reef when I convinced the institute that owns and operates it to make a little side trip."

"Quite a side trip."

"What's a thousand miles each way between friends? Needless to say, the foundation will be making another generous donation this month."

"I wouldn't have it any other way."

"How are you faring on Guadalcanal? I hear it's about as exciting as watching ice melt."

He told her about the crocodile attack. When he was finished, she was silent for several moments.

"That's terrible. Why don't you two ever pick someplace safe to go?"

"I keep trying to convince Remi to let me retire, but she's a slave driver," Sam said, stealing a glance at his wife in the rearview mirror. She glared at him and shook her head in disapproval.

"It will be three more days before the ship gets there, so you'll have to find other ways to amuse yourself in the meantime. Do try to keep away from the man-eaters. Besides the crocodiles, they have plenty of great white sharks there, too."

"That's good to know. Keeps us on our toes."

When he hung up, Remi leaned forward as they bounced down the road. "Well?"

"Selma says hello. Said to practice your shark punching, too."

Her eyes widened. "No."

"Yes. Apparently, she's been researching the area, and there are great whites in addition to the other local attractions."

"And we're going diving today?"

Sam shrugged. "Nobody lives forever."

Remi glared at Leonid. "Tell me again why we agreed to fly halfway around the world to do this?"

"Scientific curiosity," Sam tried. "Friendship. The thrill of discovery. A zest for knowledge."

"Boredom," Leonid said, and everyone smiled.

"You know we'll look like seals in our wet suits to any great whites," Remi commented.

Sam grinned. "I hear wet suits aren't very tasty. Sharks tend to avoid them."

"You're thinking of *sea otters*," Remi corrected.

"Ah, I always mix those up. Well, try to act like an otter while we're in the soup."

"At least the crocodiles aren't a problem in open water. They tend to be mostly dangerous on shore or at the mouths of rivers."

"As Benji, unfortunately, discovered."

When they arrived at the bay, a different truck was parked near the sand and only three men waited beneath one of the swaying palm trees, watching the SUV approach. A single boat was tethered to a tree trunk, floating lazily, in the strengthening sun.

After a scan of the shore to ensure no further crocodiles were lurking in the brush, Sam and Remi donned their wet suits and climbed into the boat, followed by the rest of the men. The old outboard sputtered to life with a throaty cough and they were skimming across the bay, Leonid directing the captain with the aid of a handheld GPS.

When they reached the coordinates, the captain kept the motor idling while Sam and Remi finished their preparations. Leonid regarded them in their masks, regulators in their mouths, and offered a halfhearted grin.

"Bottom's at around eighty feet. Visibility should be pretty good, from what the divers said. The water's usually exceptionally clear."

Sam spat his regulator out. "Except for the storm runoff yesterday. Still, it is what it is. Should be interesting."

Remi dropped backward off the side of the skiff while Sam lowered himself down a metal dive ladder that one of the men had attached to the stern. Once in the water, he was glad to discover that the temperature was almost bathlike. He slipped below the surface and spotted Remi ten feet away, waiting for him. He gave her a thumbs-up that she returned, and then they began their slow descent to the bottom, which was barely visible from their vantage point.

At the fifty-foot mark, the contours of the mounds drifted up to meet them from the reef. Sam tapped Remi on the shoulder and pointed to their right, where a large, hulking shape rose from the sea bottom. As they approached, it became obvious that they were looking at something man-made. The jutting rise was almost entirely encrusted with sea life, but the shape and symmetry were unmistakable—it was part of a building.

When they arrived within arm's length, Sam felt for the handle of the dive knife he'd strapped to his leg and freed it. Remi watched as he scraped away at the barnacles. After a few moments, he stopped and pushed himself back so Remi could see.

It was a seam. A joint between two blocks. Any doubts about the origin of the protrusions were now put to rest. These were indeed ruins of buildings, albeit submerged ones.

A shadow drifted across the bottom and they froze. Sam turned and looked up to see the long shape of a shark. Not a great white, but, still, at least nine feet of marine predator.

The shark orbited their position and then seemed to lose interest in them as it continued on its way. Remi's eyes had gone wide in her mask, and Sam kept control of his breathing as his heart rate settled back to normal. If they'd required any evidence of their completely exposed state, the close encounter had been sufficient, and, after a quick swim through the ruins, they ascended, pausing for a decompression stop, eyes roving the water for more uninvited guests.

Once back in the boat, they stripped off their buoyancy compensator vests and peeled off the wet suits. The tropical sun was blistering even near the cool surface of the water.

"Well?" Leonid asked expectantly.

"It's definitely some kind of a compound. And old. That's obvious."

"How can you be so sure after only one look around?"

Remi explained about the block construction, and Leonid nodded. "Then you're certain?"

"It's exactly what we suspected—a sunken complex of buildings."

"You don't dive?" Sam asked Leonid.

The Russian shook his head. "Never learned."

"You should take a crash course while we're waiting for the dive boat to arrive. You can't very well head up an aquatic expedition if you don't go in the water."

"I'm not sure at my age this old dog has many new tricks left in him," Leonid said.

"Nonsense. We'll find an instructor. What else do you have to do over the next few days?"

Leonid looked unconvinced. "Are you sure? I haven't exactly kept this"—he gestured at his body—"in athletic shape."

"It mainly involves floating around, Leonid. Jacques Cousteau was doing it at twice your age. Come on. Live a little," Sam teased.

The captain returned the boat to the shore and they disembarked onto the hot sand. Remi gazed down the beach to the grove where the crocodile had attacked and she nudged Sam.

"What happened to our big friend?" she asked in a low voice.

"The locals probably overcame their fear of the area to drag it off.

The hide's worth a small fortune," Leonid said. He turned to the islanders. "Can you make it tomorrow?"

The captain and his crew exchanged worried glances and then the old man shook his head. "No. This is a bad place," he said, his accent so thick his words were almost unintelligible.

"Come on. Nothing happened. Easiest money you ever made."

The islanders looked at one another again and the captain frowned. "Money won't do you any good here. I should never have come—this bay is cursed. If you know what's good for you, you'll leave and never return. If not, there will be more misfortune, and may God help you."

Leonid barked a harsh laugh. "Come on, old man. Cursed? You don't strike me as someone who scares easily."

The captain fixed him with a cold stare. "I did as you asked, but no more. Pay me so I can get out of here. Just because you're willing to gamble with your lives doesn't mean I am."

"Little dramatic, don't you think?" Leonid said. The captain waited in silence as Leonid peeled off several bills and handed them to him. "Remember our deal. You tell nobody about this." He fingered another bill.

"I won't tell a soul. And even if I did, nobody will want to tempt fate. I heard about what happened to Benji. He lost a leg to the curse." The captain paused. "There will be more. That's just the start."

Leonid passed him the larger-denomination bill and the man trudged back to the boat. He used the outboard to back it off the sand, and then the remaining two crew members trundled to the truck and took off, leaving Sam, Remi, and Leonid standing alone on the beach.

Remi glanced at Sam. "Did you see the old man's face? He was terrified."

"Native superstition. Mumbo jumbo. Nonsense," Leonid scoffed.

"He's heard of this bay before, though. It might be interesting to find out what the rumors are," she said.

"Doesn't really matter, does it? There's a lost city right offshore nobody knows about and we've discovered it. Who cares what some childish legends say about it?" Leonid spat.

"There's usually an element of truth to folklore, Leonid," Sam chided. "Can't hurt to ask around."

"Well, if you want to waste your time, suit yourself. Sounds like I have to learn how to scuba dive in the next three days."

CHAPTER 8

La Jolla, California

Selma looked up from her computer screen at the sound of the front door opening. Her assistants, Pete and Wendy, were at lunch, and Zoltán bristled at her feet at the intrusion. She reassured him with a stroke of her hand and then relaxed when she saw it was only Lazlo.

The bedraggled English academic had taken to stopping by regularly, she strongly suspected, because he had nothing better to do with his time now that his Laos expedition was formally over with and no treasure discovered. He'd been dejected by the outcome but had recovered when he'd gotten wind of a recently surfaced document that was purported to be written in the notorious pirate Captain Kidd's hand— in code.

"Selma, my dear woman, may I say you look breathtaking this fine day," Lazlo announced to her amused gaze. "And Zoltán, you handsome beast, what a fine specimen of canine corpulence you are."

"He's not even close to being fat," Selma said, defending the dog's honor. Zoltán tilted his head as he regarded Lazlo and then lay back down and closed his eyes, dismissing the visitor with the disdain only a purebred can master.

"Merely a term of endearment. I adore the bloodthirsty killer." He looked at her screen. "And what are we working on?"

She pressed the power button and the monitor blinked off. "Nothing of interest to you, I'm sure."

"One never knows. I suspect that if you're involved, I could muster some enthusiasm."

Lazlo had been increasingly flirtatious since returning from his trek, which amused Selma.

"Well, at your age, I suppose enthusiasm's all one could hope for." She paused. "What brings you by, Lazlo?"

"I was hoping I might help you. Do you have anything I could be of assistance with? Perhaps an unbreakable cipher? A riddle that's baffled the brightest minds of our time?"

"Still haven't decided whether you're going to chase down the Captain Kidd thing, have you?" she said knowingly.

"I'm looking into it. The owner of the letter believes it's somehow related to his lost pirate treasure, but I think that's overly optimistic."

"And of course those trying to convince others to buy obscure documents have been known to exaggerate the importance of the contents," Selma observed.

"Which is why I'm not willing to trust and need to verify. Right now I'm hopeful, but cautiously so, absent any further substantiation. However, if it turns out to be what the owner purports it to be, it could be a magnificent opportunity—and a profitable one, to be sure."

Selma shook her head. "Don't quit your day job."

"Yes, well, this rather is my day job." He glanced away. "And how are our benefactors, the Fargos, faring? What are they up to now?"

Selma filled him in on the Solomons find. "I'm researching the area for them. Volcanoes, earthquakes, a history of tidal waves—you name it. I haven't heard from them since they were going to dive the site and confirm whether there's anything to the accounts."

"Hmm. Most intriguing. There aren't many areas of the world that haven't been thoroughly explored. But I'd venture a guess that's one of them."

"True. And with all the social unrest, it's likely to remain that way. There was a civil war in the early millennium, and then widespread rioting in 2006, and then again in 2014. The poverty's off the scale, and the Australians have basically had to station a small occupation force there to keep the peace. Not really an area conducive to exploration."

"Leave it to the Fargos to find something right under everyone's noses. Amazing, that."

"If that's indeed what they've done, it's actually their colleague Leonid Vasyev who made the discovery. They're helping out."

"Leonid, eh? Good Irish name."

"Well, Laz-lo," Selma said, stressing the second syllable of his name. "Can't jump to conclusions. That's the first rule the Fargos have. A good one, I'd say," she cautioned.

"Then he's not Russian?"

She cracked a small smile. "Is there anything else I can help you with?"

He stood, taking the hint. "No, no. I was just stopping in to ensure you hadn't been swept off your feet by some rakish pretender." He nodded at Zoltán, then to Selma. "Good day to you, then, Selma. I'm only a phone call away should you need my considerable skills."

"How reassuring. I trust I won't today."

"Nevertheless, I'm at your beck and call."

She watched him retreat, his head held high, and smiled to herself. He definitely had a certain charm, even if he was full of himself and completely amoral as they came. Mad dogs and Englishmen indeed.

The front door closed and she returned to her duties, a small part of her registering that the room seemed empty now that Lazlo had left. A blur of motion from outside the floor-to-ceiling picture window facing the Pacific Ocean caught her eye and she watched as a white gull rode an updraft, effortlessly soaring into the clear sky. Lazlo was a menace, she told herself with conviction, a scoundrel, and she'd have no part in his shenanigans, but the small smile remained even as she turned back to her monitor. Zoltán shifted at her feet and she reached down and petted his massive head.

CHAPTER 9

Guadalcanal, Solomon Islands

Breakfast at the hotel restaurant with Leonid was a somber affair, the Russian sullen. He'd asked around the waterfront, trying to find another boat for the next day, but word had spread about the attack and nobody wanted to sign on regardless of how much money he offered.

"Look at it this way, Leonid," Sam said. "There's not a lot we could accomplish on quick dives by ourselves. We're better off waiting for the research ship to arrive anyway so that we have all the equipment and manpower we need. We've already confirmed the ruins are man-made. That's more than I expected on a first look."

"And it gives you time to learn to dive yourself," Remi pressed. "Who knows? You may even enjoy it."

"I highly doubt that," Leonid grumbled into his coffee.

"Not all is lost, my friend," Sam said. "While we're landlocked, we'll nose around and see what we can come up with in terms of local lore. It's hard to believe there are no stories or legends surrounding a sunken city."

"Good luck. I could barely get the locals to talk to me. Tight-lipped bunch."

"Well, my beautiful wife's powers of persuasion might be more compelling than your Russian charm."

Leonid had to concede the point. "I'm not great with people."

"Which is why we'll divide and conquer. You take scuba lessons and we'll talk to some people and see what we come up with," Remi said. "Sound good?"

"Except for the part where I have to get in the water."

They parted ways, and Sam and Remi walked to the hospital, the morning heat building as they neared it. When they arrived, they asked for Dr. Vanya, and she seemed delighted to see them when she came through the emergency room doors.

"Well, this is a nice surprise. I didn't expect you so soon."

"We were just in the neighborhood . . ." Sam said.

"When you live in a town the size of Honiara, you're always in the neighborhood."

"How's he doing?" Remi asked.

"He's stable, but probably not up to seeing anyone yet. We have him sedated. I'm sorry. But I'll tell him you stopped by."

"Thanks. We don't even know him, so he might not understand who we are," Remi said.

"I'll just tell him the people who saved his life came by to check on him."

"Thank you."

"Well, I am going to put the bite on you for a donation, so it's the least I can do," Vanya joked.

"You offered to help us last night. I hope you don't mind if we take you up on that," Sam said.

"Of course not. What can I do?"

"Keep a secret, for starters," Remi said, looking around the area.

"My lips are sealed."

"The anomalies we're here researching? They appear to be the re-mains of a sunken city."

She blinked twice. "A what?"

"An ancient city off the coast."

"Off Guadalcanal? You can't be serious."

Sam nodded. "We are. And we want to know if there are any leg-ends about such a place. I'd imagine there would have to be. One of the old captains said something about a curse? We'd like to find out what's behind it."

Vanya took a seat in the empty patient lounge and stared at the two of them as though they'd appeared from another universe. "I was born here and I've never heard of a cursed sunken city. That sounds like sci-ence fiction. No offense."

"None taken. I know it sounds far-fetched. But we're sort of in the legends business and this isn't the first time that the seemingly impossi-ble has turned out to be real," Remi explained.

"Oh, I don't doubt that you found something. I just can't believe that . . . that you found ruins around here. I mean, no disrespect, but it's not like the Solomons are known for their advanced civilization stretching back to ancient times. Look around. That someone built a city that's now underwater . . ."

"Well, city may be a bit grandiose. More like a complex," Sam con-ceded. "But, still, is there anyone you can think of who might be able to answer some questions for us? Maybe an elder? Someone who's well versed in all the oral traditions?"

She shook her head. "Perhaps Orwen might know. He socializes a lot more than I do. But, off the top of my head, nobody springs to mind."

Sam frowned. "He seemed rather down on foreigners coming to the islands and taking advantage. He might not be receptive to an overture for help."

"Oh, don't let Orwen's bluster put you off. He'll help if I ask him to."

"We'd really rather keep the circle that knows as small as possible," Remi cautioned.

"Well, if you're going to mount any kind of real expedition, you're going to need permission from the government and that's Orwen. I can't see the administration just allowing you to go around disturbing our heritage even if they don't know it exists just yet. Orwen's your best shot at getting their okay."

"We don't even know what it is we found. It might be premature."

"And better to ask forgiveness than permission? I wouldn't try that here. As you probably surmised at dinner, the islanders can be touchy when it comes to their territory. I'd do it properly from the beginning."

Sam nodded. "Good advice. Could you touch base with him?"

"I'll call right now. Do you mind waiting?" Vanya asked, rising.

She disappeared back into the hospital. Sam leaned into Remi, his voice low. "I wish we didn't have to share anything about the find."

"I know. But it's not like anyone can do anything about it even if it was on the nightly news. Look at the equipment on the island. At best, they could dive and confirm it's man-made. No harm there."

"Still, force of habit."

"The boat will be here soon enough and whatever it is will still be there. Besides, it seems like the locals are so spooked by the area that we won't have much to worry about."

Vanya returned, a smile on her face. "Orwen can see you this morning if you'll go to his office. Here's the address," she said, and handed Sam a business card with handwriting on the back.

"Thanks so much for this," Remi said.

"My pleasure. Good luck with your mystery. What an exciting life you must lead if it's always like this."

"Well, there's a lot of hurry up and wait, too," Sam said.

Manchester's office was in one of the nicer buildings on the main street, two stories that looked like they had at least seen paint within the last ten years. A pleasant woman greeted them and showed them back to where Manchester was sitting, resplendent in his suit, behind a desk the size of an economy car.

"Please, sit. Vanya was very secretive on the phone. Said you're on an adventure and need some help?"

"Well, I'm not sure about the adventure part," Remi said.

Sam told him about the sunken ruins and Manchester's eyes widened. When Sam concluded, the big man rose and moved to look out his window at the ocean.

"That's quite a tale. I'm not sure what to make of it." He hesitated. "What would you like me to do?"

"A couple of things. There has to be some kind of evidence of what the ruins are. Some historical reference, or at least a legend."

"Perhaps. But we have no written history, so I wouldn't expect much. I've never heard anything."

"Maybe an elder who knows all the old stories?"

Manchester appeared to think. "There are a few relics who might be able to help you. But they're out in the middle of nowhere. City life isn't for them—they prefer the traditional ways."

"Could you make any introductions?"

Manchester laughed. "It's not like I can send them an e-mail. But I can give you directions and a note to show them. Although they probably can't read, they might recognize the stationery."

"That would be perfect." Sam paused. "There's also the question of how to get the government's approval to investigate the site."

"That I'll need to think about. We've never really had anyone approach us to do anything resembling archaeology here, so it's a first, at least as long as I've been a MP. I'm not sure there's a procedure to follow."

"That can be both good and bad," Remi said.

"Yes. I understand. Wouldn't want to run afoul of anyone's sensibilities. I'll have lunch with some of the other members of parliament and see what I can come up with. It's not like you want mineral rights or anything, just to poke around in some sunken stones. Am I correct?"

"Absolutely. Anything we find would be the property of the Solomon people. We're here merely out of curiosity."

"I think that will go a long way to engendering support, then. You're basically working for free, helping us catalog a piece of history we didn't even know existed until today."

"That's how I'd present it," Sam agreed.

Manchester smiled. "Well, I can't guarantee a permit, but I'll do what I can," he said doubtfully.

"That's all we can ask."

"As for the oldsters, I have two people in mind. One lives down by Mbinu, halfway to the eastern tip of the island, and the other is more remote—he has a shack on a dirt road by the river east of the village of Aola. What are you driving?"

Sam and Remi exchanged a glance. "We have to find something to rent."

"Get an SUV with good tires and four-wheel drive. You'll need it."

"Where's the best place to find one?"

Manchester sat back down in his executive chair and wrote out a brief letter on official stationery with the Solomon Islands crest at the top and then scribbled several names and addresses on a separate sheet of ordinary paper. He slid both to Remi with a flourish.

"Rubo is about a hundred years old. He's the one on the dirt road. The superstitious think he's a shaman—a holy man. Tom's a former logger who knows everyone. Not as old, but he's plugged in to everything that happens around here. He probably already knows you're looking for him," Manchester said with a grin. "Both speak some English, so you shouldn't need a translator. As for the car, this guy's honest and his vehicles aren't bad. Tell him I sent you and he'll treat you well."

They stood and shook hands and Sam's was again crushed as he forced a tight smile. Once out in the swelter, he read the directions to the car rental company and shook his head.

"Quite an adventure, all right. Look at these directions. 'Take dirt road east, past washed-out bridge, look for a hut on left near big banyan tree.' How badly do you want to do this?" he asked.

Remi shrugged. "We don't have anything better to do. Might as well see the sights."

"Right. What could go wrong?"

Remi froze and then slowly shook her head. "How many times . . ."

"Oops. Sorry. I take it back. I never said it."

"Too late. The universe heard you."

"Let's hope it's not paying much attention to the Solomons today." He looked around at the shabby storefronts and sparse traffic. A rooster eyed them from across the street before darting around a corner.

"Looks like a fairly safe bet."

CHAPTER 10

The car rental company was owned by a chubby man with a Buddha-like countenance who laughed at the end of each sentence he spoke like a form of punctuation. He showed them a silver Nissan Xterra that was more dents than not and they agreed on what seemed like a reasonable price per day.

It began raining as they climbed into the cab. Sam took the wheel and within minutes they headed east at a crawl, the main road having almost instantly become a river from the cloudburst. They passed beneath a pedestrian bridge and Sam paused to look at the elaborate graffiti murals adorning the concrete pylons. Depictions of islanders from the distant past and of primitive deities ringed the concrete, the detail impressive even in the heavy rain.

Within minutes, they had left the city limits and crossed the swollen Lor Lungga creek, its rushing brown water thick with floating branches from the mountains. They passed Henderson Field, the international airport that had been built by Allied forces during the war, and soon were barreling along through dense jungle. The rain blew across the asphalt in silver sheets, and the Nissan's wipers struggled to keep up with the downpour.

After a few miles, the rain stopped as abruptly as it started. When the clouds parted, steam rose from the pavement as the water evaporated under the harsh glare of the blazing sun.

"Well, one good thing about this place," Sam said as Remi fiddled with the dashboard knobs, trying to coax the reluctant air-conditioning to action.

"What's that?"

"If you don't like the weather, all you have to do is wait a little while and it will change."

"Right. A choice of humid hot and raining hot. My hair's hopeless," Remi said, tugging at her limp locks.

"After we finish up here, I'll take you anywhere you want. Rio, Milan, Nice. Spas, salons, shopping, pampering, the works."

"Any chance we can skip straight to the fun part?"

"Didn't I tell you? This is the fun part." Sam chuckled.

A small roadside sign announced they were crossing Alligator River, and Remi gave Sam a dark look. "I'm noticing a theme to the local attractions."

"Alligators are different from crocodiles."

"A distinction that's lost on this girl at the moment. They'll both eat you."

"Well, there's that," Sam conceded.

They arrived at another bridge, this one barely wide enough to accommodate the Nissan, and then drove past a sign pointing south that said "Gold Ridge."

"I wonder if that's the mine?" Remi said.

"We can take a look on the way back, if you want. We're not on any pressing schedule."

"Let's see how we do in the wilds. If not today, there's always tomorrow."

"Whatever my lady wants," Sam said.

"That's a little more like it."

When they arrived at Mbinu, they found the little hamlet was barely more than a few modest homes along a stretch of nothing. They stopped at a tiny market and were immediately assaulted by heat and bugs. Several islanders sat in the shade of a tree by the side of the road, staring at them curiously. Sam approached, the sheet of paper with the names and addresses in his hand.

"We're looking for a man named Tom. Supposed to live around here?" he asked with a smile.

The islanders stared at him, and then one made a comment in a language neither Sam nor Remi understood and the others all laughed.

Remi stepped forward. "Do you know Tom?"

More muttered comments, more laughter, and one of the men shrugged. Remi turned to Sam. "This is going well."

"I remember reading that even though English is the official language, only a fraction of the population speaks it."

"Looks like this isn't that fraction."

They waved at the islanders, who waved back, friendly enough, and tried the market. There they had a slightly better result—the heavyset woman behind the ancient cash register spoke a little English.

"Tom? He by da church. Down da road a piece."

"Church?" Sam asked.

"Back that way."

"Oh, good. And where, exactly, is Tom's?"

"Look for sign."

"Sign?"

"Skink."

"Excuse me?"

"Skink." The woman pantomimed a crawling animal and Remi nodded.

"Ah."

They got back into the car and backtracked. It took them two return trips before they spotted a muddy sign with the outline of a lizard on it. "Want to bet that's a kink?" Sam asked.

"*Skink*. With an *s*. At least that's what it sounded like," Remi corrected.

They bounced down a rutted muddy drive for a hundred yards and then rounded a bend. A tired-looking house occupied the far side of a clearing ringed by trees. A sixties Toyota sedan, almost entirely rust, was parked at the edge of the drive. An elderly man wearing a dark green T-shirt and shorts sat on what served as a porch, staring at them as they parked and got out of the Nissan.

"Tom?" Remi asked with a smile.

"That's me," the man replied, smiling, his few yellow teeth standing out against his dark complexion like headlights.

"We're friends of Orwen Manchester."

"That thief? Always said no damned good would come of the boy," Tom said with a cackle. "What can I do for you? Skink?" He held up a green lizard that had been slumbering in his lap and Remi resisted the urge to recoil. It was over two feet long, with a triangular head and beady black eyes.

"Um, no. We're here to ask about some of the old stories. Orwen felt you might be able to help," Remi said, returning his smile.

"Well, I don't know about that, but no harm asking. Can I get you anything? Water? Maybe soda? I'm a little low on supplies, but I can probably find something."

Sam shook his head. "No, that's fine. We're good."

"Well, come on and have a seat, then. What stories you want to know about?"

They sat on a makeshift wooden bench, their backs to the front of the house, and Sam cleared his throat. "Anything that might have to do with a cursed bay on the other side of the island."

Tom's eyes narrowed. "'Cursed bay,' you say?"

"That's what the captain of the boat we were on said."

"Why you care about some old nonsense like that?"

"We're just interested in why such a pretty area would be considered taboo by islanders."

Tom stared off into the distance and then grunted. "Sorry. Can't help you."

Remi's face fell. "You don't know any stories connected to the bay?"

Tom shook his head. "Afraid you wasted your time, folks."

"That's a shame. We saved a man's life who was attacked by a crocodile there," Sam said, hoping to score some points.

Tom showed no interest in the story. "Yeah, that happens. People go missing sometimes when they're careless. Crocodiles are plenty dangerous around here." He spat to the side. "'Course lots of danger around this place if you aren't careful."

"Really?" Remi said. "It doesn't strike me as particularly dangerous."

"Oh, it is. 'Specially you go poking your nose around where it don't belong."

"Like where?"

"Like that bay you talking about, for starters. And the caves." His voice softened to a whisper. "Best not to get too close to the giants."

Sam sat forward. "I'm sorry. Did you say 'giants'?"

Tom nodded. "That's right. Plenty of them in the mountains. Best to stay away and mind your own business. Stay in Honiara. Enjoy yourself. Be safe."

"You're saying there are giants here?" Sam asked again, his tone skeptical.

Tom grunted again. "Been here forever. And then some."

"As in 'big people'?" Remi clarified, surprised by the unusual turn the conversation had taken.

"Not people. Giants. Huge. They live in the caves and eat people. People aren't their friend. Most country people know about them. They see them all the time."

"This is a legend, right?"

"Call it what you want, I'm just warning you so you don't get into trouble. You friends with Orwen. Wouldn't do to be eaten by giants."

Sam chuckled. "You honestly believe in giants?"

"Hell, boy, I seen 'em. Plenty of 'em, in my time. Over twice as tall as you, covered in hair. Meaner than that crocodile that ate your mate." Tom spat again and then seemed to lose interest in the conversation. Sam and Remi tried to get something more out of him, but, while polite, he answered their questions with cryptic comments and generalities.

"Is there anything else we should know about besides giants?" Sam asked with a good-natured smile.

"Laugh all you want, but there's strange things going on. People are disappearing. Getting sick for no reason. Up in the hills, there are areas nobody will go because they're poison. The island's changing and giants are only one of the dangers. Never seen nothing like it before, and I know enough to understand none of it's good."

"Is that what people think about the bay, too? That it's poison? Cursed?" Remi asked softly.

"I don't know nothing about no bay."

"What about stories from the old days. Anything about lost cities?"

Tom petted his skink and shook his head. "You talking nonsense now?"

"No, I just thought I'd heard something about a lost kingdom."

"That's a new one on me," Tom said, but his tone sounded guarded.

After a few more minutes of stonewalling, Tom announced he was tired. Sam and Remi took the hint and made their way back to the car, the old man's eyes boring through them as they walked.

Sam started the engine and turned to Remi. "Can you believe that?"

"What, the giants or not knowing about the bay?"

"Both. I watched his eyes. He knows more than he's letting on. I think the giants were just to distract us."

"It worked. It's the craziest thing I've ever heard. But he described them with a straight face."

"I'm getting the sense that the national pastime here is BS'ing the tourists. There's no such thing as giants."

"I know, but he was awfully convincing about there being danger around every turn and people disappearing. What do you make of that?"

"I honestly have no idea. But what I do know is that it tells us nothing about the bay or why it's cursed. More like he was trying to scare us away from asking any more questions."

A rumble of thunder sounded from the west and their eyes met. "Not again," Remi said.

"You up for another old-timer? Maybe he's friendlier than Tom."

"If it's pouring down rain, it could get awfully messy on a muddy road."

"I say we go for it."

"Why am I not surprised?" Remi fluttered a hand. "Fine. Don't say I didn't warn you."

Fifteen minutes later, the blue sky turned to roiling anthracite and dark clouds pummeled the island with driving rain. The potholes made a terrible road even slower going, and when they ran out of pavement, it quickly became obvious that their willingness to forge ahead was no substitute for a sunny day. After a quarter mile, the water neared the running boards and Sam conceded defeat. He turned around and the SUV slipped and slid back to the road, the muddy track almost unrecognizable with the flood coursing down its middle, the ruts from their tires filling only seconds after passing.

The rain didn't let up, and the trip back to the hotel took twice as long. When they finally reached the hotel lot, they exhaled in relief as they parked. Dripping, they entered the lobby, and the front desk clerk beckoned to them. Remi went to see what she wanted while Sam continued to the room. There were two messages: one from Leonid, saying he'd had his first classroom lesson and would be doing a shallow dive in the afternoon, and the second from Manchester, inviting them to dinner.

"You want to go?" Sam asked when she made it back to the room.

"Sure. Why not? We can see what he thinks about the giants."

"I know what I think about them. Boogeyman stories to scare children."

"Probably. But you have to admit the whole discussion with Tom was unsettling. He really sounded like he believed that stuff."

"He's at an age where he might not be able to tell the difference between reality and hallucinations, Remi. What did you make him as? Eighty? Older?"

"Hard to tell, but he seemed pretty sharp to me."

They met Manchester at another seaside restaurant, this one a little tonier than the prior night's. A glance at the empties on the table and the bottle in his hand showed that the big man was already through his second beer when they arrived. He motioned them over with his ever-present smirk.

"Sorry the weather didn't cooperate today. Should be fine tomorrow," he said as though he was personally responsible for the storm.

"No problem. We got to see one of the two fellows you directed us to," Remi said.

"Oh, good. Which one?"

"Tom."

"He's a character, isn't he? Did you get anything useful out of him?" Manchester asked, draining his bottle.

"Just a shaggy-dog story about giants."

"Ah, yes, the giants. A local tradition. Everyone knows someone who's seen them, but when you start trying to nail the story down, it gets slipperier than a greased eel."

"Tom said he's seen them."

"Of course he has. I mean, I'm sure he's seen something he thought was a giant. A shadow in the rain forest. An unexplained blur. He doesn't mean any harm. But did he know anything about your bay or the sunken ruins?"

Sam shook his head. "Regrettably, no. All he did was talk about people disappearing because of cannibal giants."

Manchester signaled to the waiter for two beers and then raised an eyebrow at Remi. "And what would you like?"

"I'll stick with water. The heat dehydrates me."

Manchester called the waiter over to relay Remi's request and then settled back in his chair. "So cannibal giants are running amok in the hills. I've heard that old wives' tale since I was a boy and the funny thing is how enduring the story is. Coming in the dead of night and snatching the unwary. I always wondered how the legend started. There's variations of it on most of the surrounding islands as well."

When the waiter arrived with the drinks, Manchester ordered a seafood feast for them all that could feed ten people. They took their time eating as Manchester plowed through helping after helping with the commitment of a bulldog. When they finished, Sam turned the conversation to the gold mine.

"You mentioned the mine last night. How long has it been in operation?"

"On and off for a dozen years. Up until recently, it hasn't done anything—ever since what we call the social unrest happened."

"I never associated Guadalcanal with gold, for some reason."

"Most Americans don't. The only reason they've heard of the island is because of the big offensive against the Japanese in World War Two. But gold has been one of our defining characteristics—it's how the Solomon Islands got their name."

"Really?" Sam said.

"Yes. When the Spanish arrived in the sixteenth century, they found gold at the mouth of the Mataniko River. Their leader, an explorer named Álvaro de Mendaña de Neira, came to the unusual conclusion that this was one of the areas that the biblical King Solomon must have gotten some of his legendary gold from and named us after him. Let's just say for an explorer, his sense of geography might have been a little off."

"That's funny," Remi said. "Truth is stranger than fiction."

Sam leaned forward. "Just to put our questions to rest, what do you make of Tom's stories?"

"Well, people do go missing, and it seems like such incidents have been increasing, but I'm not sure what that means. It's probably that the usual culprits are getting them—accidents, drownings, crocodiles—and that our reporting has gotten better so we're tracking the disappearances more accurately. But it's hardly an epidemic. We're talking maybe twenty people a year. Hard to survive as a cannibal on that calorie count, I'd think."

"I take it you're not in the 'giants are everywhere' camp?" Remi asked.

"Tom's a very nice bloke, but I prefer to stick to the physically possible, or at least probable. I'll leave the unicorns and leprechauns to others."

"What about his contention that certain areas of the island are cursed?"

"What does that mean? Because there's more crocodiles in certain bays and near rivers there's a curse? Or that because some of the inland cave systems are so treacherous that people disappear near them, never to be heard from again? For every curse, I can come up with a plausible explanation, and I don't require flights of fancy to do it."

"We were thinking about heading up to the gold mine tomorrow after we meet with Rubo."

"Assuming he's still alive and hasn't washed away. As for the mine, there's not a lot to see. It was closed down recently due to flooding and hasn't reopened."

"We're running out of things to do in our off time. Where are these caves with all the giants located?"

"Up in the mountains," Manchester said vaguely. "But there are no roads near them. And it's treacherous terrain. I'm not sure I'd ever get bored enough to try to explore the caves. Too much other stimulation available. Diving, fishing . . ."

When they'd said their good-nights and were driving back to the hotel, Sam turned to Remi as they passed the waterfront.

"He didn't seem impressed by Tom's yarn, did he?"

"No. But there's something off about him. Don't ask me what."

"You got that, too? I thought it was only me."

CHAPTER 11

A utility truck rolled along the coastal road, and its engine labored to climb a grade on the dogleg leading away from the shore toward the mountains. The driver hummed along with the radio while his companion dozed in the passenger seat, khaki shirt soiled from a long workday.

The two Australians had been on Guadalcanal for six months, part of the ongoing aid effort since the 2006 riots. Now a much smaller group than during the upheaval, their duty was almost boring, with none of the danger of the previous years. The island had settled into a peaceful truce after much of Honiara had been destroyed during the unrest, and the focus was now on building a better future rather than fostering the cultural differences that had led to so much dissension.

The driver made his way around the curves with caution, alert to the possibility of coming head-on with a slow-moving vehicle without lights in the evening gloom. On the road, automobiles with questionable brakes and nonexistent safety equipment were only one of the many hazards. Domestic animals, fallen trees, broken-down cars—any and all could appear out of nowhere, and the driver was taking no chances.

"Crap. What's this all about, then?" he muttered to himself as he came around a particularly sharp curve. A van was stopped in the middle of the road, its emergency lights flashing. "Alfred. Wake up."

The passenger sat up straight and rubbed a hand over his face as they slowed. The road was blocked, so they couldn't go around the vehicle.

"Bloody great, Simon. So much for getting back at a reasonable hour."

The truck coasted to a stop and Simon peered at the rear of the van. "I hope the driver's here. If he went walkabout to get help, we're screwed."

"Only one way to find out."

Both men opened their doors and stepped out of the truck, leaving the engine running and their headlights illuminating the rusting van's rear end. Simon walked to the driver's door and peered inside and was turning to tell Alfred that it was empty when four dark forms ran from the bush at the side of the road, machete blades flashing in the dim light.

Simon held his arms up instinctively to block the blows, but his flesh and bone were no match for steel honed to a razor's edge. Alfred went down in a heap as a blade severed his carotid artery, and the attackers continued to hack at him even when it was obvious he was dead.

Simon fell soundlessly from a sharp blow to his skull and crumpled lifelessly to the ground as his killer stood over him with a demented grin twisting his face. A voice called from the brush and the men stopped in their tracks.

"Enough. Get the truck off the road and drag the bodies into the bush so they aren't discovered. The animals will take care of the rest."

The men exchanged glances, their tattered clothes sprayed with blood that was already congealing in the warm night air. They sprang into action and within five minutes had cleared the scene, leaving no evidence of the massacre other than glistening black stains on the road.

"Go on, now. Get out of here. Stop at the shore and clean yourselves off, and take care to get all the blood off your weapons. And remember—not a word to anyone. I hear anything, I'll cut your tongues out and have you staked over an anthill."

The men shuddered. Nobody doubted the speaker's sincerity. They nodded and climbed into the van, which started with a sputtering puff of blue exhaust, and were out of sight before the motor's roar faded. The speaker walked to the bloody smudges on the road, considered them, and smiled. Everything was going according to plan, and the only thing that remained was to contact the papers and plant a statement saying that the rebel militia had kidnapped two aid workers and were demanding all foreign companies invested in the island relinquish their claims and leave—before lives were lost.

The surrounding jungle was quiet, the only sound the scurrying of nocturnal creatures moving toward the easy meal that awaited them. A black SUV pulled out from behind a thicket twenty yards down the road and headed for Honiara, leaving the Australians' truck and their mutilated corpses at the bottom of a nameless ravine, two more casualties on an island whose soil ran red from battles fought for its control.

CHAPTER 12

The next morning, Sam and Remi headed for the hospital. Dr. Vanya was there and this time allowed them into the depths of the building to see Benji, who thanked them profusely for their help in barely understandable English. It quickly became obvious that there wasn't anything further to talk about, and after a few minutes of assurances that Leonid would help out with the hospital bills they moved back to the patient lounge with Vanya.

"What do you have planned for today?" she asked.

"We're going to interview some locals about Guadalcanal legends and then maybe go see the mine," Remi said.

"Oh, well, be careful. Once you get outside the city, the roads can be treacherous. And you've already seen what the jungle can hold. The crocodiles are only one of the dangers."

"Yes, Manchester told us all about the giants," Sam said.

Vanya slowed and smiled, but her expression seemed brittle. "There are some colorful beliefs here, that's for sure."

"As we'd expect in any isolated rural society," Sam acknowledged. "We're respectful of the traditions that fostered them, but still . . ."

"I've heard about giants ever since I was a toddler. I don't even pay any attention to the stories anymore. I treat it sort of like religion—people are entitled to think what they think," Vanya said.

"But he did say there's been an increase in unexplained disappearances," Remi reminded her.

"I've heard rumors that there are still pockets of militia in the mountains who are hiding out. I find that far more likely than the giant explanation."

"Militia?"

"Ever since the social upheaval, when the Australians sent in an armed task force to keep the peace, there have been those who have agitated for a change in regime—who view foreign intervention as a disguised occupation of the country in order to control its natural resources. While the majority seems ambivalent about it, there are still groups of people who are angry, and some of them are militant. There have been clashes."

"Then it actually *is* risky to go explore the caves?" said Sam.

She nodded. "Not because of giants. But does it matter what gets you if you're never heard from again?"

Remi eyed Sam. "She has a point."

"Thanks for taking the time to escort us to see Benji," Sam said to Vanya. "What happened to the poor man is a tragedy."

"My pleasure. Just take care that the same doesn't happen to you. The island's still largely wild, and, like I said, the crocs aren't the only predators."

"We'll bear that in mind. Thanks again."

Heat radiated off the parking lot as they walked to the Nissan, the equatorial sun already brutal in the late morning. This time, their drive east on the only paved road was fast and relatively easy until they passed the tiny village of Komunimboko and the road they'd had to quit the prior day. It wasn't waist-deep in water any longer, but it was badly rutted and still mostly mud.

Sam dropped the drive train into four-wheel drive and they edged along, the car swaying and bouncing like an amusement park ride. The passage through the jungle narrowed until it more resembled a tunnel than a road. The canopy overhead blocked much of the sun, and the foliage framing the muddy track was dense and foreboding, brushing against the sides of the SUV as it rocked inland.

"And we don't even know if this Rubo is still alive or living here?" Remi asked.

"There are no guarantees in life. Where's your sense of adventure?"

"I think I left it back a mile ago, along with my sacroiliac and a few fillings."

"We've been through worse."

"I just hope I can keep breakfast down."

Half an hour later, they rounded a particularly ugly switchback curve and entered a clearing by the river. A traditional thatch-roofed hut rested in the shade of a tall banyan tree, no evidence of power or phone lines to be found. They rolled to a stop in front, and Remi glanced at Sam.

"Nice. And you have me staying at that crappy hotel?"

"Every day brings new surprises, doesn't it?"

"I think your quarry is peering out the doorway."

"Let's hope so."

"Maybe I'll stay in the car. That way, if you take a blowgun dart to the neck, I'll be able to get help."

"Always thinking of me, aren't you? It has nothing to do with the AC . . ."

"If you can even call it AC. To me, it feels like it's just blowing the hot air around."

"Stay, if you want. I'm going to talk to our new friend. You sure you saw someone there?" Sam asked, squinting at the hut.

"I think so. Movement. Could have been a crocodile or a skink, though, so be careful."

"That makes me feel . . . really good."

"That's what I'm here for."

Sam opened the door and stepped out of the vehicle and then slowly made his way toward the dwelling, which looked uninhabited. When he was a few yards away, a tremulous voice called out from inside in pidgin. Even though Sam didn't understand it, from the tone it was clearly a warning, so he stopped.

"I'm looking for Rubo," he said slowly. "Rubo," he repeated for emphasis. "Do you speak English?"

All Sam could hear was the soft rumbling of the Nissan's poorly muffled exhaust and the buzz of inquisitive insects that had taken an interest in him. He resisted the urge to swat at the air like an enraged bear and instead waited for a response.

A figure appeared in the doorway. It was an ancient man, stooped and thin, with sagging skin, and clad only in a pair of tattered shorts. The skeletal face studied Sam, the eyes dull in the shadows, and then the figure spoke.

"I speak some English. What you want?"

"I'm a friend of Orwen Manchester. I'm looking for Rubo."

"I heard you fine. Why?"

"I need to ask some questions. About local legends."

The old man emerged from the dark interior and regarded Sam with suspicion. "You come long way for questions."

"They're important."

The old man grunted. "I'm Rubo."

"I'm Sam. Sam Fargo." Sam extended his hand, and Rubo stared at it like it was smeared with filth. Sam hesitated, wondering if he'd crossed some social line, and the old man grinned, exposing toothless gums.

"Don't worry. Me don't like shaking hands. Not taboo. Just don't like." Rubo asked, "You sit?" motioning to a log that ran along one of the thatched walls, thankfully in the shade.

"Thank you."

They took seats, the old man's watchful gaze roving from Sam's shoes to his hair.

"What you want?" Rubo asked again, his voice quiet.

"I want to talk about the old days. Old stories. Orwen said you know more than anyone."

Rubo nodded. "Could be. Lot of stories."

"I'm interested in any about a curse. Or a lost city."

The old man's eyes narrowed. "Lost city? Curse?"

Sam nodded. "About a bay on the other side of the island that's cursed. Bad luck."

"Why you ask 'bout city?"

"I heard from someone who's exploring the island that there are ruins underwater."

Rubo looked off into the distance, watching the river's brown water surge past. When he returned his attention to Sam, his face was stony.

"There is story. Old. King who tempt gods. No good, tempt gods. He build temples in bay. But big wave destroy. Curse bay. No good go there."

"When did this happen?"

The old man shrugged his bony shoulders. "Long time back. Before white man come."

Sam waited for him to continue, but for a storyteller Rubo was short on details. After a half minute of silence, Sam tried a smile. "That's it?"

Rubo nodded, then held out a gnarled finger, pointing at the car. "Who that?"

"Oh, sorry. My wife." Sam waved to Remi and motioned for her to come over. She stepped down from the vehicle and approached.

Rubo's vision seemed to improve and his eyes stayed locked on Remi as she neared before looking away at the last second.

"Remi? This is Rubo. He was just telling me about a legend. A king who built temples in a bay that the sea then reclaimed. Angry gods."

"Nice to meet you," Remi said, beaming a smile at the old man. He stood unsteadily and took her proffered hand and shook it. Sam didn't say anything. Apparently, there were exceptions to every rule.

"Sit," Rubo invited, and she offered him another smile. She took a seat next to Sam and waited expectantly. Sam cleared his throat.

"Sounds like our ruins, doesn't it?"

"Yes. It's amazing that Rubo knows the story."

The corners of Rubo's lips tugged upward. "I know many. Stories."

"I'm sure you do. And your English is very good. How did you learn to speak so well?"

"Big war. I help Uncle Sam."

"Did you really? Those must have been rough days," Remi said.

Rubo nodded. "Bad days. Many die. Hate Japanese."

"They were bad to the islanders?"

"Some. One very bad. Colonel."

"What did he do?" Sam asked.

"Bad things. Kill many of us. And do tests. Secret."

Remi edged closer. "What? What kind of tests?"

Rubo looked away. "Med."

"Med? You mean 'medical'?"

He nodded. "Yes. With white man. But not American."

Sam stared at Remi. "Japanese experimenting on locals with white men. Want to take two guesses what nationality they were?"

They turned their attention back to Rubo. "Why haven't we heard anything about this before?"

He shrugged. "Dunno. Maybe nobody care?"

"Japanese engaging in war crimes here? I can't believe that would be swept under the rug."

Rubo gave her a blank look. "Rug?"

"Sorry. An expression."

"Back to the king and his temples. Can you tell us the whole story?" encouraged Sam.

Rubo shrugged. "Old. Not much to tell. King build temples and palace. Gods angry, destroy it. Place cursed. Everyone forget about him."

"That's it?"

"Pretty much."

Sam sighed. "What about giants? What are the legends about them?"

Rubo's eyes widened. "They real. Use to be lots. Now not same. But real."

"How do you know? Have you seen them?"

"No. But many I know have."

"Isn't it a little strange to believe in something you've never seen? I mean, it's like ghosts. Lots of people believe in them, but . . ." Sam stopped talking when he saw Rubo's face.

"Ghosts real."

Remi took over. "So you think there are really giants in the caves?"

"I don't go there." The old man shifted on the log. "Bad spirits in caves. Jap officer do things there. Many ghosts. Angry. And giants. No good in caves."

Sam exchanged a glance with Remi. Rubo was clearly not a fan of the Japanese or the caves. And he seemed to have exhausted his limited repertoire of stories about the king.

Remi cocked her head and leaned toward Sam. "Did you hear that?"

"No. What?"

Rubo was lost in his thoughts, staring into space.

"I thought I heard an engine. Down the track."

Sam shook his head. "Not me." He returned his attention to Rubo. "How well known is the story about the king?"

The old islander shook his head. "Nobody talk about the old days. Just as well."

A crack of branches sounded from the river, and Remi started. She and Sam peered into the brush but saw nothing. They listened, ears straining for any further sound, but the area was quiet other than the sound of the river rushing past and the occasional flutter of birds overhead. Rubo didn't seem to notice, and after several minutes they relaxed.

Remi took the lead in asking more questions about the legend of the lost city, but the old man's responses became even more terse. When Remi took Sam's hand and stood, he didn't resist.

"Rubo, thanks so much for taking the time to tell us about the island's history. We really appreciate it," she said, her smile lighting up her face.

Rubo studied his feet with a shy expression. "Good to see people. Talk. Long time."

They retraced their steps to the Xterra and were greeted by a blast of cool air when they opened the doors. The little motor was still chugging along and the AC with it. Remi strapped in and turned to Sam. "What did you make of that?"

"It's another piece of the puzzle. Makes sense, though. Sounds like a natural disaster destroyed the king's work and that that was interpreted by the locals as angry gods swatting him like a fly. Also explains the curse. Even if the specifics have been forgotten, legends like that have a way of lingering."

"Leonid will be pleased to have more to go on than a question mark."

"In case you haven't noticed, Leonid's hard to please. Ever."

"Leonid is a grumpy guy."

"It goes with being Russian. All the snow. Or the cold soup."

Remi eyed the shack. "He really did look like he was a hundred."

"He'd have to be close to that if he was around during the war and old enough to help the Allies."

"The bit about the Japanese colonel conducting experiments was more than a little creepy. I can't believe something like that could happen and wouldn't be recorded by history."

"It's a small island. History tends to miss a lot of the minor events. We more than anyone should know that."

"Kind of our edge, isn't it?"

"That and your charm. Judging by Rubo's reaction, that can't be underestimated." Sam smiled and slid the transmission into gear. "So? What next? Gold mine sightseeing or back to town?"

"I say let's look at the hole in the ground. Not that I'm complaining, but it's easy to go stir-crazy sitting in a hotel room all day."

"Then gold mine it is."

The drive back to the main road seemed longer, if anything, and by the time they made it to the asphalt they were both over the thrill of rural off-roading.

The pavement degraded after they turned off the coastal road until soon it was loose gravel over potholes and ruts deep enough to break an axle. Acres of trees of a palm oil plantation lined the way, one of the island's principal industries. As they climbed into the mountains, Sam checked his rearview mirror several times.

"Looks like we're not the only ones out for a drive," he said.

"I wonder if that's the one we heard back by Rubo's? That's the first car we've seen today outside of town, and this is a pretty rural area."

"In a way, it's reassuring. At least if we break down, we won't be walking twenty miles for help."

"Why do you have to jinx us by thinking negative thoughts like that?"

"Sorry. Just the way my mind works."

They passed a lagoon with a small traditional village and then a small company town of abandoned Quonset huts.

"Ghost town, isn't it?" Remi said.

"Makes sense if the mine's shut down. Not like there are dozens of ways to make a living out here."

They continued south and, when they came over the crest of a hill, saw an expanse below them that looked like a giant hand had scraped the jungle from the mountaintop, leaving only bare earth. A security gate blocked the road in front of them, but the buildings behind it were empty, their glass shattered, and the gate broken.

"Are you sure about this, Sam?" Remi asked.

"Looks like we're not the first to want to poke around."

"Right, but it's private property."

"Well, maybe, but since the mine's closed, I'm not sure that matters. Besides, it's not like we cut chains or jumped the fence. And we're not here to steal anything."

"Save it for the cops."

"I don't think they have any outside of town."

"And that's a good thing?"

Sam coaxed the Nissan forward and farther up the mountain road until they were above the main processing plant. He stopped by the massive conveyor system that had once hauled ore to the crushers and eyed the line of abandoned ore trucks.

"Not a soul around. A little eerie, isn't it?" he said, his voice low. "You want to get out or keep going?"

"Keep going."

The road twisted along the ridge, and when they rounded a curve, they came face to face with the open pits, where the land had been methodically excavated and hauled to the plant for processing. The road ended at the southernmost, largest pit, and this time when Sam stopped, Remi agreed to look around. They got out of the vehicle and the heat immediately assaulted them.

Remi turned to Sam. "It's like they cut off the top of the mountain. I've never seen anything like it. It's . . . it just seems so destructive."

A hot wind gusted across the mountain, carrying with it a low moan from the plant as it blew through the towers. Eventually, Sam led Remi back to the truck. They buckled up and Remi shook her head. "I don't know what I was expecting to see, but it wasn't that."

Sam twisted the wheel and they backtracked down the grade. When they passed the security gate, they accelerated, kicking up dust as they rolled down the mountain. Remi closed her eyes, enjoying the cool air blowing from the vents, and then Sam's voice jogged her out of her thoughts.

"We've got company."

She sat up, eyes wide. "And?"

"And either they want to race or they want to pass."

Remi glanced in the passenger-side mirror as they bounced along. "Well, slow down so they can get by. We're in no hurry."

Sam rolled his window down and motioned for the truck to pass as he slowed down. They both heard the roar of the vehicle's big engine before they felt the jarring blow as the truck's front bumper struck the rear quarter panel. Sam floored the gas and downshifted, fighting to stay on the narrow road, the tires slipping and sliding before regaining their grip.

"Hang on," he yelled as he eyed the rearview mirror, cursing silently at the coating of mud that obscured all but a hazy outline of the truck. He returned his attention to the road in front of him and glanced at the speedometer, trying to gauge how much more speed he could squeeze out of the Xterra without flipping it on one of the hairpin curves.

The truck accelerated, keeping pace, and as it tried to pull alongside, Sam twisted the SUV's steering wheel, blocking the move. They approached a winding stretch of road and he gunned the gas, hoping their smaller vehicle's agility would enable him to gain some valuable distance from the madman in the truck. The Xterra slalomed around the turns, Sam's knuckles tightened on the wheel as he piloted the SUV to within inches of its limits.

Remi craned her neck to better see their pursuers, but her side mirror, like the rear window, was coated in mud from the earlier slog down the river road. Sam swerved again as they hit a straightaway, trying to keep the truck behind him as its larger engine kicked in and it pulled closer.

Sam tapped the brakes and downshifted as he neared a tight turn, and then things happened fast. The big pickup truck rammed the rear bumper of the Nissan hard enough to snap their necks back against the headrests, and the Xterra fishtailed out of control as Sam battled with the steering wheel. Remi wedged her feet up against the dashboard as the truck rammed them again, and then the Nissan was flipping, tumbling down the steep gorge toward the river far below.

CHAPTER 13

Steam hissed from beneath the ruined hood as Sam fought to free himself from the seat belt. The SUV had come to rest on its side. River water rushed around it and through the shattered windows. Remi sputtered as she groped for the seat belt's release, but Sam got to it first and she fell against him as the water level rose, soaking them both.

"You okay?" he asked as he pushed deflated air bags aside.

She nodded. "A few bumps and bruises."

Sam tested his limbs and then gazed around the submerged cabin. "How do you want to do this?"

"Out my window."

"Okay."

Remi hoisted herself toward her door and then up through the gap where her passenger window had been as the cabin filled. Sam followed her to where she was clinging to the side of the Nissan, and then a fountain of spray exploded from the river's surface, followed almost in-

stantly by the sharp crack of a gun from the road above. They released
their hold on the SUV and slid into the river as another shot punched a
hole in its roof, and then they were carried downstream in the brown
current, the river only six feet deep but swollen from the rains.

Sam yelled at Remi, whose head bobbed above the surface. "First
bend, climb out at the far shore and take cover."

"Got it."

He could barely hear her above the rush of the water.

Their speed increased as they approached a narrower section that
churned with white froth. Rapids. Rocks beneath the surface, most
likely sharp. He began pulling for the shore as the water deepened and
found that he could beat the current. Remi followed his lead, and Sam
helped Remi onto the bank near the rapids, gasping for breath.

Sam listened for more shots as he peered up at where the road followed the ridge, now several hundred yards away. If the shooter had a
pistol, they were so far out of range they had no worries. If a rifle with
a scope, they were still in trouble.

"I thought there were no guns on the island," Remi whispered.

"Apparently, gun laws only work with law-abiding citizens. We can
assume whoever was shooting at us doesn't fit that description."

They both saw motion at the bend in the river and ducked low. Two
islanders were making their way along the bank, one clutching a revolver. They were still a good hundred yards away and apparently
hadn't spotted Sam and Remi.

Sam whispered to her, "Slide back into the brush. As long as they're
on that side, they'll never spot us."

Soon they were hidden by the dense vegetation. They watched as
the men followed the river south. Both Sam and Remi held still as their
pursuers eyed the foliage on both sides of the river and then faltered
as they neared the rapids. The pair was close enough that their voices
carried over the sound of the rushing water. The one with the pistol
gestured with it downriver as though emphasizing his point, and then

they turned and made their way back to the bend. Remi exhaled softly when they disappeared from view, but neither she nor Sam dared move in case the men had gone in search of reinforcements.

They waited ten minutes, ears straining for any sound of pursuit, but heard and saw nothing.

"Looks like they're gone," Remi whispered.

"Right. But the question is who 'they' are."

"Maybe someone associated with the mine? Or a group of the militia Manchester was warning us about?"

"Could be. But the way he described their territory, they were in the central part of the island, by the caves."

She stared up the river and shook her head. "I don't get it. Why would anyone want to run us off the road and shoot at us? Even if they were militia?"

"That's a good question."

"All we've done is talk to a couple of old men about some legendary ruins."

"Don't forget the giants." Sam took a final look at where the men had disappeared beyond the bend and then stood. "Looks like it's just you and me, kid." He inspected his wet clothes. "The only good part about this weather is that we won't freeze. In fact, once we're out in the sun, we'll be dry in a few minutes."

"That's great. But the main road's at least, what, six or seven miles away?"

"Probably. Assuming it's safe to walk to it. Didn't someone say there were crocodiles along most of the rivers?"

"Not exactly positive thinking, Fargo."

"Okay. I'm *positive* there are crocodiles along most of the rivers."

Remi smiled in spite of herself. "That's better. See how easy that was?" She struggled to her feet and felt her neck. Sam eyed her with concern.

"Did you hurt yourself?"

"Probably a touch of whiplash. But God bless whoever invented the air bag and seat belt."

Sam glanced back up to where the car was wrecked. "I'm glad I took the extra insurance. Think it covers running off a cliff?"

"Probably an exception in the fine print." She felt the side of her face, which was swelling.

"There are two ways to go—the road or the river. Which would you rather face—a thug with a gun or twenty feet of hungry croc?" Sam asked.

"What's the middle choice?"

Sam offered a pained smile in response.

Remi eyed the rushing water. "If I were our attackers, I'd have hightailed it out of here once we disappeared. That looks like what they did."

"I hope you're right."

Remi followed Sam's gaze up the river. "Me too."

"It'll probably be shallower after the rapids. We can try crossing there and find the road," suggested Sam.

"Lead the way. Mind the crocodiles."

"Thanks. I'd almost forgotten."

Sam carefully moved along the bank as they worked their way downstream. The roar of the rapids increased, and, as he'd hoped, after a deep pool with eddies swirling along the surface, the river widened and he could see the bottom. Crossing was still tricky. They held hands as they waded up to their waists, Sam feeling along the bottom with his feet as they gingerly made their way to the far shore.

Once on dry land again, they waited for their clothes to dry, and in fifteen minutes were on the dirt track that led back to the seashore road. Two hours later, a farmer heading into town with a half-loaded pickup gave them a ride. The man's wizened face showed no surprise at finding two Americans hitchhiking on a road to nowhere who looked like they'd gone over the falls in a barrel.

Remi leaned her head against Sam's arm as the truck bumped along.

"How's the neck?" he asked over the noise of the wind.

"I could seriously use a massage, but, other than that, I'll live."

"Maybe we can find you a spa in town," Sam said hopefully.

"Sure. I could see that as a viable business here."

"Maybe settle for an amateur massage after a long shower?"

"You really don't think of anything else, do you?"

"That was completely innocent, Remi. I swear."

She shifted her head and stared up at him with a hint of amusement. "It always starts that way."

As they neared Honiara, Sam grew quiet.

Remi nudged him. "What now?"

"We need to find the police and report this."

"Okay. Ask the driver to take us to the station, or at least give us directions."

Sam rapped on the rear window, startling the farmer, who slammed on the brakes, causing both Sam and Remi to bang into the rear of the cab.

Sam leaned toward the driver's-side window. "Can you take us to the police station?"

The farmer seemed to understand the word "police" and nodded before giving the old truck gas. Sam slid toward the tailgate and came to rest next to Remi.

"I think that went well."

She gave him a wide grin. "You're my hero. Crocodile Fargo, the great white hunter."

"I just hope the police can do something other than commiserate. I think it was a Dodge truck, but it all happened so fast I can't be sure."

The duty officer showed them to a waiting area, where a sergeant took down their report, nodding and asking polite questions now and again. By the end of the hour, two things were apparent to the Fargos: the police were concerned and meant well, and the likelihood of anything happening soon, or ever, was low. The officer explained the problem as politically as he could.

"We'll check on all the trucks registered on the island, but it could be a long process. And if the driver is any good with sandpaper and paint, we may never find the culprits."

"But they shot at us. It was deliberate. We saw two of them after we crashed. They were looking for us."

"Yes, I wrote down the descriptions—two men, islanders, medium height, no distinguishing marks, wearing jean shorts and T-shirts, one brown or burgundy, the other pale blue," the officer said. "The problem, as you can probably appreciate, is that describes about half the population. We'll do our best, but it's not much to go on." He shook his head. "Your rental vehicle will tell the story, I'm sure. There will be evidence you were rammed, and you say that a shot hit it, so there will be a bullet hole."

"Yes," Remi agreed, her heart sinking as she listened.

The policeman regarded both of them. "Why are you in the islands?"

"We're on vacation," Sam said, which was close enough to the truth.

"Have you gotten into any fights? A disagreement with someone here?" the officer asked, and they shook their heads.

"No. Everyone's been nice," Remi said.

"So you can't think of anyone who would try to kill you." It wasn't a question.

"No. It makes no sense," Sam said.

The man stared hard at him. "Well, it must to someone. We just don't have this kind of thing happen here, Mr. Fargo. We're generally a peaceful island. It's not like we have roving gangs of criminals going after our tourists."

It was clear from his tone that the policeman wasn't buying the tourist explanation, and neither Sam nor Remi wanted to push the issue. When they finished with the questioning, they were close enough to their hotel to walk, and once again the front desk staff seemed horrified by their appearance as they strode through the lobby.

"We're making quite an impression," Remi said under her breath. "Next time you want to go sightseeing, I'm out."

He smiled at the clerk, whose face was frozen in a disapproving expression, and leaned into Remi.

"Next time I suggest it, hit me on the head with a brick."

CHAPTER 14

When Sam called Selma, she sounded excited. "I'm glad you called. You must be psychic. I was just getting ready to touch base. I've got some research I want to send you, but I wanted to tell you about it before I did—give you the background."

"Well, I'm here. Shoot."

"I dug around, as you requested, and quickly discovered that there's almost no information online about the Solomon Islands that doesn't relate to World War Two, mineral rights, or tourism. So there isn't exactly a wealth of data to sift through."

"That never stopped you before, Selma."

"Of course not. Anyway, once I exhausted the Internet, I switched to making calls to people who might know something about Guadalcanal history. Turns out most of those are in Australia and New Zealand, which isn't surprising since those are the nearest developed countries."

"Right . . ." Sam said, his tone mildly impatient. If Selma noticed, she gave no indication.

"I contacted some friends in Sydney and it turns out that one of the foremost experts on the islands is actually in Adelaide. An anthropology professor at the university there, Dr. Sylvester Rose. Anyway, I called him and we had a long chat. Very nice man."

"I'm glad you got along," Sam said, hoping she would cut to the chase.

"Turns out he spent years summering in the islands, collecting data about the cultures, documenting their habits, recording their lore. I asked him about anything that might be relevant to cursed bays or sunken ruins and he said it rang a bell but that he needed to go back through his logs and review his notes—nothing immediately came to mind. That was yesterday. Today he called me back and said he'd located the section he was looking for and that he'd send it over."

"That's great, Selma. So you have it?"

"Yes. I wanted to read it to you."

He closed his eyes. "There's never been a better time."

"Okay, here goes. 'One particularly obscure legend appears to have been taboo to discuss, but as with most forbidden stories, the prohibition made it all the more alluring for those wishing to buck the status quo. Thus it survives, albeit with the taboo intact. It was recounted to me by a medicine man, a healer in the highlands of Guadalcanal who lived a hermetic life away from the surrounding tribes. I was introduced to him by the tribal chieftain of the neighboring village, who held him in enormous regard. Our initial meeting became an annual one until he passed away in 1997. He told me the legend on our last night together the prior year.'"

Selma paused to clear her throat. "'Many generations before the white man appeared when the island was only our people, a great king arose to lead us. This king was a sorcerer who could command the gods of sea, sky, fire, and earth to do his bidding. He rallied the disparate tribes and created a powerful island nation. He was both feared for his prowess in battle and beloved for his benevolence and wisdom in deciding difficult social and moral questions. His name was Loc, and during his lifetime his name became the most revered in the kingdom.'"

"Interesting. First I've heard of it," Sam said.

"Here's where it gets good. 'In a time of plenty, King Loc announced that he would build a royal complex the likes of which had never been seen. For many years his subjects labored to fulfill his ambition, quarrying limestone and dragging enormous blocks over rollers from the mountains to the sea. On the eve of its completion, King Loc took a wife—the most beautiful woman in the islands, daughter of a powerful chieftain from Malaita. It was said that to see her face was akin to gazing at the sun, so great was her beauty, and the king forbid anyone from looking directly at her. It is thought that this is where the cultural taboo against looking at females came from.'"

"I just thought that was shyness," Sam said.

"Apparently not. 'The following morning, the heads of all the island tribes were to gather at the site of the new complex for a weeklong celebration. For months the king had been collecting tribute from traders and his tribes and adding it to the vast treasure secreted in the royal palace. The celebrants came heavily laden with gold, jewels, and other tribute. When the column arrived at the site, the king was parading his riches in the sun, his high priests and wife nearby. The gods were so offended by this display of arrogance from a mere human that the earth shook as never before, destroying the compound as though it were made of sand, and then the sea god sent a wave the size of an island to erase any trace of the site. Most of the visiting dignitaries were lost in the destruction, only a handful survived. Those who did agreed that the gods had made their will known and that the survivors' atonement would be to live as they had before the king came to power. As punishment for the king's sins, his name was never to be spoken again and his palace and temples were to be forgotten, the site damned as a cursed place.' That's the end of his entry."

"So the Solomon Islands' primitive culture is a direct result of that event? All progress erased in one fell swoop?"

"That's how I read it. But one thing that struck me was that a treasure is mentioned as though the amassing of riches was a big part of the affront to the gods, the clear message being that wealth is also to be avoided since it brought calamity with it."

"A treasure. Well, I've never been one to shy away from a challenge. I wonder how much of the legend is real and how much invention?"

"The professor had no way of knowing. Because it was forbidden knowledge, he had no secure way of corroborating it, and the medicine man swore him to secrecy. He couldn't very well go asking around after giving his word or nobody would have trusted him ever again. He'd spent a decade building his standing in the community with his regular trips and he didn't want to destroy that trust, so he kept quiet about it." Selma paused. "But no secret lasts if more than one person knows about it. There has to be someone else the medicine man told—or, more obviously, someone told him originally—and that someone may well have told others. If you haven't heard anything after turning over rocks there, it might be pretty obscure, especially as generations die off and the new ones aren't interested in the past."

Sam nodded to himself. "Yes, the islands have undergone a big change since the war. Our other problem is that such a small fraction of the population speaks English, so we're limited to the few that do. That's mainly the residents of the capital."

"Well, now you know everything I do. The professor said he'd be more than happy to speak to you by phone if you wanted to pick his brain. I'll forward his number when I send the scans."

"Do you think it would do any good?"

"I got the impression he told me everything he knew. He wasn't at all evasive. To him, this is all just academic interest. I didn't tell him you'd found the likely site of the king's palace."

"As always, Selma, you're the real treasure in this story."

"It's all part of the job, right? The professor's account will be in your e-mail in-box in a few minutes. Call me if you need anything else." She hesitated. "I'm glad to hear you're having a less eventful time than on one of your usual forays into the wilds."

Sam debated not telling her about the recent attack but decided that it might prove useful for self-preservation if more people knew. "Up until today, I would have agreed with you."

"What now?"

"We were run off the road and someone shot at us. Other than that, it's a lovely place."

Selma's voice grew quiet. "You're joking."

"Truth is stranger than fiction, as always."

"Who's after you?"

"Don't know."

"Well, that certainly narrows it down. What can I do to help?"

"Nothing I can think of. Maybe let the State Department know in case we disappear forever?"

"A cheerful thought."

"Thanks, Selma. Don't worry about us—we'll manage, as always. I'll call as soon as we know something more."

Remi eyed him as he punched the call off. "Selma came through?"

"Doesn't she always?"

"Come on. Give."

He told her about the medicine man's legend. When he was done, she studied her reflection in the mirror and shook her head. "Even when we're just helping a friend, we manage to trip over treasure. The Fargo luck cuts both ways, doesn't it?"

"There's no telling whether it's true or not, Remi. And, frankly, what might have been riches thousands of years ago could be trash nowadays."

"You mentioned gold and jewels. Last I heard, those were still in demand. In fact," Remi said, looking pointedly at the back of one hand, "I haven't seen a nice rock in a while. I say we officially consider this a treasure hunt now that there's at least a mention of one."

Sam ignored her facetious fishing for jewelry. "Of course we tell Leonid."

"Absolutely. And, as always, we'll turn over whatever we find to the local government." Remi turned toward the window and winced as her hand flew to her neck. "Ow!"

"Let's get a doctor to look at that. I know just the place."

"I don't need to go to the hospital."

"You just flipped over in a truck and took a tumble down a river. I'm afraid you're overruled on this one, Mrs. Fargo," Sam said sternly.

Remi shrugged and winced again. "Fine. You win. But no shots. Promise me, no shots."

"All I can do is relay your wishes to the powers that be."

"Traitor."

CHAPTER 15

Dr. Vanya stepped back from where Remi was lying on the hospital exam bed. "I don't think it's anything more than some strained ligaments. Your vision is fine, you're showing no signs of serious trauma, and your neuro workup was normal."

"That's all good news," Sam said.

"You should avoid sudden movements or strain. Anything that would jar your head and neck are likely to be painful. I can get you a whiplash collar, if you like. It might help."

Remi frowned. "I hate those."

"Nobody likes them. It's up to you. It's not like you'll die if you don't wear one. Just be careful, and if you have to ask yourself whether something's a bad idea, it probably is." Vanya regarded her. "You're extremely lucky given the circumstances. The swelling on your face will subside within a few days, and you'll have a slight bruise. Unbelievable you survived a rollover with only a few scrapes." She eyed Sam. "And you look like you walked away without a scratch."

"The air bags did their job," Sam said.

"I'll say. Did the police give you any indication of what they intend to do about this?"

Sam shook his head. "Doesn't sound like much."

"Don't be too frustrated. Our islands have their charm, but nobody expects high efficiency. I tell newcomers who are thinking about start-ing businesses that if you just answer your phone and open on the days you're supposed to, you're ahead of ninety percent of the competition." Vanya shrugged. "A relaxed island pace comes at a price. You're seeing the downside. It's nothing personal."

"I just don't understand why we were targeted," Remi said as she sat up.

"There's no way of knowing. There have been rumors of armed rebel groups in the mountains. Maybe you stumbled across something or disrupted their plans? Or saw something you weren't supposed to?"

"Like what?" Sam asked.

"I have no idea. I'm just grasping at straws here. I've never heard of this kind of an attack, so I'm speculating. Who knows why crazy peo-ple do violent things?" She hesitated. "I treated someone whose hus-band attacked her with a machete. For no reason. The best she could guess was that she'd said something that set him off. It was by the grace of God she didn't die. The husband disappeared into the hills and has never been found. Could be it's he who attacked you. You never know."

"How many of the islanders have vehicles?" Remi asked.

"I can't say. The total population of the island is less than a hundred thousand, depending on which numbers you believe, and the vast ma-jority live here in Honiara. My guess is there might be five thousand cars, if that," she said doubtfully.

"Then finding the truck that did this shouldn't be too complicated."

"In theory, no. But if many of the trucks are in rural areas where the roads are basically goat tracks, you're asking whether the police will spend weeks trying to track down every one in the middle of nowhere. I suppose anything's possible, but did you get the impression they were champing at the bit?"

Sam laughed drily. "Not exactly."

"Then there's your answer. I'm sorry, but living here you quickly learn to have no expectations. Works better that way."

Remi joined Sam at the door. "Thanks for seeing me," she said, and Dr. Vanya smiled.

"I'd hoped it would be under better circumstances." She scribbled a note on a chart and put it under her arm. "You've both been through considerable trauma. I'd take it easy for a few days. What do you have planned?"

"Other than explaining to the rental car place that one of their vehicles is now a piece of modern art? Not much," Sam said.

"Well, try to relax. That's the allure of the Solomons, isn't it? Lounging on a beautiful beach, not a care in the world?"

"Other than the crocodiles."

"Hardly, in town. I'd have a cocktail on the veranda and watch the sunset. Leave the strenuous activity for someone else."

The walk to the rental car lot was grueling in the humid heat and by the time they got there they were soaked through. The owner's eyes widened to the size of moons when Sam explained what had happened and he looked like he was ready to cry at the loss of his Nissan. Neither Sam nor Remi wanted to push their luck and ask about renting another vehicle, and after giving the dejected man all the police information as well as a copy of the report, they made their way back to their hotel.

As they rounded a corner onto the main road two blocks from the waterfront, Sam leaned in to Remi and murmured to her, "Don't look back, but I think we're being followed."

"I don't think I can look back with my neck like this. Who is it?"

"Unknown. One man in a sedan. I noticed it because it's crawling along."

"Why is it that every damned time we go anywhere we wind up attracting the wrong kind of attention? Are you sure about this?"

"We'll know in a minute."

They walked along at a leisurely pace, waiting for the sedan to materialize, but it never did. At the end of the long block Sam shrugged. "Maybe I'm a little paranoid."

"A little?"

"Comes from being shot at and run off the road."

"No question. Thankfully, this time you're wrong."

They stopped at the intersection and Sam looked back. Only a few slow-moving pedestrians were shuffling down the sidewalk, moving from shady spot to shady spot in an effort to stave off the worst of the sun's effects. No questionable sedans were prowling the street, no furtive figures with earbuds were spinning suddenly to shield their faces from view.

When they returned to the hotel, Leonid met them in the lobby and they went to the pool bar overlooking the ocean. He walked like an old man and grumbled the entire way about the scuba school killing him slowly with their demands.

"They had me swimming laps—twenty of them, with no break—as my endurance testing. I was winded after two and thought I was hemorrhaging after ten," he griped.

"But you made it," Remi said brightly.

"What happened to your face?" Leonid asked, finally noticing something other than his own misery. "It's swollen."

"Oh, didn't we mention it? Someone pushed our car off a cliff and shot at us," Sam said with a nonchalant wave of the hand. "Remi bumped her head when we were swimming the rapids, trying to escape."

Leonid regarded them as if they were mad. "No, really. What happened?"

Remi smiled. "I mouthed off and Sam let me have it."

The Russian shook his head. "I don't know what to make of you two."

Sam leaned forward. "We really did get run off the road, Leonid. We don't know by whom, or why, but it's what happened. This morning."

Leonid held his gaze, eyes searching for some sign of mockery, and, when he saw none, his face grew even more somber than usual. "I can't believe it."

"I know. We just finished up at the hospital and the police. To say it's worrisome is the understatement of the year," Sam admitted. "But we have some good news, too. Or, at least, some interesting news. There may be a treasure somewhere in the ruins."

"What are you talking about? How do you know?"

Sam gave him the rundown. When he finished, Leonid looked even more upset than before. "Wait. So this is the king's compound and, in addition to a curse, there's a buried treasure?"

"You're acting like that's bad news."

"It complicates matters. And it makes me wonder if that's why you were attacked. Maybe the medicine man wasn't the only one who knew about the treasure. It's possible that word's spread and someone else wants a chance at it. The divers could have talked, or the captains, and anyone who knew the legend would have gone into high gear."

Remi glanced at Sam. "He's right. Most people here are barely surviving. The prospect of unimagined wealth can do strange things."

"Right. But we don't actually know whether there's even a treasure, much less where it might be. And let's not forget it's in eighty feet of water. In a cursed bay teeming with sharks and crocodiles. Wouldn't it make more sense to wait until we located it before trying to knock us out of the picture?" Sam said.

Remi shook her head. "You're assuming whoever did it is rational and logical. And we're also assuming this has to do with treasure. It could be that we intruded on something we weren't meant to see, even if we have no idea what it was, and they took action. It could be smuggling, drugs, anything. We shouldn't assume we have all the puzzle pieces because after only a few days here the odds say we don't."

Sam nodded. "She's right, as usual."

Leonid grunted. "So where does that leave us? What should we do now?"

Sam's brow furrowed. "I'm not sure we do anything different except keep our eyes open. We can't really dive the ruins properly until the boat arrives anyway, so it's a moot point."

"I don't like unknowns. Particularly when they shoot at you," Leonid said.

"Agreed, my friend. But that's all we have. I think a better question than trying to figure out the unknowable is how we treat our new knowledge of a possible treasure," Sam said. "If we're going to do anything more than catalog the site, we may want to consider bringing in some specialized talent. Because if we're going to conduct a more thorough search, the ship's divers aren't going to do the trick—we'll want a large pro team with related experience."

Leonid nodded. "I gather you have someone in mind?"

Sam grinned. "Not someone specific, because many of those we've worked with in the past are busy with their own projects. But we have the resources to get whatever we need. Let's put Selma on it and see who she can find. She can coordinate with the research vessel. Anything they don't have she can get flown in."

Remi took Sam's hand. "He may look like just another pretty face, but every now and then he comes up with a good idea. I agree. Let's get some serious talent here as soon as possible."

"When is the boat supposed to be here?" Leonid asked.

"Tomorrow evening."

The Russian rubbed his face and studied Sam and Remi. The dark circles and bags under his eyes lent him the appearance of an unhappy raccoon. "Then all you need to do is keep from getting killed for twenty-four hours or so while I endure the final tortures of the damned scuba instruction."

Remi smiled. "Sounds like a good plan."

"Particularly the avoiding being murdered part," Sam agreed.

"No more driving around in the boonies," Remi warned.

"My appetite for adventure is completely sated at the moment. One brush with death per day is more than enough."

"The problem is tomorrow's another day."

"Right, but technically we had two brushes today: going off the cliff and being shot at. So that takes care of tomorrow, too."

"I'll believe it when I see it," Remi said, her tone skeptical.

Sam smiled. "I'm a changed man."

"Sure you are, Fargo. Sure you are."

CHAPTER 16

Sydney, Australia

Jeffrey Grimes leaned back in the executive chair and eyed the others in the conference room, the air filled with the aroma of half-drunk coffee, tension, and frayed nerves. The end of another quarter was upon them and the publicly traded conglomerate they operated was going to report a loss—the third straight quarter the company had hemorrhaged money due to its international subsidiaries.

Grimes was a fixture on the Australian business and social scene, legendary for his high-risk strategies that had, until now, turned out to be winners. But the increasingly difficult financial landscape and tightened access to investment capital had proved more challenging than any he'd encountered and several spectacular flameouts had gutted the company's balance sheet as well as investor confidence.

Going public had seemed a brilliant idea two years earlier when the Australian economy was booming and money was flowing like water. The initial offering had raised almost a billion dollars. But Grimes's personal stock was locked up and his net worth had collapsed in the wake of bad bets in the mining and petroleum sectors when the company's valuation dropped by half overnight.

The decline triggered covenants in the company's debt agreements and now the wolf was at the door, the former golden child of the Australian investment community struggling for survival.

Grimes ran his fingers through his thick salt-and-pepper hair, worn longish and combed straight back, and sighed. "Can't we push some of the bad assets off into a subsidiary, at least for this quarter? You know, the usual game of musical chairs?"

His chief financial officer, Curtis Parker, shook his head. "The regulators will be all over us. If we transfer anything off the balance sheet, there will be fifty snoops demanding to know where it went and that will open a whole new can of worms. No, whether we like it or not we have to take our lumps and hope we can turn it around next quarter."

Grimes frowned. "What about accelerating or slowing depreciation on some of the underperforming investments? Or why don't we simply claim an inflated value for the assets with a straight face, get an accounting firm to sign off on it, and ignore that in a sale we'd get ten cents on the dollar?"

Parker gave him a humorless smile. "Because we aren't a Wall Street bank. We don't get to play those kinds of games. We're expected to behave honestly."

Grimes tossed his pen on the table. "Fine. How much of a hit are we going to take on the stock? Give me your worst-case scenario."

"Fifteen percent. Which will recover within a week—I've lined up some buyers to come in and stabilize the price at that level and they'll hype it once they've stopped the fall, turning a handy profit in the meantime—they've already established short positions to finance the purchases." Parker glanced at a spreadsheet. "But we're going to have a hell of a time with our credit lines. It's looking increasingly like we won't be able to service our debt within another two quarters and no-body's going to want to be last in line to get paid."

A beautiful brunette in her early thirties poked her head into the conference room and caught Grimes's eye.

"Yes, Deb?" he asked.

"I have a call on your private line. Said it's urgent . . . that you're expecting the call?"

Grimes brightened. "Ah, yes." He looked around the room at his inner circle. "Gentlemen, would you excuse me for a moment?" With-out waiting for a response, he rose and made his way down the hall, trailed by Deb, who had to practically jog to keep up with his long strides.

"Line two," she said as he entered his office, and he nodded as he closed the door behind him and walked to his desk. He sat in his bur-gundy calfskin executive chair and raised the handset to his ear.

"Hello," he said.

The caller's voice was flat, genderless, robotic, run through some sort of software filtering that disguised it, as it had been each time he'd spoken with his mystery accomplice.

"The first step in escalating our conflict has been taken. By the end of the day there will be articles in the Australian and Solomon papers about the aid workers' disappearance, as well as the militia's demands."

"Finally, some good news. How do you intend to resolve the situa-tion once the tension's built sufficiently?"

"Unfortunately, the workers won't make it. Which will trigger cries of outrage, demands for retribution, and travel advisories. Most im-portant, it will create a difficult situation for the sitting administration, whose approach so far to unrest has been to do nothing."

"Will that be sufficient?"

"Only time will tell."

"I presume you have an alternate course of action if this doesn't do the trick."

"Of course. But you don't want to know what it entails."

"Very well. Do what you must."

"Just don't forget the next transfer. I'll be watching for it."

"Consider it done."

The caller hung up, leaving Grimes staring at the phone. This was unlike any arrangement he'd ever had and that made him uncomfortable but also exhilarated. He'd been approached the year before by the caller, who'd had a unique proposition: participate in the formation of several untraceable corporations in far-flung jurisdictions and have them salt the Solomon Islands' parliament with donations to pliable officials so that in the event of any societal upheaval the companies would be in first position to receive any new leases or prospecting rights for oil, gas, and minerals.

At first he'd been skeptical, but when the caller had promised to shut the gold mine down, it had gotten his attention. Right on schedule, things had begun to go wrong for the operation, culminating in seasonal flooding that brought catastrophic results mainly because emergency equipment designed to protect the mine failed at critical junctures.

Almost immediately after that the foreign operators had been ejected by the government, as promised, throwing the entire country's mining prospects into jeopardy.

At that point Grimes became a believer and shunted millions from his personal accounts through a complex series of blind transfers in places like Latvia and the Seychelles. The cash wound up in the corporations that his new friend had set up, always in jurisdictions where ownership was impossible to verify. The visible entities appeared to be Solomon Island companies and would be viewed as domestic by any cursory regulatory scrutiny.

The game plan was simple: foment discontent and support a new rebel group whose aim was to eject the current players. Once that was done, allies of the caller would create a new administration that supported local involvement in key lucrative industries and would declare all prior agreements void before handing out new agreements to preferred players—Grimes's silent-partnered corporations ranking among the most desirable.

If it worked, he stood to make hundreds of millions from the oil rights alone. That the scheme required a few casualties was a necessary evil—his hands wouldn't be sullied.

As with all opportunities, one had to weigh the benefits against the costs. A few aid workers or unfriendly locals were nothing, in the scheme of things. Grimes hadn't fought his way to the top of the heap by being soft. He understood how the game was played—the bigger the money, the dirtier the dealing. He'd watched rivals get rich rebuilding countries after war had ravaged them and it hadn't escaped his attention that they always seemed to be at the front of the line when it came to lucrative contracts. All he was doing was creating his own advantage where he could, with complete deniability baked into the cake.

Grimes looked around his office, taking in the model sailboats, the awards from community organizations, the photographs with dignitaries and celebrities. He'd built it all from nothing. Along the way he'd had to do some questionable things, but everyone who'd amassed significant wealth and power had done so—there was no such thing as an honest fortune. He glanced through the picture window at Sydney Harbor and smiled with satisfaction. The difference between him and the rabble shuffling around on the street was vision . . . and daring. He saw opportunity and didn't hesitate where others might.

Grimes checked the time on his platinum Lange & Söhne Perpetual Calendar Terraluna wristwatch and nodded to himself. He felt no remorse about his countrymen meeting their fate so he might profit from the outcome. People died every day.

It was strictly business, nothing more.

CHAPTER 17

Guadalcanal, Solomon Islands

Sam powered on his satellite phone, checked his messages, and listened to one from Selma, letting him know that the Australian research vessel, the *Darwin*, would be at the Honiara port by noon. After checking the time, he called California to leave his own message, confirming with Selma that they would meet the ship when it arrived.

The police had stopped by the hotel the prior evening and asked more questions, lifting Sam and Remi's hopes that their attackers would be caught; but now, as Sam looked out over the primitive buildings and rusting fishing scows, that goal seemed as far-fetched as the tale of giants roaming the island.

"What are you staring at?" Remi asked, coming up behind him and slipping her arms around him.

"Nothing," he said, not wanting to depress her with his morose thoughts. "The boat should be here by noon."

"Well, that's good news."

He turned to her. "How's the neck?"

"If you're asking whether I can manage a dive or three, the answer's yes."

He inspected her cheek, which still had a trace of discoloration from bruising, and smiled. "You ready for breakfast?"

"With Comrade Chuckles as usual?" she smirked.

"It wouldn't be the start of a new day on the islands without Leonid's sunny disposition and sense of childlike wonder, would it?"

"He's certainly got the market cornered on pessimism. Although I did get the sense that he was enjoying his dive experience, for all his grumbling."

"Me too. But don't let on that you noticed or it'll ruin his whole morning."

"My lips are sealed."

Sam escorted her to the hotel restaurant, where Leonid was sitting at their usual table, his face sunburned, sipping coffee with an expression like the dark brew was laced with rat poison. He looked up as they approached and offered a humorless smile.

"Good morning, my friend," Sam said cheerfully, slapping him on the back. "You're looking sprightly."

"I'll take whatever you've been drinking," Leonid said sarcastically.

"I think the island pace agrees with you, Leonid. You're positively glowing," Remi beamed as she took a seat across from him.

"Make it a double," Leonid muttered, but Remi caught a barely controlled flash of a smile.

"We come bearing good news," Sam announced.

"Really?" the Russian asked, raising a distrustful eyebrow.

"The *Darwin* will be here in a few hours and then we can get this exploration kicked into high gear. And you can show off some of your newfound scuba moves."

"As long as they consist of sitting on board and directing the divers, you won't be disappointed," Leonid assured him.

"I bet you're like a fish in water," Remi teased.

"A puffer fish. It's all I can do to get into the pool, much less swim."

"Well, fortunately, Selma called this morning to tell us that she's got four ex–Navy divers flying in to help. They should arrive tomorrow," Sam said.

They agreed to meet at the boat when it was scheduled to dock. Leonid still had one final dive to do before getting his certification. They watched him trundle out to the parking lot and Remi shook her head.

"You'd think he'd just found out he only had a few days to live. Has he always been like that?" she asked.

"As long as I've known him. What's funny is that he's had a relatively charmed life. There's no logical reason for it. But that's the way he is."

"Thank goodness I didn't marry Mr. Sourpuss."

"How could anyone be married to you and do anything but smile?"

Remi grinned. "You're showing promise, young man."

The Honiara waterfront lived up to their expectations, with the pungent aroma of decaying marine life thick as fog. Rows of rusting cargo ships in various states of disrepair bumped against the concrete docks in the gentle swell, and Sam and Remi watched as a large power catamaran edged to a stop near the shipyard. The water shimmered with a sheen of oil and gas, adding a petroleum stink to the area, and Remi wrinkled her nose and leaned in to Sam.

"Charming, isn't it?"

"Hope nobody lights a match around here or we're all going up."

Leonid arrived a few minutes later and they stood together, staring impatiently at the horizon. Leonid shifted from foot to foot as the sun blazed down unrelentingly, clearly anxious to get to the bay.

"How did the dive go?" Sam asked, eyeing the Russian's still-damp hair.

"I'm here, aren't I?"

The satellite phone trilled. When Sam retrieved the phone from his backpack, he didn't recognize the number.

"Hello?" he answered.

"G'day. Sam Fargo?" The Australian accent of the cheery male voice was pronounced even over the noise of the wind and a rumbling motor in the background.

"That's me."

"Captain Desmond Francis. Des, to most. Wanted to see if you're ready for a pickup?"

"Yes. We're at the Honiara docks."

"Brilliant. We should be rounding the point in ten minutes. I'll send a tender for you, if that works."

"Of course. How will we know you?"

Des laughed. "Hard not to spot us, mate. Bright red hull and a bad attitude."

"We'll be watching for you."

Captain Des was right—they couldn't miss the *Darwin* on approach. Painted neon red, it had a stylized gaping shark's mouth emblazoned in yellow on the bow, replete with oversized teeth. Remi laughed when she saw it and elbowed Sam.

"What have you gotten us into this time?" she whispered.

"Blame Selma. I just asked for a boat."

A crane swiveled on the ship's deck and lowered a twenty-foot fiberglass tender onto the water and soon the small skiff was cutting across the small waves toward the wharf. Sam walked to the edge of the concrete dock and waved both hands over his head and the research vessel changed course to approach.

The skiff pulled alongside a metal ladder and the pilot, a twentysomething-year-old man with long unruly hair and a goatee, grinned up at them.

"G'day. Looking for a ride?" he called.

"You bet," Sam said, and they descended the rungs to where the tender bobbed on the swells.

Once they were aboard, the young man introduced himself.

"Name's Kent. Kent Warren. I'm the dive master aboard the *Darwin*," he called from his position in the stern of the craft. "I'll shake everyone's hand once we're on the ship. Which will be in no time." With that, he twisted the throttle and the tender surged away from the dock, its bow slicing through the chop as it rapidly picked up speed.

When they neared the *Darwin*, they could see she was a serious research vessel, built for rough seas, her bow impressively high out of the water, her steel hull steady in the waves. Her pilothouse bristled with antennae, and as the skiff approached a tall man wearing a red shirt waved from the bridge.

They climbed aboard and the red-shirted man, Captain Des, introduced them to the rest of the crew—a dozen men in all. His mate, Elton Simms, gave them an orientation belowdecks as the captain pointed the bow west and the big ship lumbered forward.

"These are the guest cabins. I reckon you'll be staying aboard while we map the site," Simms said, his Australian accent so thick they could barely understand him.

Remi eyed the three simple staterooms, each equipped with four fold-up bunk beds bolted to steel support beams running from floor to ceiling, and glared at Sam, who smiled engagingly.

"To be determined. We may commute out to the site," he said.

"Fair enough. But we've got room, if you're so inclined. The galley's over here, and the equipment room's astern down that passage."

They made their way to the bridge, where Des was standing in front of a wide console, eyeing the GPS and the chart plotter. He glanced at Leonid and the Fargos and stepped aside, leaving the helm to Simms.

"How was the trip?" Remi asked.

"Bit rough in the middle. Twenty- to thirty-footers in parts of the

Coral Sea—but rollers, not breaking. This here's a pond after that," Des said.

"Glad you made it in one piece. We're looking forward to diving the site and mapping the ruins. The gear on the island leaves something to be desired," Sam explained. "I trust you've got a full complement of equipment?"

Des nodded. "We do. Compressors, rebreathers, wet and dry suits, a submersible, robotic cameras—the whole nine yards."

"We're going to be joined by additional divers tomorrow," Sam said. "That will give us more bottom time as a group."

"More the merrier. How long do you figure you'll need the boat?"

"Hard to say," Sam said. "At least a couple of weeks. Depends on how it goes."

"I'll tell the crew and the bosses back home we're here for the duration, then. We're pretty self-contained. Just need to make shore runs for fruit and veggies. We've got a watermaker aboard and the sea's lousy with fish, so we can stay as long as you like."

Des gave them a quick tour of the specialized equipment along both sides of the bridge. Leonid and Sam nodded with approval. The electronics were cutting-edge, a floating laboratory and archaeological research department, with satellite Internet and communications. "We had a complete overhaul two years ago, so there's little we don't have aboard," Des said with obvious pride.

"It's certainly impressive," Remi agreed.

When the *Darwin* arrived at the site, it orbited in a slow circle over the coordinates of the ruins, and both Des and Simms hovered around the monitors as the equipment detailed the anomalies along the bottom. Des ordered the anchor dropped at the edge of the complex, close enough to easily dive but far enough away so the anchor wouldn't damage anything if it dragged. Soon four of the divers were suiting up for an initial exploration.

Once the men were in the water, everyone gathered in the bridge again to watch their progress on the screens. Their helmet-mounted cameras were sending color images in real time, recorded on hard disk for later study. Visibility was better than when Sam and Remi had dived, and soon the ruins appeared from the reef, the remains of a ghostly city swirling in the flickering light.

"There. What you're seeing is the largest mound, and others oriented around it," Leonid said.

"Makes sense. Probably the main palace, with the outbuildings temples and housing for the royal court and servants," Remi said.

"I make out, what, forty structures? Maybe more," Des said.

"At least. It appears to have been a significant compound in its heyday. Probably housed hundreds, depending on how many lived in each building," Sam confirmed.

"Amazing that this wasn't discovered during the war," Simms said.

"The occupation forces had other fish to fry," Remi said. "And the technology wasn't really up to the challenge of exploring an underwater archaeological find." She eyed the screen. "There's been a lot of progress over the last seventy-something years."

"Have you given any thought to how you want to operate?" asked Des.

Leonid stepped forward. "I have," he said, and proceeded to detail the approach he intended to use for mapping the site. Sam and Remi exchanged glances several times—the Russian might have been ill-natured, but he was clearly a first-rate archaeologist and more than capable of running the expedition now that he had the tools to work with. When he was finished speaking, it was obvious the Australians were impressed.

Two sharks put in appearances during the dive, but the Aussies seemed unconcerned. Des pointed to the image on the monitor. "See that? Sharks typically avoid divers. Something about the noise of the bubbles startles 'em and nine times out of ten they'll swim away as fast as they can."

"What about the tenth time?" Leonid asked.

"Well, that's when it's best to have a powerhead. When we're diving in waters with sharks, one of the team will always have one. It's also known as a bang stick, a small air round affixed to a speargun shaft that detonates on impact, terminally injuring the target."

"That's good to know. Seems sensible," Leonid allowed.

"But the chances of having to use 'em are low," Des reaffirmed.

"How about crocodiles?" Remi asked.

"Same effect. The damage of a powerhead isn't from the projectile, it's from the explosive gasses entering the target. So even a relatively small round will kill a huge beast. It's the blast, not a bullet, that does the trick," Des explained.

"We could have used one of those the other day," Sam said, and told him about the crocodile.

"Blimey! Twenty feet? We get 'em that big up north, but still. Did the bloke on the receiving end make it?"

"Lost a leg."

"Damn. Well, I'll alert the lads to be careful. Then again, working Australian waters, we've seen just about everything. I'm pretty sure we've got more dangerous creatures per meter than anywhere else on earth. Even the bloody pinecones will kill you down under. Our bunya pines drop a cone that can weigh ten kilos—imagine a bowling ball falling thirty meters onto your head." Des offered them a smirk. "And those are just the plants."

Sam nodded and turned to Des. "We've been there a few times and love it." He glanced at his watch. "How can we get back to town?"

"Simms here can give you a lift in the skiff."

Sam looked to Leonid. "You staying aboard?"

"Might as well. As you Americans say, it's 'prime time,' right?"

Sam took a final look at the monitor and the ghostly outline of the sunken city.

"Yes, it is. And you're in the spotlight, my friend. Front and center."

CHAPTER 18

Sam and Remi drove to the airport the next morning to meet the American divers. Even with a chartered jet from Brisbane to Honiara, the flight time from Los Angeles had taken thirty hours, and they expected the men to be stiff and tired. They were surprised when the four divers descended the steps from their plane looking chipper and rested. The tallest of the group approached them without hesitation and extended his hand.

"Mr. and Mrs. Fargo? Pleased to meet you. I'm Greg Torres and this is Rob Alderman," he said, indicating the man next to him, who nodded.

"Please. Sam and Remi," Sam said, shaking Greg's hand.

"And these two are Steve Groenig and Tom Benchley," Greg said, looking to his right where the final pair of fit young divers was standing. None was older than early thirties, and Sam recognized the unmistakable bearing of former SEALs—battle-hardened veterans who would be as comfortable in the water as sharks.

The customs and immigration clerks sauntered out onto the tarmac and did a cursory inspection of the men's dive gear and duffel bags before stamping their passports. The immigration clerk eyed the men and shook his head.

"You best be careful and stay in town, yeah? With what happened wit' the aid workers, it's not safe anywhere else," he said in heavy patois.

"What happened with them?" Remi asked. All they'd heard the day before was that the two Australians had gone missing, with no official word of explanation.

"It's all over the web. Rebels got them." The clerk shook his head. "It's bad. They threatening to kill them, they are."

"Kill aid workers? They're here to help."

"These fool rebels say they all part of the foreign plague. Dat's what they calling it. Fools blaming everything on others, like none of our problems is our doing. But they saying all the foreigners gotta go or there goin' to be big-time trouble."

"So they kidnapped unarmed humanitarians who are here to help the underprivileged and they're going to kill them?" Remi said, her tone disbelieving.

"Dat what they saying. Crazy in the head, dese fools be."

Sam's eyes hardened as he studied the divers. "Well, looks like you flew into the eye of the hurricane. All of this just happened."

"We can take care of ourselves," Greg said, his words clipped, his tone flat. Sam believed him.

"You'll be on the boat all the time in any case, so any local issues shouldn't affect the expedition."

Greg shrugged as if it was all part of the job.

Sam and Remi had rented a four-wheel-drive Toyota van from a different agency and the men loaded their gear in the cargo area before wordlessly taking their seats. The drive to the site took an hour longer than the day before. They were stopped three times by uncomfortable-looking policemen at makeshift roadblocks, who, after searching the van, cautioned them against proceeding any farther into an area of the island that was out of official control. Sam and Remi remained courteous, but firm, and each time the lead officer shook his head when he waved them past as though he were directing them through the gates of hell.

Sam looked over at Remi from the driver's seat. "They seem pretty wound up, don't they?"

"Sounds like we were lucky we didn't meet the aid workers' fate on our little drive the other day," she said.

"That occurred to me. But it wasn't for wont of the bad guys trying."

When they arrived at the bay, Greg's team moved quietly and efficiently to set their equipment out on the sand as they awaited the arrival of the skiff. Remi fished a two-way radio out of her bag and called the ship. She was rewarded by a burst of static and then Captain Des's cheerful voice.

"Good morning to you both," he said. "Ready for a ride?"

"We are. Six of us, and enough gear to sink the boat."

"We'll make room. Be there in a jiffy."

Once they were on board, Simms showed the men to the guest quarters while Sam and Remi joined Des and Leonid on the bridge.

Leonid looked up from a photograph he was studying when they entered and grunted before returning to his project. "About time," he grumbled.

"I hope you were able to get something accomplished without us," Sam said, ignoring the Russian's barb.

Des nodded. "Two dives so far. We've got the layout nicely mapped now. Leonid here was just going over the images so we could work on each building in a systematic fashion."

Leonid tapped a finger on the glossy printout. "This is by far the largest ruin. We should start there. It's easily double the size of any of the others, which indicates it was the most important."

Remi inched closer. "That would make sense, given the orientation."

Sam nodded. "It's east of the one we were looking at."

"It looks to be in better shape than many of the others. Next dive, we'll go over it carefully and see what's under all the sea life," Leonid said.

Kent Warren, the dive master, tromped up the steel steps and entered the pilothouse. "G'day. Just met the new lot. Serious gents, they are," he announced.

Leonid pushed the underwater image away and stood. "I want to clear as much of the surface area of this large structure as possible by nightfall. The more bodies in the water, the faster it will go."

"Too right. Let me run the calcs on bottom time and I'll put together some dive schedules," Warren explained.

"How many surface supplied air rigs do we have?"

"Only two," Warren said. "We're usually in shallower water and don't use 'em much. But this seems ideal, so we'll keep two men down for as long as feasible. Between them and the scuba, we should be able to make short work of clearing the worst of the clutter."

"We don't want to damage anything. And every step needs to be captured on film so we have a record," Leonid reminded.

"Absolutely."

Half an hour later, the on-deck compressor was clattering away as a member of Warren's crew fed out hoses carrying air to the divers below. They were accompanied at the bottom by a pair of the recently arrived American divers in scuba gear and their slow approach to the sunken ruin flickered on the bridge monitor, where Leonid, Sam, Remi, and Des watched.

The image was high-res, creating the illusion they, too, were peering through dive masks as the swimmers approached the mound. Light filtering from the surface lent the scene a spectral quality. They watched as the lead diver moved near the closest surface and twisted the valve on a hose, directing a blast of high-pressure air at the crust of barnacles and seaweed.

The camera distorted in a cloud of debris as the water instantly turned opaque from centuries of accumulation being blasted off. Leonid had researched the best way to clean the structures with the least chance of damage and had hit on the idea with Des—use the compressor's power to clean them.

The downside was that visibility was only a foot, and the divers had to give it a rest so the sediment could settle. The camera feeds flickered in the brownish cloud, and after a few minutes everyone could begin to make out the unmistakable shape of large limestone blocks.

Two hours later, enough of the wall had been cleared so they could appreciate the scope of the ruin—the wall measured at least one hundred feet long.

"It's huge. Hard to believe that was built by the islanders," Leonid said, his voice hushed. "Nothing hints at them having the means to construct anything like it."

Remi peered at the screen and turned to Des. "Can you communicate with the divers?"

"Yes. The surface breathers have a comm line."

"Ask them to zoom in on the area to the far right of what they've cleared."

Des lifted a microphone to his lips and gave the instruction, and they waited as a diver moved in slow motion to the section that interested Remi. As the camera closed in on the block, Sam and Remi smiled and Leonid nodded.

Remi was the first to break the silence. "Looks like glyphs, and, if I'm not mistaken, that's a totem of a sea god," she said. "And look there. Looks like a depiction of a column of men. Hauling cases."

Leonid squinted and Des cleared his throat. "What do you make of that?"

Remi sat back and smiled.

"Unless I'm completely garbling the glyph, it's a group of warriors carrying something into a temple."

"Something?" Leonid said.

When Remi spoke, it was almost a whisper. "Treasure. An offering to the gods."

CHAPTER 19

By the end of the afternoon, much of the top section of the large structure had been partially scrubbed clean. The uppermost portion of the roof had collapsed, but enough of the edges remained to be able to make out the rough shape of the building. The divers continued working even as Sam and Remi climbed into the skiff to return to shore. The plan was to continue until ten that night, using underwater floodlights, switching out the surface-breathing divers every few hours to avoid fatigue.

Once back in the van, Sam eyed the *Darwin*, floating serenely at anchor.

"What are you thinking?" Remi asked.

"What it must have been like to watch your entire civilization disappear without a trace. Imagine how that had to feel."

"I'm pretty sure that in an earthquake large enough to do that, nobody had time to feel much of anything."

"You're probably right. But I can understand why the survivors would think the place was cursed. How else could you explain that kind of devastation?"

"What do you make of the glyphs?"

"It appears to suggest the legend of a treasure, at any rate. We'll soon know for sure."

Remi gave him a doubtful look. "It's a lot of area to explore. It'll take years just to clean the ruins and then they'll have to contend with all the rubble. It might be a long time before there's a chance to hunt for any treasure."

"Well, Mrs. Fargo, I'm enjoying the Solomons' charms, but not enough to spend years here. Even in company as delightful as yours."

"Leonid seems to have it under control now. Maybe we can leave this one to him?"

The sun was sinking into the sea when they turned onto the paved road, and they hadn't been driving for ten minutes before they came to a roadblock where six grim-faced police officers were standing by their cars in the middle of nowhere. Sam coasted to a stop. Four of the policemen made a big show of making them get out of the van and checking their identification while the other two did a cursory inspection of the interior.

"What have you got in the backpack?" the oldest of the group asked, indicating Sam's bag.

"Just some odds and ends. A phone, canteen, spare shirt, that sort of thing."

"Show me."

Sam humored the man and caught Remi's eye, willing her to stay quiet. He knew her well enough to see that she was going to ask the officer whether he thought the militia was composed of American tourists and was silently thankful when she thought better of it. More than once she'd voiced her frustration at airports when a grandmother was searched by security personnel lest the woman be the world's oldest terrorist, but Remi caught the meaning in his stare and bit her tongue.

"You shouldn't be driving out here," the officer said when he was done with his cursory search. "Be very careful, even in Honiara. Things are unpredictable right now."

"Seemed fine this morning."

The man's eyes narrowed. "Yes, but the news about the aid workers' execution hadn't hit yet. People are uneasy. Just watch yourselves. I'd go straight to your hotel and not leave if I were you."

"They're dead?" Remi asked, her face revealing her surprise.

The policeman nodded. "There was a broadcast this afternoon. It's a dark day. They were unarmed, helping rural families who have nobody else."

"What will those families do?"

The officer shrugged and frowned. "We'll probably escort whatever remaining aid workers who still want to help, but I doubt there will be many takers. It's one thing to have compassion, another to risk your life to ease the troubles of others." He looked away into the thick underbrush. "Drive safely and don't stop unless the roadblock is manned by official vehicles like ours. Just to be sure."

One more roadblock treated them the same way, and by the time they reached the hotel lot, Sam and Remi were worried. They'd passed crowds of angry-looking islanders who glared at the van as it drove by. Though nobody did anything, they could sense the menace. As they pulled through the gate, Sam noted that the parking lot security guard looked as worried as he felt, although there were no signs of a mob anywhere near the hotel—perhaps because it was located near the main police station.

When they entered the lobby, the front desk clerk signaled to them. They approached and she gave them a professional smile and asked them to wait for her boss, who appeared moments later, wearing an obligatory sincerity suit.

"Good evening, Mr. and Mrs. Fargo. I'm Jacob Trench, the manager. I hope you're enjoying your stay?"

Remi nodded. "Everything's been satisfactory."

"Good, good." Trench shifted nervously and looked down at his shoes. "I wanted to greet you and introduce myself and apologize in advance for what I'm going to say. We're advising our guests not to leave the hotel grounds. The situation in town is . . . unsettled . . . and we don't think it's safe."

"Really?" Sam said. "Then why would it be safer here?"

"We have extra security coming. Don't get me wrong—I'm not saying that we expect any trouble. Purely precautionary. But it would be unfortunate if any troublemakers used the current uneasy sentiment opportunistically, and there's always a faction . . ." Trench's Australian accent was crisp, but it was impossible to mistake his concern.

"Do you really think there's a risk?" Remi asked.

"It would be better not to test your luck, for the time being. The authorities have everything under control, but I was here during the last . . . unrest . . . and it got out of hand rather quickly. A hotel down the beach was gutted."

"Right, but this is completely different, isn't it?"

Trench nodded but wouldn't meet their eyes. "It always is, unfortunately. Please. Be our guest in the restaurant tonight. I'll be happy to provide a complimentary bottle of champagne as an incentive."

Remi looked at Sam. "He's convincing me with the free champagne, Sam."

Sam smiled. "Sounds like you've got a deal. Do we need to make a reservation?"

Trench shook his head. "Just let me know what time you'd like to have dinner and I'll take care of it."

"Say . . . seven?"

"Perfect. Party of two or will you have guests?"

"Just us," Remi said.

As they continued to their room, Sam whispered to Remi, "Did you see the guy reading the paper in the lobby? Big man, khaki pants, local?"

"No, I was too busy being warned that we're all going to die."

"He seemed very interested in us."

"Maybe he doesn't get out much."

Sam grinned. "Not that I'm not used to having men take notice when you walk into a room."

She looked down at her rumpled cargo pants and T-shirt and laughed. "I am a real glamor girl today, aren't I?"

"You look pretty good to me."

"Don't think you're going to dupe me with your silver tongue, Sam Fargo."

"I was hoping the free champagne would do the trick." They approached their door and Sam paused as he felt in his pocket for the card key. "Maybe you're right. I just thought he was trying too hard at not being interested in us, especially given how much attention he was paying to us."

"I have it on reliable authority that we're in the safest place in all Guadalcanal tonight."

"That's reassuring. But I didn't get the most confident feeling from the manager, did you?"

"Probably not the A-team working the night shift in Honiara."

When Sam and Remi returned to the lobby just before seven, the big man Sam had noticed was nowhere to be seen. In fact, the area was empty except for a few nervous Australian tourists talking quietly among themselves near the entrance, their accents as distinctive as their ruddy complexions, the legacy of Scottish heritage in a subtropical climate.

The hostess checked the list, smiled when she found their name, and led them through the dining room, which was surprisingly full. Halfway to the table Remi paused and grabbed Sam's arm. Orwen Manchester was sitting at a booth, reviewing a small pile of paperwork, a sweating bottle of beer on the table beside him. He glanced up and waved them over when he caught Remi's eye.

"Well, look who's here! Are you two following me around?" he boomed as he rose.

"It's certainly a small world, isn't it?" Remi said.

"Maybe not that small. This is one of the few restaurants that's open tonight. Sam, Remi, if you have no plans, I insist that you join me. Assuming that I'm not interrupting a romantic candlelight dinner or anything."

Remi smiled and shook her head. "No, no, nothing like that. Sam?"

"Perfect," Sam said, and pulled a chair out for Remi, who sat gracefully while beaming at them both.

"Probably best you aren't out on the town tonight anyway," Manchester said as he and Sam took their seats. "It's ugly out there."

"That's what the manager told us. Why would a rogue rebel group's execution of two foreigners cause so much unrest?" Remi asked.

"Guadalcanal is polarized. Most of the population's dirt poor, but a small segment is quite well off, so there's an inevitable friction that occasionally causes violence. Scapegoats are always popular for the less fortunate, and there's also a powerful antiforeigner sentiment simmering just below the calm surface. The rebels' reprehensible actions have forced that sentiment into the spotlight and it's suddenly acceptable to give voice to the unmentionable. You have the poor and disenfranchised looking for any excuse to express their frustration." Manchester shook his head. "It makes little sense, but there it is."

Sam nodded. "Sounds like your views are clear on the issue."

Manchester swigged the remainder of his beer and motioned to a waiter to bring two more. Remi ordered a soda.

To their surprise when their drinks arrived as promised, champagne was also served. But the mood was tense as more tourists arrived and were seated, their collective worry palpable even across the room. Manchester toasted and then fixed Sam with a stern stare.

"I hate to seem like an ungracious host, but perhaps the Solomons aren't an ideal place for you until this all dies down." He shifted his eyes to Remi, his gaze changing from steely to admiring. "I'd hate for such a lovely couple to be caught in any escalation."

"We keep hearing that, but it's a little late now. We've flown halfway around the world to help our friend. It's an important project for him, and for us," Sam replied.

Manchester ignored Sam's comment. "And you're only a few short hours' flight from more hospitable lands. I hear the restaurants in Sydney are spectacular this season."

"That's not our style," Remi said firmly. "We don't turn tail and run at the first sign of trouble."

"Of course not. I'm speaking as a concerned friend. And this may all blow over. But if it escalates, you won't want to be around. Half the town burned in the last big one. The opportunists and predators come out when they think they're anonymous in the mob, and almost nothing's off limits once that dam breaks. It's the ugly side of human nature we see when things get out of control—one that's best viewed from a safe distance."

"Your point's well taken." Remi held her glass aloft. "To level heads and better times."

"Hear! Hear!" Manchester said, but the broad smile on his face never reached his eyes.

CHAPTER 20

Sam and Remi listened to the news on the radio as they ate breakfast before driving out to the bay. There had been small outbursts in the slums on the town periphery, but no large-scale unrest. Advisories were still in effect, and travelers were warned to expect delays due to roadblocks, but it seemed that tempers had cooled overnight as the reality of the murders had set in. The Prime Minister had issued a statement condemning the slayings, dozens of off-duty police were called into service, and international censure was swift and absolute. The rebels had been officially pronounced a terrorist organization and the administration declared that it would not negotiate with terrorists under any circumstance.

The lobby thronged with a crush of foreigners checking out, anxious to leave the island before the other shoe dropped. Sam and Remi elbowed through the crowd and found a table in the restaurant.

"Looks like the exodus has begun in earnest," Remi said after ordering.

"I don't blame them. We're here for a reason. If we were tourists, how appealing would getting stuck in the middle of a civil war be?"

"Sounds like our last couple of vacations."

"Oh, come on. Other than the shooting and being run off the road, it hasn't been that bad."

"I think you said that out of order. Besides, you forgot the crocodile."

"Technically, it didn't come for us, so I left it off the list."

The rental van was where they'd left it, and they noted that there were now three security guards in the parking lot instead of one. All had their batons out and were doing their best to look menacing. Other than a few stragglers loitering across the street, the area looked calm, and only a few cars were on the road.

"Let's stop at the hospital on our way out of town," Remi said. "I want to talk to Dr. Vanya. I read her presentation last night. It's pretty well thought out. I think we should plan on adding her to our donation list."

"You're the boss. She'll be over the moon at the news," Sam said.

"I admire what she's doing. It's a thankless job, and obviously she could be working anywhere else and making far more money."

"True. But I get the sense that for her it's about making a difference, not money."

"Which is why we should support her clinics."

"You'll get no argument out of me," Sam agreed, and then his eyes narrowed as he stared at the hospital street. Groups of islanders, some with machetes, roamed the sidewalk, watching menacingly as the van passed, and he could feel Remi tense beside him as he picked up speed. "You sure you don't want to just keep going to the boat?" he asked. "We can see the doctor some other time."

"We're here now. I'd prefer it in broad daylight. Morning's got to be safer than evening."

They arrived at the hospital and parked close to the main entrance, reassured to see that there was a security guard standing at the driveway. Only a few other vehicles were parked in the lot, one of them Dr. Vanya's SUV. They nodded to the nervous guard and entered the hospital, the heat in the interior already stifling.

A tall islander, wearing a white lab coat, a stethoscope draped over his shoulder, glanced up from where he was standing behind the reception counter when they entered.

"Yes? May I help you?" he asked.

"We'd like to see Dr. Vanya," Remi said.

"I'm Dr. Berry. What seems to be the problem?"

"Oh, it's nothing like that," Sam said. "No problem. More of a social call."

"I see. She's in her office. Just a second."

Dr. Berry called into the back of the building and moments later Dr. Vanya appeared, a folder in hand. She smiled when she saw Sam and Remi.

"Well, isn't this a delightful surprise. What brings you here? All's well, I trust?" she said as Remi shook her hand.

"Everything's fine. We wanted to stop by to see how Benji is doing and talk to you a little more about your project."

"I just looked in on him. He's asleep. Had a rough night, with a fever. We're pumping more antibiotics into him to try to stave off infection."

Remi said, "I reviewed your presentation and I have to say it is impressive. We discussed it and we've agreed to match your sponsorship commitments and make up any shortfalls. So, congratulations. You're fully funded!"

Vanya's eyes widened. "Are you serious? That's wonderful news. Thank you. Thank you so much . . ."

Sam smiled. "It's a worthy cause, and, God knows, the island looks like it can use some help."

Vanya's face darkened. "Yes, well, I haven't considered the effect these most recent events will have on my corporate sponsors. Big pharmaceutical companies can be skittish if there's even a hint of controversy. I'd hate for them to pull out because of the rash actions of a few zealots, but there's not much I can do about it other than hope for the best."

"Do you really think they'd pull out?" Remi asked.

"No way of knowing. But I'll say this—if there's rioting, keeping them committed will be a hard sell. Many will view it as the population destroying its own home, like a toddler throwing a temper tantrum, and will be unwilling to do anything that seems like it's rewarding that behavior."

"But surely they would be discriminating enough to appreciate that the actions of an unruly segment don't reflect an entire island's—"

"The problem is, we're small potatoes. For most of these companies, we're no more than an afterthought. It's all too easy for them to do nothing if there's even a hint of controversy. We saw that the last time around with the promised foreign aid—too little, too late." Dr. Vanya shook her head. "Based on history, I'd have to say it doesn't look positive."

"Well, we're committed," Remi said.

"That's really the best news I've had in months." Vanya hesitated. "How's your dive project coming?"

"Oh, we're plugging away at it," Sam said brightly, avoiding any details.

"You mentioned sunken ruins. Any further clues as to what the ruins are?"

"It's too early to tell. Could be nothing," Sam said, again deflecting.

Again Vanya hesitated, looking pensive. "Well, let me know if you need my help in any way at all."

On their way out of the hospital, Remi whispered to Sam, "Playing your cards close to the chest with her on the find, aren't you?"

"We've learned from harsh experience that the fewer people who know a secret, the likelier it'll remain one. This is Leonid's find. It's not ours to discuss."

"I know. I just thought it was funny how you danced around the topic."

"I've always considered myself a great dancer."

"Which medication and therapy could probably help with, but—" Remi stopped teasing Sam when they neared the van and she tensed. Her eyes roved across the street, where the random bands of islanders had gathered in a mob. "Sam, you probably want to get us out of here sooner than later. This looks like trouble."

Sam popped the locks with the remote as he assessed the situation and then slid behind the wheel. "I'm way ahead of you. Buckle up, because I'm not stopping for anything."

CHAPTER 21

The van engine roared as Sam floored the accelerator, sounding a warning to the group of islanders spilling into the street. Sam's horn honking drove any stragglers aside as he aimed the vehicle down the center line.

"Look out!" Remi hissed as she grabbed the armrest. Sam adjusted their trajectory just enough to avoid a rough-looking man toting a baseball bat, raising it as they neared like he was going to knock one over the wall. The heavy wood missed the van by inches, and then they were past the mob and heading toward the main boulevard that led out of town.

"See? No problem," Sam said, but the tightness in his voice betrayed his uneasiness.

"That was close, Sam. Maybe everyone who's been warning us to get off the island has a point."

"Nonsense. Although it's not a terrible idea to spend the night on the boat. I'm not sure I want to run that gauntlet again until things calm down."

"And what if they don't?"

"Then we may be looking forward to an extended cruise."

The police at the first roadblock they came to were jumpier than the prior day. There were more officers, fully outfitted in riot gear, as though they felt the need to make a show of force. Their admonition that driving into the rural area of Guadalcanal was inadvisable was more strident than before, and when Sam thanked the officer in charge politely for his counsel but said he was continuing west anyway, the man shook his head like he'd never see them again.

The next roadblock was more of the same, and Sam couldn't help noticing that they were the only car at each stop.

"Kind of deserted, isn't it?" Remi said as though reading his mind.

"Seems like nobody's in the mood for a drive."

"Might have something to do with the whole brink-of-civil-war thing."

"I don't know. It's a lovely day for motoring," Sam said, although Remi noted that he picked up speed as the jungle seemed to close in around them.

When they arrived at the bay, Sam parked out of sight by the grove where the crocodile had attacked and radioed Des to pick them up. The *Darwin*'s skiff sliced through the calm water and reached the beach in a few minutes, Elton Simms in the stern piloting.

"Morning. Nice day for it, am I right?" Simms said.

"It's gorgeous," Remi agreed as she climbed aboard, helped into the boat by Sam, who quickly joined her after handing her the backpack.

"Anything new to report?" Sam asked.

Simms dropped the transmission into reverse and eased off the sand. "No. Same as yesterday. Clearing off the gunk while your man Leonid looks on."

Bubbles frothed on the surface of the sea as they neared the ship, evidence of the work taking place beneath them. On the expansive deck of the *Darwin*, two crew members fed out hoses, ensuring that the surface-breathing divers had freedom of movement and didn't find themselves gasping at the end of a kinked line.

The tender pulled alongside the red hull, and Simms cut the engine after securing a line to a cleat at the stern. They clambered onto the oversized swim step and up a stainless steel ladder to where Des and Leonid were waiting in the morning sun.

"Good to see you!" Des called down. "I caught some of the news broadcasts about the excitement on the island. Can't say I'm too upset to be out here."

"We're going to spend at least one night aboard, so we're right there with you," Sam said. He looked to Leonid. "And how are you, my Russian friend?"

Leonid scowled and waved a fly away. "We're making progress," he allowed, as though unhappy with the work. Sam knew better than to query him on what was wrong and instead looked over his shoulder at the pilothouse.

"Let's see what you've been up to," Sam said.

The interior of the pilothouse was a mirror of the previous day, with the exception of the images on the monitor, which revealed considerably more of the stone blocks that composed the wall. As the divers worked along the far end of the structure, clouds of debris and bubbles filled the surrounding water until it had all the clarity of mud.

"Looks like you're getting a lot of it cleared," Remi said. "Check out the size of those blocks. It must have taken years to quarry them and get them to shore, much less build the structure."

"We cleaned off some of the base and it looks like they used a combination of landfill and smaller rock and gravel to create the islands. We're estimating that the bay was only fifteen or so feet deep when it was built, based on that," Leonid observed.

"Sounds like a safe bet," Sam said, peering at the monitor. "Can you imagine the size of the earthquake to drop the bottom almost eighty feet?"

"Assuming that there hasn't been more movement in the intervening years. Looking at this, I think it happened in stages. The first catastrophic shock, where the entire shelf shifted, possibly creating a fissure that sucked the shoreline into it. And then smaller events, each depressing the bottom farther." Leonid sighed as though exasperated. "We'll know for sure once we have more time to study it."

Sam grinned. "Patience is a virtue, my friend. Nothing happens fast in this business, as you know."

Leonid threw him a dark look. "One of the many things I hate about it. Did I mention that I'm susceptible to seasickness?"

"No, that was one of the few things you haven't complained about."

"Only because I didn't know until I tried sleeping last night."

Des snorted and tried to cover the sound with a cough. Remi smiled and Sam fought the urge to laugh.

"If you dive some, I understand that will equalize the motion and you'll sleep like a baby," Sam offered.

"You lie, don't you?" Leonid said, but his voice sounded a little hopeful.

Sam's face could have been carved from stone. "It's true."

"I know better than to trust you, American deceiver," he replied.

The quiet of the pilothouse was shattered when a tiny speaker near the helm crackled and a disembodied metallic voice with a thick Aussie accent sounded from it.

"Captain. You there?" Kent Warren, the dive leader, called.

Des moved to the microphone and lifted it to his mouth. "Yes, Kent. What is it?"

"You probably can't see it yet, but we cleared something that one of the big brains should come down and have a look at."

Sam looked to Des with a raised eyebrow.

Warren sounded hesitant. "I could be wrong, but it looks to me like an entry." He paused, and the comm line hissed with faint static. His next words sent a jolt through everyone on the bridge. "And unless I'm mistaken, it's been used recently."

CHAPTER 22

Sam slipped the dive mask over his head and glanced at Remi, standing beside him in a wet suit. "Fits you like a glove," he said, admiring her figure.

"It's too loose, but I'll manage. You ready to do this?"

"I was born ready."

"Let's not start on that again," she said as she cleared her regulator and moved to the edge of the dive platform. She stepped off the lip and dropped into the water. Sam cleared his line with a hiss and followed her into the sea with a splash.

Once they were below the surface, Sam swam toward Remi and gave her a thumbs-up signal, which she returned. He glanced to his right and pointed and she nodded. He began swimming toward the hazy outline of the ruins, bleeding air from his BCV as he descended. Remi did the same, and several minutes later they were beside Warren and one of his divers, wearing commercial diving suits and Kirby

Morgan dive helmets. Warren pointed at the gap in the wall and Sam swam toward it.

He paused and ran his gloved hand over the edge, noting the scrapes along the rim. He turned back to Warren and pointed at the marks and Warren signaled *No*. They hadn't made them.

Remi joined him and Greg Torres swam near. Sam fished a flashlight from his dive bag and switched it on, and Remi did the same. Greg tapped his watch and pointed up, his message clear: he was running low on air and would need to begin his decompression run to the surface. Sam gave him an *OK* signal and watched as Greg and his companion began their ascent.

Sam returned his attention to the gap and shone his light in it. The darkness lit up, and he and Remi could make out a passage. The floor of the corridor was littered with broken chunks of block, seaweed, and barnacles.

Remi directed her flashlight beam into the opening and waited for Sam to lead the way as Warren waited nearby. Sam pushed himself cautiously into the passage, wide enough to accommodate both Remi and him side by side. He moved slowly, his fins barely propelling him along. Remi's light bounced off the sheer face of the walls and played over the ceiling.

Slivers of daylight glinted through cracks overhead. Sam stopped at the end of the passage where it made a hard right and paused before shining his beam into the inky darkness. He recoiled abruptly as a long black form swam toward him, the creature's predatory smile eerie in the flashlight's glow. The eel's sleek body, at least four feet long, undulated in serpentine waves as it darted past Remi toward the opening.

Remi followed the eel with her light until it faded into a shadow by the gap and then turned back to where Sam waited motionless. He wiped away the edge of the corner block and pointed to where more of the distinctive scrapes could be made out.

Sam resumed his progress, brushing away a trail marker along the walls to guide their way out.

Remi was behind him. When they made the turn, they found themselves in a large, partially collapsed chamber. Their flashlight beams roamed over the floor and walls, and Remi's stopped at another gap—this one in the floor.

Sam drifted toward the opening, pausing to look around, and hovered over it, before pointing at the scrapes along the edges. Remi nodded with an exaggerated waggle of her head so he would see it and then she stopped, wincing. The doctor's warning about taking it easy had been forgotten in the fray, but it came screaming back as a lance of pain shot down her spine.

Sam, unaware of his wife's discomfort, flashed his lamp into the hole, the darkness closing in as the amount of light in the chamber halved. With another look to Remi, he swam into the opening.

Remi followed him down, the shriek of pain in her neck subsiding as quickly as it had come. They found themselves in a smaller chamber, the walls as encrusted with barnacles and marine life as the one above. Sam edged to the nearest wall and rubbed it with his glove. A smear of greenish brown came away, floating in the water like a cloud, as he eyed the stone beneath. A line a quarter inch deep ran from top to bottom.

He scrubbed again lower down and peered at where the line intersected another. Two minutes of this and he had a three-foot section cleared, enough to see that the indentations were carvings.

A glint caught his eye, and he neared the wall until his face was only inches away. The light caught the spot again and it sparkled.

Remi was nearby, also scrubbing with her glove, but along the floor. She waited for the floating residue to clear and tapped Sam's arm. He spun to where she floated weightless near the floor and she pointed to a lump on the surface. There was still too much debris in the water to see well, but he focused his lamp where she was indicating and approached.

His eyes widened when he made out what Remi had found. It looked like a long knife.

Sam reached down and freed the blade from the silt, but most of it disintegrated at his touch, leaving him holding a worn piece of wood. He inspected it for several long beats and then directed Remi's gaze to the wall as he placed the find in his dive sack. She swam closer to the lines and he joined her, taking care to shine his light along the etching so she could see what had caught his attention. The section he'd pointed to gleamed in his beam and she reached out to touch it.

After scrubbing more of the wall, Sam tapped his watch and then his air supply gauge. Remi checked hers and gave him a thumbs-up. It was time to return to the surface.

They turned and were swimming toward the doorway when a low rumble trembled through the structure. Several large blocks dislodged in the chamber above them and dropped in a cloud of debris, barring their exit as the small earthquake shifted the foundation. Sam and Remi held deathly still until the shock subsided, their light beams filtering through the cloud of sediment. They exchanged a glance through their masks—their means of escape was sealed off.

Sam swept the area with his flashlight, looking for another opening. At the far end of the chamber, the light disappeared into darkness where previously there had been wall. Sam pointed to the new gap and swam cautiously toward it, Remi by his side. They reached the opening and found themselves peering into a passageway encrusted with marine life, long tendrils of seaweed drifting in the water like wisps of green smoke. Sam looked over at Remi and gestured at his air supply gauge. Remi glanced at hers and gave him a *So-so* signal with her right hand.

They swam into the narrow corridor together, Sam in the lead, the glow of his lamp of little help through the curtain of marine growth in their path. He groped with his free hand as the passageway curved, and slowed when he came to a bend, the bottom rising in a mound of debris.

Another glance at his watch confirmed that they were almost out of time—their ascent would require a decompression stop to allow the nitrogen in their systems to disperse, which would require air to breathe. At the rate they were going, they'd run out before they had sufficient decompression time and would have to rush to the surface, risking the painful and sometimes fatal condition known as the bends.

Which assumed they'd be able to escape in the first place and didn't drown when their dwindling air supply ran dry.

Sam pushed ahead until he came to a point where the rubble pile rose so high it blocked his way forward. He looked overhead at the ceiling and spotted a narrow section of opening created by several of the stone blocks collapsing. He inched to it and groped along the rim. More sediment filled the water as he broke loose a crumbling edge.

After two minutes of painstaking effort, he'd cleared an opening large enough to squeeze through without his tank. He slipped out of his BCD, took a final deep pull of air from his regulator, and then swam up into the darkness, pulling his rig along behind him. Remi waited, and twenty seconds later Sam reappeared and gestured for her to follow him up.

She repeated his maneuver with her BCD and wriggled into the gap. Once through the breach, they were in another chamber, this one smaller than the expansive one they'd entered through. Their lights scanned along the walls, and Sam pointed to where the sea growth was waving.

Remi swam toward the corner, slid her dive knife from its thigh sheaf, and hacked away at the seaweed until she'd cleared a section. Shattered blocks littered the floor beneath, and they could both make out another opening in the ghostly glow of their lamps, this one larger than the previous one. Remi took the lead and just managed to make it without having to remove her tank. Sam wasn't so fortunate and had to remove his harness again before slipping through.

They now found themselves enveloped in a solid mass of seaweed.

Sam and Remi cut through it with their knives. His blade encountered stone, and Sam pushed himself upward, continuing to cut.

A shaft of light pierced the gloom when his knife sliced through the last of the seaweed. The glow increased, and then they were in open water, on the far side of the ruin from where they'd entered. Sam drove through the water to where Warren was waiting at the entry and motioned to him to return to the surface with them. The Australian gave him an acknowledgment, and then Sam and Remi were rising, the sun's rays seeping through the water above like a starburst.

Warren shared his air at the decompression stop, but still the tanks were empty by the time they reached the surface. Sam gasped in relief as his head popped out of the water, Remi close behind him, and they bobbed in the gentle waves, catching their breath, the *Darwin*'s distinctive crimson hull fifty yards away.

Ten minutes later, they had shrugged off their dive gear, dried off, and changed into shorts and T-shirts. After a brief discussion about how to best proceed, Sam and Remi returned to the pilothouse with Sam's dive bag in tow, where Leonid was seated by the monitors, his expression typically dour.

Sam sat next to him and told him about the earthquake and near miss.

"You're lucky you made it out alive."

"That seems to be how our fortunes run, thank goodness." Sam paused. "Your theory that there have been a decent number of earthquakes slowly eroding the ruins seems accurate. That wasn't a very big one, but it was large enough to cause damage and almost trap us."

"Why did you tell the others to come back up?" Leonid asked. "They were outside and barely felt anything."

"Because we need to discuss what we saw inside the big structure and I don't want to repeat myself," Sam said.

Warren had joined Des by the helm. The rest of the dive team stood around the area, waiting to hear what Sam and Remi would say. Sam cleared his throat, and his gaze slowly swept the room before settling back on Leonid.

"Remi found something that changes everything."

"What?"

Remi interrupted. "First, let's talk about what we didn't find. There was no treasure."

Leonid's shoulders sagged almost imperceptibly. Remi smiled and continued. "That would have been nice. But one of the things we saw were deep grooves in the walls of a chamber beneath a larger room that appeared to be a central gathering place. It's hard to know until we clean everything off, but I'd say that the building was the main temple and the chamber was a treasure vault."

"Grooves in the walls?" Des asked, his tone puzzled.

Sam nodded. "Yes. Carved into the stone. Once we get the hoses in there and clean the area, my hunch is we'll find glyphs covering every surface in the chamber. Probably depicting holy places, or maybe images of gods."

"How can you be so sure?" Leonid asked.

Remi raised an eyebrow. "Because the carvings were filled with gold."

"Gold!" Warren blurted.

Leonid appeared puzzled. "But I thought you said there was no treasure."

It was Remi's turn to nod. "That's right. There were only traces of gold left in the carvings. The rest had been removed. I could see where they'd dug it out of the etchings. But they couldn't get it all."

"They? Someone has been inside this temple before us?" Leonid asked.

"That's right. There's evidence on every wall. Probably a team of divers in surface-breathing equipment. You can make out where the hoses scraped the edges of the openings, rubbing at them. They weren't taking any care to conceal their presence, that's for sure," Remi said.

"But surely we'd have heard about a find of this magnitude. Are you saying that someone located a modern-day Atlantis and didn't tell anyone?"

"Obviously, that's puzzling. Since we never heard of it, as unlikely as it sounds, that appears to be the case." Remi paused. "It had to be a painstaking process to chip all the gold out of the walls—it probably took weeks of work with a team of divers."

Leonid shook his head. "I don't understand. Who beat us to this?"

Sam eyed him. "We can't be certain . . . but Remi found a clue."

"A clue?" Warren asked.

"That's right." Sam reached into his bag, extracted the object he'd brought from the chamber bottom, and considered it for a long moment before holding it up. The men drew nearer, pressing close to see what Sam held. Leonid was the first to react with a snort.

"What is that? A piece of junk?"

"Not junk, Leonid."

"You found a piece of wood? What am I missing?"

Sam gave him a disapproving look. "For a scientist, it amazes me that you haven't asked the key question."

"What's that?" Leonid said with a scowl.

Remi cut in. "Why would Sam bring a piece of junk to the surface and call a meeting?"

Sam grinned. "Correct. That's the question."

Leonid scowled. "What's the answer? Or do we have to guess that, too?"

Sam sighed and glanced at the seemingly insignificant piece of flotsam. "The only reason I brought this back up is because the rest of it dissolved to nothing when I tried to retrieve it." He placed the wooden scrap with metal attached to it on the counter. "Looked to me like a broken bayonet. Broken, I suspect, when whoever looted the chamber was digging gold out of the wall with it."

"How can you be sure, if it disintegrated?" Des asked.

"Because if you look closely at that piece of wood, you'll see it's the handle of a bayonet."

Remi stepped forward. "And if I had to guess, we'll find that it matches the kind used by the forces that occupied the island during the Second World War."

"The treasure was discovered during the war?" Des asked slowly.

Remi nodded. "The only uncertainty is whether it was the Allies or the Japanese. I don't know because I'm not an expert on antique bayonets. But I'm going to take a picture of it and send it to someone who is or who can find an expert in a hurry. Then we'll know who made off with the treasure—which, if the amount of gold it would have taken to fill the carvings is any hint, was probably substantial."

CHAPTER 23

Selma called them back within two hours of receiving the photographs. Sam and Remi were watching on the bridge as the surface-breathing divers worked their way into the first chamber. The progress was slow due to the lack of circulation—the debris they blasted loose just hung suspended in the water until gravity slowly pulled it to the bottom. After half an hour of frustration, Des had improvised a pump-driven suction system to use in conjunction with the blasting hose, which sucked most of the loosened debris to the surface where it was dispersed at the ship's stern. Even with this improvement, it was obvious that this phase would take just short of forever.

"You're in luck," Selma said without preamble. "Milton Gregory is one of the foremost experts on World War Two arms. It didn't take him long to identify that handle."

"What's the verdict?" Sam asked.

"Japanese army Type 30 bayonet, without a doubt. Probably

mounted on an Arisaka rifle—the most commonly issued rifle for Japanese forces during the war."

"He's sure?"

"Absolutely. The bayonets used by the Allies had a completely different handle. He's positive. And there's something else: on one end of the handle you can see faint markings. They're the Japanese symbols for Aoba."

"What?"

"One of the Japanese regiments that was stationed on Guadalcanal was the 3rd Battalion, 4th Infantry Regiment." She paused. "The Aoba Regiment."

"When did it land?"

"September eleventh, 1942."

Sam was silent for a few moments. He nodded to himself and turned from the monitor.

"I have a project for you, Selma."

"I suspected you might."

"Your ESP is working. I want you to research the Japanese occupation of Guadalcanal. Who commanded it, how many soldiers were stationed here, when they left, how they were evacuated, the whole works."

"How detailed do you want?"

"Give me everything you can find. All sources, along with a summary."

"Will do."

"How long?"

"I'll put Pete and Wendy to work as well, so if we're lucky . . . How soon do you need it?"

"As usual, Selma."

"So, yesterday?"

He smiled. "That might be a little late."

"All right. I'll get on it immediately."

When he hung up, Remi was watching him expectantly. "Japanese, I presume?" she said.

He nodded. "Good guess. But it also makes tracking down any information harder."

"History is written by the victors."

"Correct. And that assumes that any record of a Japanese operation to recover sunken treasure is not going to be in the encyclopedias."

"True. But if we're lucky, we'll pick up the scent."

Sam looked at the sun glittering on the surface of the sea. "Imagine what that had to have been like. Diving, day after day, off an island during wartime, enemy attacks taking place constantly. With technology that predates scuba. The old copper diving helmets . . . like something out of Jules Verne."

"They were obviously successful. One look at the walls proves that," Remi said.

Sam looked back at the monitor with a thoughtful expression. "No question."

The rest of the day went by slowly even with the improvised suction pump. Leonid's impatience created a palpable tension. When the dive teams finally called it a night, everyone gathered in the galley for dinner, the good-natured banter of the men lively and filled with laughter as they feasted on fresh fish.

Des tuned in to the local radio news for updates on the unrest, which appeared to have calmed somewhat over the course of the afternoon. According to the somber announcer, record numbers of police were on patrol and any disturbances were being met with a swift response from the authorities. Over twenty people had been arrested, but there was no mention of anything of significance in the hunt for the rebels. So for now, at least, it looked like they'd gotten away with murder.

The following morning, Sam used the satellite Internet to check his e-mail. There was a message from Selma with a file attached. He downloaded it and studied the pages as Remi lingered over another cup of

coffee. By the time she was done, he'd skimmed the summary and ze-
roed in on a few promising threads.

"The Japanese had a hell of a time supplying their troops here. That
was the main reason they ultimately evacuated. When the surviving
soldiers made it to the ships, they were suffering from starvation. Some
of the reports are grim. Dysentery, malnutrition, you name it."

"How long did the Japanese have control of the island?"

"Only about seven months. From June 1942 until February 1943.
And it was some of the bitterest fighting of the war."

"Then there's not a long time period for us to cover."

"No, but there's also very few records from the Japanese side."

"Right, but since we know they found whatever treasure was here, the
question is what happened to it? Why hasn't it surfaced since the war?"

"You beat me to the punch. If you'd discovered gold, and who knows
what else, what would you do? Remember, you're in the middle of a
battle zone with fighting going on every day, your side losing the battle,
starvation setting in, heavy casualties, an uncertain future."

"I'd want to get it off the island."

"Right, but that's easier said than done, with the Allies throwing
everything they had at you." Sam's brow furrowed in thought. "And
there's another wrinkle. To dive that site, there had to have been a ship
anchored over it for weeks. That would have naturally attracted un-
wanted Allied forces attention."

"Then I think we can safely assume that the mother ship wasn't an
official Japanese vessel."

Sam nodded. "It was probably a converted long-range fishing vessel
or an innocuous, seemingly empty barge. It would have had to have
been something that looked innocent or it would have been sunk by the
Allies."

Remi frowned. "And there's no wreckage." She sighed. "Are you
saying that once the Japanese were done bringing the treasure to the
surface, it just steamed out of here?"

Sam shook his head. "Highly unlikely. Especially as the Allied campaign intensified. They obviously couldn't afford the sinking or search and seizure of whatever craft they used. The Allies had created a tough enough barrier that the Japanese couldn't even supply their troops. I can't see anyone risking high stakes on the open seas."

"Then what?"

"Well, let's think this through. Imagine what it must have been like. You have the treasure, but you're starving, and the enemy's landed on the island and is preventing any vessels from reaching you. The shoreline is littered with sunken Japanese and Allied boats, but the Allies have control over the sea during the daylight hours. What would you do?"

Remi thought for a moment. "Submarine!"

"That's one possibility, but a sub would still run considerable risk of being discovered if anything went wrong or took longer than planned. Also, it's harder than it sounds to get one close to shore, presumably at night, without risking grounding it or being a sitting duck."

"Then I'd hide the treasure until I could get it off the island safely."

"Okay, fine. But get it off how? It's increasingly obvious that the Allies aren't going to give up. And no matter how patriotic you are, how devoted you are to your cause, it's a virtual certainty that Japan isn't going to be able to hold the island forever."

"I'd . . . I'd probably wait until a big push, when I had the best chance of making it off the island with it."

"Like minds think alike. If you look at the chronology of the occupation, there's only one point where it seemed certain you could get off the island alive."

Remi eyed him. "Which was . . . ?"

"The final evacuation. For whatever reason, the Allies didn't prevent the Japanese evacuation of the troops. And you would have known it looked like a sure thing, if you had communications capability, because the initial run in February went uncontested, as did the next run on February fourth. The final run was on the night of February seventh and it was also unchallenged."

"Did the Allies not want to commit resources to blocking a retreat?"

"Best I can tell, they thought the ship movements were the prelude to a big attack, so the naval forces fell back to the Coral Sea. That left the Japanese with an opening to make the run and they took full advantage of it."

"I still like my sub theory."

"I can see that. But in addition to the risk of running aground, the Japanese didn't have that many subs around the Solomons, at least that we know of." Sam ran his hand over the stubble on his jaw and shook his head. "Besides, the Japanese subs didn't have much cargo space, and in the Guadalcanal campaign, other than dropping off a limited numbers of reinforcements, they didn't play much of a role."

"Joy killer."

Sam grinned, a distant look in his eyes. "Let's assume it took the Japanese a reasonable amount of time to locate the ruins and then more time to explore them and discover the treasure—they'd have had to contend with all the same sea growth we've been battling, so it wouldn't have happened quickly. And once they did, assume it took still more time to dig the gold out of the walls, as well as raise whatever else was in the vault. The bayonet came from a group that didn't arrive on the island until September. Let's say they somehow managed to find the treasure and get it to the surface in . . . a month, at minimum. That would put them well into end of October or later—when the island was awash with Allied forces and the sea corridor basically controlled by Allied airplanes. There were massive naval battles fought on an almost weekly basis—both sides lost plenty of ships. Does that sound like an opportune time to try to move treasure off an island?"

Remi cleared her throat. "Probably not. But that's a lot of ifs."

"I know. But looking at the time line, assuming they didn't stash it on the island for pick up at a later date, I'd say they made the run during the evacuation because at any point from about September on it would have been too risky trying any other way."

Remi nodded slowly. "But your earlier point's a good one—a significant find would have been impossible to hide for long. If the treasure was recovered, why hasn't any of it surfaced? Secrets don't keep for that long, and I'd imagine that the Japanese could have used a nice infusion of riches for the war effort. Something would have made it to the market."

"I sent Selma back some direction on what to look for. I asked her to get us anything she can find on Japanese asset sales during the war, as well as details on all the ships involved in the evacuation—or that were ever near Guadalcanal for more than the time it would take to off-load supplies. Nobody was trying to get anything off until the evacuation, so that would be a giveaway. It's a tall order, but she loves that kind of challenge. If anyone can do it, it's Selma."

Sam and Remi moved on deck, where the divers were donning their equipment. Remi shielded her eyes from the sun as she studied the coastline, Sam by her side speaking quietly to Leonid. Sam noticed her attention and stopped what he was doing.

"What is it?"

Remi shook her head. "Probably nothing. I thought I saw a flash of something over by the car."

"Probably the sun on the windshield," Leonid said.

Sam looked to Des, who held a coffee mug. "Do you have a set of binoculars handy?" Sam asked.

Des nodded and ducked into the pilothouse, then returned a few moments later.

"These work for you?" he asked as he handed him a pair of waterproof Bushnell's.

Sam peered through the lenses at the coast and then handed the glasses back to Des. "Any chance you could give me a lift to shore to check on the van?"

Des nodded. "Sure. I'll run you over myself."

Sam turned to Remi. "I'll be right back."

She rubbed her neck and winced. "I'd offer to join you, but not this time. Maybe scuba diving falls under the category of things you shouldn't do after plunging off a cliff?"

Sam gave her a concerned look. "Are you okay?"

"I'll be fine. I think I just slept wrong," she said, but neither of them believed that.

Soon they were cutting across the placid sea. There was hardly any swell on the calm morning, and they reached the beach in minutes.

Sam hopped out onto the sand and approached the van, which looked exactly as he'd left it. He checked the locking gas compartment— no evidence of anyone trying to break into it. The windows were up tight and the doors all locked. His senses on alert, he inspected the vehicle, listening for any hint of movement in the surrounding jungle.

Nothing but the slight rustle of the wind tickling the tops of the trees.

After a long glance at the area around the Toyota, he walked back to the boat.

He'd spotted fresh tire tracks near the van.

Remi's instinct had been right. Someone had been watching the boat.

CHAPTER 24

Orwen Manchester sat in the rear of a waterfront bar, empty except for a desultory bartender, who was well paid by Manchester to be blind and deaf whenever he required a discreet meeting place out of the public eye. The Rusty Shrimper had been a notorious Honiara watering hole for decades, a favorite of the more unsavory elements wandering the port, but quiet that morning, its doors officially closed until nightfall.

Manchester drank his beer and checked his watch. The summons from his colleague and sometimes partner in crime, Gordon Rollins, had been abrupt, which Manchester was accustomed to. Rollins's tenure as governor-general, the largely symbolic representative of the British Crown's authority, had made him even more powerful and influential than he'd been by virtue of his considerable wealth alone and declining an invitation to meet wasn't an option.

Rollins pushed his way through the back service entrance, a hat pulled low over his forehead, and approached Manchester's table. He flicked a finger at the bartender, who nodded, and then shook hands with Manchester before taking his seat. A Bombay Sapphire gibson arrived, and the pair waited until the bartender was out of earshot before they joined in a muted toast.

"The rebels are proving to be a godsend, Orwen. I've begun probing with the foreign office, and while they aren't delighted at the idea of nationalization, they're really in no position to oppose it."

Manchester nodded cautiously. "Where does that leave us?"

"Between you and me, we stand to benefit handsomely from a movement for Solomon control of Solomon assets."

"Yes, however, I have a long-running position in opposition of the idea."

Rollins waved an uninterested hand. "Which you shall retain. While I work behind the scenes to generate support for it. That will give you considerably greater moral authority when it comes time to reluctantly change your tune—you'll have been the voice of reason against it for so long that when you capitulate, it's a guarantee that it passes."

Manchester's eyes narrowed. "You aren't in any way involved with these rebels, are you?"

Rollins studied him with a calm expression. "Of course not. But I also know how to capitalize on opportunity, and whether I approve of their tactics or not, they're forcing the administration to have a dialogue about nationalization now, when six months ago it would have been inconceivable. So the question, old man, is not how we feel about things, but rather how we can both emerge from this little episode considerably wealthier."

Manchester eyed the seedy walls of the watering hole, stained the color of mud from nicotine, and took a contemplative sip of his beer, before sitting back and fixing the older man with an avaricious stare. "I'm listening."

Upon his return to the *Darwin*, Sam told Remi what he'd discovered and she convinced him to call a meeting to alert the crew. It could have been something harmless—a curious islander killing time on a slow morning—but there was no point taking chances.

He filled the men in and they agreed to mount a watch. Everyone was more than aware of the two aid workers' deaths, and the possibility that they were at risk, working a remote stretch of the coast, wasn't lost on them.

When Sam finished, Leonid pulled him aside and spoke in what for the Russian was a low tone. "Do you think we're in danger?"

"No more than we would be on land."

"That's not very reassuring."

"There are risks to everything." Sam shrugged. "I don't believe we're going to be attacked, but it can't hurt to be watchful. We don't want to underestimate any rebels in the vicinity."

The day stretched on slowly as the divers continued their plodding work, and after a tedious afternoon Sam and Remi decided to return to the hotel rather than spend another night aboard the *Darwin*. The radio hadn't reported any further unrest, and the latest broadcasts sounded as though things were returning to normal in Honiara.

On the outskirts of town, traffic was heavier than the day before, and there was a sense of normalcy to the pace of the pedestrians making their way down the darkening sidewalks. There was still an increased police presence, with a pair of uniformed officers on every other corner, but their demeanor was unconcerned.

The hotel security guards were still at the entrance of the almost empty parking lot. The other guests had obviously chosen to play it safe and leave the island rather than stay in the uncertain environment. Sam selected a parking stall near the front doors and they entered the deserted lobby, empty except for two desk clerks. One of them waved Sam down and handed him a message slip. He glanced at it and thanked the clerk.

"Selma called," he said. "That's a good sign. Means she's found something."

"Let's hope so."

Once in the room, Sam threw the sliding doors open and stood on the small terrace, satellite phone in hand. Selma answered on the second ring.

"Oh, good. You got my message," she said.

"We did indeed."

"I scoured my sources for reports of anything resembling your treasure that was liquidated by the Japanese during the war and came up empty. Nothing. So then I checked with all the usual suspects who might have been involved in clandestine sales to collectors—you know the sort—and again found nothing. So if a treasure was discovered by the Japanese, it's the best-kept secret of the war years."

"That's not good news."

"I know. I'm still digging, though, but a significant find would have attracted attention, as you more than know."

"Selma, the bayonet confirms the Japanese were in the vault, and, based on what we saw, they dug a significant amount of gold out of the walls. And the carvings were just the decoration of the vault. I'd have to assume that whatever was housed inside were riches far more valuable than the wall ornamentation."

"Right. So after running into a brick wall tracing suspicious sales during or after the war years, I turned to the evacuation, as you asked. Specifically, that final run on February seventh."

"And?"

"I'll forward everything to your e-mail, but there's a glaring lack of data on the Japanese navy's movements around Guadalcanal. Other than accounts of the naval battles, I really had to dig."

Sam bit back his impatience. "I presume you found something that caught your interest?"

"Yes. It might be nothing, but I found an account of an Allied ship rescuing some Japanese sailors from the Solomon Sea on the morning of the eighth. From what I pieced together, the destroyer they were on sank in a storm. Most of the hands didn't make it."

"Wait. I read about the evacuation online. It's described as having gone off without a hitch."

"Maybe so. What struck me as odd was that one ship was in the Solomon Sea rather than with the main force, which was more than a hundred miles away—and it wasn't on a course for the base on Bougainville Island." She paused. "As for online research, you know what I think of most of the available sources." Selma had nothing but disdain for the sites most used as a kind of gospel. As a research specialist, she was deeply distrustful of anything that hadn't been subjected to rigorous peer review, and she openly scoffed at the web-based encyclopedias that, in her opinion, were nothing more than unsubstantiated hearsay.

"Yes, your stance is well established. That's the only oddity from February seventh?"

"Unless something happened that was never recorded. But I will say this—I almost missed the destroyer sinking. Unlike the other ships that went down around the Solomons, there's no information on this one. And perhaps most odd is that it's not listed on any of the rosters of Japanese warships involved in the Pacific theater."

"That is strange."

"Yes, it's almost as though Tokyo scrubbed its existence off the books. That got my alarms sounding. Sort of like that Sherlock Holmes story about the dog that didn't bark."

"What about the survivors? Nobody wrote a tell-all memoir?"

"No, they were taken as POWs and imprisoned for the duration."

"You know the next question . . ."

"I anticipated it. I'm trying to track down info on survivors as we speak. But that will take more time. I have to follow up on each name, and when and where they were imprisoned and released, assuming they lived to the end of the war. Many didn't. And of course anyone who made it would be older than dirt by now if they are still alive, which isn't likely."

Sam sighed. "You mentioned that the ship went down in a storm. Where, exactly? Can we narrow it down?"

"I'm way ahead of you. Based on the Allied naval reports of where the survivors were rescued, I came up with a likely area grid where it sank. I established a fifteen-mile radius from where they were picked up, allowing for the direction of the storm, which was north." Selma hesitated. "It's not good news."

"Why?"

"Depths are anywhere from seven thousand to sixteen thousand feet."

Sam's heart sank. "So if the treasure was on the ship, it's going to stay on it."

"Unless you plan to pull a *Raise the Titanic*."

"Not likely. That's not the news I was hoping to hear."

"Don't shoot the messenger."

"Why would one destroyer be so far from safe harbor after evacuating men from Guadalcanal?" Sam said, thinking out loud. "A hundred miles is hours away from port. Why brave a storm in seas that the Allies effectively controlled during the day?"

"I thought you might ask. It makes more sense if you look at a map."

"Why's that, Selma?"

"Because I don't think it was going to stop at the base at all. The boat was on a course that would have taken it all the way to Japan."

CHAPTER 25

Late that night, Sam and Remi checked their e-mail in-boxes for the last time. Sam had a brief message from Selma that said she was tracking the only living survivor of the sunken destroyer, now more than ninety years old, and hoped to have more information the following day. He glanced at the time and decided to try Selma, the time difference making it a good bet he'd reach her. He padded out onto the terrace with the sat phone, but Selma's line rang with no answer.

"What are you doing out here?" Remi asked from the sliding door, startling him. The phone seemed to leap from his hand and he watched helplessly as it dropped a dozen feet onto the sand. Remi saw the expression on his face and shrugged. "Sorry."

"No problem. You caught me by surprise."

"Selma?"

"Right. But no answer." He looked down at the phone on the beach. "I'll be right back."

"Want company?"

He smiled. "That's the best offer I've had all day."

They exited the building at the far end of the wing and slowly approached the phone, the wind dimpling the surface of the dark sea the only sound. When they reached the phone, Remi scooped it up and was turning to Sam when he murmured to her, "Don't look, but there are a couple of guys down the beach who are doing their best not to be seen. Headed this way."

Remi glanced along the sandy spit, their footprints the only break in the smooth surface. "Behind us?"

"Yes."

"I'll take your lead."

"Let's pick up the pace. With the unrest on the island, it might not be so smart to be out alone in an unlit area like this."

Remi strode quickly back along the sand as Sam hung behind, listening for any sign of pursuit. He heard the unmistakable sound of soles slamming along the hard-packed sand by the water's edge and dared a glance over his shoulder. Two islanders were closing on them, no more than a dozen yards behind.

"Run, Remi," Sam called as he poured on the steam. Remi took off like a greyhound, and Sam made a mental note to increase his gym time as his breath burned in his chest from the sudden sprint.

Remi reached the corner of the building a few seconds before Sam and was fumbling with the card key as he arrived. She looked over his shoulder as he took the key from her and swept it over the reader—the islanders were only footsteps away, but slowing as they neared the lit area by the door.

And then the heavy steel door swung in and they pushed through it, heaving it shut behind them as the welcome figure of a security guard peered around the corner from the distant lobby, alerted by the commotion.

"Everything okay?" he called.

Sam and Remi exchanged a glance, both breathing hard, and Sam nodded. "Yes. But there are a couple of tough-looking fellows on the beach outside."

The guard was by their side in moments, his baton in hand. "Are you all right?"

"Yes. But they came after us. It was close," Remi said.

"Best not to test the island hospitality right now . . . especially late at night," the guard said, holding a radio to his ear. He spoke into it and then returned his attention to the Fargos. "We'll deal with this."

"Come on, Remi," Sam said, touching her arm as another guard made his way down the hall toward them.

Back in the room, Sam inspected the phone and then set it on the dresser before opening the terrace door and stepping out. The beach was empty, their tracks the only evidence of their nocturnal jaunt, the faint imprints of the islanders' feet already washing away from the gentle swell.

"Probably not such a good idea going for a moonlight walk," he commented as Remi joined him.

"You had to get the phone."

"Yes, but dropping it in the first place was careless. It's easy to forget just how precarious the local situation is."

Remi leaned her head against his arm. "That which does not kill you . . ."

"Atta girl."

They awoke to a light rain, the morning gray and bleak, the sea churning into an ugly froth. When Sam connected to the Internet again, there was another message from Selma, this one containing a name and address in a town forty miles south of Sydney. Sam called Remi over and read the information aloud.

"Toshiro Watanabe, Wollongong, New South Wales. Number eighteen Brighton Ridge Gardens."

"Wollongong?" Remi asked. "That's a real name of a place?"

Sam nodded. "Apparently so." He checked the time. "I wonder what time the next flight to Australia leaves?"

Remi pulled up a travel website. "There's a flight in two hours, but they all go through Brisbane, and there's nothing until the following day to Sydney."

Sam walked to the closet, where his travel bag was stowed, and pulled it out. "Sounds like we're going on a little trip."

"Wonderful. I need some new clothes."

"Nothing like seeing the world, is there? Come on. Last one out the door buys breakfast."

"We don't have time to do anything but get to the airport."

"Fine. Then cocktails in Brisbane."

"Are we keeping the room?"

"Sure. Just bring what you need for a couple days."

The flight to Brisbane was only half full, and when they arrived in the city of more than two million souls, they booked a hotel and spent the remainder of the afternoon relaxing and shopping on fashionable James Street. Or, rather, Remi shopped and Sam attended her with amusement, providing commentary on several new outfits.

The following day they arrived in Sydney and set out on the road to Wollongong, figuring the drive to the sleepy suburb would take about an hour and a half. Selma had contacted the nursing home where the elderly Watanabe was living out his golden years and used her powers of persuasion to arrange for the Fargos to meet with the former sailor that afternoon.

When they arrived at the home, they saw a two-story brick complex, on a tree-lined lane near the hospital, with all of the charm of a prison. Entering the lobby, a stout woman with the no-nonsense demeanor of a drill sergeant met them and showed them to what she referred to as the card room. Once they were seated, she went in search of Watanabe. She returned five minutes later with a reed-thin Japanese man in a wheelchair. Wisps of silver hair were brushed straight back off

his liver-spotted forehead, and the skin on his taciturn face was trans-
lucent as parchment.

"Mr. Watanabe. Thank you for meeting with us," Remi said in English after learning that Watanabe had lived in Australia for many
years. She and Sam had discussed it and had agreed that the feminine
touch would likely elicit a more positive response than Sam's direct
approach.

Watanabe nodded but didn't speak.

"My husband and I are archaeologists."

Nothing. Remi gave him her warmest smile. "We're interested in
talking about the war. About the ship you were on when you were captured. We've traveled a long way to hear your story."

The Japanese's eyes narrowed, but he remained silent. Remi decided
to try again.

"I read the account of the submarine that rescued you and the other
four sailors. It must have been hard in the open sea with a storm like
that raging around you."

That elicited a reaction. Watanabe nodded. "Three sailors. One soldier," he said, his voice soft.

"Right. But five of you, correct?"

"Yes. Out of hundreds."

"It sounds like quite a story. Can you tell me what happened?"

Watanabe shrugged and shifted in his chair. "Our ship sank in the
storm." The Japanese's English was good, if tinged with an Australian
accent.

"Yes, we know that. A destroyer, right?"

He nodded. "Only a year old but already damaged several times."

"What happened?"

"The repair didn't hold. Water poured in. No way to fix. Big seas
sank her."

"So it was an old repair that let go. I see," Remi said. "Why were you running on that side of the islands? Apparently, it was calm to the northeast, near your base."

"We picked up soldiers on Guadalcanal. Our orders were to return to Tokyo. So a long trip ahead of us. The storm was a surprise." The ancient Japanese sailor stared at the floor. "The last surprise, for most of us."

"Tell me about that night," Remi coaxed, sitting forward on the sofa, her tone quiet. "You're the last person alive who was there. It must have been agonizing."

The old man closed his eyes with a flutter, and when he opened them, he was staring at a point a thousand miles away. He cleared his throat, and when he began to speak, his voice quavered.

"We did the trip from our base in the afternoon, knowing the Allied planes wouldn't get within a hundred miles of Bougainville because of their range. We ran at thirty knots. The seas were confused, and a squall was coming from the west, but nobody knew how bad it would turn out. We were at the rendezvous point off Guadalcanal by ten-thirty and picked up the men we'd been assigned to evacuate in about an hour before steaming away."

Remi nodded encouragingly.

"The seas began to build a couple of hours later, but it was only clear how rough it would get in the end. Breaking waves the size of cliffs. Wind and rain blowing sideways." He paused, the memory clearly vivid. "But we'd been through worse. We were fine until the repair gave out. From there, it was a losing battle. We never had a chance. We got lifeboats floated, but there weren't nearly enough because of all the soldiers we'd evacuated. And, in that weather, most didn't last long. We did . . . we did what we could, but it was no good." Watanabe drew a long breath. "Many of the soldiers couldn't swim. Those that could . . . There were too many in the water. The waves were thirty, forty, fifty feet. It was . . . it was a miracle anyone survived. The lifeboats were overloaded, torn to pieces." He closed his eyes. "And then the sharks came."

"And you were heading back to Japan?" Sam asked.

"Yes. Our captain had his orders."

"Why?"

Watanabe shook his head. "I don't know. When you're a sailor, you do as you're told."

Remi offered another smile. "You only picked up men on Guadal-canal?"

Watanabe's brow furrowed. "Yes. It was an evacuation. Our men were at the end of their rope."

"Is it possible any cargo was brought aboard?"

Watanabe looked puzzled by the question. "What would have been worth bringing? The solders' clothes were rags. They were starving. They were days away from dying."

"But was there time to load anything?"

He appeared to consider the question and shook his head. "We barely had time to get the men on board."

The card room door burst open and an Asian woman in her sixties barged in, a furious expression on her face.

"What are you doing here?" she demanded, staring at Sam and Remi like they'd been beating the elderly Watanabe.

"We're just talking. He agreed to it," Remi started, but the woman stepped between her and the old man.

"Talking? About what? What could you have to discuss with my father?"

Watanabe looked at the newcomer, his gaze growing dull. "The war. We were talking about the war."

The daughter glared at Remi and shook her head. "You've talked enough. Leave him alone. He's not well, and he doesn't need to have strangers making him relive that nightmare."

Sam rose. "We're sorry, it's just that—"

The woman cut him off. "Go on. Leave. He's tired. Look at him. What's wrong with you—don't you have any compassion? He's been to hell and back. Just leave him in peace."

Chastened, Sam and Remi moved to the door. "We meant no harm," Remi said in a quiet voice.

"I grew up seeing what that war did to him. He moved away from Japan after ten years there—the war broke him, as well as the country he loved, and he never went back. What do you know about anything? Just . . . go. He's been through enough."

Sam led Remi outside, his expression grim. When they reached the car, he hesitated before opening his door.

"Maybe she was right. That didn't really tell us much, did it?"

"Sam, we've done this often enough. We had to talk to him. He was our only lead."

"I know. But she was furious. I hope we didn't upset the old man."

"She was the one who seemed bent out of shape. He didn't. Maybe she's just being protective."

He shook his head and popped the locks using the remote. "I can see her point."

"Sam, we didn't do anything wrong."

He slid behind the wheel and slid the key into the ignition. "I know. So why does it feel like we did?"

CHAPTER 26

The streets of Honiara were slick from a recent cloudburst when Sam and Remi arrived the next afternoon. They dropped their bags at the room and Sam eyed Remi, the hint of a smile tugging at the corner of his mouth.

"What?" she asked.

"I was just thinking it is a nice day for a drive."

Her eyes narrowed. "Oh, really. Where did you have in mind?"

"We might want to go back and talk to Rubo. He was around during the Japanese occupation. He may know something."

"Unless it's how to find a ship that's a mile and a half below the surface and raise it off the bottom, I doubt it."

"Perhaps," Sam said. "But we don't have much else to do. We can hang out on the boat and watch the divers blow sediment all over, but that doesn't feel particularly useful, does it?"

Remi shuddered involuntarily, the cold air-conditioning prickling her skin. "As I recall, the last time we did that trip, we came back without a car."

"I promise not to get run off the road."

"Or shot at?" She sighed. "I suppose there's no point in trying to talk you out of it."

"We'll be fine. What could . . ." Sam paused with a slight wink of his eye before continuing in a firm, deliberately bright voice. "What could be nicer than a drive along the coast?"

"Close, Fargo, close."

He looked at her innocently, his face a blank.

There was one roadblock on the road out of town, but the police waved them through without interest. Apparently, the state of emergency was over and things were back to as routine as they ever were. When they ran out of pavement, the van bumped down the dirt track that ran along the river and Sam had to slow to a crawl.

After a particularly memorable bump, Remi glanced sideways at Sam. "Whatever you do, Sam Fargo, promise me we won't get stuck."

"I'm doing my best not to."

"Not to promise or not to get stuck?"

"Neither, hopefully."

"You aren't convincing me on either count."

When the hut finally came into view, Rubo was lounging in the shade, watching the river rush by. He looked up at them when the van pulled to a stop. They got out and Remi waved.

"Rubo. Are we disturbing you?"

Rubo cackled and shook his head. "Every day the same as the last out here. You want to hear more stories?"

"We do."

Watching as they approached, the old man motioned to a spot on his log bench. Remi sat next to him and Sam took a stump opposite. The heat was sweltering even in the shade. The old man waved a fly away and raised an eyebrow. Remi leaned nearer and waited for Sam to speak.

"Rubo, you said you were here when the Japanese occupied the island. That they treated the locals badly."

Rubo nodded. "That's right. They mean as crocodiles."

"All of them?"

"Hard to say. But the officer who ran things . . . he a monster."

"What can you tell us about him?"

"He a devil, he was. Kuma . . . Kumasaka. Colonel Kumasaka. Never forget that name, I won't."

"What did he do?" Remi coaxed. "Specifically?"

"I told you. He bad. Do bad things to us."

Rubo repeated his prior account, and nothing in the story changed on the second telling. Sam then pressed in a different direction.

"Did you ever hear or see anything out on the west side of the island? With the Japanese?"

"Like what?"

"Anything strange. Maybe diving in that bay that you told us about," Sam said.

"In the end, there was lot of fighting, so can't say for sure. But I remember sometime before they leave for good there was big killing in the village near the bay. Those bad times."

"The Japanese killed islanders near the bay?"

"I just say what others talk about. I wasn't there."

Remi nodded. "We understand. What do you believe happened, Rubo?" she asked softly.

"I hear things. One of the things is that whole lot of island men killed by Japanese. They make them slaves, then kill them before they leave the island."

"Slaves? For what?"

"I don't know. Some kinda work."

"Was that normal?"

Rubo shook his head. "No, they leave us be, mostly. But this man . . . he in charge of west side and he like to kill. Everyone know he a bad one." Rubo spit into the dry leaves by his side. "Only two islanders get away. All the others . . ." He shook his head with a sad frown.

"There were survivors?" Sam asked, his voice quickening.

"Like I said, I think one still alive. Tough as rock."

"Really? Do you know him?"

"You live long enough, you know everyone, sure do."

"Where is he?"

"Still in the same village, I think." He eyed Remi. "But he don't speak no pidgin. Just local talk."

"Would you be willing to take us to him?" Remi asked.

Rubo stared at the van distrustfully. "Long way."

"Bad roads?"

He laughed and spit again. "*No* roads. You not going in that."

"If we get a bigger truck, something for off-road, would you help us, Rubo? We'd pay you for your time."

Rubo studied Sam and then his gaze wandered to Remi. "How much pay?"

Sam did a quick equation in his head. "Solomon dollars or American?"

Rubo didn't blink. "American."

"I don't know. What do you think is fair?"

The old man appeared to give it deep thought and then sat back with a grunt. "Hundred. Hundred American dollars."

Sam and Remi didn't know whether they were expected to negotiate, but Remi didn't chance it. "That's fair." She glanced at the time: still five hours until dusk. It was an hour and a half from the bay, the way Sam drove. Allowing for time to rent something more rugged . . . It would be too close. "We can pick you up tomorrow morning. Will that work for you, Rubo?"

He nodded slowly and smiled his toothless grin. When he spoke, he savored each word like rare wine. "Hundred dollars."

CHAPTER 27

Sydney, Australia

Jeffrey Grimes frowned as he studied the topside of his yacht while his captain stood stiffly a few feet away. With a practiced eye, Grimes squinted while peering down at the shining surface, the sun gleaming off it like a mirror, and then he straightened and grunted.

"Bloody wankers. Couldn't be duller if they'd used sandpaper instead of polish. Why do I pay these thieves?" he complained.

"Well, sir, you didn't like the last lot, either, so I changed them out, didn't I? These are the ones your friend recommended. Supposed to be right masters at it," the captain said.

"How can you look at this and not cringe? I mean, seriously? You can't tell they did a crap job?" Grimes stalked to the stern, fuming, and the captain followed, a pained expression tightening his face. Grimes inspected the brightwork, freshly sanded and varnished, and nodded. "At least the buggers got this bit right. Small miracles and all."

His cell phone chirped and he glanced at the screen. No caller ID. His stomach tightened as he regarded his captain. "That will be all for now."

"Yes, sir."

Grimes waited until the man was out of earshot before thumbing the phone to life. "Yes?"

The voice was the usual robotic, heavily filtered drone. "Things are proceeding apace."

Grimes exhaled with frustration. "I wouldn't say that. I don't see any progress, do you?"

"These things take time, as I said before. However, I agree that we will need to increase the pressure."

He looked around the marina as though checking to verify he was not being watched and lowered his voice. "You really needed to . . . take such drastic steps?"

"The end justifies the means. Great fortunes are never made without blood being spilled. Why would this one be any different?"

"They were innocent aid workers."

His words were greeted with a pause. "I hope you're not losing sight of the stakes," the mechanical voice said.

"Of course not. I just hoped . . . that matters wouldn't escalate to this point."

"Indeed. Well, they have. What's done is done. And you should prepare for more . . . unpleasantness."

"I see. That's necessary?"

"There is nothing that I do that isn't necessary. I trust I still have your full, unquestioning support?"

Grimes eyed the other yachts—each millions of dollars of excess on the water, tributes to their owners' egos, monuments to their willingness to squander fortunes on frivolities. The human struggle was about pecking orders. He needed to be at the top. Anything less was failure.

He couldn't afford for his life's work to crumble to nothing, and time and circumstance were working against him. He sighed. "Yes. Do whatever needs to be done. But, for the love of God, hurry, would you?"

"We have never been closer. The island's at a tipping point. Like dry kindling in summer—any spark could set it off."

"I don't need to ask about the spark, do I?"

"You're better off not knowing any more than you already do."

The line went dead. He stared at the little phone—the latest technology of course—and shook his head. He'd steeled himself for some difficult moments in bringing his scheme to fruition, but the waiting was proving to be the most trying for him.

The captain returned, but Grimes had lost his taste for nitpicking the imperfections of his workers' efforts. He waved the man away and stepped down to the dock, oblivious to the tranquil beauty of catamaran ferries in the distance slicing through the Sydney Harbor chop as his mind worked at a thousand miles per hour.

Guadalcanal, Solomon Islands

The wheels of the Toyota Land Cruiser spun in the muddy ruts of the trail that wound into the hills. Remi gave Sam a sidelong glance for the twentieth time that day and turned to look back at Rubo, who seemed to be enjoying their bouncing progress.

The jungle encroached on all sides of the track they'd been following since leaving the main road twenty-five minutes earlier. Honiara had been gridlocked due to a protest in town, carefully monitored by the police, and it took an hour longer to traverse than they'd hoped.

Sam hit an ugly bump and Rubo bounced on the seat like a toddler, a look of delight on his face.

"Is it much farther?" Remi called out to him as Sam concentrated on following the faint game trail.

The old man shrugged. "Been long time since I come out here."

"But surely the distance hasn't changed."

"We get there soon," Rubo assured her.

Remi sat back in her seat. She'd already more than learned that in the islands the term "soon" had an amorphous quality, much like the Mexican *mañana*, which could mean anything from "tomorrow" to "never."

Sam caught her eye and grinned. "Patience a virtue and all," he said.

"Tell that to my sacroiliac."

They arrived at a small stream and Sam rolled to a stop at the gravel bank. The trail forked in two directions, one across the stream to the left, the other continuing up the slope to the right. Sam glanced at his watch and then twisted in his seat to look to Rubo.

"Which way?" Sam asked.

Rubo appeared to consider the question, tilting his head. "Need to get out and look."

Sam and Rubo opened their doors and Sam helped the old man out of the vehicle. They trudged together to the water and Rubo closed his eyes and did the odd head tilting again. Sam waited patiently, resisting the urge to prod him into a decision. After several moments, Rubo straightened and nodded.

"Stream wasn't here last time."

Sam blinked. "And?"

"I think village is that way," Rubo said, pointing to the left.

"How do you know?"

"Didn't say I know. Said I *think*," Rubo corrected.

"Then you're not sure . . ." Sam said, glad Remi wasn't there to hear Rubo's admission.

"We on island. If not that way, we come back, and then I'm sure it the other way."

"Very practical. But I thought you knew where the village was?"

"I do."

"But not well enough to get us there on the first try."

"You wanted translator, not guide." Rubo peered up the hill, and then at the other fork, before nodding sagely. "It either that way or this."

Sam exhaled, seeing the wisdom of the practical old man's approach. They had a full tank of gas and all day. It was probably to the left. Or maybe to the right. At least they didn't have to worry about it being straight ahead.

They moved back to the mud-splattered Toyota and got in.

"Well?" Remi asked.

"We've never been closer," Sam assured her. "Rubo thinks it's to the left."

Sam put the transmission in gear and, with a skeptical glance in the rearview mirror, gave the big vehicle gas. Water splashed high into the air as they crossed the stream, and then they were climbing again, the thick canopy nearly blocking the sunlight as they crawled up the slope.

They stopped again five minutes later when the trail became barely wide enough for a bicycle. Sam regarded Rubo in the rearview mirror, keeping his voice even and his face impassive.

"Still think it's up ahead?"

"Keep going. Should be over this hill."

They continued on. Branches and vines rustled and scraped along the exterior of the SUV. Remi jerked when a particularly aggressive branch swatted her side window, and she gritted her teeth as she whispered to Sam, "How is this a good idea again?"

Sam was preparing to answer when they broke through into a clearing, where a scattering of huts was arranged around a central fire pit. Rubo smacked his gums in satisfaction as they coasted to a stop on the grass.

"See? Rubo right," he said. Sam and Remi exchanged a relieved glance and then peered through the windshield at the humble thatched structures climbing the rise into the rain forest on the other side of the clearing.

"Should we stop here?" Sam asked the old man.

Rubo nodded, his expression as peaceful as an angel. "We walk now."

The muggy heat enveloped them once they were out of the air-conditioning. Sam waited with Remi by the hood as Rubo hobbled to them, and they walked as a group toward the nearest huts, where curious eyes peered from the interiors.

A man in his sixties, wearing ancient shorts and a T-shirt faded by the elements to an indeterminate color, stepped from one of the huts and smiled when he saw Rubo. They exchanged a greeting that neither Sam or Remi understood, and the man gestured to one of the far huts. After another few words, Rubo turned to Sam and Remi.

"He very sick. Up there," Rubo said, waving a limp hand at the hill.

"Sick? Can we talk to him?"

Rubo shrugged. "We try."

Rubo shambled up the faint path to the next cluster of dwellings and hesitated at the entry of the one farthest up the hill. The villagers in the lower tier watched Sam and Remi with curiosity. The adults lingered by their huts, joined by their children, as the village turned out for the unexpected excitement.

Sam said to Remi, "Everyone seems friendly enough. If the rebels are hoping to recruit from rural villages like this one, they're not going to do very well. I'm not getting a lot of anger and resentment, are you?"

"Let's hope our luck holds, at least until we're back in Honiara."

"So far, so good."

An elderly man with skin the color of tobacco stepped down from the nearest entryway and eyed Sam and Remi distrustfully from his position on the raised wooden porch. Rubo stepped forward and nodded to the man, who descended to the path.

A quiet discussion ensued. Rubo pointed at the Toyota parked at the clearing's edge and then made a sweeping gesture with his hands. The man appeared to consider whatever Rubo had said and then shook his head. More back-and-forth finally elicited a cautious nod, and Rubo gave Remi a sly smile that was all gums.

"He the holy man. Says Nauru very sick for a while. Will be in spirit world soon. Not sure he able to talk much," Rubo explained.

"But it's okay if we ask him some questions?"

"I had to promise holy man some American dollars."

"How many?" Remi asked.

"Twenty."

Sam eyed Rubo skeptically. "Fine."

"But we only have little time. Nauru close now."

Neither Sam nor Remi needed to ask what he was close to.

Rubo took a long look at the hut's porch and then stepped aside. "You go inside and sit. I follow and talk to him."

Remi nodded and cautiously stepped up the wooden stairs to the small porch. She peered into the dark interior of the hut, Sam by her side, and then they entered the small room.

CHAPTER 28

Dust motes hovered in the beam of sunlight shining from a slit in the roof as they made their way past a crude rustic table crafted from rough-hewn tree trunks to a cot near the far window, which was nothing more than a rectangular opening in the woven-leaf wall, a thinner woven shade hanging over it.

The interior smelled of death. It was all they could do to breathe without gagging as they neared the makeshift bed upon which lay a small man. He was naked, except for a pair of ratty shorts, and withered like a prune, the years having sucked the juice of life from him, leaving only a barely animated husk.

A pair of eyes squinted at them through the darkness, and the man's labored breathing rasped ominously as they approached. Sam looked at Rubo, who took tentative steps until he was by the bedside.

Rubo bent toward the dying man and murmured for a few moments. He then straightened, awaiting a response. The air was still, heavy with humidity, the sunbeam on the far side like a dagger of light through the gloom around them. The only sound was the rattle of the sick man's lungs as he struggled for breath. Rubo stood motionless, and after a few minutes the man muttered a few words.

Rubo nodded and indicated a bench along one wall. Sam and Remi sat while Rubo moved closer to the cot.

"This is Nauru. He said he would try to talk." Rubo paused. "What you want to know?"

Sam sat forward. "Ask him about the Japanese colonel. The slave labor. Ask him to tell you everything he remembers about it—and the massacre."

Rubo stared at Nauru, seeming to contemplate the best way to frame his questions, and then began speaking, the words alien to Sam and Remi's ears. When he was done, Nauru grunted and mumbled for half a minute. Rubo sat back once Nauru finished and turned to Sam.

"He say it was long time ago. Nobody care about it for many years. Most people he know from back then die that day. He the only one left. Other man who live die maybe twenty years back. Kotu. A cousin."

"Yes, but we're interested in the story. We're studying that time on the island and this is the first we've heard of any forced labor or mass murder by the Japanese on Guadalcanal. Ask him to start at the beginning. What did the Japanese forces have the islanders doing? What was their job?"

Rubo returned his attention to Nauru and spoke softly. Nauru's chest rose and fell, and he raised a leathery hand to his face, trembling as he rubbed his cheek before dropping it back onto the mat, his energy spent. When he began talking, it sounded to the Fargos almost like a chant, like some primitive death song as old as time itself.

Rubo listened and nodded until Nauru's voice trailed off like a motor running out of fuel, sputtering to a halt as he wheezed sporadically. Rubo looked at Remi, and then his gaze drifted to the entry as he began to speak.

"The man who came for the male villagers was the commander of this side of Guadalcanal—an officer—colonel—who they call the dragon. He like a devil, an evil man, and he kill islanders for nothing. Most the Japanese leave us alone, but he different."

Rubo described a monster of a man who dragged children from their beds and tore men from their wives, forcing every able-bodied male to work from first light to nightfall as slaves while their sisters, spouses, and children disappeared. Rumors circulated about experiments in the caves, horrors too dark to imagine, whole families dying in unspeakable agony, their bodies carted away by their relatives at gunpoint and thrown into the ocean for the sharks to feed upon once their usefulness was over.

Toward the end of the occupation, a group of about a hundred of the most able islanders were forced to cart what Nauru described as many dozens of extremely heavy crates, made from crude planks cut from the local trees, into the mountains. The trip took days in the extreme heat with the impossible loads and only survival rations of water.

At the end of their journey they deposited the crates deep in a cave, a forbidden cleft in the earth that was avoided by the locals because it was believed to be one of the entrances to the land of the giants. Once the trove was hidden, the Japanese devil ordered his men to slaughter all the workers, and it was only through stealth and luck that Nauru and his cousin escaped undetected back into the system of caves, where they hid for days before daring to venture out. When they did, they came upon the rotting bodies of their kinsmen, every man murdered where he stood, the corpses bloated in the heat—those that hadn't already fallen prey to local scavengers.

They stayed in the mountains, hiding from the Japanese, for weeks, afraid to go anywhere near their old village, wandering the jungle and living off the land. When they finally made it back to their home, they found it deserted, the population eradicated down to the last baby. None of the villagers was ever heard from again, and the village was gradually reclaimed by the jungle. Eventually, the Allies controlled the island, and Nauru and his cousin went to work for them, and when the war ended, they settled down with girls in nearby villages—living in simplicity until called to the afterlife, as Nauru was even now.

Sam and Remi tried to keep their expressions calm as Rubo ended his monologue. Remi cleared her throat.

"That's so sad. He's lucky to be alive." She hesitated, trying to figure out how to frame the question delicately. "Does he know what was in the crates?"

Rubo asked Nauru the question in a gentle voice and the ancient islander grunted in a way that required no translation. Sam shifted and fixed Nauru with a steady gaze.

"Where is the cave?"

Another exchange with Nauru produced a few sentences, and then more rasping as he struggled to fill his collapsing lungs.

"He no know. Up in the mountains. Bad place."

"Can he be any more specific? Anything you can get that would help us locate the cave would be . . . important. Please. Ask again."

Rubo did as requested, and this time there was no answer but the wheezing. After a time, Rubo shook his head. "Best leave him find way to his reward. He tell you everything he ever will."

The swelter in the confined space seemed to intensify as Sam and Remi stood. If Nauru knew anything more, it was clear that he'd be taking that knowledge with him.

Remi moved to the front entrance and Sam trailed her. Rubo stood by the cot, whispering words in his native tongue, perhaps a prayer, possibly a blessing, while Sam and Remi waited by the threshold. After a few contemplative moments, the old islander nodded to himself and followed them into the near-blinding sunlight. The air smelled sweet and pure after the hut, and even Rubo was obviously relieved to be out of it.

Sam felt in his pocket for his wallet and extracted a fifty-dollar bill and handed it to Rubo. "For the holy man."

Rubo pocketed it. "I see him around," he said, giving the holy man's dwelling a sidelong glance, and tottered down the path to the lower huts.

"Rubo is quite the entrepreneur," Remi commented as Sam took her hand.

"Well, he has been around for a long time. Probably knows a thing or two."

Remi dragged her feet as they slowly followed Rubo back to the vehicle. "Sam, what if Nauru did tell him where the cave is located and he's holding out on us?"

"I don't get the idea that Rubo is at an age where he's particularly adventurous. Even if he was, he seems genuine in his dislike of the caves. I have a hard time believing that he'd be all that interested in trying to find the mysterious crates on his own, and my bet is there aren't a ton of locals who don't share his sentiment about the caves—not to mention that the rebels are roaming the mountains, along with giants and who knows what else."

"Well, he seems to appreciate the value of a dollar. What if he sells the information?"

"Anything's possible, but to whom? I mean, look at the island. Who could mount an expedition, or would even want to, based on some third-hand account from a delirious villager?"

They trudged along in silence, and Sam turned to her and whispered conspiratorially, "So we let him live? You sure?"

Remi sighed as they neared the SUV, Rubo off to the side, glancing furtively in the direction of the huts. "Sam Fargo, what in the world am I going to do with you?"

"Are you looking for suggestions?"

Remi ignored the innuendo. "We need to talk about Nauru's story."

"Maybe once we've dropped Rubo off. It can wait," Sam cautioned as he neared the vehicle, and then he raised his voice as he called to the islander, "Rubo? Ready to guide us back to civilization?"

Rubo nodded, obviously anxious to get in the car. "We go now."

Sam grinned. "We do indeed. Hop in."

The police roadblock a few miles outside Honiara waved them through after a cursory inspection, and by the time they dropped Rubo off at his shack it was midafternoon. Remi had tried to make light conversation with the old islander several times, but his interest was non-existent, and he seemed to have aged several years since his visit to the village.

They watched him shuffle to his porch as though carrying the weight of the world on his shoulders and Remi sighed. "Looks like a rough day for everyone."

"That can't have been pleasant for him."

"All right. Now that you've had some time to think about it, what do you make of the story of the commander and the crates?" she asked.

"Sounds promising, you have to admit. Of course there's the small problem that the mountains are covered in jungle, the caves are un-mapped, the entire area may be crawling with hostiles, the crates might have been moved again after the massacre, it's possible that the crates have nothing to do with the sunken complex, and we have no idea where to even begin. Other than that, I'd say we have the treasure in our hands."

"So we're almost done here?"

Sam grinned and put the car in gear. The Land Cruiser's suspension groaned in protest as they returned down the mud road as though it, too, had had enough of the outing and was ready to return to civiliza-tion. "Compared to some of our other adventures? Piece of cake."

"Why do I get the impression you're actually enjoying this?"

"I do like a challenge."

Remi looked at the brown river racing past and recalled their brush with death on the mine road and then tilted her head back and closed her eyes as the Toyota lurched and bounced. "Make it stop."

"That's the spirit."

CHAPTER 29

Guadalcanal, Solomon Islands

Lilly, her faded summer dress a hand-me-down from her sister, coughed as she made her way to the stream that ran along the southern side of her village. Only just turned fourteen, she'd been sick for weeks, and while the new medicine she was taking was supposed to make her better, it seemed to have the opposite effect. It was only on good days over the last week that she felt well enough to emerge from her family's shack and help with the chores.

Lilly had always been slim, but since the illness she was a wraith, having shed twelve pounds that she couldn't afford to lose. Her high cheekbones jutted beneath ebony skin stretched like rice paper over bones, and now that her baby fat had dropped away, she was all coltish knobby knees and elbows, caught somewhere midway between adolescence and womanhood.

She was almost to the stream when she heard the crack of a branch somewhere nearby—possibly behind her, although when she spun to see who was there, the trail was empty. Puzzled, she called out.

"Who's there?"

Silence answered her, the only sound the rustle of leaves in the canopy overhead as a bird hopped from branch to branch.

Lilly continued on her way, ignoring the rising sense of anxiety in the pit of her stomach as she heard the unmistakable crunch of footsteps on twigs. She turned, hands on her hips, chin high in defiance. It was probably one of the annoying boys from the village who'd been showing an interest in her since she'd begun to bloom last summer. They were persistent but harmless, and she'd successfully rejected their clumsy advances just as her mother, a God-fearing woman who'd warned her more than enough about the devil's presence in boys' hearts, had advised her.

But the track was deserted.

"I hear you, you know, so you're not fooling anyone," she said, her voice sounding stronger than she felt. She waited a few moments, and when there was no response, she called out again. "You best run back to the village or I'll crack you on the head when you show yourself."

Nothing.

"This isn't funny. Just stop it," she said, and this time her voice broke on the last word. If this was that Jimmy boy who'd been dropping off little gifts anonymously, she hoped he'd either show himself or lose interest in the game. One of her friends had told her she'd seen him skulking around the shack, and she wasn't entirely displeased with the attention.

When she didn't see or hear anything more, she continued to the water's edge, the burbling of the current as it washed over large smooth rocks in the middle of the stream musical. She was kneeling to rinse her hands off when a pair of powerful hands clamped over her mouth and around her waist, and her scream of alarm was muffled. Lilly struggled for all she was worth until a blow landed on the side of her head and a spike of pain shrieked through her skull, and then everything faded as the viselike grip of her attacker cut off her air.

The drive back was slow going. For much of the way, Sam and Remi were stuck behind an overloaded truck that had been around since the war, black exhaust belching from its hopelessly eroded tailpipe in toxic clouds as it occupied the middle of the road without regard for the faded yellow line marking the two lanes. The few times Sam tried to pass on the narrow strip of pavement, he had to duck back in order to miss an oncoming car. He quickly tired of the island version of chicken and resolved to accept the trip taking as long as it took.

When they reached the hotel, Sam called Selma on the sat phone from the room's terrace. After several seconds of popping and clicking, Selma answered on the first ring in her customary cheerful voice.

"Hello, there," she said. "How's island life?"

"Hi, Selma. Never better. How's it going back home?"

"Nothing unusual. We're still digging through any records that would shed some light on the phantom destroyer, but so far it's a dead end."

"That's frustrating. It sounds like if it weren't for the survivors, nobody would know the ship ever existed."

"I've never seen anything like it before. Then again, there's no way of knowing how much of that period's history is anywhere near complete, because if the Japanese did this with other boats, they'd already be lost forever, as far as we're concerned."

"Well, if you have the time, I have another project for you."

"I live for new projects," she said, only half joking.

"This one involves giants and the Japanese."

"I can't wait to hear the punch line."

Sam smiled to himself. "I think we touched on it before, but now I'm serious. There are persistent legends on the island about giants that

live in the mountain caves, showing themselves only when raiding remote villages or abducting people."

"I see," she said, her tone flat.

"I know it's far-fetched, but the part of the legend that interests
me is the constant reference to a network of caves that supposedly runs
the length of Guadalcanal and is used by the giants to traverse the
island."

Selma took a deep breath. "What, exactly, do you want me to research?"

"See if you can find the earliest references to giants in accounts of
the Solomons and then work forward. And I'm also very interested in
any map or description of the cave system. I know that's a long shot,
which is why I think you may have better luck leading with the giant
legend rather than the caves. My bet is that nobody's ever done much
exploration, if any."

"Right. Giants and caves. You also mentioned the Japanese?"

"Yes. I want everything you can find relating to the last days of the
occupation."

"Didn't we already cover that with the evacuation?"

"No. I'm most interested in the time frame from October to February, before the evacuation began."

"Care to narrow the search for me? Anything in particular you're
looking for?"

Sam told her about Nauru's account. "I want to see if there's any
mention of slave labor or secret experiments. Even unsubstantiated accounts or rumors. I'm hoping you can come up with something because
our link to the past is on his deathbed and I don't think there's going to
be anything more forthcoming from him."

Selma was quiet for a few moments. "What did you say the name of
this commander was?"

"I didn't. Why?"

"It may be nothing. But a colonel on Guadalcanal . . ."

"Selma, what is it?"

"I was just thinking that there couldn't have been dozens of them. I mean, we're talking about a total force of only a few thousand men at the end."

"Right. But how does that help us?"

"When I researched the survivors of the destroyer that sank, I remember one of them was a high-ranking officer. Army. I'll have to go back, but I think it was a colonel. Hang on just a second and let me pull up the file."

Sam could hear the sound of keys clicking in the background in a flurry of activity and then Selma came back on the line.

"I knew it. Here it is. A Colonel Kumasaka was rescued, along with four seamen."

"On a ship bound straight for Tokyo, best as we can figure."

"Right. It could just be a coincidence . . ."

"Or it could be he was the reason for the detour."

More typing and then Selma sighed in exasperation. "Oh. Well, that's not so positive."

"What, Selma?"

"According to the search I ran when you asked me to investigate survivors, he died in a POW camp in New Zealand before the end of the war."

Selma was silent as Sam digested the news. "Get me everything you can find on him," he said. "If there's a record of his internment, a file on him, I want to see it. Anything at all no matter how seemingly insignificant. Service records, decorations, family, education, the works."

"Will do. But as I've already discovered banging my head against the destroyer wall, the documentation for that period is lacking, to say the least."

"Do the best you can."

"You got it." Selma paused. "Do you have anything new we can use Lazlo for? He's driving me crazy. Stops in every few days like a lost puppy. I think he's bored out of his mind."

"If you think he can help with Kumasaka, sure, put him to work."

"I'm not sure that would be his strong suit. There's nothing more . . . intricate? Some puzzle he can solve?"

"Not so far. But I'll keep it in mind. He's not in poor spirits because of Laos?"

"A little down, but he's already evaluating a new project, or so he says."

"Can you give me a hint?"

"Pirate treasure."

"Are you pulling my leg?"

"Do I sound particularly playful?"

Sam considered possible responses, then opted for a safe one. "I'll give him a call when we come up for air. Let me know as soon as you have something on the colonel."

"I will."

Sam hung up and gazed at the fishing boats moored off Honiara, their hulls a rainbow of blues and greens and oranges. Remi slid the glass door open and joined him. "Selma or Leonid?" she asked.

"Selma. But it doesn't look good." He told her about Kumasaka.

"If there's anyone who can track down information on him, it's Selma. Let's hope she gets lucky."

Sam turned and kissed her. "Those are the magic words."

"Track down information?" Remi asked innocently.

"Something like that."

At dusk, Sam called Leonid on the *Darwin* for an update. When Des put the Russian on the line, he sounded typically morose.

"How's the seafaring life, my friend?" Sam greeted him.

"I can't wait to get off this scow. It never stops rocking. It's like a kind of living hell, only worse."

"Did you try diving like I suggested?"

"I won't be toyed with for your amusement."

"How's the exploration going?"

"The divers are making progress, but it's going to take years to clear the total complex. Just this main building will be weeks of work."

"No crocodiles or sharks?"

Leonid ignored him. "Perhaps it's worth getting a larger, better-equipped ship here now that we know there's a genuine find?"

"I can look into it. But what's wrong with the *Darwin*?"

"Nothing. Only, the more hands we have working, the faster this will go. I don't want to spend the rest of my life in this place."

"Noted. I'll see what we can do, although we're in about the most remote point in the world. It could take weeks to get a big mother ship there." Sam grinned. "You should savor the time, Leonid. You're going to be a national hero for making this discovery. They'll probably re-name the bay in your honor and declare a holiday. So plan on being here for a while."

"I really do get seasick."

"Come on, Leonid. You're Russian. From a long line of seafaring warriors."

"My ancestors were farmers. They lived in the snow. The closest they got to water was when the ice melted."

Sam finished the call and plugged the phone into the charger before going to where Remi was sitting up on the bed, accessing the Internet with her tablet. She glanced up at him and then continued what she was doing.

"So? How is he?"

"Claims to hate the boat and needs a bigger one."

"In his usual good mood?"

"More cheerful than usual."

Remi smiled. "It might not be such a terrible idea to look into a large vessel."

"I know. Since you're on the web, could you send Selma an e-mail so she can get the ball rolling?"

Remi tapped out a quick missive and then stretched. "Hungry yet?"

"I could force down some fish."

"Hotel restaurant?"

"I was thinking about that place we ate at the first night."

"Do you think it's safe?"

"I see no reason why not. It's only a few blocks from here. Why not live a little dangerously . . . ?"

She gave him a sidelong glance. "So help me, if you say what's the worst that can happen, I'll scream."

"It never entered my mind."

The streets were empty except for a pair of stray dogs, loping in the shadows. Sam pulled into the restaurant parking lot and looked around—there were only three cars.

Remi frowned. "I hope you know what you're doing."

"If I let that stop me, I'd never go anywhere."

When they entered the dining room, the waiter looked at them like they'd descended from a spacecraft, but he quickly recovered and approached.

"Sit wherever you like," he said with a thick island accent.

They ordered the seafood special again, and this time the fish was freshly caught, lightly seared yellowfin tuna with a black pepper crust. They took their time eating, enjoying the balmy wind off the ocean.

When they finished their feast, Sam paid the check and left a generous tip, and they made their way to the Toyota, the surrounding palm trees swaying in the breeze. When they reached the vehicle, Sam stopped, squinted at the SUV in the gloom, and cursed under his breath.

"What is it?" Remi asked.

"Flat tire."

"Are you joking?"

"I wish."

He moved to the rear cargo door and swung it open. Twenty minutes later, soaked with sweat, he finished with the jack and stowed the tire and gear. Remi stared up at the full moon before looking back at Sam. "Look at the bright side. At least this didn't happen on the trail. Can you imagine trying to change a tire in that mud?" she said.

He nodded. "True. One of life's small blessings I should be thankful for." With a final glance at the new tire, he opened the driver's-side door, beads of perspiration streaming down his face. "Hop in."

She made a face. "I'm hoping there's a shower in your future."

"Safe bet."

The security guards smiled as they pulled up to the hotel gate and one of them directed Sam to a spot near the front entrance like he was guiding an airplane into a Jetway. When he and Remi entered the hotel, the staff studied them warily, faces frozen in polite expressions but eyes wide at the apparition of Sam looking like he'd fallen into the sea. Remi nodded to the night clerk and the man smiled reluctantly as they passed the reception desk and made their way to the room down the gloomy hall.

"Light must have burned out," Sam observed, looking up at the dark ceiling.

"Classy joints you take me to, Fargo."

Remi stopped when they were only a few yards from the room and her hand flew to Sam's arm and gripped it, halting him, too. She cocked her head, listening, and then leaned close to him and whispered, "Did you shut the door well when we left?"

"Yes."

She didn't say anything for a few long seconds. "Then we have a problem." She pointed at the darkened doorway. "It's open."

CHAPTER 30

Sam edged toward the door. He was only steps away when a figure burst through it and tore at full speed down the hall.

Sam hissed, "Get help. Have the hotel call the police," and took off after the thief. His shoulder slammed into the wall as he rounded the corner just in time to see the steel exit door at the far end of the corridor swing shut. He drove himself harder, only slowing when he reached the door. He stopped, listening, and then pushed through, out into the darkness.

Sam's eyes swept the edge of the parking lot and locked on the man, running across the boulevard. Sam covered the distance to the street in a matter of seconds, but his quarry was fast and he disappeared into an alley on the other side. Sam bolted after him, laser-focused on the thief, and he barely registered a dark form hurtling at him from down the street before he was falling, his left side flaring with pain.

An islander on a decrepit bicycle tumbled next to him with a loud clatter. Sam had hit the ground hard. He lay on the pavement for a few seconds with the wind knocked out of him, trying to understand what had happened, and then realized that the bicyclist had been invisible in the darkness because he had no headlight or reflectors.

Sam pushed himself to his feet as the man on the bicycle swore at him from the asphalt in pidgin. Sam's knee was throbbing, and he could feel scrapes where he'd landed, but he was in one piece, nothing broken.

And the thief was getting away.

He glanced at the fallen rider, a young man who appeared to be fine, if disgruntled, and took up his pursuit of the thief, sprinting for the dark gap that was the alley's mouth. He paused when he reached it—there was no light, and he could barely make out the far end. Sam glanced to either side and, seeing no hiding places from which he could be ambushed, set out at a flat run. When he reached the other end of the alley, he was on a narrower street, with a handful of small shops on the near side and industrial buildings on the other.

His eyes roved over the buildings, searching for motion or anything out of place. From the far corner, the sound of metal scraping against cement reached his ears. Sam covered the distance in a blink.

And found himself looking at a black-and-white cat perched on a pile of refuse by a garbage can. The feline glared at him, annoyed at being interrupted on its nocturnal rounds, and hopped down, before scurrying off.

Sam froze, straining his ears for any sounds of running human feet. The buzz of a distant motor scooter echoed off the waterfront, but there was nothing else. The area was deserted. After several long moments, he took a final look down the street and sighed.

The thief had escaped.

He made his way back to the hotel, where two police cruisers were parked in front, their light bars flashing blue and red on the building façade. Sam made his way into the empty lobby and continued on up to the room.

When he arrived, Remi was standing outside the door, an annoyed expression on her face. She turned to him with a raised eyebrow.

"Any luck?" she asked.

"No. He got away."

She nodded and returned to watching two officers gingerly walking through the room, the smaller of the pair scribbling in a small notebook in between taking photographs with a digital camera. The bathroom door was open, as was the closet, and their clothes were scattered across the bed and floor. Sam frowned as he took in the ransacked area and then led Remi down the hall, where the desk clerk and the night manager were standing in the shadows.

The manager came forward, obviously distraught.

"I'm so sorry, sir. Please accept the hotel's apologies. This has never happened before."

"Just our luck, then," Remi said. "It's been that kind of a trip."

Documenting the crime scene took half an hour, during which time the pair of officers established that the room's safe had been broken into and Remi's tablet stolen but the passports left behind. Once Sam and Remi were allowed in the room, Sam's eyes strayed to the satellite phone still charging on the table. Remi's gaze followed his to the phone, and then he turned to the officers.

"Does it strike you as strange that they didn't take that?" Sam asked, his tone neutral.

The taller of the two shrugged. "Maybe they were afraid the telephone could be tracked. We do have TV here, you know."

Sam kept his tone even. "And our passports?"

Same shrug. "Nothing they could do with them on the island."

"They couldn't sell them?"

The cop shook his head and looked at his partner. "Who'd want to buy your passports?"

Apparently, there wasn't a thriving market for stolen documents on

Guadalcanal because the officers looked honestly puzzled by Sam's question. Sam didn't push it and allowed them to finish their report before signing, as requested, at the bottom. Remi went to the door, peered into the hall, and then turned and addressed the taller of the two policemen.

"Maybe there's a security camera that caught something?" she suggested. "I see a mirrored dome mounted to the ceiling. That's probably what it is."

They appeared surprised by the suggestion, but he nodded. "We'll go check with the manager." With a final look around, the taller officer shook his head. "It's a shame this happened—we'll do everything we can to recover your possessions. But with the town agitated like it's been lately, people behave in strange ways. I'm sorry your trip to the Solomons was a bad one," he said as though he personally was to blame for the robbery.

"I'm sure you'll do your best," Sam said, trying to maintain a calm demeanor.

Sam and Remi followed the officers to the front desk. The night manager was standing behind the seated night clerk, fidgeting. When the police asked him about the security cameras, he studied his shoes with a sheepish expression before answering.

"System's been down since last week."

"What?" Remi blurted.

"It died on us. Takes forever to get parts. Thing's twenty years old," he explained.

"Tell me this is a bad joke," she said.

"I'm sorry, ma'am. Believe me, I wish it was working as much as you do."

Sam touched her arm, and, after a moment, her shoulders relaxed.

"Come on. Let's get the room cleaned up." He turned back to the unhappy manager. "I'm assuming you can find another room for us."

"Of course, sir. Call when you're ready to move and I'll come personally to show you your new suite."

Remi didn't say anything until they were almost to the room. When she did, it was in a low voice.

"Do you have the same feeling I do?"

"Being violated?"

"No. That this wasn't a simple robbery."

He waited until they were inside the room with the door closed behind them. "We're probably one of the only occupied rooms. Could it have been an inside job? Maybe. But was it something besides thievery? If it was, what? What was the point?"

"It's awfully convenient the cameras that would have nailed him aren't working," Remi said.

"My hunch is it's hardly noteworthy when something doesn't work here. It probably hasn't worked for years, not days."

Remi moved to the safe. "Whoever did this came prepared. The lock was drilled open."

Sam inspected the safe and nodded. "Yes, but look at the thing. It's made out of tinfoil. If they've done this before at other hotels, which is a safe bet, they know the equipment's junk. I could get that open with a can opener."

She looked at her watch. "It's still early. So they had to know we were out to dinner." She stopped. "And the flat tire delayed us returning. Think that was a coincidence, too?"

"Maybe not, but I'm not sure how we'd ever know for sure." He shook out a shirt and folded it. "What was on your tablet? Anything relating to Leonid's find? Passwords? Financial info?"

She gave him a dubious look. "Of course not."

"So what did the thief really get? A little money I left in the safe—I had my wallet at the restaurant, and you had your purse with you. A tablet that can be replaced in seconds. No credit cards, nothing sensitive, and he didn't even want our passports. Seems like amateur night, other than the drill. For all we know, it was the two from the beach the other night—opportunistic thieves looking for easy prey."

"Then explain how he got into the room."

Sam walked over and inspected the lock. "You could pick this in your sleep."

"It's a card key."

"Right, but look at the latching system. That's the problem with going high-tech on the equipment and then cheaping out on the installation. It's garbage, Remi."

She shook her head in frustration. "You really aren't worried?"

He shrugged. "Sure. But then what? If this is more than a robbery, what has the mystery intruder learned? Nothing, except that you've got excellent fashion taste." His tone softened. "I say we keep our eyes open, don't take anything for granted, and go about our business. I don't see any alternative, do you?"

She closed her eyes for a second. "No. I just feel . . . unsafe."

"That's natural. So do I. But it's over. And we got off light."

Sam dialed the desk and told the clerk they were ready. The manager arrived shortly thereafter and escorted them to a room in the other wing of the hotel. After apologizing again, he left and they unpacked in silence. When Remi finished hanging up her clothes, she turned to Sam.

"So did you get a decent look at him?"

"Not really. I told the police everything. An islander. Medium build. Fast. Wearing dark shorts and a striped polo shirt. Messenger bag. Not really a lot to go on."

"There aren't many people out at this hour. Maybe we'll get lucky and they'll spot him."

Sam gave her a small smile. "Anything's possible, but I think the first order of the day tomorrow is to try to find you another tablet."

"That's not going to be easy."

"I saw an electronics store when we drove through town. My bet is they'll have something. Might not be cutting-edge, but we'll make do."

She frowned and sat on the edge of the bed. "I suppose it could have been worse."

"Of course." He eyed her. "Are you going to be able to sleep tonight?"

"Sure. I have a big, strong man to protect me."

CHAPTER 31

Boyd Severin took a final sip of coffee before pushing back from the dining room table and smiling at his wife, who was cleaning pots and pans in the kitchen. "Thanks for making breakfast," he said, a morning ritual he'd been repeating for eighteen years of marriage.

"You're welcome. You want more coffee?" his wife asked, also part of the ritual.

"No, I should get to the office. There are clients to cheat."

Severin was a prominent Guadalcanal attorney, as well as an outspoken member of parliament well known for his scathing diatribes about the government's incompetence and corruption. He'd been beating his head against the public service wall for two years, during which time he had succeeded in alienating many of his peers with his views. Severin believed that the only way the Solomon Islands would ever make significant progress would be if they created a hospitable climate for foreign investment—a position that rankled those for whom national pride was the basis of their platform.

Like most of the professionals on the island, he had been educated in Australia and was under no illusions about the competence level of his fellow natives. His mission was to force the island to recognize its limitations and then take on qualified partners who could help unlock the value that was the Solomons' birthright.

"What time are you going to be home? Remember, it's Toby's birthday."

"Right, then. Sorry, I've been so busy lately . . . Did you take care of gifts and the like?" Toby was their seven-year-old son, their pride and joy, who had walked to school twenty minutes earlier, as he did every weekday.

"Of course. Just try to be here at a reasonable hour. I'm making a cake."

"I will." He carried his plate and coffee cup into the kitchen and set them on the counter and then leaned toward his wife and kissed her. Even after eighteen years he still marveled that she'd agreed to marry him and he reminded himself that he was the luckiest man alive. "What kind of cake?"

"Mocha. His favorite. What else would I make?"

He sighed. "He's getting so big. Time really flies, doesn't it?"

"Which is why it's important to be home early for the important moments," she warned, her tone stern.

"I know. I promise I'll be back by . . . six."

"Okay, then. But no later, Boyd. I'll plan an early dinner and then he can unwrap his presents."

"I swear."

He took a final look at her and then moved to the foyer, where his satchel sat waiting next to the door. He scooped it up and grabbed his keys from a bowl on the side table, studying his reflection in the gilded mirror as he did so. His hair was thinning now and graying at the temples, and he was carrying a few more pounds than he should, but overall he wasn't in terrible shape. Perhaps not exhibition condition, but serviceable.

Severin pulled the door closed behind him and made his way to the detached garage. He was almost there when he heard the crunch of feet running on gravel. He turned, an exclamation just beginning to sound from his mouth, and then a machete blow to the side of his head cut his cry off, along with most of his skull. He collapsed, dead before he hit the ground, his satchel tumbling next to him. Two assailants hacked at him for another few seconds before stopping, satisfied that Severin was finished. After a final blow to his head, they ran down the block to where a van waited beneath a tree, its license plate obscured by a layer of mud.

Orwen Manchester was arriving at his office when his cell phone rang. He eyed the screen, but there was no caller ID. He thumbed it to life.

"Hello?"

"Can you talk?" Governor-General Gordon Rollins's voice sounded tense.

"Yes. What can I do for you?"

"Orwen, we've known each other a long time. You need to tell me the truth. Are you involved in any way with these rebels? Passive support, maybe slipping them some information . . . ?"

Manchester stopped outside his office door and stared at it in puzzlement before raising it back to his ear.

"I've been wondering the same about you, old boy. No offense."

"That's not an answer."

Manchester sighed. "No, Gordon. I have no contact or affiliation with them. Can you assure me it's the same with you?" He paused. "Why? What happened?"

"You haven't heard?"

"I'm walking to work. All part of my new healthy living program. But stop talking in riddles—what is it, Gordon?"

"Boyd Severin was murdered this morning. Hacked apart like a fatted calf. There's going to be hell to pay."

"You can't be serious."

Rollins told Manchester what he knew, based on a phone call he'd just received. When he was done, both men were quiet. Manchester digested the information, the blood drained from his face.

"And you have nothing to do with this?" he asked, his tone ugly.

"Orwen. What do you take me for?"

When he hung up, Manchester stood for a long moment, staring at his office door, lost in thought. Rollins was ruthless and utterly without conscience, but he didn't think he'd go as far as to support assassination. And the man sounded genuinely shocked, and . . . worried.

Things were spiraling out of control, and what had seemed like a harmless bid to capitalize on the local unrest had suddenly taken on far more ominous weight as he realized that he had no idea what his counterpart was actually capable of—and, by extension, had involved Manchester in.

He swallowed hard and twisted his key in the lock, furrows of doubt creasing his face. Neither man trusted the other, that much was clear. As he pushed his way into his office, Manchester's mind was racing at the implications of his colleague being butchered in his drive—an atrocity, to be sure, but one that conveniently removed one of the last obstacles to nationalization.

Sam stood by the pocket doors, staring through the glass at the ocean. The morning sun was warming the surface of the sea, glinting off the waves like liquid fire.

"You ready to hit it?" Remi asked from behind him.

He turned to her. "Always. I'm thinking about diving the temple again to see if I can spot anything new. You're invited."

"Let's see how it's going on the boat. No point in getting wet if they're just blowing barnacles off the walls."

"Where's your sense of adventure?"

"On my tablet. Which we need to replace, if you remember."

"Right. Bite to eat before we go?"

"I could use some coffee."

Sam took care to lock the door, painfully aware of the futility of the gesture but doing so anyway, and then they made their way to the lobby. A few guests were standing by the front desk, huddled around a radio with the staff. The day manager looked up as they approached, his face drawn and tight.

"Good morning," he said, and then turned his attention back to the radio. Sam and Remi joined the listeners as the broadcaster spoke in somber tones.

"Reports are coming in that MP Boyd Severin was attacked outside of his home this morning at eight-fifteen and was dead on arrival to Honiara hospital from machete wounds. Severin was unarmed.

"The rebel militia is taking responsibility for the gruesome atrocity and promises more to come if its demands aren't met. In a statement sent to the station only moments after the attack, the rebels repeated their conditions—that all Solomon Island resources be returned to Solomon Islanders and that foreign involvement in our government and our industry be terminated immediately.

"The administration condemned the outrage and is taking steps to shore up security for its members. Calm is counseled, and martial law is being considered if unrest surfaces on the streets of Honiara. The government reemphasized that no lawlessness will be permitted and made clear that anyone attempting to use this tragedy as a pretense for looting or rioting will be prosecuted. Australia and New Zealand have offered to send a peacekeeping force to assist in maintaining order and protecting its citizens and interests, but no word yet on whether the administration intends to invite the force to our shores.

"More to follow as details are available. This is a sad day for the island. One of its favorite sons has been stolen in a shameful episode, and the tragedy will not be soon forgotten."

Sam took Remi's hand and squeezed it. The manager cleared his throat, and when he spoke his voice quavered.

"Ladies and gentlemen, rest assured I will be arranging for additional security today. However, I would caution you that nothing is certain, and if there is widespread disorder, we may not be able to guarantee your safety."

Silence smothered the lobby. An Australian woman was the first to speak, in a panicked voice.

"Can't guarantee our safety? What does that mean? How do we get to the airport without getting killed?"

The beleaguered manager made a visible effort to keep his tone even.

"Madam, it means that while there is no clear and present danger, staying at the hotel does not guarantee that you will remain safe. We will do everything to ensure you do, and there's no reason to believe you won't be, but if emergency conditions prevail, the men and women here are unable to promise anything."

"So you'll give us up to the mob?" the woman screeched.

"There is no mob. There has been a regrettable incident by terrorists. I'm merely suggesting that if you feel you're in any danger, you should plan on going elsewhere. We will contract security on your behalf to get you to the airport. But as is the case for everyone here, employees included, there is no way to ensure you will be safe under all circumstances, no matter how unlikely."

The woman clearly wanted more assurance, but the manager turned and disappeared into the back office, leaving a small throng of worried guests to pepper the reception clerk with questions. The woman, no more than twenty-five, did her best, but her answers were even hollower than the manager's.

Sam and Remi watched the assault for several minutes and then moved to the empty restaurant, where a lone waiter took their order. When he'd gone to the kitchen, Sam shook his head.

"This makes no sense at all. People are losing it for no reason. Nothing on the island has changed except for an isolated incident of lunatic behavior," he said.

"Maybe we're just more used to craziness than the average person," Remi suggested.

Sam looked through the large window at the parking lot, which boasted only a few cars, theirs included, along with two sleepy-looking security guards.

"It could be this is a classic case of man bites dog. News that everything's fine doesn't really grab your attention like warnings that there's an imminent emergency."

"Seems to me you're downplaying the danger."

Sam shook his head. "Not at all. I'm just pointing out that aside from the murders, nothing else has happened."

"What about whoever was watching the boat? That happened."

"It did, but as far as we know that was just a curious islander. The car wasn't touched. No harm came to it. Of course we were paranoid after being run off the road, but it doesn't mean that every new face is a homicidal enemy."

"The guy in the lobby?"

"Who did nothing but give me a weird vibe? A nonevent."

Remi sighed. "You can't dismiss our hotel room being broken into."

"Of course not. Of everything, other than being shot at by rebels, that's the most disturbing—although there was an obvious motive. Poverty is serious here."

They ate in silence, the large dining room quiet as a tomb. When they finished, they paid the bill and moved back to the hotel entrance, where the manager was waiting for them.

"Mr. and Mrs. Fargo, not to be alarmist, but I was here for the last civil unrest. It was . . . Words cannot describe how ugly it got. And it happened very quickly. Before it was over, half of Honiara was in flames. At the risk of repeating myself, I'd really look at leaving the island until things settle down."

Remi took Sam's hand. "Thank you for your concern. We'll discuss our options this morning. But in the meantime, is there an electronics store anywhere around here that sells computers?"

The manager said, "Yes, a block and a half from the hospital, on the right-hand side. Sedgwick's. Expensive, but well-stocked."

"Sedgwick's," Sam repeated, the Toyota keys in his hand. "Very good."

Sam and Remi could feel the manager's eyes burning into their backs as they made their way to the SUV. The guards came awake at the sound of the big motor starting, and one of them raised the barrier that barred the driveway so Sam could pull out.

Remi pointed at a brightly painted two-story building on their right as they neared it. "That's got to be it—Sedgwick's."

"Seems like a lot of people outside, don't you think?

Remi took a hard look and nodded. "Keep going, Sam. That looks like trouble."

Several dozen tough-looking islanders were thronging around the store entrance, which was protected by steel roll-up shutters. Several of the men had machetes, and one had a crowbar, his intent clear. Sam accelerated and gave the crowd wide berth, continuing on toward the road that led out of town.

"Maybe the manager isn't being overly paranoid," Remi conceded as she watched the men in her side mirror. "That looks like looting about to happen, doesn't it?"

"I wonder where all the police are? We're only, what, six blocks from the station?"

"Maybe they're eating breakfast? Or dealing with other problems?"

Sam applied the brakes. "This looks bad, Remi."

Thirty yards ahead, several hundred islanders were milling around a makeshift barricade. Black smoke belched from a drum by the side of the road, and two sedans were wrecked nearby. Their windows had been smashed in and glass dusted the surrounding pavement.

As they slowed, Remi cried out, "Look out."

A rock completed its arc and smashed into the windshield on the passenger side, starbursting instantly in a shower of safety glass.

CHAPTER 32

Sam gunned the accelerator and screeched into a sidelong drift, fighting to keep the SUV from rolling as he abruptly reversed direction. Another rock struck its top, and then they were roaring away, going the wrong way down the one-way street.

"Are you okay?" Sam asked, daring a glance at Remi.

"Yes. Just some glass on me. But no cuts." She hesitated. "What are we going to do?"

"Get off the road. Somewhere safe."

"The hospital's right there. They have guards, don't they?"

Sam didn't need to be coached. He made a hard left, aware that the crowd was running down the street following them. "I'd say we should try for the other end of town, but there are no guarantees trouble hasn't started there, too."

"This is crazy."

Sam nodded. "It is. Let's get to the hospital and wait for the authorities to show up. This strikes me as parasites looking for an excuse to cause mayhem. That will only last until the cops arrive and then it will lose its fun value pretty quick."

"And if they don't arrive?"

"That's a whole different problem. But right now I have to believe these are isolated incidences. That looked to me like a bunch of poor islanders trying to figure out how to get free computers, using the MP's murder as a pretense. Which is way different than the kind of social outrage that was apparently present during the riots in the mid-2000s."

"Let's hope you're right."

They arrived at the hospital, where a security guard raised the gate to admit them and then froze when he saw several bicycles and an ancient motor scooter leading a running throng toward the lot. Sam pulled in and the guard dropped the gate and followed the Toyota to the main hospital entrance. Sam jumped out with his backpack as Remi swung the passenger door open and all three bolted for the hospital as the rush of islanders neared the parking gate.

"Is there some kind of security barricade for the entrance?" Sam asked the terrified-looking guard. He seemed not to understand Sam's question. Sam turned, his eyes roaming over the few patients waiting in the emergency room area, and then Dr. Vanya emerged from the rear of the ER, a puzzled expression in place.

Sam explained to her what was happening in a few short sentences and she sprang into action, barking orders to the guard and the staff as she hurried to the doors. Sam helped her free a thick cloth ribbon that ran floor to ceiling along one side of the entry and they lowered heavy set of steel shutters designed to protect the hospital in big storms.

They moved to the side windows and barely repeated the procedure before the first loud thumps pounded against the steel.

The security guard and the nurses hurried to the rear of the building to lower the barricades there, and after a few minutes a tense Dr. Vanya declared the building secure. Vanya eyed the Fargos as the frightened patients looked to her for reassurance and then used her cell phone to alert the police that the hospital was under attack. When she hung up, her face was tense.

"You're lucky you made it in. After the last riots, we fortified the hospital so it could withstand a direct hit from a Category 5 hurricane. Those entry shutters wouldn't budge even if you ran a car into them. We're safe—for now."

"Won't the police put a stop to this?" Remi asked.

"That's the hope. But it could take a while, depending on how stretched they are," Vanya warned. "In the meantime, I have patients I need to attend to."

Another loud crash sounded from the front entrance, but the metal shutters held. Sam lowered his voice and tilted his head toward Vanya.

"Might not be a terrible idea to push any metal desks and cabinets that are nearby to create another barrier just in case that one gives."

She shook her head. "If they manage to get through the shutters, a few obstacles in their path won't stop anyone."

A woman rose from one of the waiting room benches and approached Dr. Vanya, obviously distraught. "Doctor, I've been waiting an hour. It's Lilly—my daughter's gone missing. You know how sick she is. We need to do something."

"What do you mean, gone missing?" Vanya demanded.

"She disappeared yesterday. She's the third one in my village in the last month. And she needs her meds. You warned her about taking them on time . . ."

Vanya led the woman to a remote area of the waiting room and spoke with her in low tones. Another thump echoed from one of the windows, but it lacked the violent urgency of the previous blows. The crowd was probably tiring of the sport and deciding what easier targets might be in the vicinity before the police arrived and dampened their fun. Free tablets and TVs held far more allure than being arrested for trying to break into the area's primary health care facility.

The woman's voice rose in pitch, and even across the room her hysteria was obvious. "But, Doctor, she's sick. I can't just wait to see if she returns. Too many of these kids are disappearing and we never hear from any again. And now my Lilly . . ."

Vanya said something unintelligible and led the woman back into the treatment area.

"How are you doing?" Sam asked, settling down on a bench next to Remi, the heat in the room rising now that all the doors and windows were shut.

"I'm fine. But that was too close for comfort."

"With any luck, this will be over soon."

"I don't feel very lucky right now," she said.

Vanya returned five minutes later followed by the woman, who seemed calmer. When she sat down heavily at the edge of the bench, Sam realized she had probably been given a tranquilizer—her lids were heavy and her movements hesitant. Vanya took a seat across from Sam and Remi and exhaled a frustrated sigh. "I hope the police arrive soon. The construction company never got around to installing air-conditioning in any of the areas but the patient treatment rooms. Makes for an ugly afternoon."

"Is she going to be all right?" Remi asked, indicating the woman.

"Oh, I suspect so. She's worried about her daughter. Fourteen. Seems like she's run off. They do that at that age around here if they can't take the rigors of adolescence. You know what it's like—they meet a boy, decide they're tired of going to school and working all day, then coming home and having Mom and Dad order them around . . ."

"She sounded pretty upset," Sam observed.

"Yes, well, I'd argue we have more pressing problems at the moment," Vanya said, eyeing her watch and standing. "I'm going to check the radio and see what's going on."

She moved to the admissions counter, where several of the nurses were huddled around a portable radio. A burst of static cut across the waiting area when Vanya turned the volume up and the deep baritone of a male announcer's voice came over the tinny speaker.

"Looting has been reported in some of the downtown areas, but it appears to be contained to a few blocks. The chief of police has issued a statement that anyone violating the law will be dealt with swiftly using the full weight of the department. All officers have been called up, including reserve forces, and are being deployed as we speak. The chief's statement stressed that there will be a zero-tolerance policy for criminality and that anyone on the street in the affected neighborhoods can be expected to be taken into custody unless they can show good reason for being there.

"The administration is expected to make an announcement shortly.

"In related news, troubling reports are circulating that the rebel militia is strengthening, gaining members as alienated villagers in remote areas of Guadalcanal join their force. The government has condemned the rebels as terrorists and vowed to pursue them into the mountains until they have been eradicated. As reported earlier, the prime minister has officially requested the assistance of coalition forces to deal with the imminent threat and the first of the troops are expected to land within the next twelve hours."

Dr. Vanya frowned at the news, her concern replaced by shock at the announcer's next words.

"We're very fortunate to have one of the members of parliament here with us in the studio—a popular public figure who's been a public servant for as long as I can remember. I am of course referring to our good friend Orwen Manchester. Orwen, thanks for stopping by."

"My pleasure. I just wish it were under happier circumstances."

"As do I. But this isn't a social call, is it?"

"No, I come to speak as a concerned islander, a business owner, and a member of the government. I'm deeply troubled by the recent unrest and by how certain segments of our society are using any excuse to disrupt the hard work of good, honest islanders, who are trying to make ends meet and to build a better future for our children. Today's murder of Boyd Severin is an atrocity of the lowest order, an act of cowardice that should be condemned by everyone regardless of their views. I'm an outspoken opponent of nationalization, but I'm first and foremost an islander, a citizen, who wants the best outcome for all. Boyd and I disagreed on numerous occasions, but I still respected him, and we resolved our disagreements through discussion and the use of reason."

Manchester stopped, his voice tight.

The announcer waited several long beats before coming back on the air. "That was Member of Parliament Orwen Manchester, Esquire, a leading Guadalcanal politician and attorney. I join with him in pleading to everyone listening: behave responsibly. Do not let this day be one where lawlessness rules our land. Please. We're better than that."

The broadcast returned to normal programming, with the promise of more updates as the situation developed. Vanya shook her head, scowling. "I feel like such a fool. I'm afraid I might have been wrong about Orwen. In spite of his posturing, I see his hand behind this latest unrest."

"What?" Remi said. "Manchester? What do you mean?"

"I was talking to a close friend of his yesterday and he painted a completely different picture than the one Orwen presents. I mean, don't get me wrong, I like him and I want to believe otherwise, but the truth is that I've suspected for some time that he's aligned with those wanting a change in regime. Nationalizing the valuable industries would make him a very wealthy man. He's a top attorney who specializes in corporate work and no doubt he has connections to many companies that would benefit from the nationalistic sentiment."

"He seemed pretty opposed to it over dinner, not to mention during this broadcast," Sam said.

"Well, of course he would seem to be. The whole point is that he says one thing publicly but another privately." Vanya paused. "I don't want to gossip, but let's just say that our friend might do very well in-deed if the administration were to be overthrown and the nation's min-eral rights reverted to local ownership."

"You truly believe he could be working in league with the rebels?" Remi asked.

Vanya shook her head. "Oh, goodness, no. That wasn't what I was implying at all. But Orwen's a lawyer and a politician, which means he's as tuned in as anybody on how to benefit from a seismic change in how business is conducted here. Right now, everything of any real value is licensed to or owned by foreign groups. While I can see how that would upset many, I also understand that if the islands nationalized those industries, it would have a catastrophic effect for years to come. Only, not for everyone."

"No?"

"Well, if you're Orwen and have the contacts to scoop up the plum rights and then negotiate a deal with someone who could step in and make a go of the industries that are stalled right now, like the gold mine, it doesn't require an active imagination to see that even a sliver of that profit could make one rich."

Remi and Sam exchanged a glance. "Is there any evidence that he's involved, other than speculation?"

Vanya rose. "I've already said too much—we islanders love to gos-sip. I'd feel terrible if Orwen proved to be blameless. Hopefully, this will all blow over soon." Changing the subject too quickly, Dr. Vanya offered to have a new tablet delivered to their hotel room. Turning, she hurried back to the patient treatment area, leaving them to their thoughts.

"I told you I got a weird vibe from him," Sam said. "If Manchester's lying about his true motives . . ."

". . . that could be what we picked up on," Remi finished.

"But, even so, there's a world of difference between seeing an opportunity and seizing it and fomenting some kind of island revolution. I can't see a guy like Manchester being in bed with murderers, can you?"

Remi didn't answer for several moments. "As we've seen more than enough, people will do strange things when money's involved."

A crash from the front entrance highlighted the difference between the rhetoric on the broadcast and the very real anarchy only footsteps away. Vanya reemerged from the rear and stared at the shuttered entrance. Sam and Remi stood and approached her.

"What can we do?" Remi asked. "Is there a secure area within the hospital we could fall back to if they're able to breach the shutters?"

Vanya shook her head. "No. We're a small facility, and all the rooms are filled with patients or equipment. We're lucky that the storm protection is keeping us safe." She eyed the front doors and sighed. "The only thing you can do now is pray."

CHAPTER 33

Rivulets of sweat ran down Sam's face, and Remi fanned herself with a public health pamphlet taken from a small pile on the reception counter. Half an hour had gone by since Dr. Vanya called the police. The sounds of intruders trying to get in had faded and then ceased completely ten minutes ago.

The swelter in the waiting area drained everyone's will to do anything but breathe. The ill, as well as those accompanying them, suffered in silence—all except a six-month-old child, who was crying nonstop in between bouts of coughing.

Remi leaned her head against Sam's shoulder and whispered to him. "Sounds like the bad guys have moved on."

"I hope the car's in one piece." He paused. "I was thinking about Manchester's words. It's possible the unrest is being orchestrated by the rebels in order to undermine the current administration. Chaos and looting would make the government look like it doesn't have control over the island and that could result in a vote of no confidence and a regime change."

She pulled away and studied his face. "And the new government might be for nationalization, giving the rebels exactly what they want."

Dr. Vanya approached from the back of the hospital, her cell in hand. "Good news. The police are here and they've cleared the parking lot and run the mob off. So for the time being, it's safe." She gazed at the security gate with a frown. "The hospital's never been in danger before—even during the worst of the riots, it went unharmed. This is something new."

"I'm afraid we might have been to blame. We sort of led them straight here."

"Nonsense. What could you possibly have done differently? Stayed out there and been . . ." Vanya didn't need to finish the thought. Her cell phone trilled and she raised it to her ear and then moved away and had a hushed conversation. When she hung up, she turned to Sam. "Mind giving me a hand raising the shutters?"

"See daylight again? My pleasure."

They heaved on the strap and the barrier slowly rose, the bearings in the mechanism compensating for the thousands of pounds of weight and making raising them surprisingly easy. When the door was clear, they could see several dozen police standing by their patrol cars, lights flashing, arranged in a semicircle around the parking lot. Vanya unlocked the entry, and relatively cool air flowed in when she pulled the doors open, drawing sighs of relief from the occupants.

A short, stout officer with the physique of a brick approached and gave Vanya a small salute.

"Everyone okay in here?" he asked.

"Yes. What happened to the mob?" Vanya asked.

"It dispersed when we came up the street with our lights and sirens on. Same in the other areas. The good news is, we're not seeing the kinds of numbers we've seen in previous emergencies and the people who are causing the problems take off at the first sign of opposition."

Remi turned to Sam. "That's a relief."

Sam focused on Vanya. "Thank you so much for taking us in. I don't know what would have happened . . ."

"My pleasure. But do consider giving Guadalcanal a rest until things stabilize. I don't want to read about you two in the paper."

"We'll definitely take it under advisement," Remi said. She turned to the policeman. "Is it safe to drive to our car rental agency?"

"Which one?" he asked.

"Island Dreams."

"That's, what, maybe six blocks away? There haven't been any reports of trouble between here and there, but I would advise against it. Wait until later. You were lucky once. Don't push it," the officer said, his tone gruff.

Sam took her hand. "Come on. Let's get it cleaned up enough so we can drive it."

They walked to the Toyota and considered the windshield, which was opaque on one side from the rock. The passenger seat and dashboard had tiny glass shards on them, and Remi returned to the hospital to get a broom and a wet rag while Sam extracted the sat phone from his backpack and called Selma.

"Selma. What's the word?" he asked when she answered.

"Your man Kumasaka was a colorful character. Graduated with a degree in microbiology and then went career military."

"Really? That's an unusual vocational path for a scientist."

"Yes, well, there's obviously more to that story. I had a hard time finding any coherent records for him, but when I did, the information in them is conflicting. Some records put him as part of the infantry, others have him as a communications specialist, still others have him as part of the emperor's trusted inner circle of military advisers."

"Strange."

"Perhaps the oddest part is that the Allies had him listed as part of the Meiji Corps."

"I've never heard of it."

"Nobody has. I couldn't find any information about it."

Sam paused. "That doesn't sound like the Selma I know and love."

He could almost hear her grinning over the phone. "So of course I dug deeper. Tunneled. Pulled out all the stops, including contacting my shadowy government sources."

"The suspense is killing me."

"The Meiji Corps, as near as I can figure out, was a special projects group that was responsible for nontraditional warfare. It took its name from one of the most famous emperors in the last two hundred years."

"Nontraditional warfare," Sam repeated. "What would that consist of in 1942? Nukes hadn't been invented yet."

"Correct. I'm filling in blanks here and speculating, but that leaves espionage, and . . . biological warfare."

The silence on the line hung heavy, a faint background hiss like the sound of the sea's receding tide pulling sand from the beach.

"Which would explain the rumors of experiments. Bioweapon development . . ." Sam said, his voice low.

"I didn't tell you the most troubling thing I discovered, though," Selma said.

"Which is?"

"Even now, seventy-something years later? All DOD and intelligence files on the Meiji Corps and on Colonel Kumasaka are still classified. Top secret. So there's no hard information to corroborate my hunches. My main contact at Defense called back and said he couldn't help me. This is a guy who's always been nothing but friendly. When I first called him, he was his usual self, but in our last discussion his voice could have frozen fire."

Sam eyed Remi and then the hospital behind her.

"Top secret even now? I wonder why? What could still be classified from that long ago?" he said.

"I don't know, but I have a feeling that your colonel was anything but an ordinary soldier." Selma answered.

Sam nodded to himself as he pulled the driver's-side door open. "Sending a destroyer to take him straight to Tokyo would seem to confirm that." He paused, eyeing the street for any signs of trouble. Nothing. The mob had vanished like the morning mist that hung over the harbor. "Selma, I know I don't have to belabor this but you absolutely have to get me everything you can about this man."

"Peter and Wendy are working on it, as am I. I'll have more for you shortly and will send it to your e-mail." She hesitated. "Am I reading this correctly? I just saw a headline flash on my screen that there's been an assassination and rioting on Guadalcanal?"

"Yes. But, thankfully, we're fine."

Another long pause stretched uncomfortably. "See to it that you stay that way. Otherwise, my research will be for nothing."

Sam slid into the seat and pulled the door closed as Remi got the last of the glass off her side and joined him. He glanced at the white starburst where the rock had hit the windshield and closed his eyes.

"Will do, Selma."

CHAPTER 34

They returned to find that the hotel now had the air of a fortified camp. The security guards brandished their clubs nervously, as the attendant raised the gate, watching the road, which was empty except for emergency vehicles. To their surprise, a new tablet had already been delivered to their room and was lying on the bed. Sam and Remi spent a half hour cleaning up. Remi changed from her glass-dusted clothes while Sam busied himself online.

"So now what? Do we have lunch or risk our lives going out to the boat to see what Leonid's up to?" Remi asked.

"I'd say lunch is a safer bet. Pretty sure that Leonid can supervise the dive without us, don't you think?"

"No question," she said, joining him in front of the tablet screen. "What are you looking at?"

"I was browsing the web to see if there were any reports of rebel activity before the aid workers' kidnapping. But, no, it's a new development."

"What can we conclude from that?"

"That it just started since we arrived. Timing's everything."

"Right. But wouldn't you think if this was a popular uprising, some-one would have said something? Sounds fishy to me." Sam sat back and stared out at the water. "There's a lot of money involved in the mineral rights. The gold is a big deal, sure. But the petroleum dwarfs that. We're talking many billions, potentially." Sam rose and turned to her. "Fortunately, it's not our fight. We've got other fish to fry. Sunken cities. Hidden treasure."

"Grilled mahi mahi with mango chutney," she said, then tiptoed and kissed him. "Why are you always spoiling me?"

"All part of my evil plan to bend you to my will."

Service was slow, and by the time they'd finished lunch it was two o'clock. After a brief chat with the manager, who cautioned them that although the morning's unrest appeared to be over they should still be careful, they returned to the Toyota and made their way to Island Dreams.

The car rental agent was understanding about the damage to the vehicle, once a wad of hundreds materialized in Sam's hand. The agent apologized for the unrest as though he'd personally been responsible for it and then escorted them to a dark blue Nissan Pathfinder that looked like it had circumnavigated the globe. They climbed aboard and strapped in.

"It sounds like the muffler's shot," Remi observed as Sam accelerated.

"An authentic island vehicle in every way," Sam agreed with a grin.

The sat phone rang as they were parking and Sam answered it while they strolled to the lobby.

"Hello?"

Selma wasted no time with small talk. "We got a hit on Kumasaka. His daughter lives in Tokyo. Well, in Sawara, in Chiba prefecture. She's in her seventies, retired, no children."

"Have you made contact?"

"No. I thought you might want to do that."

Sam considered the question. "How's your Japanese?"

"About as good as my Bulgarian."

"Do you have any friends that could help you with the daughter?"

"Of course. What do you want me to say?"

"That you're working with historians documenting the stories of Japanese POWs imprisoned in Australia and New Zealand. That her father, being a high-ranking officer, is of interest and we want to speak to her." Sam paused. "Remi and I can be in Japan at the drop of a hat if you can get us a meeting."

"Okay, boss. But she must have been a child during the war. She might not know anything worth traveling for."

"I know, but she's our only lead so far and we're running low on options. Just see if she'll agree to meet us."

"Don't turn the phone off," Selma said, and hung up.

Once in their room at the hotel, Sam strolled out onto the terrace and called the *Darwin*.

Des answered, his voice typically chipper. "G'day, Sam. Heard on the radio there was a bit of excitement this morning."

"Yes, we got caught up in a little of it, but it's quiet now."

"All's well, I trust?"

"Never better. Listen, Des, I have to apologize. We were hoping to make it out today, but time got away from us. How's everything going?"

"All good. Your man Leonid's on the ball. Slow but steady wins the race."

"Is he nearby?"

"Just a sec." A few moments later, Leonid came on the line.

"Leonid. How's the exploration going?" Sam asked.

"It's going," Leonid said, his tone sour. "Were you able to get a bigger boat?"

"Working on it, my friend. Any news on the ruins?"

"No. Just clearing barnacles and seaweed off the main temple. It's

going to be a long process, even with better equipment and more divers." Leonid didn't sound excited at the prospect.

"Well, good things come to those who wait. Patience is a virtue,
right?"

A faint hum of static was the only reply. Leonid eventually sighed.
"Are you coming to torment me in person?"

"No, my friend, not today. But soon." Sam hesitated. "There was
some more unpleasantness in town this morning. Does Des still have
the men watching the shore?"

"Yes. There's nothing to report. Just jungle and more jungle."

"Consider yourself lucky." Sam gave him an abridged account of the
near miss at the hospital.

"Do you think we're still safe out here?" Leonid asked when Sam
finished.

"Yes, but it can't hurt to keep an eye out for trouble. You're in a
desolate spot, so best not to let down your guard."

"I'll add the risk of being beheaded by madmen to my list of worries. After seasickness, it's actually beginning to sound like a relief."

"The secret is to dive, Leonid. You'll see."

"What I'm hoping to see is a much, much bigger boat."

Sam couldn't help smiling at the crusty Russian's tone. He was
nothing if not persistent. "I spoke with Selma earlier today. I hope to
have news on the new boat soon," Sam said, reminding himself to ask
Selma about it when she called back. "You'll be the first to know."

Sam had just hung up when the phone rang.

"Selma! That was quick."

"A friend of mine at Scripps is half Japanese. She made the call for
us and said we needn't have bothered—the daughter speaks good English. She agreed to meet you whenever you can get to Japan or you can
call her. Your choice."

"We'll fly to Tokyo. Is she expecting our call?"

"Yes, we told her that someone would contact her. We left it open-ended. You want her number?"

"Shoot."

Selma read off the information.

Sam repeated it, and then he remembered the boat. "Have you made any progress on finding us a larger research vessel? Leonid's driving me a little crazy, asking about it."

"That was the next item on my list. I'm in final negotiations to get a two-hundred-sixty-footer, fully equipped with the latest gear. It can be there within a week." Selma mentioned a price. "Will that work?"

"They understand we want to rent it, not buy it, right?" Sam joked.

Selma paused, and when she spoke again Sam recognized the tone: she'd learned something and couldn't wait to share with him. "Are you sitting down?"

"Yes, Selma. What's up?"

"I did some more digging on your Japanese colonel's history. Or, rather, on Japanese history that might be relevant to your man. I think I discovered the reason nobody wants to talk about the mysterious Meiji Corps. Have you ever heard of Unit 731?"

"No."

"Unit 731 and several associated groups were units of the Japanese military that engaged in experimentation on prisoners and civilians. They tested every depravity you can think of—vivisection without anesthesia, freezing or burning victims to death to see how long it took for them to die, injecting them with poisons and chemicals for the same reason, you name it. They operated in China, mostly out of the Ping-fang District, where they had a complex of one hundred fifty buildings just outside of Harbin, China. Unit 731 was run by a Japanese general named Shiro Ishii."

"Shiro Ishii," Sam repeated with a slight grin.

"The complex was disguised as a water purification facility. The atrocities went on for ten years. Besides the experimentation, they were also involved in germ warfare, where the Japanese dropped special bombs containing contaminated fleas into Chinese populations to spread the plague. To make a long story short, the Japanese made infamous Nazis like Josef Mengele look like Mother Teresa."

"Why haven't I heard of any of this? You're describing war crimes that went on for a decade."

"Well, that's where it gets interesting. And, I mean, really interesting. After the Japanese were defeated, the Allies granted the Unit 731 scientists blanket immunity from prosecution. And apparently many of the worst offenders went on to become rich and powerful in postwar Japan."

Sam's tone hardened. "Do you have proof of that?"

"Well, it depends on what you mean by proof. The Japanese government claims it has no documentation on Unit 731."

"How convenient."

"Exactly. And the way I understand it, under Japanese law, all the eyewitness testimony and confessions from Unit 731 personnel are considered inadequate to prosecute. There were plenty of accounts from workers, even some photographs, but nobody wanted to pursue it. Especially when the people who were responsible for it became bigwigs— I'm talking owners of pharmaceutical and technology companies, seriously highly placed politicians and lawmakers, the whole nine yards."

"Why on earth would the Allies grant those animals immunity?"

"At the end of the war, the Americans wanted to keep all information on biological and chemical weapons to themselves, out of Soviet hands. There was only one way to accomplish that—and to acquire the knowledge that years of inhuman research had generated. The Soviets wanted to prosecute all the Unit 731 scientists, but the Americans refused for the ones in their custody. The Soviets had a trial for a dozen they'd captured and the evidence was irrefutable, but it was dismissed by the U.S. as Soviet propaganda until the 1980s, by which time it was ancient history."

"And you think that the same thing was done with the Meiji Corps?"

"It would certainly explain why everything related to it is still top secret."

"And you're sure about all of this?"

"Hundred percent."

Sam hung up, and filled Remi in on the Tokyo contact and Selma's research. When he finished, Remi was shocked.

"I don't want to believe it, but if it came from Selma . . ."

"I know—it must be true. We can probably research more online—at least the Unit 731 stuff. She said there's now plenty of information about it, after decades of total secrecy."

Remi shook her head in disgust. "We need to talk to Kumasaka's daughter, Sam. Sooner, the better."

"I know. You want to make the call or should I?"

"I'll do it. Don't want to scare her off."

"I've been told I can be very persuasive," he said, handing her the phone.

"Then put all that persuasiveness to good use and book us a flight to Tokyo. Since you were the one who decided not to bring the Gulfstream to Guadalcanal . . ."

Sam sighed. "I'll look at the flight schedules."

"Good idea."

CHAPTER 35

Tokyo, Japan

The customs line at Narita International Airport moved at a rapid clip. Sam and Remi were waved through, after a cursory study of their passports and a few disinterested questions in perfect English, and were blinking in the sunlight a few minutes after changing money at an airport kiosk.

It had taken them a full day to get from Guadalcanal to Japan since all flights went through Australia first. Remi had poured on the charm with Kumasaka's daughter in their brief phone conversation the prior day and found her to be friendly but cautious in her replies.

Sawara turned out to be closer to Narita Airport than to the proper city of Tokyo. Sam took one glance at the map of train lines and instructions Selma had e-mailed him and then headed to the waiting line of taxis.

"No train?" asked Remi. "Afraid to navigate the system?"

"Time is money," replied Sam, "and I'd rather not spend the better part of the afternoon puzzling out which train is the local and which is the express. It's only about fifteen kilometers from here. How hard can that be?"

The first cab in line pulled up, the passenger door swung open automatically, and the white-gloved driver jumped out to help them with their carry-on bags, stowing them efficiently in the trunk before slipping behind the wheel again. He nodded vigorously several times when Remi showed him the address printed neatly on the paper. He spoke limited English, learned from watching American movies and YouTube, he said, and pointed to the GPS unit in his dashboard when Remi asked if he knew the quickest route.

The trip took longer than they'd expected, as the taxi wound around country lanes bordered by rice fields. They were a good forty-five minutes late when they finally rolled to a stop in front of a modest wooden house in a residential neighborhood. The driver told them he'd wait for them, after pocketing Sam's generous tip. They stepped out onto the sidewalk and made their way to the front door, eyeing the crumbling concrete steps that led to the porch without comment.

The door opened before they had a chance to knock and a diminutive woman wearing a sweater and dark slacks offered a tentative smile from the shadows. Remi smiled at her as the woman fiddled with the screen door, Sam standing slightly behind her, having agreed that Remi would take the lead in the questioning.

"Mrs. Kumasaka?" Remi asked.

The woman nodded. "Yes. But, please, call me Chiyoko. You must be Remi-san. I recognize your voice."

"This is my husband, Sam," Remi said.

"Nice to meet you," Sam said with a small bow.

"Come in," Chiyoko said. Remi smiled again, her expression offering no reaction to Chiyoko's profile when she turned to allow them to step past. The Japanese woman's face was puckered scar tissue on the left side, artfully repaired at some point in the past but still obvious even with a layer of heavy foundation applied in an attempt to mask it.

"Thank you for agreeing to see us," Remi said as they entered. They slipped their shoes off and left them by the front door, where several other pairs, most likely Chiyoko's, lay on the floor.

"My pleasure. I'm just not sure I'll be able to help you much. I hardly knew my father," Chiyoko said. "Please. Help yourselves to slippers," she said, motioning to a neat rack of house slippers behind the shoes. "This way, please," she said, leading them up the little step that separated the entryway from the hall. "Let's go to the living room."

Remi and Sam sat on a stuffed chintz couch and looked around the room. The overhead lights were dim, but even in the faint light they could see the scar tissue on Chiyoko's hand as well as her face.

"I'll be right back. I have made some tea. I hope that's all right," Chiyoko said, and disappeared through a doorway.

Sam and Remi sat wordlessly, waiting for Chiyoko to return, the only sound the whirring of an overhead fan. When the Japanese woman reappeared, she was carrying a tray with three small cups, a teapot, and a plate of sweets.

Once the tea was prepared and they had sipped appreciatively from their cups, Chiyoko sat back in the shadows and eyed them expectantly.

Remi leaned forward and cleared her throat. "Thank you so much for the hospitality," she began.

"It is nothing. You have traveled a long way."

"Well, it's true, we have. We're so glad that you agreed to meet with us." Remi paused. "Your English is very good."

"I was a secretary for an international company that did considerable business with the United States. I studied it in school, which proved wise, because as Japan changed after the war being an English speaker became a valuable skill. But it has been some time since I have had a chance to practice, so forgive me if I am a little rusty." Chiyoko touched a hand to her beautifully styled gray hair. "You mentioned you are researching my father. I hope you haven't come so far to go away empty-handed."

"Yes, we're trying to piece together his story. He was one of the highest-ranking Japanese prisoners of war in Australia and New Zealand. But we're having a difficult time creating a coherent account of his time before being captured or during his imprisonment. All we have about his stay in the camp was the account of his illness, and later his death, from the camp physician's records. There are no real details."

"I am afraid there is not much I can tell you about his time before the war. He was already in the service when I was born in 1939 and was gone most of the time on one campaign or another. I only have the vaguest memories of him."

"But surely you looked into his life as you grew up?"

Chiyoko shook her head. "After the war, there was no real mechanism in place to do so. The country was busy reinventing itself as it rebuilt, with no interest in revisiting the past. I did spend a little time investigating him when I was in college, but it was like chasing ghosts. There were no records left—almost nothing to go on."

"Did he have any siblings? Anyone he was close to?"

"Yes. A sister." Chiyoko swallowed hard before continuing. "She raised me. But she passed away twenty years ago. The only things she could tell me about my father were that he was a very brave, honorable man who died doing his duty and that he had been a scholar and a fine husband to my mother, who also passed away during the war."

"I'm sorry to hear that," Remi said in a soft voice.

"It is still hard to talk about even after all these years. I was six. The Allies bombed Tokyo regularly, but in the final days of the war there was a huge firebombing campaign that destroyed whole residential neighborhoods." Chiyoko stopped and drew a ragged breath. "She was caught in the fires. I was lucky. She wasn't."

"It must have been terrible," Remi said.

"Nothing I say can describe it. Miles of Tokyo burned to ashes.

Over a million lost their homes, and it's said that over a hundred thousand civilians died. My mother one of them." When Chiyoko looked
Remi directly in the eyes, they were moist, the pain still fresh. "It was a
vision of hell I'll never forget. Nobody who went through it could."

"I'm . . . I'm so sorry, Chiyoko," Remi whispered.

"It was a long time ago. Regrettable acts were committed on all
sides. I'm grateful to have lived, and that there has never been another
war like it. I grew up and lived in a time of relative peace and prosperity. A rebirth of Japan as a world power, but without the need to conquer militarily. A better time, I think."

Remi sat silently for several moments before she spoke. "What
about photographs? Letters?"

"Most were lost in the fires. Although I do have some very old ones
that my aunt salvaged. I'm not sure they would be of any help. Mostly,
him as a young man." Chiyoko hesitated. "Would you like to see them?"

"That would be wonderful," Remi said. Chiyoko stood and left the
room, and Sam gave Remi a hopeful look. She returned several minutes later, carrying a cardboard box. Sam leapt to his feet and approached her.

"Please. Let me help you."

Chiyoko reluctantly handed him the box. "Thank you. It's easy to
forget that I'm not as fit as I once was. Time is a thief. It steals our
memory, our hopes, and our strength, leaving only the sense there's
never enough of it." She pointed to the low table in the center of the
room with a scarred hand. "You can put the box there."

Sam complied and sat beside Remi again, watching as Chiyoko removed several tiny metal picture frames. She stared at them for a long
moment and then handed them to Remi.

"These are the best ones. My father as a young boy, then as a student, graduating from university. And that one is his wedding photograph. That is the only one I have of my mother."

Remi and Sam gazed at the picture. A stern-faced young man stood by his diminutive bride, who seemed to glow in the faded black-and-white picture. Remi gasped as she held the frame. "Oh my . . . she was breathtaking."

"Yes, she was considered a great beauty. My aunt reminded me all the time." Chiyoko's voice was oddly flat. She lifted a final frame from the box and passed it to Remi with trembling fingers. "This last one is my favorite—I keep it by my bed. It was taken by his sister at the cherry blossom festival in Arashiyama before the war with America began. She said that the trees bloomed late that year because it had been an especially cold winter. They were there on the final day before the blossoms began falling. She said when they did, it was like the air was filled with pink snow."

Remi and Sam studied the photograph of the martial Kumasaka in uniform, staring off into the distance beneath a canopy of cherry blossoms, figures in the background adorned in traditional Japanese garb. The image had an otherworldly quality to it, something from a different era. They both regarded it with intense concentration, trying to reconcile the accounts of a savage monster with the serious man in the shot, about mid-thirties, his profile pensive. Sam noted the insignia—Kumasaka was already a colonel by that point, already a veteran of Japan's foray into China, which had begun in 1937 with the start of the bloody Second Sino-Japanese War.

"Do you know anything about your father's service? His involvement with Unit 731 or the Meiji Corps?" Remi asked.

Chiyoko looked confused. "I've never heard of either. Do they have some significance?"

"They're army groups that were involved in medical research."

"Medical? My father was a soldier, not a doctor."

"He had a degree in microbiology."

"Yes, but he became a career officer. He never put the degree to use. It was a strange time, according to my aunt. Many educated Japanese pursued military careers instead of their trained professions."

"Do you know anything about what he did in the army?"

"My aunt said he was in communications. I'm not sure what that involved, to be honest."

Sam was looking in the box. "What's that?" he asked, pointing to a small leather-bound notebook, battered and scarred almost beyond recognition.

"Ah, I was going to mention it. My father kept a journal while he was a prisoner. I have read it numerous times. There is not much in it. Some poems, his thoughts on being a prisoner. Nothing very detailed that relates to his captivity. One of the men in the building where he was imprisoned gave it to me after the war. He said that the prisoners were allowed to keep diaries, but they were regularly raided and read to ensure that nothing seditious was being written. It is pretty bland."

"May I see it?" Remi asked.

"Certainly. But I must warn you, it is all written in kanji."

Chiyoko handed her the book. The pages were badly yellowed and stained in many places, covered in neat, tight Japanese symbols from top to bottom. Remi handed the journal to Sam and lowered her voice. "Is there any way we can get a copy made and return the diary to you? It might provide some information we can use. We'll guarantee it isn't damaged in any way."

"There is nothing in it, but if you want to make a copy, I have no objection."

They continued their discussion for another half hour, but as friendly and helpful as Chiyoko was, she really had no material information that they didn't already know. When it was obvious that there was nothing further to be gained by continuing the questioning, Sam and Remi stood and Chiyoko showed them to the door.

"Thank you so much, Chiyoko," Remi said. "We both appreciate the time and your sharing painful memories."

The Japanese woman looked down at her small feet. "It's been a pleasure. I'm sorry I don't have anything more I can offer."

"You've done more than enough. Thanks again."

The taxi was still parked where they'd left it, and when they got into the car, they were both silent. Only once they were under way did Remi lean forward and speak to the driver.

"Can you take us to the nearest place that would have a scanner and a printer?"

CHAPTER 36

Three hours later, they had returned the diary to Chiyoko and were sitting in the Narita Airport departure lounge, awaiting their flight. They had e-mailed the scans of the pages to Selma with the instruction to find a translator as soon as possible. Both were quiet. Chiyoko's story weighed heavily on their minds. Remi intently paged through a site on her tablet, preoccupied.

Sam studied her face. "You okay?"

"I suppose so."

"A lot to think about, isn't it?"

"Yes. I can't shake her description of the firebombing. Imagine what that must have been like—to lose your mother at such an early age. And the scars . . ."

"According to Selma's research, Chiyoko never married. I can't help but think that the scarring might have played a role," Sam said. "It had to have been terrible to grow up like that."

"I'd bet the external damage is nothing compared to the baggage she's carrying around inside."

"No question."

They watched the busy crowd rush through the terminal, countless anonymous faces on their busy way to important destinations. Remi shifted in her seat and edged closer to Sam.

"Anything interesting online?" he asked, peering at the tablet screen.

"Oh, just a litany of horror. One historian estimates that the Japanese killed thirty million. It's mind-boggling."

"Hard to comprehend," Sam agreed. He sat back in his chair and checked the time. "I wonder if I can get a clear line of sight for the sat phone over by the window?"

"Only one way to find out."

Sam retrieved the phone from his bag. After half a minute, the device had acquired a satellite and he dialed Selma's number. She answered on the fourth ring.

"Good morning," he said.

"Same to you."

"Did you get the file we sent?"

"Of course. We're already working on it."

"You found someone who can translate it that quickly?"

"Call it serendipity. Lazlo was here first thing today, nosing around, and he volunteered. Apparently, he reads and writes it fluently. He's a man of many surprises."

"So I've heard," Sam said drily. "Did he give you any feeling for when he'd have it done?"

"He said he'd get right on it. Poor man seems bored out of his mind. He practically ran out of here with the file." Selma hesitated. "Your new boat's on its way."

"Super. What's the ETA?"

"Four days."

"Leonid will be ecstatic."

"Then my life has meaning. Is he still as cheery as ever?"

"Practically giddy with good humor."

An announcement for the flight blared over the speakers in three different languages. Sam finished up with Selma, and a few minutes later the Fargos were aboard the plane.

Their connection in Australia put them back into Honiara midafternoon the following day, the flight almost empty. Apparently, there was little rush to vacation on an island on the brink of civil war. The hotel was equally quiet, the clerks eager to please, the manager typically reserved when he saw them.

"Mr. and Mrs. Fargo. Welcome back," he greeted, sounding unenthusiastic.

"Thanks. Any new developments?" Sam asked.

"No. All is quiet, thank goodness."

"That's a bit of luck, right?" Remi said.

"Let's hope it holds," the manager agreed.

Once settled in their room, Sam powered up the sat phone and called Selma.

"We're back in Guadalcanal. What's the good word?" he asked.

"Good timing on your part. Lazlo's right here. You want to talk to him?"

"Sure."

Lazlo's British-accented voice came on the line. "Sam, my good man. Globe-trotting around the world, I hear?"

"Hardly. More like puddle-jumping from island to island. How's the translation going?"

"About halfway through. Tedious stuff, for the most part. Bad haikus, dreadful poetry, long passages lamenting living in captivity."

"Anything catch your eye?"

"Since you mention it, yes, there's something odd about the prose. I can't be certain, but it seems like there's an underlying pattern to some of the entries that's deeper than the maudlin sentiments the author is expressing."

"A pattern?"

"Too soon to say for certain of course, but my sniffer is on alert."

"You think there could be some sort of code embedded in the text?"

"That would be my first guess, but it's just a hunch. Let me get the entire text translated and I'll run it through some of my programs and see what I can spot. I'm hoping to have it done by late tonight."

"Keep us informed."

"As always. Enjoy the swaying palms and tropical breeze."

"Thanks. We'll try."

Remi eyed Sam expectantly when he returned from the terrace. "Well?"

"Lazlo's hard at work. Thinks there might be a code. Or there might not."

"That sounds promising. Or not."

Sam grinned. "If it were easy, everyone would be doing it." He checked the time. "You want to go for a ride?"

"What did you have in mind?"

"I want to pay Rubo another visit. Probe him for more info and see if his story stays the same—if his buddy told him more than he let on, he might slip up now that it's been a few days."

When they pulled up to the shack, two vehicles blocked the way: a police truck and an ambulance. Sam and Remi exchanged a worried glance and stepped out of the Pathfinder, only to find themselves facing a burly island policeman, hands on his hips, his eyes inscrutable behind aviator sunglasses.

"What happened? Is Rubo all right?" Remi asked as they approached.

"I'm afraid this is as far as you go," the officer said.

"We're here to see him. What happened?" Sam explained.

"Accident. Looks like he slipped and hit his head."

They were interrupted by two paramedics pushing a gurney onto Rubo's porch from inside the house. A sheet pulled over Rubo's slight frame, provided all the explanation necessary. The policeman glanced over at the body as the men carted the gurney across the uneven muddy terrain to the ambulance and then turned to Sam and Remi. "Was there anything else?" he asked.

"No. Poor man. I hope he didn't suffer," Remi said.

"No way of knowing for sure, but the techs say he probably didn't," the cop said.

Sam and Remi walked slowly back to the car. Sam slid behind the wheel and glanced over at Remi as he started the engine. "Old Rubo managed to live to be nearly a hundred without any issues, and right after he goes with us to ask about the past, he has a fatal accident. Am I being paranoid or is the timing suspicious?"

"You're asking the woman you were in the river with, dodging gunmen after being run off the road, whether you're paranoid?"

Sam's grin was humorless. "Good point."

CHAPTER 37

The next morning, Selma called as Sam and Remi sat on the ocean-front veranda, enjoying their coffee, the fishing fleet rocking at anchor in the harbor as the sun rose out of the sea. Sam lifted the handset to his ear and punched it to life.

"Selma! Tell me you have good news. We could use some."

"Why? What happened?"

Sam told her about Rubo's demise.

Selma's voice quieted. "I'm sorry to hear about it. Definitely sounds fishy. Although you did say he was old . . . Still, I hope you and Remi are watching your backs."

"There isn't a lot else to do here, Selma. Now, how about your news?"

"I have Lazlo with me. He wants to tell you."

"Put him on."

When Lazlo spoke, he sounded exuberant. "Greetings and salutations. Your Japanese diary definitely held some surprises."

"I presume you're not talking about particularly resonant poems, Lazlo."

"Actually, the prose was agonizing—a lot of bloodred sunsets and still water, that sort of thing. Terribly amateur. But the substitution cypher wasn't."

"Substitution cypher," Sam repeated.

"That's correct. But even once I cracked it with my program, I'm not sure it makes a huge amount of sense. It's rather oblique."

"Why don't you tell me what it says?"

"I'll do one better. I've shot my findings to your e-mail. Check it as soon as you can and see if it means anything to you. It's possible I missed some key parts. I'll continue checking, but I doubt it."

"Can you summarize?"

"Rather a lot of blather about a village, a waterfall, that sort of thing. Seems like directions, but I'd think longitude and latitude would have been more useful."

"It's possible he didn't have access to his notes or a GPS when he wrote it," Sam joked.

"That's certainly one explanation. The other is that he was wary that someone would crack the code. I should say that's unlikely, given the technology in use during the war, but it's a possibility. Nowadays, of course, a car has more computing power than the entire Allied cryptology effort, so for a seasoned pro like me it's child's play."

"Which is why we're glad you're on our team, Lazlo," Sam assured him.

"Take a gander at it and call Selma or me if you have any questions. Meanwhile, I'll stay on it."

"Thank you, Lazlo. Nice work."

"I hope it helps. Selma is as tight-lipped as the Sphinx when it comes to what you two are up to over there. It's all I could do to drag a few tidbits out of her."

"We've located a sunken city, and it looks like there was a treasure of some sort the Japanese located and hid before they evacuated the island. Your contribution may be the key to finding it." Sam smiled at Remi. "Lazlo, are you busy with anything at the moment?"

"I'm debating writing the great American novel. But then I remember I'm British and watch the telly instead."

"Think you could stomach a flight to the lovely Solomon Islands to help us on our treasure hunt?"

Remi gave Sam a sidelong glance and sighed. There was no hesitation when Lazlo answered. "I'll be on the next plane out."

"That would put you here in a couple of days."

"Don't go and find the treasure without me."

"Might want to have Selma get you a can of crocodile repellent and some giant spray. Oh, and a Kevlar vest in case there's more rioting or assassinations."

"What's that you say?"

"Never mind. Dress for the tropics. Let us know when your flight arrives so we can roll out the welcome committee."

"Will do."

Remi signaled to the waiter for a refill of coffee as Sam hung up and she fixed him with a skeptical eye. "We really need Lazlo here?"

"He's bouncing off the walls with nothing to do. And he did decode the diary." He told her about the cypher and the e-mail.

"So our suspicions were correct. Kumasaka hid the treasure, planning to come back for it after the war," Remi said.

"Or once the Allies were driven back by the might of the Axis powers."

"That didn't quite work out as planned." She waited as the server topped off her cup. "But why Lazlo, at this stage? It sounds like we're close."

"I think it would lift his spirits to be in on the hunt."

She gazed at a gull, riding an updraft over the water. "I don't know, Sam. With the rebels knocking people off left and right . . ."

"He can always hop on a plane out just as easily as we can. Or join us on the boat."

"Speaking of which, are we heading out there today?"

"I think it would be good to show our faces. Moral support for Leonid and all."

Back in their room, Remi pulled up the e-mail and they read Lazlo's attachment. When they were done, Remi shook her head. "Just once, I'd like to have a clear set of directions. Just once. Is that too much to ask?"

"It would take all the fun out of it."

"Maybe, but come on. This could be anywhere. He doesn't even identify which village he used as his starting point."

"Lazlo did say he might have missed something. Could be a starting point yet to surface. Even so, we're way ahead of where we were just a few days ago. He places the cave near a waterfall."

"There's some ambiguity there, I think. Lazlo makes a point of indicating that it could be plural, as in caves."

"Cave, caves, at least we have something to follow now."

"I know." She checked her watch. "How hard do you think it will be to round up some decent spelunking gear on the island?"

"Basics? Shouldn't be too bad. I'll make out a list and send it to Selma, just in case. Lazlo can bring anything we can't locate."

There was only one police checkpoint just outside of town and little traffic as they followed the winding road to the turnoff that led to the bay. They were again the only vehicle parked by the shore and there were no fresh tire tracks, their old ones long since washed away by the regular cloudbursts. Des arrived in the skiff five minutes after they arrived and gave them a progress report as they bounced over the mild waves toward the *Darwin*.

Once on board, Des led them to the bridge, where Leonid was in his customary position in front of the monitor display, watching the divers go about their work. He glanced up when Sam and Remi entered and then went back to staring at the screens.

"Morning, sunshine," Sam said as he neared.

"More like afternoon now, isn't it?" Leonid said.

"When you're in the islands, time slows down. Don't you know that?" Remi said with a smile. "How's it going?"

"Agonizing. It'll be years, at this rate," Leonid said.

"I have good news for you, my aquatic friend," Sam announced. "There's a much larger ship en route. It should be here in no time." Sam told him about the research vessel and, uncharacteristically, a hint of a smile played across the Russian's taciturn face.

"Won't be a minute too soon," Leonid said.

"But, in the meantime, we have a related project to which we need you to bring your considerable skills." Sam described the encrypted clues Lazlo had discovered. "We were hoping you might want to get off the boat for a little while and help us find King Loc's treasure. Unless you've got your hands full here," Sam said, eyeing the cloudy images on the monitors.

"Back on solid ground? When do we leave?"

"Shortly. We have an associate coming from San Diego with some supplies we'll need. Figure in two days, tops." Sam smiled. "In the meantime, we can do a little diving together. Remi's been bugging me about seeing you in action. I hate to deprive her of anything."

Remi nodded enthusiastically. "That's right. We'll stay overnight so we can get in some morning dives, too. You ready to suit up and put those newfound skills of yours to work?"

Leonid closed his eyes and shook his head. "I hope you're joking."

Remi waited until his eyes flittered open and gave him a wicked grin. "I never joke about diving."

Sam shrugged. "She's the boss. Come on, Aquaman. Time to get wet."

CHAPTER 38

The next morning, after breakfast with the crew, Sam and Remi returned to shore accompanied by Leonid, whose relief to be off the *Darwin* was obvious. He trudged up the sand toward the Nissan with the enthusiasm of a prisoner released from death row, and Sam exchanged a smile with Remi.

"Be sure to make plenty of noise, Leonid. Remember the crocodiles," Sam warned.

Leonid slowed and glanced around. "Are you making jokes again?"

"No, he's serious. It's a well-established fact that crocodiles are sensitive to sound. I usually sing and flap my arms. Better than being eaten alive," Remi assured him.

"That's right. Remember Benji. He was quiet and paid for it with his leg," said Sam.

Leonid stopped. "I think you're pulling on mine. My leg, I mean."

"Did you know a male crocodile can run faster than a racehorse?"

Remi shared. "I don't know where I read that, but they're called land barracudas by the natives."

Once at the SUV, Sam did his usual inspection of the exterior as Leonid and Remi climbed in. After confirming that there were no new tire tracks or footprints around the vehicle, he slid behind the wheel, started the engine, and pulled onto the rutted track and made for the main road.

Getting Leonid a room at the hotel proved easy. It was almost completely empty now, the news of the assassination and the murder of the aid workers having chilled interest in vacationing on Guadalcanal.

"We got Lazlo's itinerary and confirmation," Remi said. "He'll be in at eight-ten tomorrow morning."

"Great. Assuming he's up to it, we can head into the mountains by noon. I'm anxious to see whether we can find that cave."

"That makes two of us. We can expect to keep news of Leonid's find secret for only so long, and once it becomes public knowledge the island will be swarmed by researchers who'll want to study it. You know the kind of speculation our continued presence here would cause at that point. We'd be followed everywhere by speculators convinced we were in search of treasure."

"I really hope for Lazlo's sake we find something. Leonid's going to be a rock star for the city discovery. Lazlo could use a win, if only for his reputation's sake."

"I doubt there's much that could redeem him after his little adventure with his student and the resulting scandal," Remi said.

"Discovering a lost treasure would go a long way."

"You don't have to convince me. Now we just need to get to the part where we find it."

"Always more difficult than it sounds," Sam agreed.

They spent the afternoon wandering Honiara with Leonid, gathering supplies for their cave expedition. They were able to locate rubber boots and strong rope, as well as LED flashlights, but unsurprisingly had no luck with carabiners or any specialized hardware. Fortunately, Lazlo was bringing the more obscure elements so that when he arrived they would be ready to hit the ground running.

The mood of the city was apparently back to normal, with none of the brooding menace that had been present earlier in the week. There had been no further violence since the machete attack, and despite lingering tension, life went on. The arrival of the Australian-led civil defense force was largely met with welcome by the locals, although there was still a vocal segment of the population that viewed it as a further subversion of the islands' autonomy.

Sam and Remi were up early the next day, waiting outside the small arrivals terminal at the Honiara Airport while Lazlo cleared customs. When he appeared through a double doorway, followed by a porter with an overloaded cart piled high, he looked every bit the stereotypical Englishman, in a crisp khaki shirt and matching shorts, desert boots below scrawny white calves, and a pith helmet perched precariously on his head.

"There you are! Buggers nearly didn't let me through with all the equipment. I'm fortunate they didn't strip-search me for pitons or whatnot," he called out as he approached.

Sam grasped his hand and shook it, then released him so Remi could give him a tentative hug.

"Were you planning on auditioning for the local production of *Lawrence of Arabia*?" Sam asked.

Lazlo looked down at his outfit. "What? You've never seen proper tropical wear before? I should think you'd be happy your associates are trying to set a good example for the natives."

Remi eyed him. "I thought it might be Halloween and nobody told us. It's easy to lose track of time in the islands."

"The last time I saw one of those hats was on Katharine Hepburn in a film," Sam added.

Lazlo's face could have been carved from stone. "I'm glad that I'm able to provide amusement for you two."

Sam clapped him on the shoulder and grinned. "We're just having a little fun, Lazlo. How was the flight?"

"Over twenty hours of white-knuckle flying, stone-cold sober. It was so turbulent from Hawaii on that I was afraid I'd lose a filling. Need I say more?"

"Well, you're here on terra firma now. Are you adequately rested to go spelunking?" Remi asked.

"It's been a long time since a woman made me an offer like that," Lazlo quipped, but then his expression grew serious. "I'm sure I can muster some energy. I trust that my directions meant something to you?"

"That remains to be seen. We think we know the starting village Kumasaka refers to as his orientation marker, but there's no way of confirming it other than going for a hike," Sam said.

"Lovely day for it. What is it, about a hundred degrees and ninety percent humidity?"

"I thought the Brits used *Celsius*," Remi corrected.

"Just tell me it gets more comfortable inland," Lazlo said.

"Oh, between the mosquitoes, the crocodiles, the rebel forces, and the giants, it feels positively breezy," Sam assured him.

"I don't suppose there's a chance you're joking about any of that lot?"

"Maybe the bit about the giants. But the rest . . . haven't you been following the news about the area?"

"Now that you mention it, Selma did say something about rebels, but I thought she was just trying to dissuade me from a cracking good adventure." He paused and lowered his voice. "The woman's mad about me. I don't think she can bear for me to be away, you know. But don't let on I said anything. I'd hate to embarrass her."

Remi rolled her eyes as Sam led the way to the parking area. Lazlo's luggage occupied the entire cargo area and much of the backseat, and he looked cramped in the rear, with barely enough room for his helmet, his knobby knees pressed nearly to his chest.

"I hope the air-conditioning works in this relic," he said as Sam and Remi climbed in.

"Like a charm. This is the fourth vehicle we've gone through since we arrived and easily the hardiest," Remi said.

"Really? Dare I ask what happened to the others?"

Remi and Sam exchanged a glance and she eyed Lazlo in the rear-view mirror. "You don't want to know."

"Ah. Quite. I'll just content myself with swatting at insects, then. Carry on."

Remi perked up. "Oh, you don't know Leonid, do you?"

"Haven't had the pleasure."

"Then you're really in for a treat. He makes you look like a starry-eyed optimist."

"Given the line of work I've taken up, a deluded dreamer might be more accurate," Lazlo said. "Laos was a bust, and I'm not confident that the letter purported to be from Cooke is genuine. So right now my prospects aren't stellar."

"That's all going to change, Lazlo. Without your decrypting the diary, we wouldn't have anything, so if we find a treasure at the end of this rainbow, it will be credited to you."

Lazlo frowned as they hit another rut and he was jarred sideways in his seat. "Well, then. I'm practically already rich, aren't I?"

Remi couldn't help but laugh. "That's what we like about you, Lazlo. Ever the optimist."

CHAPTER 39

At the hotel, Sam introduced Leonid and Lazlo. They loaded the equipment into the Pathfinder as storm clouds darkened the sky.

"How do you know where to start the search?" Leonid asked as they rolled past the first police roadblock.

"We know that the Japanese moved the treasure from the bay and we know where we met with the only living survivor. We're hoping we can enlist someone in that village to show us where the old deserted village site was," Remi said.

"And if not?"

"Then it gets harder," Sam said.

"What about the language issue?" Leonid pressed. "I thought you said that none of the villagers spoke English or even pidgin."

"That was our impression, but my suspicion is that some of the older villagers must," Remi reasoned. "Even if they don't have a lot of contact with the outside world, they have to have some, and if they want to do business, they have to speak something in common. Probably pidgin. In which case, we can wing it. Plus, we have the mighty Lazlo with us—master of a thousand dialects."

Remi pointed at the opening to the trail that led to the bay as they passed it. "There's the bay road. The village is about three miles down the coast. According to the survivor, it took them a full day to haul the treasure to the cave."

Leonid did a quick calculation. "What, exactly, are the directions that Lazlo found hidden in the diary?"

Sam glanced at Lazlo in the rearview mirror. "Care to demonstrate your photographic memory?"

"Ahem. It said 'Toward the rising sun from the last hut, to the goat's head, then into enemy territory to the small waterfall. The way lies beyond the falls.'"

Leonid shook his head. "Seriously? That's what we're going on?"

"He obviously intended it to be a reminder to himself, not a series of directions to be followed. But it should be enough," Remi said. "We've worked from more obscure clues than this."

"Right," Leonid snorted. "So we have to find a village that's no longer there, which may or may not be the only one in the area, then locate whatever a goat's head is, then find a waterfall. Assuming it's still there. Somewhere beyond that, which could be ten meters or ten kilometers, there's a cave. Which may or may not be visible and could well be crawling with murderous rebels. Did I get this right?"

A deafening roar of thunder exploded overhead and moments later the road darkened with gray rain, reducing visibility to no more than twenty feet.

"You left out where we're going to probably have to camp out at least one night, and possibly several nights," Sam said. "But don't worry. We got a couple of tents and some supplies."

"And plenty of bug spray," Remi added.

"In this soup?" Lazlo asked. "I say, nobody said anything about camping. I'd rather hoped to try the blackened ahi for dinner tonight. Looked smashing on the menu."

"Then there's an incentive to work fast," Sam said. He glanced off to his left and slowed. "I think this is the trail to the village. Remi?"

She peered through the rain at an unmarked gap in the jungle. "Could be. It's hard to tell."

"Well, we've got nothing but time. Might as well give it a go," Sam said, slowing further as golf-ball-sized raindrops hammered the Nissan. He engaged the four-wheel drive and they lurched off the pavement, the tires slipping in the mud before gripping sufficiently to propel them forward.

The rain stopped just as they arrived at the stream that had proved such a challenge to Rubo on their last trip. Sam slowed and gazed at it. "Now, was it across the stream or up the hill?"

"Are you kidding?" Leonid muttered.

"I think it was across the stream," Sam said, goosing the gas. The overloaded vehicle splashed through the stream. The jungle closed in around them as they climbed the bank.

When they rounded the bend and the village appeared, Remi exhaled a silent breath of relief—they'd taken the right trail from the road. The SUV coasted to a stop in the clearing at the base of the first cluster of huts, and several curious villagers stared at them as they disembarked. Sam led them up the hill to the group, where he recognized the shaman from the prior trip. The man nodded to them and pointed to the hut far up the hill where they'd interviewed Nauru and shook his head. Sam nodded and fished in his pocket and then extracted a fifty-dollar bill and handed it to the man.

"Rubo," he said, then shook his head as well. The old man's eyes widened in understanding and he hesitantly took the bill. "You speak English?" Sam asked.

The man shrugged in denial and then pointed at one of the youths sitting nearby. The young man rose and approached. Sam repeated his question and the youth nodded.

"Little speak," he said.

"We're looking for an old village. Abandoned," Sam said. The youth's eyes were confused. Sam tried again. "A village. Where Nauru used to live. We need to find it."

This time, it appeared that the message got through because the youth turned to the elder villager and a short discussion ensued. After some back-and-forth, the youth squared his shoulders and addressed Sam.

"Nothing there. Bad."

"We know. But we need to go," Remi said, stepping forward.

More discussion between the youth and the old shaman and then the same impassive stare from the young man.

"No road."

"Right. We can walk." Remi paused. "Can you show us where it is?"

Sam withdrew a twenty-dollar bill, deciding the matter as the youth's eyes lit up at the windfall. He had another brief exchange with the old man and then snatched the money from Sam's hand like he was afraid it would disappear into thin air.

"Now?" he asked.

Sam nodded. "Yes."

They returned to the SUV, unloaded the backpacks and sacks containing the camping gear and spelunking equipment, and divided it among themselves. When everyone had a pack and a sack, they set off into the brush, following the barefoot youth as he marched into the rain forest with the ease of an antelope. Lazlo exchanged a troubled glance with Leonid, who looked even more glum than usual, and they followed, struggling under the weight of their burdens, as Sam and Remi strode effortlessly up the faint game trail.

The trek took a solid hour. The last vestige of the squall intermittently drizzled on them, making the slippery ground more treacherous.

The sun was just breaking through the clouds as they entered a clearing at the base of another hill, the area soundless except for the cries of birds in the surrounding jungle. The boy gestured toward a brook running along the far side of the clearing, near several crude, man-made stone formations, almost completely overgrown but still distinct from the landscape.

They took a break in the shade of the trees and the youth nodded at the structures.

"Tables."

Remi nodded. The only things left of the hapless village were the worktables used for cleaning fish and laundry and built using indigenous limestone carved from the nearby hill.

"Looks like the same rock the king used for his islets and temples," Leonid said.

"Makes sense. Relatively easy to cut and plenty of it," Sam agreed.

Lazlo gazed around the clearing. "Nothing else here. Bloody amazing it can all disappear—if this fine lad hadn't shown us the way, we'd have never known what we were looking at."

Remi nodded. "According to Nauru's account, everyone was slaughtered. So there was nobody left to keep the elements at bay."

Sam moved to the brook. He eyed the sun overhead and pulled a compass from his shirt pocket. After glancing at it, he returned to the group and regarded the youth.

"Thank you. We stay here now," he said. The young man seemed puzzled and Sam repeated his statement, augmented with some simple sign language. Understanding played across the youth's face and he shrugged. If the crazy foreigners wanted to camp in the middle of the Guadalcanal jungle, it was none of his business—he already had his prize. "You go back," Sam said, pointing at the trail.

Their escort nodded and with a wave disappeared into the rain forest, leaving them alone in the clearing. Sam pulled a portable GPS unit from his pack and turned it on, then entered a waypoint for the village site so they'd have coordinates to return to if they had to retrace their steps. After ten minutes in the shade, he glanced at his watch and shouldered his gear. "Might as well get going. East is over there. 'Toward the rising sun from the last hut.' That says east to me."

"What about the goat head?" Lazlo asked.

"That's a little more problematic. I'm hoping we'll know it when we see it."

"What if it was referring to something that's long since been blown or washed away?" Lazlo pressed.

"We'll cross that bridge when we come to it."

Leonid gave them a dark look and waved away a mosquito. "Goats' heads. Villages that are no longer there."

Sam took the lead and led the group across the brook to where he'd spotted a faint game trail leading in the desired direction. Once they were back in the brush, the heat quickly rose to a stifling level, the faint ocean breeze stopped dead by the vegetation. Sam slowed every few minutes and cocked his head, listening for any hint of followers—he didn't think they had anything to fear from the youth or the villagers, but he wasn't taking any chances.

The slope steepened as they worked their way east, and the trail eventually veered off in a northern direction, rendering it useless. Sam and Remi unsheathed their machetes and hacked a way through the thick underbrush, their progress slowed to a crawl as they fought the jungle and the terrain.

The afternoon wore on, the swelter almost unbearable, and when they reached another opening near a larger stream, they took a break beneath the spread of a banyan tree, all four panting from exertion.

"How far do you think we've come?" Remi asked, blotting her brow with a bandanna soaked in lukewarm river water.

"Maybe half a mile. No more." Sam retrieved the GPS, waited until it acquired a signal, and peered at the screen. "Actually, a little more than a half mile, but not much."

"And we have no idea how much farther until we're in goat head neighborhood," Leonid muttered.

"All part of the challenge," Sam said.

"Don't forget that we have no idea what the goat head refers to," Lazlo chimed in. "Lest anyone think we're doing this the easy way."

Remi cleared her throat. "The reason I ask is because it seems like this stream, assuming it's been here for a while—which, judging by the erosion, it looks like it has—would be a natural place to rest, just as we have. And while taking a break, it might also be a good spot to memorialize somehow as a marker."

"Yes, well, that's all very good, but I'm afraid the diary didn't say anything about any stream. And I don't see a waterfall," Lazlo said.

"And no goats," Leonid grumbled.

"Sometimes the answer is right in front of your face," Remi said. Sam followed her gaze to a rock outcropping.

After a few moments, he grinned broadly. "Have I bragged about how perceptive and smart my wife is today?" he asked, his tone nonchalant. He rose slowly and pointed at the boulders. "What does that look like to you, Lazlo?"

Lazlo peered at the outcropping. "Like a bunch of bloody rocks."

Remi smiled. "In the land of the blind, the one-eyed man is king."

Lazlo turned to her. "That's as may be, but—" He stopped dead and stared again at the rocks.

They sat quietly for several moments and then Leonid broke the silence. "Forgive me, but are you all talking in code? Because I don't understand any of this . . ."

Sam shook his head and gestured to the rocks. "The boulders look like a goat's head, Leonid."

Leonid gaped at the outcropping. "Well, I'll be . . ."

Lazlo nodded. "Quite likely, we all may be, old chap, but apparently not just yet."

CHAPTER 40

Sam set another waypoint on the GPS and zoomed in on the satellite map of the area. After studying the terrain, he shook his head. "Looks like it's going to be a low-tech hike for us. The images aren't any help—it's all rain forest canopy. You can't even make out this stream—too much overhang."

"What's the rest of the line from the diary?" Remi asked. "Something about 'into enemy territory'?"

Lazlo nodded. "That's right. 'Into enemy territory to the small waterfall.' Any ideas?"

Sam looked up at the top of the nearest mountain, where wisps of clouds hovered around the peak like a halo. "The Allies held the area around Honiara down to where the airport is. That would be more northeast from this point. Assuming that's what he was referring to."

"Actually, they also had most of the eastern part of the island, not to be a killjoy," Lazlo observed.

"Right, but since Kumasaka felt it noteworthy enough to write in his diary, I think it's a safe bet that the wording signaled a direction change at the goat head—from east to northeast," Sam said. "Otherwise, why say anything?"

Remi peered at the slope beyond the rocks. "Looks like it's going to get harder from here. That's pretty steep."

"Remember that they had to lug heavy crates, so all we have to do is think like the Japanese," Sam said.

"Then we're looking for a natural passage—a path of least resistance," Lazlo said.

They studied the landscape, from the dull gray of the goat head to the neon green of the lush vegetation around it. There was no obvious way forward—or, rather, up the mountain that stretched endlessly into the afternoon sky. Sam and Remi headed up to the base and slowly walked along the edge of the brush. It was evident from the abundant tall grass that the area hadn't seen human feet for eons.

When they returned to where Lazlo and Leonid were resting in the shade, Sam's expression was pensive. "It may be as simple as following the stream. It looks like it heads in a roughly northeast direction, and it could well be that's what the Japanese did," he said.

"Why wouldn't Kumasaka have simply said 'follow the river,' then, instead of all the nonsense about going into enemy territory?" Leonid demanded.

"Maybe he was worried about the stream changing course over time. Rubo mentioned that the stream that now runs across the trail leading to the village wasn't there the last time he was. On a tropical island, that's a distinct possibility. Or he might have been paranoid that someone might get their hands on the diary and somehow decrypt it. There are a number of possibilities . . ."

". . . any of which could be wrong," Leonid finished.

"Look at the bright side. We found the goat head. So we're doing something right," Remi said.

"Ever the diplomat," said Sam. "Reality is, it's a decent guess. Unless you have a better suggestion." He eyed Leonid and Lazlo.

Lazlo pushed himself to his feet. "I'm with you. We follow the stream. If we're wrong, we'll figure it out sooner or later. We're on an island, after all. Eventually, all directions lead to the sea."

Sam checked the time. "We should get going."

"I don't suppose there's any way of arguing for going back to our nice, safe hotel and picking this up tomorrow?" Leonid asked. "You have the waypoints."

"We're on the hunt now, my Russian friend. We have the scent. We keep pushing," Sam said, ending the discussion.

The streambed of loose gravel was at first a welcome relief from the endless mud of the trails, but after a short time it proved the more difficult path as the slope steepened. After an hour of hiking along the bank, the stream widened and then forked, one tributary stretching to their left, the other to their right. They stopped and eyed the two choices. Sam turned to Leonid. "Which do you like?"

"Neither."

"Come on, choose one," Lazlo said. "Be a good sport."

They waited while Leonid studied the two branches, and he eventually grunted and pointed at the one on the right. "That goes more eastward."

"Well, there you have it," Remi said. "But perhaps now it's more obvious why the colonel didn't simply write 'Follow the stream.'"

After a brief rest, Sam led them along the stream as it climbed into the mountains. The sun was beginning to sink into the trees behind them when they arrived at the base of a steep expanse of sheer rock that the stream cut through. They stopped to catch their breaths, and Sam looked up into the mist.

"No way they climbed that. I think we might be on the wrong path here."

Remi nodded. "He's right. They were hauling heavy crates. They must have followed the other branch."

Sam looked to the sky. "We should be able to make it back to where it forked before dark. We can set up camp in that little clearing and take this up tomorrow."

Lazlo eyed Leonid. "No shame in guessing wrong, old boy. Happens to the best of us."

"That's why I try to avoid guessing about anything important."

They made it back to the clearing with just enough time to set up the tents. Building a cooking fire was out of the question, given the waterlogged soil and moist vegetation, so they settled in for a dinner of energy bars, electrolyte-replacement tablets, and tepid water, silently consumed in the ghostly glow from their LED flashlights.

As night fell, the mosquitoes swarmed them. They retired early, liberally doused with insect repellant, serenaded by the hoots and squawks of night creatures beneath the stars.

The following day they were up at dawn, trudging up the second stream, trying to get a head start before the heat of the day hit with full force. The jungle was blanketed with a hazy mist and visibility was down to twenty meters, the humidity heavy in the air even in the relative cool of morning. The only sound was their breathing and the crunch of gravel beneath their boots as they marched determinedly upward toward the distant, fog-enshrouded peak.

Sam stopped at a bend and held up a hand. The group paused behind him as he stood listening, his head cocked.

"There. You hear that?" he whispered to Remi beside him.

She shook her head. "No. What?"

"I thought I heard splashing."

Lazlo pushed past them and strode farther up the stream. "You aren't imagining things. I think we've found our waterfall," he called from around the bend.

They hurried to join him, where he was gazing at the white froth at the base of another steep rise, this one a cliff with water rushing over its edge, forming a waterfall easily twenty feet wide. Off to their right, another, smaller waterfall tumbled into a small pond. A ridge stretched eastward, jutting through the jungle that covered as far as they could see.

"Look. That feeds into at least two more streams," Remi said, indicating the pond.

"Now the question is which waterfall Kumasaka was referring to when he said that the way lay beyond the fall," Sam said.

"How will we know?" Lazlo asked.

Sam eyed the various falls and grinned. "That's the tricky part, isn't it?"

Leonid grunted as he stared at the tumbling water. "We're looking for a cave, right? Unless I'm seeing things, there's a cave over there by those boulders," he said, pointing to their right, past the smaller waterfall.

"'Beyond the fall . . .'" Remi whispered.

"Leonid, I don't care what they say about you, you aren't all bad," Lazlo said, clapping him on the back. The Russian looked at him disdainfully and took a step away from the Englishman.

Sam fished his GPS from his backpack and entered in another waypoint. "Come on, gang. We're almost there. Remi? Care to do the honors?"

"I think Lazlo should lead the way since it was his decryption that brought us here in the first place," Remi said.

"Very well, then. No point in dawdling," Lazlo said, shouldering his pack and setting off toward the cave.

They skirted the water's edge, crossing two streams, and made their way to a mushy stretch of bank near the boulders. The cave opening yawned like a giant mouth, the gloom beyond its threshold impenetrable, vines having overgrown across part of it. Sam and Remi freed their machetes and set to work and three minutes later had cleared enough of it to enter.

"Flashlight time," Sam said. They paused outside the rent in the rock, took out their lights, and switch them on. "Lazlo? No time like the present."

Lazlo cautiously moved into the cavern, followed by Sam and Remi, their machetes still in hand, with Leonid bringing up the rear. The entry was long and narrow, stretching for fifteen feet, but no more than five high, requiring them to stoop as they crept forward. Lazlo's light shone ahead of him, and as he moved deeper into the cave, they saw that it opened into a small chamber with water pooled on the ground, the light reflecting off its surface. The source dripped from a fissure in the stone above, rippling the placid surface.

"Be careful, Lazlo. That could be a hundred feet deep, for all we know," Sam cautioned.

"Ah, yes, the dreaded cenote. Noted," he said. "Pun intended—" He stopped midsentence and held his lamp aloft.

"What is it?" Remi asked, his body blocking the passage.

"Looks like we're not the first visitors," he said as he stepped aside. Remi and Sam followed his gaze to where a pair of skeletons lay on the cold stone floor, their sightless eye sockets fixed accusingly on the entryway.

Leonid brushed past them and neared the bones. "Murdered villagers," he whispered as if afraid he might rouse the dead with his voice.

"Perhaps," Sam said, stepping forward and illuminating the pair with his light. "But I seriously doubt the Japanese did this unless they had a time machine. Look at the smaller one's feet."

Remi gasped. "Are those . . . ?"

"Yes," Sam answered. "Flip-flops. Judging by the size and pink plastic, worn by a very small woman or a girl."

"What are they doing here?" Lazlo asked, his voice hushed.

Sam shrugged. "Don't know. But they've been here a while." He

paused as he eyed the remains. "Animals and rot got their clothes, unless they were naked when they died. But look—no visible injuries,
nothing broken, no cracked skulls or bullet holes. It's possible they died
of natural causes . . ."

Remi shook her head. "I doubt it. Look at their wrists. See the
plastic?"

"What is it?" Leonid asked.

They all peered down at the skeletons and then Lazlo straightened
and spoke softly. "Zip ties. Their wrists were bound when they died."

CHAPTER 41

Sydney, Australia

Jeffrey Grimes sat back in his executive chair, his shirt collar open, his Armani jacket hanging from a coat rack in the corner of his office. He smiled at the young blond journalist sitting across his desk from him, her aqua eyes intelligent and quick, her bone structure a testament to fortunate genetics, her slim form a tribute to long hours in the gym.

"I'm afraid that the rumors are always more interesting than the truth," Grimes said with a wave of his hand. "We've had a few difficult quarters, but all businesses experience ups and downs. It's impossible to operate with sustained growth every quarter in this business. Any thinking person realizes that—it's only the stock market that focuses on short-term profitability rather than long-term sustainability."

"Your critics say that you've lost your Midas touch and that the recent quarters are more attributable to risky strategies gone wrong than normal business fluctuations," she parried, her smile lighting the room even as her eyes remained locked on his.

"Oh, I'm sure there's a cadre of hopeful short sellers who are spreading all sorts of alarming rumors. After all, they profit only if the stock loses value. So it's in their best interests to make it seem as though the world's ending for us." Grimes chuckled at the thought. "To hear them talk, every day is a new nail in our coffin."

"Right, but what do you have to say about the specific criticisms? That you were caught overextended when the value of the derivatives you were speculating in lost much of their value?" she asked, her tone reasonable.

"Anyone familiar with our operations understands that we're always adequately hedged. That the doors are still open underscores that we were in that instance as well."

The woman nodded and shut off her recorder, then slipped it into her purse before smoothing her dress and standing. "I think that should do it. You've given me more than enough to work with."

Grimes took in her long tanned legs with a quick glance and offered a sparkling, chemically augmented smile. "Ms. Donovan, it was a pleasure meeting you," he said, rising and offering his hand.

"Likewise, Mr. Grimes. Thank you for taking the time to meet with me," she said, shaking it.

"A refreshing departure from the usual drudgery of my day," he assured her, his hand lingering on hers. "I hope you got what you wanted out of it."

"I think my readers will be fascinated with the human face of the ruthless corporate raider portrayed by your critics."

"There are two sides to every story," he said, and then glanced at his watch. "If you'd like to get together after my day's over, perhaps to have a drink and tie up any loose ends, I'd be delighted to answer any further questions you might have."

She batted her eyes and appraised him with interest. "Why, Mr. Grimes, that's very . . . generous of you. I know how valuable your time is."

"Please. It's Jeffrey. And I make time for the things I find important," he said, squeezing her hand slightly before releasing it. "It would
be my pleasure. I'm planning to take my boat out for a sunset cocktail
cruise—something, regrettably, I don't get the chance to do nearly
enough. Would you join me in watching the sun set over the city?"

She smiled broadly. "You're very persuasive, Jeffrey. And it's Cynthia. What time were you thinking?"

"Six-thirty at the dock. My assistant will give you all the information and security codes." His eyes roved over her figure before his gaze
locked on hers. "Do you have any favorite beverages?"

Cynthia blinked and shook her head slightly. "Surprise me."

Grimes escorted her out of his offices and instructed his assistant to
arrange for her access to his dock. She was beaming as she left, and
Grimes congratulated himself on another conquest, only hours away.
He'd successfully converted a potentially hostile interview into a romantic pursuit, the conclusion of which was foregone for a wealthy,
handsome bachelor like himself.

He pulled his door closed behind him and was startled out of his
reverie by the chirping of his cell phone—a tone he'd programmed that
chilled his blood whenever it sounded. He rushed to his desk and lifted
the phone to his ear.

"Yes," he answered.

"There will be another event tomorrow that should seal the island's
fate," the robotic voice announced without preamble.

"It's taking too bloody long. I thought the last 'event' was supposed
to be the tipping point," Grimes complained.

"This isn't an exact science. It's more of a cumulative process. Each
drip of water wears the stone away."

"That's all well and good, but I'm being eaten alive here by margin
calls and demands from my bankers. Something needs to happen fast
or there will be hell to pay."

"There should be substantial progress within forty-eight hours, at the outside. I'm alerting you so you can be ready to move quickly, as discussed."

"I've been ready for a week," Grimes snapped.

"Then your wait is almost over," the voice said, and the line went dead with a click.

Grimes punched the phone off and tossed it on his desk before taking a seat. The call was good news. He was juggling a lot of balls and running short on both maneuvering room and time.

When it would be announced that he'd negotiated deals with the supposedly nationally owned shell corporations that would soon have most of the islands' mineral rights in their portfolios, his company's stock price would skyrocket. There was literally incalculable value locked beneath the jungle and the sea for the fortunate group that was granted permission to exploit those rights—in this case, Grimes being the sole member of that exclusive group.

He'd doubled down on his bet by buying call options on his own stock, and part of his impatience centered on their expiration date— they'd expire worthless within three more weeks. But if he was able to announce the news of the deals, his million-dollar option play would net him an easy six or seven—not a bad payday for idle speculation.

He smirked as he sent a short message to his captain and alerted him to have the yacht fully stocked and ready to sail that evening. He suspected he would get ample opportunity to explore the nubile Ms. Donovan's charms before the night was through and he wanted everything in place for another perfect evening on the water.

Grimes eyed the sparkle of Sydney Harbor from his picture window, his thoughts once more on his mystery caller. To the victor in this struggle would go impossible spoils. That he would be the victor was preordained. He'd made sure of it. Although it was taking longer than he'd been assured, which had his fortune, and nerves, teetering on the brink.

His intercom buzzed and he pushed the doubts from his mind, donned his jacket, and marched to his conference room for another awkward meeting with several of his largest creditors. There would be time enough to revel in victory in the days ahead. Right now, he needed to keep the wolves at bay for just a little longer.

Guadalcanal, Solomon Islands

"They were captives?" Leonid blurted, eyeing the bindings that loosely ringed the skeletons' wrists.

"I'd say that's a given," Sam said quietly as he crouched by the remains.

"The question is, whose?" Remi finished the thought for him.

"Maybe . . . rebels?" Leonid said.

"Could be," Lazlo said. "How long have they been active here?" he asked.

"I don't know," Sam admitted. "But I got the impression that they were a relatively recent development."

"That's my understanding," Remi said. "There was no mention of them in any of the accounts from the civil war in 2000."

Lazlo shined the light beam on the far wall of the cave, which stretched into darkness beyond the water's edge. "Not to be a materialistic pig, but back to the immediate concern—the treasure. Shall we continue into the void and see what we find?"

Leonid stared at the skeletons. "They certainly aren't going anywhere."

"Lead on, Lazlo," Remi said.

"Wait," Sam said, eyeing the surface of the pool. "I want to see how deep this is."

"Why?" Leonid asked.

"In case our Japanese friends decided the best place to hide a treasure was back underwater." Sam approached the pool, knelt, and probed at it with his machete. The blade hit stone. He continued until he was standing near the center of the pool in no more than three inches of water. "I think it's safe to say there's no treasure here."

The group moved to the other side of the cavern, the walls lit with the eerie blue-white of their flashlights, and Lazlo took careful steps into the narrower passage at the far end. A few moments later, he stopped, speechless.

"What is it, Lazlo?" Remi whispered.

When he found his voice, it was tremulous. "Rather a lot more dead in here."

The scene in the second, smaller chamber was one straight out of a nightmare: at least thirty skeletons of all sizes were strewn around the cave, their dead grins greeting the newcomers in humorless welcome. Sam stepped past Remi and focused his flashlight on the piles of bones. Remi shuddered at the grim spectacle.

"It's a massacre," she said in a quiet voice.

"Look at the size of them," Leonid murmured.

Sam shook his head. "They were children." He examined several of the skeletons. "But these weren't bound when they died."

"Some of them were," Lazlo said from the wall near the entry, where he was regarding three more skeletons. "Same treatment here—zip ties, wrists bound behind them."

"But no sign of what killed them," Sam said under his breath. "That's odd. Maybe there was some sort of deadly outbreak and the natives decided to take care of their own? A mass grave?"

"Doesn't explain why some of them were tied up," Remi said.

"There are a few shoes in here, too. Modern," Sam said.

"Why would the rebels kill mostly children? That makes no sense," Lazlo said.

They stood, puzzled, at a loss for words. Eventually, Sam edged to the narrowest section of the cave and peered into it, and then he called out, "Look at this."

They moved to where he was staring at another skeleton, this one not completely decomposed. A swarm of maggots were finishing with their meal in the corpse's rib cage. Remi frowned in revulsion. "Recent," she said, her voice tight.

"Yes, and an adult, male probably, judging by his size—or, if not an adult, at least older than the rest of them." Sam crouched by the bones and pointed at the skeleton's shattered spine. "But check out the vertebrae . . . I'd bet money that was the cause of death. He died from a broken neck. Although look at his ribs and his left arm—also broken. And his ankle."

Sam stood and played his light farther into the cave. He gasped at the spectacle before him and took a step back. Remi drew close to him and took his hand. Hundreds of skeletons were collected in a pit, the bones dull in the flashlight beams.

Lazlo's intake of breath was a groan. "Good heavens . . . it *is* a massacre."

They took careful steps into the new section of cave, Sam leading the way. When he neared the edge of the bone pit, he paused and examined the skulls closest to him. "These look older. And they're adults. Larger." He peered at the nearest skull. "This one died of a gunshot wound to the head. See the entry wound?"

"This one, too," Remi said.

"Look at this chap," Lazlo called out from their left. "Both his legs were broken, looks like, and only partially healed. You can see the calcification."

"What's that?" Remi said, directing her light at one of the skeletons. Sam's eyes narrowed as he regarded where she was indicating.

"Looks like manacles. Rusted beyond recognition. They've been here a long time—probably from the war years," Sam said.

"The murdered villagers?" Lazlo asked.

"Doubt it," Sam said. "They were left where they fell, according to

Nauru's account. And I don't think the Japanese would have found much use for slave labor that couldn't walk because of broken legs. No . . . this is something different."

"Maybe this is where the victims of the medical experimentations wound up?" Remi said softly.

"That makes more sense." Sam shuddered involuntarily at the thought, the sheer number of dead difficult to comprehend. He moved around the edge of the pit to where the cave continued deeper and lit the connecting passage. After several moments, he turned back to them.

"The ceiling drops to next to nothing and it gets impassible. Looks like there might be another cavern on the other side, but if there is, we aren't getting in through here."

"If we can't get through, neither could the Japanese. Whatever horror this is, it doesn't have anything to do with the treasure," Remi said.

"No, I don't think it does," Sam agreed. "But it does create several more mysteries."

"Ones we need to get to the bottom of," Remi whispered.

"Agreed," said Sam, his expression grave.

Lazlo glanced at Sam. "I understand the war dead, at least intellectually. But the children are more than puzzling." He stood, lost in thought, and then continued, his words quiet. "I wonder if there's any truth to the stories of the giants. Didn't you say that the legends have them stealing villagers and eating them?"

Remi stared at him. "Lazlo. There are no such things as giants. Come on."

"Right. Of course. But what I'm suggesting is that perhaps the stories are based on some sort of fact. That perhaps there's an element of truth to them. I don't know . . . maybe there are surviving soldiers from the war who never surrendered, who went mad and became mass murderers. I remember a movie like that—the blighter was still going years after the war had ended because nobody ever told him it ended."

Remi gave him a perplexed look. "They'd be in their eighties or nineties. You really think that's realistic?"

"Preposterous," Leonid spat.

"I agree, although one might have said the same thing about a sunken city just off the coast."

They retraced their steps until they were back in the sunlight, the mass grave left behind, and Sam checked the time. "There have to be other openings along this ridge if the diary is accurate."

Lazlo nodded. "It makes sense. We have the water sources to create the cave system, we have the right sort of limestone . . . but how do we proceed from here? And what about the skeletons? Surely we have to report them to someone."

"When we do, we can expect the authorities to take this area apart," Leonid observed. "Any chance of us locating the treasure is lost at that point."

"But this is mass murder," Lazlo said.

"Yes, it is. And we'll report it." Sam hesitated, his gaze locked with Remi's. "In due time. For now, we're here, but we haven't found what we came for. I think we have to stay focused on our objective. Once we find the treasure, we'll have every cop in the islands crawling through these caves. But we need to continue our search before that happens." He stared at Lazlo. "Agreed?"

Lazlo nodded. "How much more daylight do we have left?"

"At least half a day. It's only eleven-thirty."

"'The way lies beyond the fall,'" Remi quoted, gesturing at the waterfalls. "There are the falls. We need to keep going along this ridge until we find the right cave."

As Sam glanced at the jungle, the hair on the back of his neck stood on end. He scanned the dense brush for any signs of a threat but saw nothing. Still, he couldn't shake an uncomfortable sensation as they continued hiking along the ridge, following the creek that paralleled the rise, Remi leading the way.

A feeling like they were being watched.

"I know it's a little strange, but I can't help but feel like we're not alone," he said softly.

Remi turned and fixed him with a deadpan stare. "Are you hearing voices again?"

"I'm serious," he said, glancing around.

"Sam, honestly. There's nobody out here but us giants."

"Very funny."

CHAPTER 42

After another half hour of hard going, the jungle thickening as they made their way east, Remi stopped and pointed. "Look. Another cave," she said, indicating a dark area between two groves of trees midway up the ridge. The group regarded the opening—small, by any measure, barely large enough for a human to squeeze through.

"You're right," Sam said. "Come on, gang. This could be it."

They worked their way up the rocky slope, the terrain rough underfoot. Sam slowed after nearly going down when his foot shifted an unstable rock. "Be careful. Some of this is loose. Probably a recent landslide," he warned.

"We're right with you," Remi said.

Sam continued up to a small flat area just outside the cave and waited for them to make it up. Lazlo was huffing by the time he arrived, and Sam was about to say something, when Leonid cried out from down the slope.

"Gah!"

Sam and Remi hurried to where Leonid was face down on the rocks, his left leg bleeding where it was wedged between two flat boulders. "Are you all right?" Remi asked.

"Stupid. I should have been watching where I was stepping instead of looking around," Leonid said through clenched teeth as he pushed himself up to a sitting position.

"How bad is it?" Sam asked.

"Hurts. But I don't think it's broken." He winced as he tried to pull his ankle free. "It's stuck in there pretty well."

"Lazlo, we can use the machetes to shift the smaller of these rocks so he can get loose," Sam said, and then looked to Leonid. "When you feel the pressure ease, try to pull your foot out."

"I understand the concept," Leonid muttered as his eyes teared.

Using both blades, they were able to move the flat rock enough so Leonid could pull his leg free. Blood ran down his calf to his ankle where the rough edge had savaged the skin, and the white sock and tan boot were now crimson. Leonid tried to stand, testing his weight, and grimaced. "Not broken, but it hurts like hell."

"Let's get it bandaged and stop the bleeding," Remi said, reaching into her pack for the first-aid kit. Two minutes later, she'd cleaned the abrasions and, using butterfly strips, closed the worst of the gash. Eyeing her work, she swabbed the entire area with antiseptic and wound gauze around it. "There."

"Think you'll live?" Sam asked as he helped Leonid to his feet.

"You'll still have me around to torture for a while longer."

"Can you walk?" Remi asked.

Leonid tried, pain obvious on his face. "Barely."

Sam looked up at the cave mouth. "Lazlo, you and Remi have a look in the cave and let us know if you find anything. But be careful."

Leonid grimaced again. "I'm sorry. I should have been more careful."

"No worries. We'll be back in a jiffy, treasure in hand, I'm sure,"

Lazlo said brightly. Remi looked less confident but offered a wan smile.

"You're going to wait here?"

"Unless you need me," Sam said.

"I think I can manage," Remi replied.

"Go on," Leonid said to Sam. "I can be trusted to sit here without killing myself."

"Are you sure?" Sam asked.

"If you're not back in a few days, I'll make sure a suitable memorial is erected."

"Thoughtful, as always," Remi said. With a final glance at the morose Russian, she resumed her ascent, Lazlo and Sam close behind, all of them eyeing the rocks underfoot with renewed caution.

At the cave mouth, they switched on their lights and directed the beams inside. Remi sniffed and crinkled her nose. "Stinks. Sulfur."

"They don't have bears here, do they?" Lazlo asked in a whisper.

"I don't think so. But you never know. Could be some of those octogenarian Japanese holdouts in there, too."

"Right," Remi said. "They probably trained the bears to attack."

"Very amusing, as always," Lazlo said with a sidelong glance at them.

"Remi?" Sam asked.

"You can go first this time," she said.

Sam stepped forward and ducked down. The gap was no more than four feet high, and, stooped over like an old woman, he inched forward with careful steps. The space widened but the ceiling was still low. The main cave was tiny compared to the first one, barely more than ten feet wide and twice that length. Sam glanced around the area and shook his head as his light bounced off the flat walls. There was no continuation like in the first cave. Just the one area.

Remi shuffled in next to him, followed by Lazlo, and Sam turned to them. "Well, the good news is, there are no skeletons."

Lazlo took in the cavern. "Not much to it, is there?"

"No. We can scratch this one off our list," Remi said.

They did a cursory inspection to ensure they weren't missing any-thing and filed back out, blinking in the bright sunlight as they exited.

"Now what?" Lazlo asked.

Sam's gaze roamed over the ridge stretching into the distance and drifted down the slope to where Leonid sat. He checked his watch and sighed. "Much as I'd like to keep looking, it will be dark in about five hours, and with Leonid's leg cut up like that, he'll be risking infection if we stay out here. So I'd say we head back to the truck, get him taken care of, and live to fight another day. Now that we have the GPS coor-dinates, we can easily return later and resume the search."

Remi smiled. "I don't know that I'd agree with the term 'easily,' but the rest of it makes sense."

"Which I take to mean that we don't report the killing field we stumbled across just yet," Lazlo said.

"Correct," Sam said. "But we will. First things first."

They returned to Leonid and helped him to his feet. Sam explained his reasoning for calling it quits and Leonid offered only a token objec-tion. They set off back down the hill, following the stream again, Lazlo and Sam taking turns supporting Leonid as he limped along, his dis-comfort obvious.

When they got back to the village, the sky's vibrant blue was turn-ing purple as dusk approached. The villagers watched as they made their way to the Nissan and Sam stopped short before they reached it, hands on his hips.

"That's not good news," he said, staring at four flat tires. He crouched down and examined the nearest one. "Someone cut the valve stems off. This was deliberate."

"Why on earth would they do that? And who is 'they'?" Remi de-manded.

"Obviously, someone who doesn't like us, for whatever reason," Lazlo said. "Could also be kids amusing themselves—"

"What are we going to do now?" Leonid interrupted, beads of sweat rolling down his pale face. The journey had obviously taken its toll on him.

"Not to worry," Sam said. "I'll call Des and see if he can get one of the lads to go into town and rent a vehicle to pick us up. Leonid, do you think you can make it another mile or so to the main road?"

"Why didn't you call earlier?"

"It's not like there was any way to get to us. That area's impassable," Remi explained. "Worst case, we can give Des directions and hope he can find his way here to the village." She eyed the trail they'd driven up. "Although he's never been here before, so he might get lost."

Leonid shook his head. "I can make it. We're in no rush now, correct? So we can take our time?"

"I'd imagine it will take a few hours to take the skiff in to Honiara, rent a truck, then drive here, especially at night," Sam said. "So you're correct that we're in no hurry. Although I don't like the idea of trekking through the jungle at night."

"We have flashlights," Lazlo reminded.

"Which will make us great targets for any predators," Remi said. "Let's just hope there are no rebels around."

"Did you have to say that?" Lazlo said.

Sam powered on the sat phone and reached Des. After explaining the situation and agreeing that the Aussie would embark for town while it was still light out, he hung up and turned to them. "We should stay quiet as we hike to the road. Whoever did this might be waiting for us to try to get back that way."

"Maybe it would be worth another twenty to have our escort show us an alternate route to the main road?" Remi suggested.

Sam smiled. "Excellent idea." He looked over his shoulder to where the youth was sitting with several others, watching them, and waved him over. The young man practically bolted to them and for an instant Sam wondered whether the vandalism wasn't part of his moneymaking enterprise and then dismissed the thought. They'd never know for sure so no point in wasting energy on speculations.

After a quick negotiation, they set off down the slope, taking a game trail rather than the main track. Half an hour into it, the sky rumbled ominously and rain began pelting them, making the ground slippery and slowing their progress even further. Leonid's limp was more pronounced as time stretched on and he cried out in pain several times when he misstepped in the darkness, twisting his ankle, punctuating his intakes of breath with a Russian curse.

When they finally made it to the pavement, their surroundings were pitch-black. Leonid sat by the road shoulder with a sigh of relief and Lazlo and Remi joined him, their energy spent. Sam called the *Darwin* and confirmed that Des had gone to town, and after paying their escort and watching him disappear back into the jungle, they settled in for a long wait on the desolate road.

CHAPTER 43

By the time Des picked them up in a bedraggled Mitsubishi SUV and drove them into Honiara, it was after ten p.m. The town was all but closed down as they negotiated the empty streets. Sam instructed Des to drop them off at the hospital so that Leonid could be attended to and Des decided to stay with them.

"No point in trying to make it all the way back to the *Darwin* tonight on the skiff. Better to do it first thing in the morning when there's light," he explained as he pulled into the hospital parking lot. "I also have to deal with returning the car and the office doesn't open until eight tomorrow."

"We'll gladly put you up at our hotel, Des," Remi said. "There won't be a problem. Since the assassinations, it's been empty."

"Good deal." Des peered through the windshield at the darkened hospital, the only light visible filtering from the emergency entrance. "Sure the place is open?"

"Yes. It's the only game in town," Sam said.

They helped Leonid into the hospital, where after a short registration process he was taken into the back in a wheelchair by an orderly. Sam and Remi followed him, leaving Lazlo and Des to wait in the reception area.

Dr. Berry greeted them with a tired handshake.

"What seems to be the problem?" he said as the orderly helped Leonid onto the exam table.

"Hiking accident," Leonid said.

"I see. Let's have a look, shall we?" he said. He reached for a pair of scissors and trimmed away the bandage and then examined the wounds. "Ouch. Probably hurts," he observed.

"I was able to walk on it, so I didn't break anything," Leonid said.

"That's good to know. But we'll want to get an X-ray, just to rule out any fractures." He inspected the butterfly sutures and looked at Sam and Remi. "Nice job."

"Thank you," Remi said. "Dr. Vanya isn't working tonight?"

"No. Do you know her?" Dr. Berry asked.

"Yes. She's a friend."

"She's a good physician," he said, removing Leonid's blood-soaked shoe and sock. "We'll probably want to use some proper stitches on this upper gash. Looks like, oh, ten should do the trick. The lower looks like only two or three." He glanced up at Leonid. "I'm going to have to clean this out. It's going to sting a little."

"Why am I afraid that's the understatement of the year?" Leonid asked.

Ten minutes later, Leonid was sewn up and on his way to the primitive radiography department. Sam and Remi rejoined Lazlo in the waiting area, where he was regaling Des with a story from his dubious past. Remi heard enough to blush and Lazlo immediately cut his account short.

"How's our Russian bear?" Des asked.

"I don't think he'll be doing any ballroom dancing in the near future, but it looks like it's all repaired," Sam reported.

"That's good news, then," Des said. "So the blighters flattened all your tires?"

"Yes. And I suspect it's going to be tough getting a tow truck up that track," Sam complained.

"Probably kids. That's the kind of crap they pull," Des said. "Same the world over. Bored, too much time on their hands."

"Maybe," Sam said.

"Certainly shut your exploration down, didn't it?" Des said to Lazlo.

"Maybe that was the whole point," Remi muttered with a veiled glance at Sam.

"Des, I think we'll want to borrow one of our divers to keep watch over our vehicle while we're exploring," Sam said.

"No worries. We've got a good rhythm going now. We can spare one."

"Good," Sam said, and then remembered about the new boat. "Oh, and some news: we have a large vessel en route to take over from you. So your stint in the Solomons will be over shortly."

Des nodded. "I know. Selma already notified my headquarters. We're out of here on Saturday." Des smiled. "I don't think Leonid will be sad to see us go."

"Underneath that grumpy exterior is a morose and unhappy inner core," Sam assured him. They all laughed, and then Sam grew serious. "If you don't think it will pose a problem, we'll take your rental off your hands, Des. Seems like a hearty vehicle, and we'll need one if we're going to finish up our little adventure in the hills."

"No problem. We can coordinate it tomorrow at the office." He named a rental agency—fortunately, one that Sam and Remi hadn't used yet.

"I hope our reputation hasn't preceded us," Remi commented. "We don't have a great track record with rental cars here."

Leonid appeared in the doorway twenty minutes later, Dr. Berry behind his wheelchair. "Your friend's all patched up. No breaks, so just the stitches and some blood loss to contend with. I told him to stay hydrated and drink plenty of fruit juice and to stay off that leg for a few days. Come by to get the stitches out in a week."

"So no diving," Leonid said, smiling for the first time.

At the hotel, the night manager recovered from his surprise at having another guest check in and quickly processed the paperwork while they waited. The restaurant was still open, only two patrons lingering over after-dinner drinks in a quiet corner, and the group ordered a seafood platter and plentiful beer. "For medicinal purposes," Des said.

Lazlo shook his head sadly. "Alas, that medicine has bitten me for the last time."

Remi smiled as she leaned toward Lazlo and whispered, "We're all proud of you, Lazlo."

"Yes, well, I will say that most people I meet are singularly uninteresting, now that I'm sober. An unavoidable by-product of all this newly acquired virtue, I suppose." He glanced around the table and toasted with his soda. "Present company excepted of course."

The next morning, they met in the lobby at seven for coffee. Leonid agreed that he would stay on land until the stitches were pulled, obviously relieved to be excused from the *Darwin* for the duration. Sam and Des left Lazlo and Leonid with Remi on the veranda while they went to swap licenses at the rental agency, after which Sam dropped him at the docks.

"We'll see you before you go," Sam said.

"Going to have another go at the caves, are you?" he asked.

"You better believe it." They hadn't shared their discovery of the mass grave with Des.

"Well, good luck. Call me when you want to pick up one of the lads. I'll ferry him to shore for you. Any preference on who goes?"

"Greg seems like he can handle himself, doesn't he?"

"I wouldn't want to go up against him," Des confirmed with a nod. "You thinking about heading into the hills again today?"

"No, probably tomorrow. We need to coordinate a tow truck, and at the pace this island operates, that could be half the day. I'll give you a buzz when we're on our way."

"Good enough," Des said.

Upon Sam's return to the hotel, he was surprised by the heated discussion under way between Leonid and Remi. She turned as he neared, a frustrated expression on her face—a look Sam knew to be cautious around.

"Would you tell your Russian friend he is under no circumstances going to try to go with us to the caves again?" she demanded.

"What? Of course he isn't," Sam said.

"You think I'm going to let you shut me out of finding the treasure? Not a chance, as you American capitalists say."

"You heard the doctor. You're to stay off your leg."

"I have. For twelve full hours. Why, are you planning to go right now?"

"No, not until tomorrow . . ." Sam conceded.

"Then what's the problem? I heal quickly. I'm Russian, remember? You can't hurt me."

Sam exchanged a glance with Remi. "It's nothing personal, my friend, but we don't want you injuring yourself further."

He waved the concern away with a sneer. "A few scrapes and cuts. Nothing broken. I'll be ready tomorrow. You don't have to worry about me."

"I don't think it's a good idea," Remi said.

"He *is* an adult male," Sam said.

"Who almost got himself killed."

Leonid snorted. "I wasn't watching where I was going. Believe me, that won't happen again."

Remi shook her head, exasperated. "Fine. I'm not going to fight you on this. But if you slow us down, we'll leave you to the crocodiles."

"I hear they can smell blood a mile away," Lazlo chipped in.

"Then it's decided. What time do we leave?" Leonid asked.

"To be determined. Probably early," Sam said.

"I'll be ready."

Remi stood and looked to Sam. "We going to deal with the tow truck?"

Sam sighed. "I suppose we have to, don't we?" He glanced at Lazlo. "Can you keep our Russian friend here entertained for a few hours?"

"I think that's within my considerable abilities," Lazlo replied with a mischievous grin.

The trip to the rental car agency was as painful as they had expected. The owner of the lot was considerably agitated by the report that one of his prize vehicles was stuck in the middle of the rain forest with four flat tires.

After dealing with that chore, they headed over to the hospital, hoping to find Vanya. When they entered the now-familiar building, she was behind the reception counter, talking to the attendant, the waiting area empty.

"Well, hello! What brings you here?" she asked, smiling as she rounded the counter to greet them.

"We were just in the neighborhood."

"I was looking over yesterday's entries and I saw that you brought in your colleague. Dr. Berry left comprehensive notes."

"Yes. He had a hiking mishap," Remi said.

"Those happen all the time around here. I'm glad it was relatively benign. You should stick to the trails—the island can be dangerous. Where was he hiking?"

"Over on the other side of the island," Remi replied vaguely.

"That can be especially challenging."

"So we learned," Sam agreed. "Listen, Dr. Vanya, we wanted to talk to you about something. Do you have a minute?"

"Of course. Fortunately, it's a slow day. Although that can change at any time." She motioned to the seats. "What can I help you with?"

They all sat, and Sam lowered his voice. "I remember you discussing that woman's missing child the other day."

"Ah, yes. The runaway. Always sad for the parents."

"It sounded as though there have been others."

"Constantly. All part of growing up and wanting to escape, I suppose."

"Do you have any idea how many?"

She shook her head. "Not really. I'm a physician, not a social worker." Her tone softened. "That sounds harsh, and I don't mean it to be. What I meant is that I confine my activities to health care because otherwise there aren't enough hours in the day. It's a matter of priorities."

Remi nodded. "I understand. We're just trying to get an idea how many children have gone missing."

Vanya's eyes narrowed. "Put that way, it sounds sinister. What are you getting at? Do you suspect foul play?"

Sam leaned back. "Oh, no, nothing like that. We were just talking to some of the locals and it came up. Since we're going to be funding the clinics, we're trying to learn as much about the islands as possible while we're here and we want to understand if there's a dynamic we're missing. That's all."

"I'm afraid I can't help you. As I said, whenever a child runs off, the parent is sure it's not what it obviously is. You can always check with the police. I'm sure they would know more than I do."

"Of course. We just don't have a contact there and it seems like they have their hands full with the social unrest of late . . . and the rebels . . ." Remi said.

Vanya rose. "The chief is named Fleming. If you like, I can make a call and let him know you'll be stopping by. Although I have to warn you that he can be quite territorial."

Sam and Remi stood as well and they all shook hands. "Any help you can offer, we'd appreciate."

"I'll make the call. No promises he can help, but, for my new patrons, nothing is out of the question," Vanya said with a bright smile.

Heat waves distorted the surface of the parking lot as Sam and Remi trudged back to the Mitsubishi. Remi took Sam's hand and sighed. "That didn't tell us much, did it?"

"Not really. Think we'll have any success with the cops?"

"Based on the lightning results we've seen to date on the theft investigation, much less being run off the road and shot at? Mmm . . . no."

"I was afraid you'd say that. What's our alternative?"

"Lunch."

They had fresh fish at a simple waterfront restaurant that was packed with locals. The tables were plastic, the napkins paper, and the fresh yellowfin tuna seared to perfection and heaped on their plates. When they were done, Remi pushed back from the table. "Why don't we see if Manchester knows anything more? He always seems willing to talk."

"Assuming he's not busy running the government. Or drinking lunch."

Fortunately for them, the politician was free and welcomed them into his office like they were long-lost relatives.

"Isn't this a lovely surprise. How's the marine archaeology going?" he boomed at them.

"Slow, but we're making progress," Remi said. "We were hoping you could elaborate on something you said the other day—about the missing children?"

"Did I say something about that? I don't recall," Manchester said, his eyes darting to the side.

"Yes, I think so. What's your take on it?" Sam pressed.

"I'm not sure I have one. I think in any society you're going to have a few kids running off. I don't necessarily see it as a Solomon Islands problem," he said, choosing his words carefully.

"What have you heard, exactly?"

"Why the interest, if you don't mind my asking?" Manchester parried.

"Just a few things we picked up here and there," Remi said, keeping it vague. "We're going to be funding Dr. Vanya's clinics, so we want to understand any issues affecting the island. Disappearing children seems like an issue."

"I'll grant you, it sounds like one, but I don't get the impression it's nearly as large or as pressing as the rebel problem, or the crushing poverty endemic to the Solomons, or the lack of coherent responses to public health or social problems, or unemployment, or fiscal irresponsibility, or civil unrest . . ."

"No disagreement. We were just hoping to find someone who could give us an idea of how long it's been going on and how large a problem it really is."

"I don't know that it's even a real problem. Again, I hear a myriad of complaints about a multitude of issues every week and that was just one of many. If I made it seem like it was a substantial issue, I apologize. It must have been the beer talking." He studied them, his smile as genuine as a mannequin's. "As to who to direct you to, I have nothing to offer. Perhaps the police?"

"That's already on our schedule. Do you have anyone specific we should speak with?" Remi asked, not telling him about Vanya's offer.

Manchester suddenly seemed anxious to move on to other tasks. "I'll look into it. I'm afraid I don't know who would handle missing persons, off the top of my head." He smoothed his hair with a bear-sized hand and changed the subject. "I'm delighted you've decided to play a large role in Dr. Vanya's clinics. That should improve life for many on the island. It's a sad state of affairs, at present."

"Yes, so we gathered. It's a worthwhile cause," Sam agreed. "Anything more about the rebels? Any sense of how public opinion is running?"

"Most condemn their actions, if not their sentiment. At least so my colleagues would have me believe. Still, there are a few who are seriously considering the merits of nationalizing all exploration and prospecting efforts. Madness—but to some, attractive madness, it would seem."

"Did you have any chance to discuss our archaeological project with your colleagues?"

"Unfortunately, not yet. As you might imagine, with the rebel crisis, that's all anyone has time for. But I haven't forgotten about it," Manchester assured them.

When Sam and Remi left the politician's office, Manchester watched them walk to their vehicle from his window, his expression troubled. His receptionist eyed him as she worked on a sheaf of documents. "Don't forget you have a five o'clock meeting with Gordon Rollins," she said.

"Oh. Right. That's today, is it? Thanks for the reminder." While Manchester had kept his clandestine meetings with Rollins secret, he couldn't avoid all public contact with him or that, too, would seem suspicious. They'd agreed to continue to have periodic meetings, as before, so if scrutinized, their behavior would seem normal. So far, the plan was working perfectly.

Manchester checked his watch and, with a final glance at the Fargos pulling out of the parking lot, returned to his office, his footsteps heavy on the polished wooden floor.

CHAPTER 44

Gordon Rollins's neighborhood was the very best in Honiara. His home, a sprawling affair sitting on a bluff overlooking the ocean, was an area landmark. When Orwen Manchester arrived in the brick drive, the gardening staff were finishing up for the day, their khaki shirts soaked through with sweat, their skin chocolate brown from the relentless sun's rays.

A blue 1963 E-Type Jaguar roadster sat in the driveway, its chrome gleaming—one of Rollins's eccentricities but one he could well afford, coming from old money as he did and having invested wisely during his long life. Rollins turned from the discussion he was having in front of the house with his assistant, a shapely island woman named Sandra who had been with him for a decade, and offered Manchester a wave. Manchester shut off the motor of his Honda sedan and smiled as he slipped from behind the wheel—Rollins had always had flair and he'd lost none of it as he'd aged. "Orwen, old man, good of you to come,"

Rollins called, shaking his silver mane of hair. He leaned into Sandra and said something. She smiled at Manchester, displaying two rows of blindingly white teeth, and then sashayed up the steps to the front entrance, leaving Rollins and Manchester to their business.

"Always my pleasure, Gordon. Lovely day, isn't it?"

"Not as hot as yesterday, fortunately." He held up a silver key on a fob. "I was thinking we might want to nip down to one of the pubs and have a quiet draft. Have you joined the ranks of the temperate lately or can you fit that in?"

"I'll do whatever I must to make you feel comfortable," Manchester said, smiling.

"Good man. That's the spirit," Rollins said, approaching the Jaguar.

"I take it this isn't entirely a social call?" Manchester asked quietly as he opened the passenger door.

"Regrettably, no. But I see no reason not to mix business with a little pleasure. Besides, all this seriousness is a thirsty affair. I'm parched."

"We make the sacrifices that are necessary," Manchester agreed. "What have you got up your sleeve now?"

"The Crown is concerned about our recent unrest and the direction these beastly rebels have taken—most alarming, I think you'll agree. And if she who must not be mocked is concerned, that means that I am—and you should be as well."

The Jaguar exploded in a blinding flash when Rollins turned the key. A fireball shot into the sky like an orange fist, and a door flipped lazily through the air before landing on the immaculately groomed lawn. The staff stood transfixed in horror as the Jaguar belched black smoke, the cockpit and engine engulfed in flame, the chassis crumpled like a discarded soda can.

Sirens keened in the distance several minutes later, but by then it was obvious to the gathering crowd that the only job remaining for the emergency crews would be extinguishing the wreckage.

Remi shifted in frustration as she and Sam sat in the Honiara police station, talking to the police chief, Sebastian Fleming, a forty-something islander with a face like a losing fighter and a gaze that was quickly distracted. Vanya had arranged for a meeting, but from the very start Fleming had been defensive and standoffish, and the discussion had quickly degraded from there.

"Wait. So you're saying that you have no idea how many missing persons reports have been filed over the last five years involving children? How is that possible?" Remi demanded. "Don't you have computers?"

"Mrs. Fargo, that's not how it works. I'm afraid you have some misunderstandings about the system," the chief said in a condescending tone.

Remi fought to control her temper at Fleming's brusque dismissal. "Really? You're the police chief. People have been filing reports. But somehow *I'm* confused when I ask you how many have been filed?"

Sam knew Remi was simmering and that it was only a matter of time before she'd explode in the face of obdurate stupidity. He quickly moved to intercede, heading off a potential disaster.

"What my wife means to say is, surely there's a record of any open missing persons cases, isn't there?" Sam tried.

"Oh, well, put that way, of course there is." Fleming stared at them with dead eyes.

"Now we're getting somewhere," Sam said. "Our question is, how many are still open after five years?"

"Oh, I understand your question perfectly. I'm afraid I'm not at liberty to disclose that."

"Why not?" Remi snapped, her color rising.

"Because it's police business, ma'am, and you're not a member of the force."

"Why is it confidential?" Sam asked, his color rising as well.

"Because it is," Fleming said as though that explained everything.

"Wait. We're members of the public you serve and we're asking a direct question and you can't answer it?" Remi fumed.

"It's not that I can't answer it," Fleming corrected. "I *won't* answer it. To be precise, I'm choosing not to." Fleming held up a hand to counter any objection. "And before you start protesting, let me clarify something you seem confused about. I don't serve you. You're visitors here, guests to the island. You aren't citizens and you don't pay my salary and I don't have to answer any of your questions, especially when they're framed in such an insulting manner. So I'd reconsider your tone. I agreed to see you to humor Carol Vanya, but I didn't agree to be interrogated by you or to entertain rude demands."

Sam could practically hear the safety flip off Remi's detonation button and he quickly interceded. "Officer Fleming—"

"It's Chief Fleming."

"Chief Fleming. We're looking into a troubling trend here of missing children. Surely you don't mind helping us?"

"Mr. Fargo, let me make my position clear. The number of missing persons reports filed with this department will remain confidential unless you get a court order requiring me to divulge it, which is unlikely given that you're not an islander." He frowned and looked at the clock on the wall. "Now, is there anything else?"

"Don't you care about missing children?" Remi demanded in a low voice.

"Deeply. What I don't care about is two privileged foreigners showing up in my office, telling me what I have to disclose to them because they've appointed themselves special investigators. Now, if you'll excuse me, I have other demands on my time. Thank you for dropping in and good luck with your research."

Remi was seething as they descended the steps from police headquarters and Sam knew better than to say anything. They walked the block and a half to the hotel, and Remi had calmed down somewhat by the time they reached the room.

"I can't believe nobody's worried about a rash of disappearances," Remi fumed, her temper stoked by Fleming's lack of interest. "If my kids vanished, you can bet I'd raise holy hell."

"True, but you saw the chief's attitude. I got the impression he didn't like us much."

"It's infuriating. There's a cave full of dead kids and these idiots don't care."

"Well, we're the only ones that know about that right now, so we have information they don't. I have a feeling that attitude will change in a hurry once we break the news."

"It's their job to have the right attitude now."

"I agree. But there's nothing we can do about it." Sam studied Remi, who was holding her tablet, a satellite image of the waterfall area on the screen. "Since that didn't go anywhere, what's the word on the caves?"

Remi had been looking for alternatives to parking at the village and traversing the ground to the waterfall from there.

"I think I've found an old logging road that ends about a half mile from the waterfall. If it's still passable, it should cut hours off the hike."

"That's great news. I've been worried about how Leonid is going to make it. For all his bluster, he's only human and his leg took quite a beating."

"We won't know for sure that it's viable till we get there, but it seems like our only alternative."

The sat phone rang and Sam hurried to the table by the sliding glass doors, where it was charging. He punched the line to life. "Hello?"

"Did you hear the news?" Selma asked, her voice concerned.

"Which news is that, Selma?"

"Another assassination. This time, the Governor-General and one of the members of parliament."

Sam froze, eyeing the darkening harbor. "Which member?"

"Orwen Manchester."

Sam closed his eyes and shook his head, then opened them and turned toward Remi. "When?"

"It just came across the wire a few minutes ago."

"What happened?"

"Car explosion. The rebels were quick to claim responsibility. Said that the puppet of colonial imperialism had been executed for the better of the islands, as would be all foreigners responsible for the nation's subjugation. I quote, obviously."

"Then Manchester's dead?" Sam asked in a hushed voice.

Remi sat up on the bed, her eyes wide. "What? Let me talk to her."

Sam handed her the phone as she stood and padded onto the terrace with bare feet.

"Tell me exactly what happened, Selma," Remi said, her words dangerously calm. Selma recounted the news. When she was done, Remi was speechless.

"Are you all right?" Selma asked.

"Yes. I think so," Remi said. "We just saw him. Not three hours ago. We were sitting only a few feet from him and now—"

"I'm sorry," Selma said.

"Thanks. I wonder if he had family?"

"Doesn't say on the news."

"It's . . . it's just unbelievable." She looked out over the water and her gaze drifted to the town. "This spells big trouble for civil unrest. I've seen enough of this place to know it's going to blow wide open once word spreads. Manchester was a moderating force—a voice of reason. Without him—"

"You two should get out of there. Now," Selma said. "While you still can."

"We can't, Selma. Not yet." She took a few moments to collect her thoughts. "Any word on the missing children?" Remi had sent her an e-mail earlier detailing their discovery.

"I couldn't find anything. There's nothing on the Internet. Which doesn't surprise me—Guadalcanal isn't exactly a hotbed of tech so-phistication. Even most of the businesses don't have websites, so it's still a few years behind everywhere else in that regard."

"That's what I was afraid of."

"You really should take some protective steps. If rioting starts—"

"I know. I'll talk to Sam about it."

"Call me if you need anything. And please . . . be careful."

"I'll pass the message along. Thanks, Selma."

Remi hung up and handed the phone to Sam. "Selma's worried. She thinks that the island could erupt in another bout of violence. I think she's right."

"So what do you want to do? Try to get to the airport and catch the first flight to anywhere? Make for the boat?"

Remi shook her head. "Would it kill us to spend the night on the *Darwin*? And then head for the caves at first light?"

"Not at all. In fact, it seems like a reasonable precaution, in light of past events. I'll call Leonid and Lazlo and have them meet us in, what, fifteen minutes?"

"And I'll call Des and let him know he's going to have guests."

Twenty minutes later, the Mitsubishi was rolling out of town, leav-ing Honiara to its fate. The Australian-led peacekeeping force was on high alert, as were the police, and a curfew had been put in place for the capital, effective within the hour. The authorities had learned a thing or two over the last few rounds with the rebels and were taking a zero-tolerance policy to any instigating by their sympathizers.

Once on the *Darwin*, they settled in for a fresh crab dinner with Des and the crew while listening to the radio. The town was quiet, by all accounts, with only a few isolated cases of attempted looting that had been quickly quashed, and with official condemnations of the murders from various government officials as well as the island's religious leaders. But most troubling were the early reports that several Australian corporations had suspended plans to invest in infrastructure for their operations in light of the ongoing unrest, as well as news that a bill was being sponsored by an opposition leader in parliament to nationalize several key industries. Manchester hadn't even grown cold yet and his worst fears were being realized.

CHAPTER 45

It was barely light out when the Mitsubishi turned onto the logging road, which was overgrown and in poor repair but passable. An hour and a half later, the SUV ground to a halt at the end of the road, stopped in its tracks by a wall of dense jungle.

Sam held the GPS up in the morning sunlight and studied the screen. "Looks like we're close. It's a little over a half mile that way," he said, pointing at the nearest peaks. "Think you can manage it, Leonid?"

"I'm a locomotive. A battering ram. Unstoppable," the Russian said, his eyes red from a restless night at anchor.

"That's good to hear," Sam said. "Greg, you've got guard duty here."

Greg had ridden out in order to watch the vehicle and ensure no harm came to it. He nodded once. Greg didn't talk much, but he looked lethal with his weapons, a machete on his belt and one of the ship's twelve-gauge flare guns in his hand, and they were confident that the Mitsubishi would be in good shape when they returned.

The waterfalls might have been closer to the logging road than the village, but the terrain wasn't accommodating. It was tough going, with none of the game trails they came across heading in the right direction. They were forced to hack their way through the underbrush as the heat rose—cutting through the jungle and then pausing every twenty minutes to rest. Their clothes were soon drenched, and their water supply was dwindling at a rapid clip.

Eventually, they broke through into the clearing at the base of the large waterfall and sprawled in the shade of a grove of trees, studying the ridge for signs of another cave.

Remi stared at the sheer rock face and after several minutes pushed herself to her feet. "We know it's got to be there somewhere. What was the final line from the diary?"

"'The way lies beyond the fall,'" Lazlo repeated from memory.

"You can't get much more beyond the fall than the ridge, so it's a question of where, exactly, the entrance is," Sam observed.

"Well, we're not going to find it, lounging around here," Remi said. "How's the leg, Leonid?"

"I'm strong as a bull. I feel nothing but impatience at being denied the treasure," Leonid said, his tone as serious as a eulogy. Remi held his stare and then they both laughed simultaneously as he struggled to rise.

"Perhaps a *wounded* bull," Sam corrected with a chuckle.

"That's not a terrible nickname," Lazlo said. "Wounded Bull. It somehow fits."

"I'm not so badly off I can't overtake you, you colonial oppressor," the Russian growled good-naturedly.

"Yes, well, save your enthusiasm for the hunt. I suspect you'll need it."

"You know," Remi said, "I don't mean to be negative, but I had a thought last night. What if the Japanese hid the cave entrance once the islanders had loaded in the crates? I mean, it's not impossible. If they really wanted to conceal their stash, it would have been easy. A grenade, a mortar . . ."

"That's a good point. But it would have left a trace, I'd think," Lazlo said.

"Probably. All I'm saying is, we shouldn't discount any irregularity in the terrain no matter how unlikely it may appear."

The trudge along the base of the ridge was agonizingly slow in the blaze of late-morning sun, over the treacherous ground. They passed the two caves they'd already explored and continued east, eyeing the landscape. Near another small stream, Leonid pointed to the rise. "Do you see that?" he asked.

They followed his finger to a collection of boulders, trailing down the hill, evidence of a landslide.

Sam nodded as he regarded the ridge. "Could be. Let's have a closer look."

The group climbed across the loose shale, the stones getting larger as they neared. At the top of the irregularity, Sam and Lazlo scraped away at the rocks, prying with their machete blades, trying to loosen the rubble. Leonid and Remi stood back, letting them work. Ten minutes later, Sam looked over his shoulder at her. "There's a space behind it. You're a genius."

"I just have a devious mind. It's what I would have done. After all, they had no way of knowing whether the Allies would investigate every square inch of the island or not once they had full possession. Better safe than sorry . . ." Remi said.

"Let's clear this and see what's inside," said Sam, now fueled to greater effort. Remi and Leonid joined them and in another few minutes a gap had been opened.

"Definitely a cave," Lazlo murmured, gazing into the darkness. Motes of dust hovered in the still air.

"Want to do the honors, Lazlo?" Remi asked.

"You know, I just had a thought. What if they booby-trapped it?" Lazlo mused.

"I highly doubt that anything they could have rigged that long ago would still be operational," Sam said.

"Fine. Follow me," Lazlo said, his voice trying for a conviction he clearly didn't feel.

They entered the cavern, trailing Lazlo, their lights illuminating the space, which was larger than the prior caves. The floor was uneven and stretched into the darkness, sloping lower as they moved deeper, with the surface slick in places from water dripping from the ceiling and leaching through the walls.

"At least it's cool in here," Sam said as they pressed forward.

"But no crates," Remi said.

"Look at the bright side. No skeletons, either."

Lazlo slowed as the passage turned to the right and he held his light up. Stalactites hung from above like giant fossilized icicles, dripping relentlessly, as they had since the cave's birth. The team edged around piles of debris, where sections of the ceiling had collapsed over time, and soon found themselves in a larger natural chamber.

"But still no treasure," Leonid reminded, his expression sour.

"Good things come to those who wait," Sam said, turning slowly, his lamp raised in his hand.

"Look over here," Lazlo called from their right. Their heads turned to where he was gazing into yet another cave through a smaller opening. "This appears to continue for some distance."

"That would make sense. Remember that the legends of the giants claim there's an entire system that stretches across the island. Those tales are likely based in some sort of fact," Remi said.

"Then how do we find the right cave? This could take forever," Leonid griped.

"What happened to Raging Bull?" Sam teased.

"*Wounded* Bull," Lazlo corrected.

As they continued down through the caves, the temperature dropped steadily, and soon the oppressive heat at the cave mouth was a distant memory, replaced by a dank chill. Lazlo continued leading the way, Sam and Remi behind him, and Leonid bringing up the rear, as they edged along a narrow rise that stretched along the side of a tunnel-like passage, easily fifty yards long, the darkness at either end absolute.

The crash of Leonid's light hitting the stone cave floor shattered the stillness as he cried out. The group spun to where he'd slipped on a slick spot and gone over the edge, dropping down the steep slope into the chasm below.

"Leonid," Sam cried out, dropping to his knees, careful to avoid the wet patch. Lichen clinging to the stone made it as slippery as ice.

"Can you see down there?" Lazlo asked, his light trained into the black depths.

"No. It looks like it twists around," Sam said, transferring his lamp to his right hand. "Remi, hand me one of the rope bundles. I'll tie it off and go after him."

"Sam?" Remi said, her voice low.

"What? Didn't you hear me? He's probably hurt."

"Sam . . ."

Sam exhaled loudly and twisted around and froze when he found himself staring down the barrel of a pistol held by a tall islander a dozen yards away.

CHAPTER 46

Three men stood in the gloom beyond the gunman, machetes in hand. The islander with the pistol grinned malevolently and thumbed back the hammer on his weapon. The snick was as loud as a firecracker in the sudden quiet.

"Well, took you long enough," the gunman said, and pointed the weapon at where Lazlo was trying to inch away. "Don't any of you move."

"We don't mean you any harm. Our friend slipped and fell," Sam said. "We have to get him. He could be badly injured."

"Saves me a bullet. Now, don't you be trying anything or I'll blow your fool heads off. Any of you give me trouble, the little lady gets it first. Boys? Search them."

The thugs made short work of a cursory frisking, confiscating their machetes and kicking their bags aside. The gunman kept the pistol trained unwaveringly at Remi the entire time, watching as she glared at him. When the islanders were finished, they manhandled everyone, pushing them forward. The gunman backed up, a flashlight in his other hand, while his companions directed them toward a dim glow at the far end of the massive space.

"Who are you?" Sam demanded as he passed the gunman.

"Your worst nightmare," the gunman snarled. "You been sticking your nose into business that don't concern you. Causing a heap of worry. That all over now."

"What are you talking about? What is this place?"

"Shut up. No more talk," the thug nearest Sam ordered, and gave him a hard push between the shoulder blades, causing him to stumble. Sam barely maintained his balance, his equilibrium thrown by the lack of a reference point in the gloom, and he could hear Remi's breathing quicken.

"Don't worry," Sam said. His captor clipped the back of his head with the handle of his machete, knocking him to his knees.

"I say shut up, I mean it," the man snarled. "Up," he growled, kicking Sam in the ribs.

Sam struggled to his feet and felt the back of his skull. His fingers came away with a smear of blood.

"Sam," Remi whispered.

He shook his head, instantly regretting the abrupt gesture and wincing in pain. The thug stepped back and raised his machete, the muscles in his arm bulging. "Move or I chop you right here."

Sam staggered forward in the faint light. The others trailed him, as their captors radiated menace, machete blades glinting, as they made their way to a gap in the cave wall. Another armed islander stood to one side of the opening, watching them.

Once through the gap, they looked around in surprise—they were in a lit area. Cables ran along the wall to low-wattage bulbs mounted in industrial enclosures, wooden crates served as tables, a half dozen cots rested near one wall, and a marine refrigerator hummed quietly in a corner.

The gunman motioned with his pistol. "All of you. Sit down there." He pointed at a clear area near the cots.

They sat where instructed. Remi quickly inspected the back of Sam's head and cringed at the split in his scalp. Eyeing the gunman, she wordlessly withdrew a wad of tissue from her pocket and pressed it against the wound to stem the flow of blood.

"There are plenty of people who know where we are. If we don't return, they'll come looking," Remi said quietly.

"Ha. You liar," the gunman said, but Remi could see a flicker of doubt in his eyes.

"Why are you—"

"Silence!" the gunman roared, taking a step forward, bringing his pistol to bear on her. "I ask questions. You answer when I say."

"Do as he asks," Sam cautioned.

The gunman's eyes narrowed. "You bring this on you. Why you here?"

"Here, on the island? Or here, in the caves?" Remi asked.

The gunman's eyes narrowed. "You think I stupid?"

Remi shook her head. "No. I don't understand the question."

"Why you look for?" he asked.

Sam cleared his throat. "We're exploring the cave system. They've never been mapped."

"Lies!"

"It's the truth. Why else do people go caving? It's our hobby."

"You make big mistake."

"Why are you doing this? Are you rebels?" Lazlo demanded.

The big man laughed with genuine amusement. "Rebels. Yes, we rebels. I rebel!"

"We mean you no harm," Remi tried.

"You come. Now you all mine," the gunman said, his gaze roaming over Remi.

"There are people who know we're here. If anything happens to us, it will be disastrous for you," Sam said.

The man laughed again. "Where are you?"

"We gave our headquarters the latitude and longitude before we entered the caves. If we don't reappear, they'll come search," Remi said, her voice calm. "We're well-known explorers."

"Maybe they pay for you?"

"A ransom? I'm sure something could be arranged," Sam assured the man.

The gunman exchanged a glance with his accomplices and then refocused his attention on Sam. "Who you with?"

Remi looked confused. "With? What do you mean 'with'? We're with ourselves. We explore remote places. We're archaeologists. Our interest is scientific."

"Who send you?" he demanded. "Who pay me for you?"

"We have a foundation. Nobody sent us. We choose where we explore."

The man looked at his cheap plastic watch and signaled two of his henchmen. "Tie up."

"You're making a big mistake. Our hurt friend is a famous archaeologist. We need to help him," Remi said.

The gunman's face could have been carved from mahogany. He watched impassively as his men tied the captives' hands behind their backs, and then their ankles, immobilizing them. When he finished, the leader slipped his weapon into the waistband of his ratty shorts and turned to the rest of his men. They had a brief discussion, in a local dialect, the gunman giving instructions, and two of the islanders went back to the passage where the Fargos had been discovered. The gunman watched them go and then stepped closer to Remi and leaned over her. She winced in anticipation of a blow. He tilted her head up with his hand, studying her, and offered a grin that froze the blood in her veins. "Pretty."

Sam struggled against his bindings. "Touch her and you'll die."

The gunman sneered at Sam and backhanded him, the move nonchalant yet lightning quick like the strike of a snake. Sam's head snapped to the side and he fell backward.

"No!" Remi screamed, the sound amplified by the cave walls, echoing over and over.

"Shut up or I hurt you." He glared at Remi. "You first."

The gunman crouched down and grabbed a handful of Remi's hair, causing her to cry out. He brought his face down next to hers and whispered in her hair, the stench of his breath and sour sweat overpowering. "I going to hurt you good."

He released her and stood, watching Remi. After a few moments, he barked terse orders and pointed at the captives, then stalked off after his departing men, leaving one islander to watch the prisoners, machete in hand.

They remained silent until the guard drifted to one of the crates and poured himself a cup of coffee from a jug. Sam slid nearer to Remi and murmured to her, the sound covered by the hum of the refrigerator.

"You okay?" he asked.

"Yes. What about you?"

"I could use some aspirin."

"What is this?"

"I don't know. But it's bad. We need to get loose."

"How tight are your wrists tied?"

"Tight," Sam said. "But I already found a spot on the wall that's got a jagged edge. Just a matter of time until I saw through the cord. We're lucky they used rope."

"What do you want me to do?"

"Shift over in front of me so he can't see what I'm doing." Sam leaned over to Lazlo. "Did you hear all that?"

"Barely. I'll move to your left so you're covered if they come back."

The men didn't return, though, and after a long hour Sam eyed the guard, who was reading in his corner, and whispered to Remi, "I'm free. Let me get my ankles untied and then I'll deal with our friend there."

"You want to get me loose first?"

"They could be back any second. I'll take him down, then cut you two free. It'll be faster."

"How are you going to do that?"

"Improvise." Sam inched farther back from Remi. "Move away from me so I have some room. You too, Lazlo. But don't be obvious."

When they'd done as he asked, Sam called out to the guard, "I have to use the bathroom."

The man looked over at him and laughed. He went back to what he was doing and Sam called out again. "Please."

The guard ignored him.

Sam decided to try something different. "You'll hang for this. They'll come for us and you'll dance at the end of a rope."

"Shut up," the guard snarled.

Sam shook his head and muttered audibly, "Idiot. Stupid piece of garbage."

"Not stupid. You the one tied up."

"Big talk, moron. What rathole did they find you living in?" Sam glared at the man. "I can buy and sell you a thousand times over, low-life. You're an insect."

The man rose, his face twisted with anger, and stormed toward Sam. "I say shut up!"

Sam spat at the man's feet and gave him a dismissive look. "You can barely pronounce it, you dolt." Sam glanced at Lazlo. "No wonder this island's stuck in the Stone Age."

The man took another step toward him and Sam made his move, a lightning-quick sweep kick that knocked the guard's legs out from under him and sent him pitching backward. Before the guard hit the hard stone floor, Sam leapt up and threw himself on the man, cracking ribs with his elbow and slamming the side of his fist into the islander's face. The guard made a wet, gurgling sound as his head cracked against the floor. His eyes rolled back into his head until all Sam could see were the whites.

Sam stood and, after a glance at the unconscious guard, rushed to Remi and Lazlo. With the machete, he quickly severed their bonds.

Remi whispered to him as he finished Lazlo's leg bindings. "How are we going to get out of here?"

"We can try backtracking through the cave, but they're probably in there somewhere." He peered toward where another passage was just visible in the gloom. "How about door number two?"

Remi moved behind Sam and quickly inspected his head. "It's scabbed over."

"One less thing to worry about." Sam hefted the machete, considering the working blade's sharpened, nicked edge, and then his eyes roamed over the room. His gaze stopped at one of the crates, where a collection of tools lay, along with a coil of rope. Remi glanced at the potential weapons and moved to them, selecting the most lethal, before heading back to Lazlo, rope also in hand.

"Here's a hatchet. Grab a light and let's get out of here."

"What about that bloke?" Lazlo asked, tilting his head at the downed guard.

"I'll make short work of him," Sam said. He scrounged among their discarded bindings and found a length of cord that looked promising. A minute later, he'd bound the man's wrists and ankles and stuffed a rag in his mouth. "That should keep him out of trouble for a while."

A faint clank sounded from the passage they'd come down. Sam's head swiveled toward it and then he gestured to Remi and Lazlo. "Follow me, and don't make a sound."

"Sam. A machete's no match for a gun," Remi whispered.

"A gun's only as good as the shooter," he said, his face serious. "Come on."

Sam crept to the far end of the cave, where a cavity led deeper into the mountain. He waited until it was too dark in the passage to see from the glow behind them and then switched on the flashlight he'd grabbed. To their right, the narrow cave forked in two directions, and he stopped, listening. He sniffed at the dank air and pointed to the right branch. "It smells fresher this way. More humid," he said.

"What if it dead-ends?" Lazlo asked.

Sam shrugged. "That would be bad."

They kept moving, the ground angling lower before leveling out. A faint hiss ahead of them grew louder as they crept forward, and, after another minute, they arrived at a rushing torrent of black water. They eyed the current and Sam directed his beam beyond it. "Looks like this continues on the other side. But the water's moving pretty fast."

"The good news is, it's not that wide," Remi said.

Lazlo frowned. "The bad news is, I haven't swum since I was a teenager."

Sam glanced at him. "It's like riding a bike."

"Haven't done that in forever, either."

"I don't see any way around it," Sam said. "Remi? Hand me the rope."

Remi did as asked. "No telling how deep it is."

"It's only the last few inches that'll kill you."

"Very comforting, Fargo. Be careful."

He uncoiled the rope. "You and Lazlo hold on to this end. Wish me luck."

The sound of angry voices reverberated from the other end of the cave. Sam frowned and quickly tied one end of the line around his waist. "Here goes nothing."

The water was surprisingly cold and stronger than he'd imagined. Almost immediately, it pulled at his ankles like an angry dog. The soles of his boots slipped along the smooth stone riverbed, polished by thousands of years of rushing torrent, and he fought to stay upright as he inched farther into the current. Spray splashed his thighs as he tested the bottom, moving cautiously, and then suddenly the current pulled him down and he was tumbling into the river, stunned by the force.

Water rushed into his nose and mouth and he choked as he lost his bearings, the lack of light now deadly. He fought to reach the surface, thrashing with all his might—but in the dark there was no hint of which way the surface was.

The cord went taut, stopping him from being washed into oblivion. Remi and Lazlo had reacted quickly and were holding him—but even their combined strength wouldn't be a match for the river for long.

Sam's arm broke from the water and he pulled himself upward, battling the rushing froth as his head shot into the air. He gasped as he struggled to cross to the far side, the surge pulling him toward where the water disappeared beneath a limestone drop. He fought its powerful draw with steady strokes, as Remi and Lazlo fed out line, the river a roar in his ears, and then light played across the darkness—Remi was shining her flashlight on the far bank to guide him.

Sam's knee bashed against rock and his leg went numb. Just then, his fingers felt cold stone—he'd made it to the other side. He scrabbled onto the bank, sensation returning to his leg, with a throbbing in his knee, and he lay on his back, catching his breath.

His relief was interrupted by an urgent tug on the rope. He looked across the water where Remi stood—he'd been washed ten yards downstream in the blink of an eye. She gestured to the area behind her and cut her light, plunging the cave into darkness. Sam understood. Their pursuers were coming and she didn't want to offer any clues to which passage they'd taken.

Sam retrieved the plastic flashlight from his pocket and flicked it on and, thankfully, it illuminated. He made his way directly across from Remi and tugged back on the rope as he looked around for anything he could tie his end to. Failing to find anything obvious, he rose and anchored himself against the eroded remains of a boulder. Lazlo wrapped the cord around his waist and did the same. The line went taut a few feet above the rushing river's surface, and Remi wasted no time. She stashed her light in her waistband, gripped the rope with both hands, and edged into the water, using the rope to guide her.

When the bottom went out from beneath Remi's feet and she was in the full surge of the current, it was all Sam could do to maintain control over the rope. He was forced to wind in several feet of rope when Lazlo skidded on his side, losing ground. He felt the jolt of the line as Remi's hands struggled and exhaled a loud sigh of relief when she regained her footing and moved to join him, dripping wet but unharmed.

"Lazlo. Tie the rope around your waist and swim over. We'll pull you to this side," Sam called out, his words amplified by the stone walls.

Lazlo did as instructed, and Sam whispered loudly to Remi, "You ready to do this?"

"Yes, but we don't have much time. They sound close."

Lazlo made his move, and Sam began reeling in the rope with Remi's help, the uneven surface near the boulder providing the necessary traction for their boots. Lazlo splashed into the water like an ungainly stork picking its way through a marsh and then he was in the current, flailing and sputtering on the end of the line as Sam and Remi pulled with all their might.

He was halfway across when Remi's grip slipped and a yard of rope burned through Sam's hands as he fought for a hold. As Lazlo's head went under, Sam's fingers locked on the cord. He stopped the slippage, sweat beading on his forehead, as he wrapped the rope around his forearm. Remi regained her footing and resumed pulling, but Lazlo's weight combined with the power of the current presented an almost impossible challenge.

After a few frantic moments, Lazlo broke the surface near them and coughed, his hacking like gunfire in the cave as he fought for breath. Sam and Remi heaved him the rest of the way out of the water and he stared up at them in the gloom like a wet dog. Water dripped from his hair and mustache, lending him the appearance of an emaciated walrus.

Boots clomped from in the passage, and Sam whispered to Lazlo, "Bring the rope and follow me."

Lazlo pushed himself to his feet, trying to contain his coughing, as Sam tossed the rope aside. Lazlo gathered it quickly and darted after Sam and Remi as they disappeared into the recesses of the elongated cave, following the passage around a natural bend. Sam kept his light off as he felt along the wall, the way burned into his memory from the one quick glance he'd had in his flashlight's beam.

They didn't have to wait long. The glow from the islanders' lights approached from the far reaches of the cave, and Sam signaled for them to stop, once around the bend, so he could peer back and see whether they were being pursued.

The islanders arrived at the riverbank—four or five, by the sound of it. Sam could hear their frustrated voices reverberating in the cave, the angry tone of the leader more animated than those of his men, who sounded subdued. Sam couldn't understand what they were saying, but he didn't need a translation as they neared the water—they were going to try to make it across the river.

One of the lights flashed along the bank and stopped at the wet footprints leading to the recess where the Fargos had taken cover. Sam swore under his breath and turned to Remi. "They spotted our trail," he whispered.

"Think they can make it?"

Sam shook his head. "Not unless they do the same thing I did."

"Think they'll figure it out?" Lazlo asked.

"We'll soon know."

"They didn't strike me as particularly bright," Lazlo said. "And unless I'm mistaken, they're all high as kites on something. Amped out of their gourds. Did you see their eyes? I don't think we have to worry about them catching on quickly."

"Let's hope you're right."

Sam resumed his vigil. The gunman was pointing at the river with his weapon and having a hurried discussion with one of his men, who looked unconvinced. The gunman barked an instruction and the other man quickly removed his boots and padded toward the river, his bare feet silent on the stone.

He waded into the water up to his knees and, after testing the current, glanced back over his shoulder to the gunman, who made a curt gesture. The hapless man edged in deeper and then went under with a loud splash, sucked down by the current as it strengthened nearer the middle. Sam watched as the others' lights roamed over the water, but after a few moments there was still no sign of the swimmer. Sam remembered the uncontrollable rush of the relentless undertow that had nearly pulled him to the bottom and shuddered. There was no way anyone could have survived.

He turned back to Remi and Lazlo. "They won't be trying that again anytime soon. That's one down." Sam glanced at the depths of the long connecting cave beyond. "Let's put some distance between us and the river before they figure out how to get across."

Sam took the lead and felt his way along the walls until the faint light from the islanders' flashlights was a memory and then switched on his lamp and picked up the pace. After several minutes, he stopped, listening. The only sound was their breathing, which filled the silent passageway.

Remi's eyes met his. "We lost them."

Sam shook his head. "Not for long. We need to keep moving. Eventually, they'll figure it out, and I want to be long gone by the time that happens."

"It's a bit mad that they're so determined to get us, isn't it?" Lazlo asked.

"Looks like we stumbled across their dirty secret and they want to keep us from telling anyone. Can you imagine the uproar if it was known that the rebels have been slaughtering dozens of children and that we have a pretty fair idea where they're hiding out?"

"There would be an army up here within hours," Remi said.

"Which may blow our search, but I'd say that's a foregone conclusion now," Sam agreed. "Of course we need to get to civilization for any of that to happen, which isn't as certain."

"What if this cave system has only one way in?" Lazlo asked in a quiet voice.

"That wouldn't be good," Sam said grimly. "Come on. Let's find a way out of here."

Remi nodded and glanced back over her shoulder. "Poor Leonid. We'll have to try to rescue him when we return with the police. Can you imagine what it must be like for him? Stuck somewhere in the dark, nobody around, probably injured . . ."

"Let's just hope he isn't too badly hurt."

"And that he's smart enough to keep quiet when the bad guys come looking," Lazlo added.

The caves were connected, comprising a series of chambers created by underground streams, which had carved tunnels between the larger areas. Sam led them into a massive cavern, the ceiling easily thirty feet high, where another smaller river cut along both sides, continuing the erosive process that had been under way for countless millennia.

Sam's flashlight was beginning to wane as they crossed a stone bridge near the far side. He slowed, and he and Remi exchanged a worried look. "Let's see if your light made it through the river intact."

She removed it from her waistband and tried it, but no light greeted the click of the switch. "It's dead. Better hurry up."

"Lazlo?" Sam asked.

"I'm afraid I lost track of mine while going for my dip," he said.

Sam studied the beam's waning intensity and pointed it toward the next connecting passage. "Then we've got no time to waste."

The ground sloped upward as they entered the long tunnel-like cave. Sam led them hurriedly through the maze of stalagmites that jutted from the floor like fangs. The precious light faded with every step. The flashlight was dimming to the point where it was more a comfort than an illumination when they found themselves in another large cavern, with a glimmering pool of water at the far end. Sam was halfway to the water when the batteries died and they were plunged into complete darkness. He reached out his hand to Remi, who sensed his proximity and took it. She repeated the gesture with Lazlo, and together they crept slowly nearer to the water's edge.

"Now what?" Remi asked when Sam stopped.

"We rest while we figure out our next move," Sam said.

Remi bit her tongue, as did Lazlo—there was nothing to say that would help their situation and complaints wouldn't do any good.

They sat down, and Remi leaned forward to touch the surface of the pool. The water was cool, and, after sniffing her fingers, she cupped her hand and brought some to her lips.

"It's fresh," she whispered. "Which means it's being fed by a source."

"At least we won't die of thirst," Lazlo muttered.

"We're not going to die," Sam said, conviction in his voice, as he peered around the cave.

"That's reassuring, but it would be more so if we knew where we were or had any hope of finding a way out," Lazlo groused.

Sam ignored him as he slowly stood. "Remi, is it my imagination or is there a tiny bit of light coming from about three-quarters up the wall to our right?"

Remi's eyes scanned the same direction. "I don't see anything."

Lazlo shook his head in the dark. "Afraid not, old man."

"I'm sure I see something. I'm going to try to get up there. There's a rubble pile along that wall. Hopefully, it will support me," Sam said.

"Are you sure rock climbing in the dark is a good idea?" Remi asked softly.

"What's plan B?"

Sam felt along the edge of the water, following it around to where it met the cave wall. He steeled himself as he willed his eyes to adjust, but he couldn't see his hand in front of him—only a pin spot of faint light from somewhere up the jumble of rocks and debris, now gone due to the angle. Unless it was all a hallucination.

Sam instinctively glanced at where his watch would have been if his captors hadn't stripped it from him and swore under his breath. He had no idea how long they'd been prisoners, much less in the caves. It felt like at least half a day, possibly more, and he realized that he didn't know whether it was still light out or not—or whether the light he believed he'd seen was a new dawn or some new unthought-of danger.

Sam felt along the rock pile, testing the rubble for stability, before pulling himself up a few feet. Visions of venomous snakes nesting in the crannies flashed through his imagination, as his fingers touched the edges of another rock, and he willed the image away.

He heaved himself up another couple of inches, but one of the rocks he was using to stabilize his feet gave way and he slipped in a shower of gravel and dust, scraping his hands as he grappled for a hold. His fingers locked onto another, larger rock and he stopped his fall, taking a moment to catch his breath once he was sure he wasn't in any immediate danger.

Remi's voice floated across the water to him. "Are you okay?"

"Just a little slip. Wouldn't be any fun if there wasn't a challenge to it, right?" Sam said.

He'd give anything for thirty more seconds of light, but those were the breaks. If he ever wanted to see anything again, he'd have to earn it.

Another hold, another few inches of progress, then another, and another, as he painstakingly moved up the rubble pile, the occasional clatter of a loose stone tumbling to the bottom his only reward. As Sam ascended, he noticed that the rocks were getting smaller and he allowed himself the luxury of hope—perhaps on the other side of the imposing wall lay freedom and the landslide he was now climbing had created a breach in the stone.

He groped with his left hand above him and edged higher and then stopped, afraid to breathe. Just above his head was a chink in the rocks. Only a hairline crack, but he could smell jungle wafting through it—and he could feel the humid heat of the outdoors, faint but real.

Sam felt for any loose rocks and was able to shift a football-sized stone half an inch. He worked it back and forth and a scant moment later the rock fell down the pile, leaving a hole he could just fit his arm through—and from which drifted the unmistakable rustling of vines and dim glow of moonlight.

He redoubled his efforts and within minutes had created a large enough opening to squeeze through. He turned and looked down to where he could now make out the shadowy forms of Remi and Lazlo in the gloom. "Well, don't stand there all night. Our chariot awaits."

"I don't suppose you have any tips for the best way to scale this mound of debris?" Lazlo asked.

"Carefully," Sam shot back.

"I'll bear that in mind."

Remi came first and, not unexpectedly, made it to Sam's position in just a few minutes. Sam helped her climb through the aperture, ignoring the trickle of small rocks knocked loose by her passage, and she pushed through the vines into the night.

Lazlo took three times longer, climbing gingerly toward Sam and freezing in place every time a stone gave way and tumbled below. When he finally made it to Sam, he was panting like he'd run a marathon and he had to stop to rest before making the final effort to clamber through the gap.

Sam followed him out, the temperature increasing at least thirty degrees once he was in the jungle air. A thin scythe of moon hung overhead, bathing the area in a pale wash. Sam brushed dirt off his shirt and then moved to Remi and hugged her close, whispering in her ear as he held her.

"That didn't go exactly as planned."

She pulled away and held his gaze. "But we're out. And Leonid could be lying in a crevice with a broken back." She glanced around the hillside. "Time to earn your keep, Fargo. Which way do you think the road is?"

Sam thought for a moment and then tilted his head to their right. "That way. I caught a glimpse of ocean through the trees as I climbed out."

"Then let's get going. Vengeance may be a dish best served cold, but after being kidnapped, tied up, threatened, and chased, I'm impatient for a little payback."

Sam nodded. "Me too."

CHAPTER 47

Sydney, Australia

Jeffrey Grimes sat on the terrace of his lavish contemporary home on the waterfront of Sydney Harbor, watching the sun sink into the southern ocean. Smooth jazz pulsed from hidden speakers near the floor-to-ceiling pocket doors as he admired the play of light on the waves that stretched to South Head and the Hornsby Lighthouse in the distance. He took a long pull on his Cuban Montecristo Gran Corona cigar and studied the glowing ember with satisfaction before resting it in a crystal ashtray and leaning back in his chair.

The call he'd received earlier had put a smile on his face. Guadalcanal was in turmoil: rioting and looting had started shortly after the most recent rebel action, and several pliant MPs had advanced a bill in an emergency meeting of Parliament that effectively nationalized the key industries he was interested in. His mystery partner had assured him that now the primary opponents to nationalization had been neutralized (he liked that word—"neutralized"—a term that was far more civilized and professional than the more vulgar "murdered" or "assassinated"), it was just a matter of a little more time, and a few more dollars spread in the right places, and their scheme would come to successful fruition.

The entire exercise had been stressful for him and he was glad it was finally ending. Grimes was accustomed to having total control over his projects and taking a backseat to a disembodied voice on the telephone had gone against the grain. He told people what to do, he didn't listen quietly like a serving girl being issued her day's chores. Playing nice with his partner had been one of the hardest things he'd ever done, but it looked like his high-stakes gamble was about to pay off as handsomely as he had hoped.

"Jeffrey? Are you going to sit out there all night?" a female voice called from inside the house.

Grimes glanced over his shoulder to where a young woman with impossibly long tanned legs, wearing one of his T-shirts and nothing else, stood by the picture window, a frown of discontent on her flawless face. Another expensive vice, he thought, as he took a small sip of the port and rolled the mahogany nectar in his mouth, savoring the toffee and hazelnut notes, before rising with a final look at the waning sunset, cigar clutched in his hand.

Guadalcanal, Solomon Islands

Finding a trail that led toward the coastal road proved more difficult than Sam had hoped. He led Remi and Lazlo down the uneven slope, taking care to avoid the area near the ridge for fear of running across a rebel search party. The memory of dozens of skeletons tossed into the caverns like so much firewood was still vivid in all their minds and their passage through the brush was quieter for their recollection.

"Wish we had one of those machetes right about now," Lazlo complained under his breath as a branch pulled at his shirt.

"If we're going to wish, I'd want a few AK-47s and some grenades," Sam replied.

"And a helicopter. Don't forget the helicopter," Remi said.

"Never," Sam assured her and then slowed. "I think there's a trail ahead," he whispered.

They approached the opening in the underbrush cautiously. Sam eyed the trail and nodded. "This looks good. Hopefully, it will get us close."

They hadn't discussed what to do next, other than find the logging road and pray that Greg was still there. Everyone knew it was a long shot, but there was a chance that the rebels wouldn't move against Greg until the situation in the caves was resolved, in which case the Mitsubishi was their best shot. The alternative was to try to hitch a ride on the coastal road—an ugly proposition under the best of circumstances, given that they hadn't seen another vehicle on the way there.

Their progress was slow, and more than once they almost lost their footing to an unseen rut or a lurking vine, obstacles nearly invisible with the clouds obscuring the moonlight.

After hours following the wandering trail, they emerged in a clearing, where the first dim pink of dawn was lighting the sky through gaps in the canopy. Remi pointed at the strip of asphalt beyond the tree line and sighed. "There's the road."

"Thank goodness," Lazlo said. "I don't suppose either of you has a fully charged sat phone in your back pocket, do you?"

"Afraid not, old badger," Sam said, affecting his best British accent. "But maybe we'll get lucky."

"That's been rather a poor expectation so far, hasn't it?" Lazlo countered.

"Killjoy."

Remi cocked her head, listening intently. Sam raised an eyebrow. "What is it?"

"I hear a motor. Faint, but there."

Remi took off at a dead run, making for the road, Sam close behind her, and Lazlo, as was customary in the bush, bringing up the rear from a considerable distance. Sam caught up to her and grabbed her arm as they neared the road. "Let's stay out of sight until we're sure it's not rebels."

She nodded, her eyes fatigued but acknowledging the wisdom in his words. They crouched behind a large banyan tree as Lazlo caught up. Remi's face lit up with relief when she saw the source of the engine noise approaching on the road.

"Look. It's an ambulance, from town," she said.

Sam stepped from behind the tree as the ambulance neared, waving his hands over his head. The ambulance slowed, its emergency lights flashing red and blue, the driver probably surprised to come across three foreigners in the middle of nowhere just after dawn. The vehicle rolled to a stop on the roadside ten yards from where they stood.

"It should have a radio. Finally, a lucky break—we can get help a lot faster," Sam said, and then his voice trailed off when the doors at the rear of the ambulance swung open and a familiar figure stepped onto the pavement. The shape of the pistol in the man's hand was unmistakable, in the unlikely event any of them had forgotten the lead gunman's face.

"Oh no . . ." Remi said, preparing to bolt. A second gunman descended from the rear of the ambulance with an ancient rifle, an evil grin twisting his features, stopping her in her tracks. At that distance, a pistol shot might miss, but not a rifle.

"Well, well, well. Look what we found," the gunman said, approaching them with his weapon held casually by his side. "Small world, no?" he asked as he neared, and slammed Sam in the side of the head with a brutal blow from the pistol's stock before he could raise his hands to defend himself.

"No!" Remi screamed, lunging at the gunman, but it was too late.

The sky spun and the world faded from Sam as he crumpled to the road, unconscious.

CHAPTER 48

Sam shifted on the hard stone floor as awareness seeped back into his brutalized cranium. His eyes fluttered open, unfocused, and then the blur of indistinct objects resolved itself into the concerned face of Remi, staring down at him, Lazlo looking over her shoulder. Sam blinked, and his head felt like someone had broken a two-by-four over it. He raised a tentative hand to his temple and drew a sharp breath when pain radiated through his skull from the swollen bump, crusted over with blood where the pistol had broken skin.

Sam tried to sit up, but the room spun, and a sound like a freight train roaring through a tunnel filled his ears. He thought better of it, deciding that a few more moments remaining supine wouldn't hurt, and then his brain began processing the words that Remi was urgently whispering.

"We're back in the caves. But this one's different," she said. He tried to make sense out of that. Last thing he remembered, he was on the road, waving down an ambulance . . .

His memory came rushing back in a jumble of images. The gunmen. A blow to the head. Darkness.

Sam struggled up, leaning on one elbow, and regarded Remi. "Are you all right?" he asked, his voice a croak.

"Yes. They roughed us up some, but you got the worst of it."

"I feel like I wrestled a bear." He blinked again. "The bear won."

"Not far from the truth," Lazlo said. "You look a trifle played."

"That's what happens when they use your head for a punching bag," Sam said, and sat up. This time, the room didn't spin—it tilted—and the nausea that accompanied that sensation surged before slowly receding. He looked back at Remi. "What do you mean, this cave's different?"

"It's not the same one we were in. It's better lit, and has multiple chambers . . . one of which has some hospital beds in it, along with medical equipment."

"Medical equipment?" Sam asked, trying to make sense out of hospital beds in caves. "What kind of medical equipment?"

A rusting iron slab at the far end of their empty chamber creaked open and Carol Vanya stepped in, a pleasant smile on her face like she'd dropped by to chat. Two gunmen followed her, brandishing their weapons with ugly expressions.

"Oh, mostly vital signs monitors, IVs, oxygen tanks, that sort of thing," Vanya said. "We've got a solar array set up in a clearing with a considerable battery bank, and a wind generator, as well as a water-driven generator that's surprisingly powerful."

Remi glared at her in shock. "You! Why have you kidnapped us?"

Vanya shrugged. "I did try to warn you to leave the island. Several times. But you wouldn't pay heed. This is what happens when you think you're so superior that you don't have to listen to the well-intentioned advice of those who care about you."

"That's not an answer," Sam managed. Vanya shrugged again.

"You stuck your noses where they didn't belong. That created a problem. Again, you were warned."

"What are you talking about?" Remi demanded.

"Apparently, you believe I'm here to answer your questions. You've got that backwards. So let's start with why you were rooting around in the caves. What were you looking for?"

"We weren't looking for anything," Lazlo lied unconvincingly. "Just exploring."

Vanya sighed. "My associates here are waiting to take you apart, limb by limb. I'd hoped to have a civilized discussion, but if you want to progress to the ugliness, so be it . . ."

Remi shook her head. "We were looking for artifacts. Some of the evidence we found in the sunken city pointed to the caves," she said, offering a partial truth.

"Ah, yes. The infamous sunken city." She regarded them curiously. "What artifacts?"

"Items of potential archaeological significance," Remi fired back.

"Well, I hope it was worth it to you because it cost you your lives."

Sam fixed her with a hard stare. "You'll never get away with this. Too many people know we're here."

Vanya laughed. "In case you haven't noticed, the island's awash with rebels. Foreigners and politicians are falling like bowling pins. So a few misguided, pampered dilettantes disappear into the jungle in the midst of a civil war? I'm sure the memorial service will be touching. Perhaps I'll deliver the eulogy—about troubled times, adventurous souls, generous spirits."

"Why are you doing this?" Remi whispered.

"You've intruded into matters that are none of your concern. Unfortunately, once seen, your discoveries can never be unseen, so even if you swore to remain silent, there's no way I could allow you to leave."

Sam's eyes widened. "You're involved in the skeletons? The children?"

"Regrettably, some of the more aggressive medical treatments result in terminal side effects. When dealing with incurable illnesses like malaria, it's often necessary to try experimental approaches in order to advance the human condition. It's a necessary by-product of discovery, of developing new cures."

"You'd kill some of your patients," Lazlo said, almost in awe. "The disappearing village children . . ."

"I've been fortunate enough to work in an unofficial capacity with some visionary pharmaceutical companies. But, as with most industries, they're hamstrung by arcane rules and regulations that prevent them from creating cures that could save millions. So they seek out medical professionals who understand that the greater good sometimes requires regrettable sacrifices." Vanya offered another smile, but instead of warming her face, the effect was chilling. "Don't look at me like that. I assure you it's nothing new. For decades, Africa has been a testing ground for new vaccines and treatments. Nobody cares what happens over there—or even knows anything is happening at all. A few villages nobody's heard of suffer casualties, but disastrous human plagues are averted. It's the way of the world."

"It's monstrous. A violation of international law," Remi stated flatly.

"Spare me your high moral tone. Your country refuses to abide by international law and flouts it constantly. Why should I be any more bound by it than you?"

"You're insane," Sam said, his voice quiet.

"Oh, right. Of course I am. That's always the reaction of the uninformed when you confront reality. You don't want to know the truth, preferring to live in a dreamworld." Her face darkened. "In Guinea and Liberia, there are 'defensive' bioweapons laboratories that are funded by your country. Why? Because those nations never signed the bioweapons proliferation treaties your government did, so your military-industrial complex can develop nightmares there without technically violating the treaties. It's a shell game designed for one purpose—to carry out research the civilized world has agreed shouldn't be continued. But how much outrage does that cause in you? None. What I'm doing is far more benign."

"It isn't the same as murdering children," Remi spat.

"Are you kidding me? I just told you that the same thing has been done in Africa for most of the twentieth century."

"That's a rationalization for taking money from the same drug companies you claim to despise and conducting research that would land you in prison for life. It's got nothing to do with idealism, and everything with money," Sam countered.

"You can't be that blind. This is the way the world works. The appetite for medical miracles is insatiable, and there are large tracts of the planet that are off the radar, where shortcuts can be had, saving years, and sometimes decades, so developed nations can enjoy breakthroughs. Do you really believe that ethics and morality, which shift depending on which side of a border you're on, guide behavior all over the world?"

She frowned. "Your government, your corporations, are guilty of so-called crimes as bad, or worse, than anything I've done here. For all your self-righteousness, you're no better than I am. You want the benefits—you just don't want to hear about how the sausage is made."

"You swore an oath—the Hippocratic oath. Which you're violating every day," Lazlo said.

"I merely grasp that in order to progress, one needs to make accommodations. Compromises. I'm focused on results. We're no different at all. I simply admit what I have to do in order to get things done. You want to remain ignorant." She snapped her fingers and the gunmen stepped forward. "I'm tired of this. Good job capturing them. You have my permission to use whatever means necessary to obtain the information I'm after." The chilling smile returned as she fixed Sam with a hard stare. "Artifacts indeed. Before you join the skeletons in the cave, you'll tell my men the truth about what you were doing here."

"We told you the truth."

"You told me fairy tales. But we'll get to the bottom of it."

"So now you're going to have your rebel associates torture us? Is that also in the interests of medical expediency?" Lazlo demanded.

"Think of that as a fringe benefit of being the leader of the so-called rebels."

Understanding settled over Remi's face. "You're behind all this? But Manchester was your friend . . ."

"Orwen was a drunk and a fool. For the only time in his life—in death—he served a productive purpose."

"You sat with him, ate with him, joked with him . . ."

"And enjoyed myself. But he was standing in the way of progress. That's always a dangerous stance to take and he paid the price."

"You really are nuts," Sam muttered disgustedly.

"Perhaps. But your opinion on the matter is irrelevant. Soon you'll be part of the boneyard, dead and forgotten in a mass grave."

"Then you're nothing but a common murderer," Remi said. "After all the lofty rhetoric, you'll murder to protect yourself, to keep your evil from becoming known."

"Don't forget to make money," Sam said. "Why do I suspect that this whole popular rebellion is nothing but a pretense for a swindle? Remember who's talking—a woman who will experiment on her fellow islanders for a buck while coloring it as some noble way of getting cures to market."

Vanya sneered at them. "Say what you like. This discussion is finished. It was nice knowing you. I would have enjoyed taking your money for the clinics, if that's any consolation."

"You won't be able to keep your crimes secret," Sam said. "We've made a find that will put Guadalcanal on the national news and have scientists swarming over the island. It's just a matter of time until they come across your misdeeds and then you'll be judged harshly by the same laws you believe don't apply to you."

"Right. Assuming the Solomon Islands government allows them access to the island. Which is doubtful at this point in light of the antiforeigner sentiment ruling the day." She eyed Sam like an owl would a mouse. "And at some point soon I can see the caves being destroyed by demolition charges I've already had placed, erasing any evidence. And before long I'm going to be rich beyond anyone's wildest dreams, so I won't have to bother with chasing pennies from pharmaceutical companies for doing their dirty work. I'll be a billionaire many times over, at which point all this becomes an unnecessary distraction."

"You don't have to do this," Sam tried, struggling to hide the distaste he felt. "Once the caves are destroyed, there's no proof of anything. You said so yourself."

"True, but I don't need a pair of multimillionaires claiming I'm the Antichrist. I'm not so provincial that I don't understand you could stir up enough interest to drive an investigation. No, I'm afraid there's only one way this ends. You and your colleagues must die. Think of it as a noble sacrifice, if it makes you feel any better, makes your deaths seem meaningful to you." She checked her watch. "And now I'm afraid I have a hospital to run and politicians to counsel. Good-bye, Sam and Remi Fargo. And you—whatever your name is," she said, eyeing Lazlo.

The nearest gunman held the iron barrier open for her and both men followed her out, shutting the heavy door and locking it behind them. The sound of the bolt sliding into place was as final as the closing of a coffin lid. As Vanya's and the men's footsteps echoed down the passageway, Sam and Remi shared a bleak look with Lazlo.

Sam was the first to speak. "Tell me about what you saw when they brought us in here."

Remi collected her thoughts and eyed the door. "This cave is farther down the ridge from the one with the bodies and the one we were ambushed in. This is probably all part of the same cave system, though—maybe the fork we didn't take when we were making our escape."

"How far in are we?"

"We went through two smaller caves after we entered the mountain." Remi shuddered. "The one on the other side of the door has the medical equipment and beds in it. It smelled like death."

Sam nodded. "Think hard. Is there anything we can use, anything either of you saw, that could help us?"

Remi and Lazlo were silent for several moments and then Lazlo shook his head. "I'm afraid not. Bit of a bind this time, I'd say."

Sam looked at Remi. "Anything at all?"

"If we could get into the next room, some of the equipment could be used as weapons. The oxygen tanks. Some of the cleansers and solvents . . ."

Sam grunted. "Help me up. I want to look at the door."

Remi and Lazlo did as Sam asked and they approached the iron door, Remi supporting Sam. He ran his fingers over the hinges, examined where rust was bleeding down the seams, and gave Remi a sour look. He didn't have to say that there was no way they could work the oversized pins loose—the door had to weigh hundreds of pounds and had been competently installed, framed by concrete rather than the softer limestone of the cave walls.

"They built quite a bunker here," Lazlo said. "The door and the cement look old. Might have been the Japanese."

Sam studied the metal slab. "Probably. The Japanese built a lab for their experiments and the good doctor took it over. Makes sense—if the Japanese did it correctly, they probably bored ventilation shafts and ran wiring. All Dr. Vanya had to do was step in and modify it, depending on its condition when she found—"

Sam's rumination was interrupted by the lights shutting off with a snap, plunging the cave into darkness.

CHAPTER 49

They stood frozen in the pitch black, afraid to move. A muffled thump echoed from the other side of the door, followed by silence.

"What do you think this is? Desensitization technique?" Sam whispered to Remi.

"Could be they just want to save their power for more important things than prisoners they plan to torture and kill," Remi said.

"Doesn't sound optimistic," Lazlo said.

Their speculations were cut short by a scrape, followed by the bolt sliding free. They stepped back just as the heavy door swung wide, hinges creaking. The cave beyond was also dark and they couldn't make anything out.

"Which one of you is the better shot?" a familiar voice asked from the doorway. "I managed to relieve one of the natives of his pistol, but there are more where that came from," Leonid said.

"Leonid! You're alive!" Lazlo whispered in surprise.

"Barely. So who's best with a pistol?" Leonid repeated.

"Remi is," Sam said.

"Where is she?" Leonid asked.

"I'm right here," Remi offered from Sam's left.

Leonid took a step into the room and held out the gun, which Remi felt for and then took from him.

"Are you hurt?" Sam asked.

"Nothing broken, but I'm not going to win any beauty contests."

"You killed the lights?" Lazlo asked.

"Yes. Machete to the main power cable. Took three tries."

"Where's the machete?" Sam asked.

"Buried in a guard." He paused. "I have a flashlight, but I don't want to turn it on. Better to wait for the others to return and shoot at their lights."

"I keep forgetting that you were in the Russian army," Sam said.

"And I've been married three times," said Leonid.

A glow bounced from the far end of the cave as a flashlight approached. Remi stepped in front of Sam and pointed beyond a row of beds at the oxygen tanks lined up against the wall. She held her fingers to her lips as the light drew closer and said softly to Sam, "Take cover. I'm going to close the door so they don't see anything wrong. It might buy us a few seconds."

"I'm coming with you," he said.

There was no time to argue. She and Sam moved into the cave with the medical equipment, pulled the door shut, and bolted it. Remi ducked behind a wooden crate and Sam hurried to a portable monitoring system near the beds, hoping the apparatus would hide him.

They didn't have long to wait. A flashlight appeared in the opening at the other side of the cave and they could make out three islanders toting pistols. The beam moved directly to the door, as Remi had hoped, stopping at the bolted lock. The men muttered unintelligibly among themselves and took cautious steps toward it, and both Sam and Remi held their breaths as the gunmen moved past them to the door.

Remi's shots were as loud as cannon fire in the cave. The first caught the flashlight bearer between the shoulders and the second hit his companion as he was spinning to shoot at her. She squeezed off two more shots at the third gunman as he threw himself behind another crate. Hers missed as he fired two of his, one of which splintered the wood by her head, the other ricocheting harmlessly off the stone walls.

The flashlight lay on the ground, shining into nothingness, providing just enough illumination for Remi to make out the far crate. The gunman's leg shot out and kicked the flashlight into the wall, shattering the bulb and plunging the cave back into darkness. Remi's night vision took several seconds to adjust and her reaction was too slow as the gunman rolled from behind the crate, pistol in hand.

Sam pushed the cart over and the heavy monitor landed on the stone floor with an explosive crash, buying Remi critical moments for her eyes to fully adjust. The gunman froze at the unexpected commotion fifteen feet from where he thought the threat lay, exposing himself for an instant.

Which was all the opportunity Remi needed. She fired two more times, emptying the revolver. The gunman slumped over and his gun clattered harmlessly to the floor. Sam moved from behind the cart to where the first two islanders lay dead by the door and groped around until his fingers found one of their guns—another revolver.

"See if you can find the other pistol," Sam whispered to Remi. "I'm going to get the door open so we can use Leonid's flashlight. After this, we've lost any element of surprise."

"Okay," Remi agreed, moving cautiously toward the sound of his voice.

Sam worked the bolt free and swung the door wide as Remi neared. Lazlo and Leonid were crouched inside. "Time for your flashlight," Sam told Leonid, who switched it on.

Remi located the other gun, a Beretta 9mm semiautomatic, and scooped it up. She quickly checked the magazine, which was full, as Sam retrieved a fallen flashlight. She felt in the gunman's shorts for a spare and noted without emotion that the dead man was the lead islander who'd captured them, the one who had brutalized Sam's head with the same weapon she now held.

Now that there was light in the cell, they could see the extent of Leonid's injuries. Sam didn't react to the Russian's appearance, but his stomach tightened when he saw the patchwork of scabs and cuts covering his face and arms. It was a minor miracle Leonid had managed to recover from his spill into the chasm, but he was clearly the worse for wear and every visible inch of skin sported a contusion or scrape.

Lazlo followed Sam and Leonid out of the cell and moved to where the third gunman's weapon lay near his dead hand. Lazlo leaned over and picked it up, distaste written across his face, and held it out to Leonid. "I suspect you might be able to make more productive use of this than I," he said. Leonid took the revolver without comment and quickly checked the cylinder.

"Only two rounds," he said, then grunted and directed the beam at the cave entry. "Who wants to take the lead?"

"I will," Sam said, but Remi shook her head.

"You're hurt. I'll do it. Leonid, give me your flashlight."

Leonid nodded and handed her the light. Sam looked ready to challenge her, but she cut him off with a determined look. "No arguments, Fargo. I've got the most firepower with the automatic. Back me up." She glanced at Lazlo. "Give him a hand, would you please?"

Remi shone the light around the chamber and froze when a moan drifted from another doorway—which was bolted shut. They moved to the heavy door and Sam pulled loose from Lazlo, a determined expression on his face. Remi stood by the side of the door, pistol at the ready, as Sam worked the bolt loose.

They exchanged a glance and Sam nodded. He swung the door

wide as Remi aimed into the darkness, Sam shining his beam into the gloom. When no attack came, he took a cautious step toward the threshold, and then another moan came from inside the chamber.

It sounded like a girl.

"What on earth . . ." Remi whispered as she moved into the cavern. She scanned the interior with her light, holding the pistol in one hand and the flashlight in the other, and then gasped when her beam settled on one of a dozen beds along the wall. A figure lay prone there, one thin arm shackled to a chain dangling from the stone wall.

Sam played his beam along the surface, where manacles hung from rusting chains clasped to iron rings. In one corner, an iron box stood open and he shuddered when he saw what it was—a coffin-shaped contrivance just large enough to imprison a human. Next to it stood a metal cage backed against the wall, its surface grooved from hands scratching at the stone in a futile effort to get free. Rust-colored streaks ran down the wall and again Sam shuddered—it was dried blood, some of it probably decades old, but enough of it relatively fresh to send chills up his spine.

Remi moved to the bed, where a young female islander was laboring for breath. Empty IV bags littered the stone floor, along with discarded syringes and medicine vials. A cockroach scuttled near Remi's foot and she grimaced.

"It's . . . it's like some kind of medieval torture chamber," she murmured.

"I think we've found where the Japanese did their dirty work," Sam agreed, leaning over to examine the girl. He touched her forehead and looked at Remi. "She's burning up."

"We have to take her with us, Sam."

He took a deep breath and nudged the girl's shoulder. "Can you hear me?"

She moaned again, a pitiful sound filled with pain and fear, and her eyes fluttered open. Her gaze was unfocused as it settled on Remi.

"Sweetheart . . . Do you understand me?" Remi asked quietly.

The girl managed a weak nod.

"We're going to get you out of here. What's your name?"

She struggled to form a word, and both Sam and Remi leaned closer in an effort to make it out.

"Lil . . . ly . . ."

Sam stepped away from the bed and Remi joined him. "She's too sick to walk, Remi."

"Then we'll have to carry her."

"We need to come back for her."

"I'm not leaving her in this living hell, Sam. Look at the poor thing. She's skin and bones." Remi thought briefly. "I'll ask Lazlo to help me, if you think you can make it on your own."

Sam winced as he nodded. "I can try." He glanced back at the shackle. "How do you plan to free her?"

"One of the guards must have keys. Stay with her while I go check."

Remi returned several long moments later with a key ring. She tried two keys before finding one that worked. The manacle opened with a metallic click and Lilly's arm fell across her thin body. Sam moved aside as Lazlo approached the bed and, together with Remi, lifted her frail form.

"Will you be able to manage her?" Sam asked.

"She's light as a feather. Between us, we'll do it," Lazlo said, his voice confident.

Lazlo carried Lilly in his arms as Remi walked beside him, helping Sam. Leonid brought up the rear, weapon in hand. As they emerged from the chamber of horrors, Remi moved into the lead, but then stopped short at the passage that connected the chamber with the medical equipment to the entry cave, pausing to glance at the dead islander lying on the ground with a machete buried in his chest before continuing past—evidence of Leonid's resilience even when injured.

When they reached the entry cave, a blur of motion flew at them from the shadows. Gunfire exploded as Remi and Sam fired at the at-tackers. Seconds later, four islanders lay dying, machetes and axes no match for quick reflexes and bullets. Remi stood, sweeping the space with her pistol, wary of another attempt—just because these islanders hadn't had guns didn't mean there weren't more gunmen nearby, wait-ing for their chance.

Sam pointed to the entry, a gap in the stone, with five yards of pas-sageway leading to the outside. Light streamed through the curtain of vegetation that covered it. Remi nodded and moved to the side of the opening, gun at the ready, while Sam crept to the opposite side of the entry and listened for any hint of ambush, his ears still ringing from the gunfire. Lazlo hung back with Lilly as Leonid eyed Sam and Remi, who gestured for him to move into the passage while they covered him.

At the opening, sensing nothing, Sam whispered to them. "There could be more out there, waiting for us to show ourselves. Anyone have any ideas about how to keep from being sitting ducks?"

Remi regarded the vegetation that hid the opening. "We wait them out."

"We can't wait here all day," Leonid said.

"Why not?" Remi asked. "Let time work against them. Assuming there are any of them left."

They settled in near the entrance, guns clenched in tired hands. Soon they heard the thump of footsteps on stone approaching—faint, but clear. Remi squeezed her body into a depression along one side of the entry, her pistol trained on the gap, as Sam and Leonid took cover behind rocks deeper in the passageway.

The vines rustled and Remi cocked the hammer back on the Be-retta, willing her breathing to slow as her pulse pounded in her ears. She relaxed and lowered the gun when Greg's head poked through the vines and smiled as she called out to him.

"You scared the—"

Sam's gun bucked in his hand twice, deafening in the confined space. The gunman who had been holding his pistol in the small of Greg's back fell backward, his skull obliterated as the first shot caught him in the forehead, and Greg dove to the side. Leonid's pistol barked once and a round tore through the man's torso and he dropped, dead before he hit the ground.

Remi's voice had a tremor in it as she regarded Greg. "Was that it?"

"No. One more by the car, but he only has a machete. Might be long gone by now, with all the shooting," Greg answered, struggling to his feet. She eyed the gash on his head and the dried blood in his hair and nodded. "They ambushed me."

"Can you make it back?"

"Sure."

She turned to Sam and Leonid. "Nice shooting."

"I only have one bullet left," Leonid complained.

"Hopefully, you won't need to use it," Sam said, rising unsteadily.

They moved to the entrance and pushed through the vines into a clearing. A dead islander lay sprawled a few feet from the opening. Greg knelt and retrieved the man's gun—another revolver easily as old as he was—and then pointed to a trail. "We're about five minutes south of the logging road."

"Did you see a woman there?" Remi asked.

Greg nodded. "She's gone. Left before the fireworks started."

"Damn," Sam said.

Remi glared at the trail. "Don't worry. This isn't over. She's not going to get away with it."

Sam studied her face and nodded grimly. "I believe you."

CHAPTER 50

Carol Vanya looked up as her assistant entered her office. The heavyset woman's face was ashen and her hands shook as she fidgeted. Vanya bit back her annoyance and sighed impatiently. The long day patching up islanders injured in the increasing looting was wearing at her nerves. "Yes, Maggie? I thought I left instructions that I wasn't to be disturbed."

"I know, Doctor. I'm sorry. But the police need to talk to you."

Vanya put down her pen and gave Maggie a withering glare. "Can't you deal with anything? What do I pay you for?" she snapped irritably.

The police had left a half dozen officers at the hospital to protect it in the latest round of civil unrest driven by the rebel instigators. The impoverished islanders were easy to manipulate into looting, the class anger like dry kindling for her agents' sparks. The plan was working perfectly: the violence was increasing throughout the day, and by midnight she expected a vote of no confidence in Parliament for the current administration, creating the opportunity for a swift regime change.

"I think you need to see them," Maggie repeated, obviously shaken.

Vanya stood up behind her desk and was rounding it when the imposing figure of Chief Fleming filled the doorway, his face impassive. Maggie stepped around him and scurried off as Vanya approached him, her professional smile firmly in place.

"Yes, Sebastian? Another emergency?" She was used to charming the chief of police, as she charmed most of the island males, with a combination of flirtation and flattery. She drew closer but stopped at the hardness of his stare. "What is it?"

"You're under arrest. Turn around. You have the right to remain silent—" Fleming began, the disgust in his voice barely contained as he held up a pair of handcuffs.

"What? Have you gone mad, Sebastian? What is the meaning of this?"

"Turn around. I'm not going to tell you again."

Her eyes widened and she clamped her mouth shut, her lips a thin line as she submitted to the indignity. She had no idea what had gone wrong, but she was confident she'd be able to talk her way out of whatever the confusion was. She was, after years of thankless public service, one of the most respected figures on the island, with many allies in the government.

"I don't know what you think you're doing, Sebastian—"

"I'd keep my mouth closed, if I were you," Fleming said as he locked the cuffs in place on her wrists and turned her to face the doorway. She gasped, and her vision swam, at the sight of four officers, glowering in the corridor, waiting to take her into custody—and Sam and Remi standing behind them. Her mouth worked like a beached fish, producing nothing but a choking sound, as realization dawned on her.

The two nearest officers pulled her roughly into the hallway. Sam and Remi watched wordlessly, Lazlo by their side. Vanya finally found her voice as she neared them, managing only a single word.

"You . . ."

"Name's Lazlo. I don't think we were formally introduced when you were telling your pet killers to murder us," Lazlo said, his British clipping of each syllable joyous in its precision.

"What's that old expression about he who laughs last?" Remi asked Sam as the doctor was dragged away.

"Something about laughs best," Sam replied, watching Vanya's humiliating final exit from the hospital she'd ruled with absolute authority for years.

Fleming shook his head as he approached. "I have to apologize again. I'm sorry I was so rude in our meeting . . ."

Remi shrugged and took Sam's hand. "We've all been under a lot of stress. Apology accepted."

Sam glanced over his shoulder at Dr. Berry, waiting in the doorway of one of the exam rooms, and turned his attention back to the police chief. "How's the crowd control going?"

"Better. The Prime Minister was on the radio a few minutes ago, exposing the bones of Carol's scheme, alerting the islanders that they had been duped. He didn't name names, but distress calls from my men have already slowed. I'd expect that our forces will make short work of any remaining looters, once word spreads."

"And the exhumation of the skeletons?"

"I have two forensic teams at the caves as we speak, but, because of the scope, it will be a while before they're done and we can begin removing the bones and identifying the remains." He shook his head in disbelief at the memory from earlier that afternoon when he'd arrived at the scene with two dozen of his top officers, led to the caves by Sam and Remi after they'd barged into his office and confronted him with their evidence. "What kind of a monster could do that . . . ? I still don't understand any of it."

"She's not like you or me," Remi said. "She's a sociopath. No sense of right or wrong, only an instinct for manipulation, and a ruthlessness unlike anything you've probably ever seen before."

"Or ever again, if you're lucky," Sam said softly. "She's a serial killer, plain and simple. Perhaps with a more structured mechanism for her killing, but, make no mistake, that's what you're dealing with. Someone who has zero compunction or remorse about taking lives."

"I'm partly to blame," Fleming growled, and his voice caught. "She's obviously been getting away with it for years on my watch. I'll never forgive myself—I didn't pursue the disappearances with nearly the vigor I should have . . ."

Dr. Berry glanced at his watch and signaled to them. It was busy at the hospital and he had an unending stream of patients continuing to arrive with every variety of trauma from the rioting. They left Fleming to his recriminations and approached Berry, who needed to finish stitching up Sam's head now that the results of the CT scan were in.

"I wish I was seeing you again under more pleasant circumstances," Berry said, and then his demeanor changed to all business. "As I suspected, you've suffered a minor concussion from the blows, but nothing you won't recover from. You may experience dizziness and weakness over the next few days, but it should pass." He eyed Sam disapprovingly. "I wish you'd consent to staying overnight for observation like your Russian friend."

"How is he?"

"He also has a concussion, more severe than yours, but nothing terminal. And, as you know, many cuts and bruises. I've given him painkillers and antibiotics and he's resting comfortably."

"After complaining every step of the way, I'll bet," Lazlo said. "What about the girl?"

Berry scowled. "She's in pretty bad shape, but I think she'll make it. We've got to figure out what poison they were pumping into her and take measures to counteract it, but right now we're focusing on keeping her hydrated." He studied Sam's head with a disapproving expression. "Sit down here and I'll finish cleaning this gash up and stitch it closed. It's clotted, but it will need sutures."

Remi offered Sam a smile and looked to the doctor. "While you're busy with him, do you have a phone I can use for a long-distance call?"

Berry fished under his exam coat and handed her a cell phone. "This shouldn't take more than a few minutes, then he'll be right as rain again."

"I'll wait in the lobby," Lazlo said. "Bit squeamish and all."

Remi went into the hall and nodded in satisfaction at the sight of the remaining police sealing Vanya's office with crime scene tape in anticipation of evidence collection. She was raising the phone to her ear when Lilly's mother materialized at the end of the hall and rushed toward her.

"Thank you. Thank you so much for saving my baby," she said, hugging Remi, tears in her eyes. "I knew she not run off like that evil woman say."

"I hope she'll be okay," Remi managed between heartfelt squeezes from Lilly's mother.

"God will provide. Lilly's one of His children. He not send you if He not want her to live."

Remi offered a smile. "She's a beautiful girl. You're very lucky."

"Today a good day for everyone, I say. 'Cept that demon woman. Devil stokin' hellfire for her, that for sure."

Remi nodded in agreement, and then a nurse waved to Lilly's mother from the other end of the corridor. The relieved island woman gasped and hurried to the nurse, leaving Remi to make her call. She dialed Selma's private line from memory and waited as it rang.

"Oh, good. Did you get everything sorted out?" Selma answered. Remi had phoned her earlier to give her a hurried update.

"Sort of. They just took Carol Vanya into custody. Sam's being tended to, and Leonid's in the hospital for the night."

"And Lazlo?" Selma asked, a slight softness in her voice.

"Hardly a scratch on him. The man has the luck of the devil," Remi said.

Selma chuckled. "That he does." Her tone grew serious. "I've been researching your doctor's background and I've found something you'll be interested in."

"Nothing would surprise me about her."

"This might." Selma paused. "It's actually about her grandfather. Apparently, he was charged with war crimes by the Allies, but once the war was over, the charges were dropped. There aren't many records, but, near as I can tell, he had been working with the Japanese and was accused of coordinating medical experimentation on his fellow islanders, as well as on prisoners." Selma let that sink in. "He was also a doctor."

"My God . . . the other bodies—the older ones. Hundreds of them. Her grandfather . . ."

"That's my guess. He probably took her into his confidence when he recognized the psychopathology ran in her, too."

"What about the father?"

"Died a decade ago. It appears he spent his entire life trying to atone for his father's sins, doing community work for free, tending to islanders . . ."

"And the grandfather?"

"I haven't found anything about his passing yet. It's like he disappeared once the war was over."

"You . . . you don't suspect he's still alive, do you?"

"I'm not going to speculate. He'd be older than Moses, though, if he is, so it's unlikely."

"Keep on it, Selma."

"Oh, you can depend on that. I'm sorry you didn't find the treasure."

"Don't be. We've been able to confirm a remarkable historical discovery and we foiled a monstrous plot in the bargain. I'd say that's a full day's work, wouldn't you?"

"Absolutely. I'm thinking more of Lazlo. He must be dejected."

"Oh, I wouldn't say that. He'll recover easily enough. He's nothing if not resilient, I'll give him that," Remi conceded.

"Still. It's out there somewhere."

Remi stared off down the hallway at the police going about their grim business and nodded to herself.

"Yes, it is, Selma. Yes, it is. But you can't win them all, right?"

"I'm sorry. You must have dropped out, I didn't catch that last bit . . ."

They laughed together, the sound musical and easy, and Selma reminded Remi again to call that evening and let her know how Sam was faring, and to be careful—she'd been following news of the rioting online and was clearly worried.

"I will, Selma." Remi smiled. "And thank you. For everything."

"What did I do now?" Selma asked warily.

"Just for being you."

CHAPTER 51

Morning mist hung thick in the air the following day as Remi motored along the logging road into the mountains, Lazlo and Leonid in the backseat, Sam riding shotgun. Sam had slept fitfully but after an early breakfast insisted he felt fine, and when they'd stopped in at the hospital with Lazlo before heading to the caves at Fleming's request, Leonid had been waiting to be released, grumbling at the staff as he signed the discharge papers.

As Fleming had predicted, the civil unrest had run its course once the Prime Minister had addressed the nation and by morning the only evidence of the prior day's rioting were a few smoldering storefronts on the southern end of the city and a notably increased police presence in town. The police chief had called on the Fargos that morning at their hotel to invite them back to the caves to walk him through and offer their impressions, which they'd only briefly discussed during the controlled chaos of the previous day.

Remi looked over at Sam as they neared the end point of the logging road, where a wall of police vehicles was visible in the distance.

"How's the head?" she asked. She'd been trying to minimize the bouncing by swerving around the worst of the potholes—a tactic doomed to failure because of the deep grooves scored into the mud by the police trucks.

"I'm not going to be taking up the drums anytime soon, but I'll manage," Sam said.

"How about you, Leonid?"

"Compared to sleeping on that Australian rust bucket, I feel fine," the Russian griped.

"Tell us again how you managed to get back to the main cave and then track us down and save us," Lazlo said.

"Easy. I came to, climbed up, followed the islanders, and then whacked one when the rest were outside with the woman," Leonid explained as though it was all as ordinary as taking a stroll around the hotel grounds.

Lazlo stared at him in amazement and shook his head. "Must be all the vodka."

"My body is temple," Leonid declared, exaggerating his Russian accent.

"Yes, well, mine too, albeit heavily supplemented by the fermented grape until recently."

The Mitsubishi rolled to a stop near a forensic van, and a stern-faced island cop stared them down as they climbed out of the SUV. A dozen journalists sat in the shade, their vans nearby, watching the police watch them.

"Is Chief Fleming around?" Sam asked. "He invited us out."

"Up that way. Who should I tell him is here?" the officer asked, holding his radio.

"The Fargos."

The officer's face changed. "Oh. Of course. One moment." He

mumbled into the radio and was greeted by a burst of static followed by a terse instruction. He eyed the journalists briefly and then pointed the way to the first cave. "You know how to get there?"

"I think we can find it," Sam said. Remi had to bite her tongue to keep from laughing.

Fleming was standing at the cave entry when they arrived, talking to two other officers with dour expressions. When Fleming spotted the Fargos, he broke off his discussion and moved down to greet them.

"Thanks for coming," he said.

"You're welcome. How's it going?" Sam said.

"Slow but steady. Forensics should be done soon enough." He scowled up at the cave. "We've compiled a list of all missing children and we've begun matching them to skeletons."

"No doubt you've seen that some were bound with zip ties."

Fleming nodded. "Yes." The distaste on his face conveyed more than words could.

"Has she talked?" Remi asked.

"I can't discuss an ongoing investigation, but let's just say that she denied everything, and then changed her story three times, before admitting that she might have been an unwitting pawn in several foreign drug companies' schemes."

"Unbelievable," Sam said.

"Oh, you don't know the half of it. She's quite a piece of work."

"How many on your list?" Lazlo asked.

Fleming looked away. "Thirty-eight. Spanning six years." His eyes darted to the side before settling on Remi. "Off the record, she admitted that sometimes the drugs she was experimenting with caused unexpected complications, but she insists that she was just trying to save lives."

"Of course. By killing some of her patients with medicine she hadn't told them was experimental and then hiding the evidence," Remi fired back.

"Don't forget the grief she caused by covering up their disappearances," Sam reminded. "Imagine how the parents felt when their sick children just vanished."

"Yes . . . Actually, that's one of the prosecutor's big fears—retribution by relatives. It's a very real danger that she'll be lynched."

"Ironic that you'll wind up having to protect her," Lazlo said.

Fleming gave him a dark look. "The islanders who were working for her all tested positive for stimulants. She was supplying them with speed, keeping them dependent on her for their fixes, which we believe was part of how she was controlling them. They were addicts, and dangerous ones—it explains why they were willing to live out here and risk everything to torture their fellow man."

"She probably also promised them that they'd be rich. She was bragging about how she'd be worth billions, when she held us captive," Sam said.

"Any progress on matching the bones in the cave with the list?" Remi asked.

"We started with the largest skeletons, figuring they'd be easiest to identify. The one that's not completely decomposed was named Aldo Cosgrove. A teenager who disappeared a couple of weeks ago after undergoing treatment for malaria by the good doctor." Fleming shook his head. "The abuse he was subjected to . . ." His voice trailed off and he rubbed a hand across his face, his eyes bleak. "Lilly's fortunate you got to her when you did. She wasn't far behind him."

"We believe that the older skeletons in the pit were victims from the war," Remi said. "Our researcher discovered that Dr. Vanya's grandfather was helping the Japanese with medical experiments on islanders." She told the chief about Selma's findings.

"It just gets worse, doesn't it?" Fleming said, staring at the cave opening.

"Do you know if the grandfather's still alive?" Sam asked.

"I don't think so—he'd have to be ancient—but I'll check. I remember her saying something about all her relatives being dead."

"We think the grandfather might have shown Carol his old stomping ground, probably bragging. That's the likeliest explanation for how she found the cave used for the experiments."

"It's funny," Fleming said. "I grew up here and heard plenty of stories about monsters in the caves. I never suspected that the monsters were walking among us every day." He paused, thinking. "We're going to be getting help from Australia. They're sending a team to work the pit with us and try to make sense out of the skeletons. But it sounds like that will be a long process, trying to match bones to POWs or islanders killed during the war."

They moved to the second cave where the medical experiments had been conducted and paused at the entry. Down the hill, a diesel generator rumbled, providing power to the spotlights strung through the caverns. Sam saw Remi shiver as they drew near the opening and he took her hand.

"Do you need any more for the police reports?" Sam asked. They'd given their statements the prior day, explaining the obvious self-defense in the rebel killings.

"No. Nobody doubts what happened here. I just wanted to hear from your own lips how it all went down as we walk the site."

"I'll just as soon stay out here, if you don't mind," Lazlo said, fidgeting with his cell phone as he peered into the cave.

"No problem," Fleming said. "How about you?" he asked Leonid.

The Russian shrugged. "All the same to me."

The caves looked smaller in the wash of light from the work lights. The corpses of the gunmen were gone, replaced by chalk outlines and crime scene tape. They moved through the area slowly, noting the number of beds and the age of the equipment, before entering the cell where they'd been imprisoned only a day earlier, rust-colored smudges on one of the walls evidence of Sam's head wound.

When they had finished with the nightmare scene an hour later, Lazlo was pacing excitedly outside, his face flushed as much from agitation as the sun. The Fargos could see that he was waiting for them to detach themselves from the police so he could talk to them in private and they wrapped up their time with Fleming before joining Lazlo on the trail leading to the logging road.

"I'm a fool. A blind fool," he blurted as they made their way through the brush.

"What are you talking about?"

"The diary. Something's been eating at me and I couldn't put my finger on it. But now I have."

Remi eyed him. "And?"

"The translation of the encoded message. I botched one of the words. As it turns out, a critical word."

"Botched?" Sam said, eyebrows raised.

"Yes. Botched. The key to the whole riddle."

"Out with it, Lazlo," Remi said.

"It wasn't 'beyond' at all. 'Beyond the fall,' remember?"

"Yes, Lazlo. Very well," Sam said impatiently. "What was the word?"

Lazlo paused and slowed to a stop. "It was an easy mistake to make. I was going too fast. Too sure of myself."

"Spit it out, Lazlo," Sam urged.

"'Behind.'"

"'Behind'?" Remi repeated, puzzled.

"Behind the fall," Lazlo said solemnly. "*Behind* it, not *beyond* it."

CHAPTER 52

Sydney, Australia

Jeffrey Grimes leaned back in his executive chair, a distracted expression in place, as his subordinates gave their reports of ever-worsening financial results. The mood in the conference room was panicked as the assembled executives described a financial empire slowly running off the rails.

"With commodity prices slipping and our tankers sitting unused twenty-seven percent of the time, we're literally bleeding money on our shipping company, as well as the commodity trading entity," a stern man in his forties said from beside the overhead projector, where a graph that was mostly red glowed accusingly on the screen. "The gold bet was disastrous, and with another nine billion in notional value of related options contracts maturing this month, it looks like at least twenty-eight million dollars net loss."

That got Grimes's attention. "Get us out of those contracts early. The trend's not our friend now. Someone's selling large amounts of gold into the market every day when trading's thinnest, driving prices down. That has to be a central bank, probably the Americans trying to prop up their dollar, given the volumes—there aren't a lot of players who can sell twenty-five tons of bullion every day and I don't want to wait until they're finished with their play—it could ruin us."

"Could be the Chinese," the vice president of the commodities trading firm observed. "Net accumulations through Hong Kong are way up. They could be selling paper options contracts to drive the price down for their bullion purchases. Nobody wants to pay top dollar, and they're sitting on a trillion dollars of currency they want to unload. So they buy bullion, pay the loss on the paper contracts with dollars they don't want anyway, and bolster their bullion holdings to wind up net even."

Grimes waved the insight away. "Doesn't matter. We're the ant and they're the elephant. The bet's run the wrong way. Time to cut our losses and move on." He eyed the chart. "As for the shipping, we'll have to temporarily reduce our prices to drive demand."

"We can't. We'll lose money on every shipment."

"I'd rather lose ten million this quarter with full ships than twenty with them sitting unused."

The discussion went on, but Grimes was only half listening. He'd been following the events in the Solomons for the last forty-eight hours and, as far as he could tell, something had gone badly wrong. The predicted massive social unrest and resultant regime change had fizzled, and there were troubling local reports that the government had declared the unrest the direct result of a plot to advance a nationalization agenda, which sounded precisely like his mystery partner's scheme unraveling before his eyes.

The implications for his personal fortune were dire. This had been a winner-take-all proposition, and if it was cratering, he'd be left with nothing. Or at least, by his standards, nothing. Perhaps ten million in offshore accounts, three in gold in his oversized floor safe, a few hundred thousand here and there. But his yacht was a liability, not an asset, as was his home, which was twice mortgaged, and his vacation condos had been pledged as collateral for bridge loans he'd been forced to secure over the last few weeks. As with most entrepreneurs, most of his net worth was tied up in his company's stock, and the day he sold his first share, the second share would be worth half as much—after being decimated when he filed the mandatory disclosures in advance.

The situation in the Solomons was a disaster. And it was unfolding in real time. Something had obviously gone badly wrong and he was fully exposed, his personal fortune at risk.

"Gentlemen, we need to find buyers for the shipping company," Grimes said. "I want to divest ourselves of that albatross as soon as possible. It was a good bet when oil was high, but with all the volatility lately, it's dead money and we need to—"

He was interrupted by three stern men in suits throwing the conference room door open.

Grimes's heart rate increased rapidly as the lead man looked around the room and then settled his stare on him.

This can't be happening . . .

"Jeffrey Grimes?"

"Who's asking? And how dare you interrupt a corporate meeting?" Grimes demanded.

"Chief Inspector Collins with the ACC—Australian Crime Commission. You're under arrest."

"Arrest?" Grimes demanded. "What are the charges?"

"We'll get to that soon enough, but we're starting with money laundering, conspiracy to commit murder, murder, kidnapping, and numerous violations of international law."

"That's absurd!"

Collins glanced around the room. "Meeting's over, gents. Your boss is going away for a long time. Say good-bye, because you won't be seeing him again."

"I want my lawyer," Grimes said.

"Perfect. Now, stand up so I can cuff you."

"Surely that won't be necessary," Grimes objected.

"Mr. Grimes, stand up or I'll drag you out of here by your hair. Fair warning." The expression on Collins's face left little to the imagination.

Grimes complied and minutes later he was being guided to a waiting police van by his humorless escorts. His mind was working furiously to calculate damage control. They couldn't have anything. None of his involvement was documented. He'd kept everything verbal, and the shell corporations had been created in a smorgasbord of jurisdictions that would take years for any law enforcement agency to untangle. This was probably mostly bluff by the ACC—the rough Australian equivalent of the Americans' Homeland Security—but he couldn't underestimate them.

He was processed at police headquarters and placed in a holding cell. Nobody spoke to him other than to assure him that his attorney had been contacted. Four hours later, the cell door opened and a harried Simon Whistock, Esquire, entered, briefcase in hand. Grimes started to rise from the steel chair he was sitting on, but his attorney shook his head and took the only other seat, setting his briefcase beside him on the floor.

"Simon. What the hell is going on?" Grimes demanded.

Simon adjusted his round steel-rimmed spectacles and sat forward. "I just spent two hours with the team that will be prosecuting you. Two of them are fairly close friends, so I was able to get a glance at what they have." Simon hesitated. "Jeffrey? It's as bad as anything I've seen."

Grimes swallowed hard. "That's impossible."

"We'll forego my observation that you aren't denying anything and skip to the evidence. They have all the financial records of some six corporations domiciled in the Solomon Islands, including bank transfers from companies controlled by you."

Grimes began to protest, but Simon held up a hand to quiet him. "That they're controlled by you will be problematic to establish but not impossible, based on the testimony of your partner in the Solomons— one Dr. Vanya. Does the name ring a bell?"

Grimes shook his head. "Never heard of him."

"*Her*," Simon corrected. "No matter. They have telephone records from a burner cell phone of hers making multiple calls to a cell that was seized in your office."

"What! You have to get that tossed. There has to be a way."

"I'll do my best, but it looks airtight, at first glance. Jeffrey, this woman murdered dozens of children. She organized a rebel group that killed Australian citizens. She was trying to overthrow the government so your companies could profit." Simon exhaled. "How on earth did you get involved in this?"

"Simon, I had no idea . . ."

Simon removed his glasses and smoothed his hair. "They're talking extradition."

"You need to stop this dead, Simon. Whatever the cost."

Simon nodded and sighed. "Which brings me to the next bit of housekeeping. This will be enormously expensive to defend. We're talking millions. Many millions. I'll need a substantial retainer to proceed. Say . . . two million Australian, within twenty-four hours?"

Grimes snorted. "That's highway robbery!"

"How much is your life worth, Jeffrey? They want you as badly. And if they extradite . . ." He didn't have to finish. "I'll be battling this for years."

"Fine." Jeffrey gave him the combination of his safe. "There's a little over three million in maple leafs and one-kilo bars in the safe. I should think that will suffice. How soon until you can get me bail?"

Simon stared at Grimes like he was mad. "You don't understand, do you? There will be no bail. You're to be transferred to solitary confinement and put on suicide watch. You're considered to be not only a flight risk but also guilty of crimes against humanity, in addition to all the other charges."

The air suddenly felt overheated and heavy. Grimes struggled to breathe as perspiration beaded his forehead. Simon didn't seem to notice as he rattled off a few immediate requirements he'd need to address with Grimes's board of directors. When Simon finished and stood, he seemed anxious to be rid of his client.

Grimes rose and shook hands with his attorney, his palm sweaty. "Simon. You have to get me out of this. Whatever it takes. I . . . I can't spend my life in prison."

Simon averted his gaze and nodded. "I'll do my best, but you've really gone and done it this time, Jeffrey."

The sound of the steel door closing behind the attorney echoed like the detonation of a bomb as Grimes glared at the walls. The entire episode had been surreal. A pulsing throb in his jaw radiated down his left arm as his sweating increased and he was trying to call out for help when his chest seemed to explode and he slipped out of the chair, gasping as his heart faltered, a chunk of plaque the size of a pencil eraser clogging one of the arteries.

By the time the medics arrived, Grimes's body was already cooling, his sightless eyes staring at the ceiling in puzzled amazement and his handsome face frozen in an expression that could only be described as fear.

CHAPTER 53

Guadalcanal, Solomon Islands

Remi eyed the impenetrable rushing of the waterfall and turned to Lazlo, who was standing between Sam and Leonid.

"Are you sure about this?" she asked.

"Never more so."

"But Nauru never said anything about going through a waterfall," Sam said.

"Be that as it may, I'd bet money there's a cave behind that water."

Sam glanced at the puffs of clouds drifting across the sky, glowing white in the noon sun. "The Japanese may well have moved the crates, once they were in a nearby cave. Or the old man might have just been forgetful. We tend to remember the dramatic moments and forget the rest—and having your entire village slaughtered in front of you is certainly dramatic enough."

"So how do we get around the water?" Remi asked.

Leonid pointed at the falls. "It looks like there are a few feet of rock that we can traverse over on the right side."

"No time like the present," Sam said, and led them toward the edge of the small pond the waterfall fed.

"Wouldn't this be exactly the kind of place you'd expect to find crocodiles?" Lazlo asked as they moved along the spongy ground.

"Oh, I'd think they'd find only you," Remi said.

"They're saltwater, aren't they?" Leonid asked.

"Technically, but they do seem to like coastal rivers and lakes, too."

"That's reassuring," Lazlo muttered.

Sam grinned. "Relax, Lazlo. You only live once."

"The problem is, rather more that you only die once, unless you're a cat. Or a Fargo, apparently."

They skirted the water and approached the waterfall, the roar increasing until it was practically deafening. Sam peered along the side of the solid white stream of water and nodded. "There could be something back there. Lazlo, care to do the honors?"

"I'd hoped you would, being a seasoned adventurer and all."

"This is how you gain all that valuable experience, my friend."

"Like pneumonia. Or hypothermia," Remi added helpfully.

"Come on, Lazlo. Fame and fortune await," Sam coaxed.

"Sometimes called crocodiles and snakes by the locals," Leonid quipped.

Lazlo gave him a dark look and nodded. "Very well. Here goes nothing."

He edged past Sam along the narrow strip of rock that framed the waterfall and moved toward the rushing white foam, the spray soaking him as he pressed himself flat against the rock face of the cliff and inched sideways until he was out of sight.

Remi checked her watch. "If he isn't back in two days, we go in after him."

"Unless something else comes up," Sam agreed.

They didn't have to wait long. Lazlo emerged, sopping but excited, from the waterfall's edge.

"There's a cave, all right. Come on, then," he said.

"Any crates?" Remi asked.

"I didn't do anything besides confirm that the cave's there."

Lazlo disappeared behind the waterfall and Remi followed him, glad her backpack was waterproof. Sam was next and Leonid last, a frown of distaste tugging the corners of his mouth as the water doused him.

They found themselves standing before a narrow gap five feet wide. The roar of the falls was amplified by the acoustics in the entry, making the sound almost unbearable. Remi unzipped her backpack and extracted two flashlights and Sam did the same, handing his to Leonid and Lazlo before taking one of Remi's. "Lead on, Britannia!" he called out.

Lazlo turned to face the darkness and switched on his light, then took the first steps into the opening.

The narrow entry quickly widened and the floor sloped upward. Their flashlight beams played across the walls, and Lazlo was walking toward another gap at the far end when Sam grabbed his arm.

"Freeze."

Lazlo did, and Sam pushed past him and crouched down, eyeing the floor. He directed his light at the wall, where there was a small cavity, and crept toward it while retrieving a Swiss Army knife from his back pocket.

"What is it?" Lazlo said.

"Booby trap. Probably no longer works, but no point in pushing our luck, right?"

"Can you disarm it?" Remi asked.

"Looks like a simple trip wire—so, yes. I just want to make sure there's no spring that will detonate it if we cut the wire." He paused, shining his light into the tight space, and then snipped the wire with a snap.

"Seems like we're on the right track," Leonid said.

Lazlo's right eye twitched, and he brushed droplets from his brow with the back of his arm. "Good catch, old chap. I didn't see it."

"Maybe I should take point from here, just in case?" Sam suggested. Nobody objected, so he moved ahead to the opening directly in front of them. He stopped at the threshold and shined his light all around the rock edge, checking for more traps, and then turned to his companions. "There are a bunch of crates in there covered with dust and rot. We need to be careful, though, because any of the crates might be wired to blow. Don't touch anything," he warned. "And watch the floor. There might be more trip wires."

"Brilliant," Lazlo murmured.

"Let me do a quick recon while you stay out here," Sam said, and, without waiting, took several steps into the cave toward the crates, his flashlight beam roaming over every inch of floor.

When he'd satisfied himself that there was no danger, he returned to the gap and smiled at Remi. "Looks clear. Let's go see what all the fuss is about."

Remi nodded and joined him, trailed by Lazlo and Leonid.

A pile of at least fifty wooden crates, three feet by two feet by two, were piled in the center of the small grotto. Lazlo kneeled in front of the nearest and brushed away a layer of mold, then turned to Sam and Remi. "It's kanji. Identifies the crates as property of the emperor. Bit cheeky, that . . ."

"How can we open some of these safely?" Leonid asked.

"Good question," Sam said. "If we're careful and on the lookout for pressure plates, spring-loads, and the like, we should be okay. We can work on a couple of them, but I'd like to get spotlights in here, as well as some specialists, before we try to open more than a few. The good news is, I can't think of many booby traps that would still be operational years after the fact. But still, don't touch anything, just in case they used a contact poison on the surfaces or the contents. Anything's possible—I just don't know enough about what was in use during the war to be certain."

Remi pointed at a crate near the edge of the pile. "Let's try this one."

Sam moved to her and set his backpack down. After eyeing the crate, he handed Remi his flashlight and removed a crowbar from the bag and set it on the ground next to his machete.

"How are you going to do this?" Remi asked.

"I'm thinking I core a hole in the top rather than try to pry the lid off. Prying would be the obvious way of opening it, so that's the way I'll avoid."

He went to work with the machete, scraping away the soft outer wood, and then grinding the harder inner area until there was a fist-sized hole in the top of the crate. He sat back, put the machete down, and took his light back from Remi as she kneeled next to him. They exchanged a long glance, and then he leaned over the hole and blew away wood dust and chips. Remi shined her light inside while they both looked through the opening.

"Well, what is it?" Leonid asked impatiently.

"Yes, do tell," Lazlo said.

"Fabric," Sam said, unfolding his knife again. "Looks like a sack." He reached into the hole and sliced at the fabric, which crumbled to dust at his touch, and then pulled his arm back with a look of revulsion on his face. A large black spider was crawling up his forearm, raising its legs in menace as it neared his elbow. Remi swatted it away with the back of her hand and it scuttled off into the darkness as Lazlo jumped back. Sam's eyes met hers. "Thanks."

"Don't mention it."

Sam took a deep breath and they both leaned over the hole again, their beams shining into the interior. They stayed that way for a few moments and then sat back. Leonid stepped closer. "Well?"

Remi shook her head and Sam shrugged. "Sometimes you win, sometimes you lose. That's how it goes."

"What's in it?" Lazlo demanded, drawing nearer.

Sam's serious expression cracked and he grinned at Lazlo and winked. "It's gold, my friend. The crate's filled with gold."

CHAPTER 54

Three days later, Fleming and a cadre of police ringed the area in front of the waterfall. Greg and Rob, having experience in demolitions from their Navy SEAL days, had been drafted to confirm the crates weren't still booby-trapped from eons ago. Lazlo helped document the contents of each crate under the watchful eyes of Chief Fleming and a gemstone expert he'd brought in from Australia. In addition to the gold shaved off the temple walls, the treasure consisted of crudely formed gold icons and hundreds of pounds of raw gemstones.

Roadworking equipment had been brought in and had cleared access to the waterfall. Soon, police vans, two official government SUVs, and a fleet of media vehicles were parked in the clearing.

Sam and Remi stood beneath a makeshift fabric shelter that shielded them from the spray of the waterfall. Lazlo's head poked out of the brush by the edge of the waterfall. He waved and made his way to the tent, wiping his brow and smiling in triumph. Leonid appeared a few moments later, trailing the Englishman.

"Sorry to interrupt, but I wanted to tell you that we opened three more crates and all have raw diamonds and rubies in them," Lazlo said in a low voice to Sam as though he didn't want Fleming to hear.

"Nice to know the hoard keeps growing," said the chief with a big smile. He was standing behind Leonid and had caught every word.

"How's your case against you-know-who coming?" Remi asked.

Fleming glanced around and leaned toward them. "There's talk of a special tribunal. The scope of her crimes is so massive that nobody's completely sure how to proceed. The Aussies have already put in an official request to charge her as an accomplice to the murder of the aid workers. And then we have all the families, who are demanding immediate justice. So everyone wants a piece."

"Any chance she gets off on a technicality?" Sam asked.

"None at all. The only question is whether Solomon Island law can be changed to allow the death penalty for crimes against humanity. Apparently, that's being discussed. Public opinion is crying for her head, so it could happen. Our people are shocked and angry."

"I don't blame them for an instant," Remi said. "Any news on the evil old grandfather?"

Fleming nodded. "Died in his sleep in 1988. He changed his name after the war and kept to himself on a ranch in the Australian outback."

Sam and Remi had to pause to answer more questions about the treasure trove from a score of reporters as cameras flashed like strobe lights in a disco.

When they had finished, Sam turned to Lazlo and smiled. "You'd better prepare your speech."

"Speech? What could I possibly say?"

"I'm sure you'll come up with something."

"Why me?"

"Because you'll soon be a national hero as soon as it's announced that the treasure will be used to build schools, a new hospital with clinics all around the island, and of course a first-rate road system. Then once we're done splitting the percentage the island is giving all of us . . ."

Lazlo's mouth dropped open. "What percentage?"

Remi raised an eyebrow at him in amusement. "Oh, didn't we mention that? The government's giving us ten percent. Even the most conservative valuation after paying expedition expenses should net you many millions."

"Blimey."

Sam smiled at Lazlo's reaction. "Congratulations, Lazlo. Your days as a pauper are behind you."

"Does Leonid know?"

Sam shook his head. "Not yet. I was just getting ready to tell him."

"This I have got to see for myself."

They made their way to where Leonid was studying an image carved on a flat piece of rock. Sam and Lazlo watched expectantly as Remi broke the news. The Russian's face didn't even twitch.

Sam nudged him with his elbow. "Come on. Tell me you aren't happy about this."

There was no mirth in Leonid's eyes. "Not if I have to participate in primitive displays of gratitude. Or if I'm going to have to work here for at least another five years."

"But you'll have all the money you can spend on future expeditions," said Remi.

"I'll believe that when I see it."

"It's a done deal, my friend," Sam assured him.

"They'll probably cheat us on the valuation."

"I doubt it," Sam tried again.

"You watch."

Lazlo caught Remi's eye and shook his head. They both laughed as Sam sighed in frustration.

Leonid swatted at a mosquito, his expression as somber as a mortician's. "I'll probably catch malaria or some sort of weird jungle fever, before this is over, and spend all the money on air evacuation and hospitalization."

"Or enjoy treasure hunting from your own research vessel," Sam mused.

"More likely I'll be targeted by corporations and relatives, all with their hands out. Cousins I never knew existed. Lady friends I don't even remember."

They all watched the poker-faced Russian mentally construct a future where untold riches became an intolerable burden. Then his expression shifted and he looked at Remi, his mouth spreading into a rare grin. "Would you care to join me, Mrs. Fargo, in conducting a search into a passage we haven't entered yet?"

Remi searched Leonid's face for any sign of deviousness. Seeing none, she smiled. "Why me?"

"Your husband and the limey are too busy playing celebrities to get their hands dirty again. Besides, I prefer your company to theirs."

"Go ahead," said Sam with a chuckle. "Just scream and Lazlo, Chief Fleming, and I will come charging to the rescue."

Without another word, Leonid took Remi's hand and gallantly led her behind the waterfall and into the cave. Once inside, she followed about ten paces behind, until he stopped and shone his light on a massive vertical stone embedded into the cavern wall.

"Here it is," he announced. "I found an inscription on a rock that suggested another passage."

Remi swept her light around the stone. "I see nothing but a big rock."

"More than simply a large rock—it's a door," Leonid said confidently. He stepped forward, put his shoulder against one side, and dug his feet into the cavern floor.

Holding her light on Leonid, Remi frowned, "You're wasting your time. It's twenty feet tall and must weigh at least that many tons. . . ."

Her voice trailed off as the great stone made a grinding sound and began to move, twisting slowly as if it were hung on a vertical shaft like a revolving department store door.

Remi lent her weight to Leonid's and helped shove the stone until it shifted enough to permit a human body to slip past. They shined her flashlight into the darkness and Remi whispered, "It's a tunnel."

Leonid squeezed through and extended his hand to Remi to guide her through the narrow opening. "Easier for you," he said. "I'm fifty pounds heavier."

Remi's shoulders barely brushed against the rock wall and stone door as she slipped through the gap. She gave him a knowing look as her beam played across the stone floor. "How far have you explored the tunnel?"

"Not more than thirty yards. My flashlight was dying and I wasn't about to poke around in the dark."

Remi directed her light ahead into the darkness. At first she saw nothing but a hollow shaft leading into the gloom. Then she saw the walls of the tunnel glow a soft gray as though they were painted. She aimed her beam farther into the tunnel, expecting it to fade, but instead a glimmer of light flickered from far down the tunnel. It came and went in less than a second before disappearing again into nothingness.

"Leonid!" Remi blurted.

The Russian had been studying the faint carving of a serpent on the rock wall and had failed to see the distant light. "Yes, pretty lady, have you made an interesting find?"

Remi didn't immediately reply. Her gaze was still fixed on the blackness looming from the opposite end of the passageway. "I saw something . . . shimmering."

Leonid's tone was unconcerned, his attention still focused on the engraved stone in his hand. "Perhaps a reflection off a smooth rock from your light? Or maybe your imagination?"

Remi shook her head. "I'm sure it was real."

Leonid turned from his discovery and peered into the tunnel and then switched off his light. "All right, turn off your flashlight and see if your ghostly illumination is still there."

She switched off her light and the passageway was plunged into blackness. A minute went by and . . . nothing.

"Say what you want, I saw a gleam somewhere down the tunnel," Remi said in frustration. A feeling of dread slowly crept through her as the walls seemed to close in on her. She was feeling for the flashlight switch when a glimmer streaked faintly in the distance.

"There!" she cried out. "You must have seen it."

Leonid spoke as if in a trance. "I saw it."

"We've got to investigate," Remi urged.

Leonid stood frozen, his expression showing more bewilderment than fear. He flipped his flashlight back to life. "You wait here. I'll find Sam and return with more lights and muscle."

Remi did not argue. She sat down while Leonid swiftly passed out of the tunnel and ran through the cavern to the waterfall, anxiety and fear building with every step.

Sam and Lazlo finally managed to break away from the reporters. All the major news bureaus from Australia, Europe, Asia, and the United States were represented, as well as many smaller ones, bringing the total close to ninety. The reporters watched from beyond a hastily erected barricade as Chief Fleming's main force of forty policemen began loading the treasure into trucks for the trip to the central bank's main vault.

Sam and Lazlo stood to the side as the trucks pulled away over the rugged path leading to the main roadway. A cloudburst drizzled warm rain on them as the last vehicle disappeared around the bend, and Sam glanced at Lazlo with a tired smile.

"Looks as though Remi and I are finished here," Sam said quietly. "We can finally head home."

"I wish I could say the same, but there are too many inscriptions that need translation. I'll be here for bloody years."

Leonid burst from behind the waterfall, his face as white as a meadow after a snowfall. "Hurry! Come quick!" he gasped.

"Remi!" Sam cried. "Is Remi all right?"

Leonid nodded. "Yes, yes. She's fine. But we found something. We need floodlights and a generator—she's still in the cave, so there's no time to lose." The Russian didn't wait for a response and instead spun and raced back to the waterfall and ducked behind the endless stream of water.

Sam and Lazlo exchanged a puzzled look and then Sam moved to where the equipment was piled. "You heard the man. Grab some lights."

"What in blazes has gotten into his head?" Lazlo griped.

"We'll know soon enough," Sam said. "But Remi's still in there and Leonid's acting like it's an emergency. We'd better go find out what the fuss is about."

Sam and Lazlo rushed to join Leonid in the cavern, each carrying two Cascadia high-intensity discharge floodlights. Rob and Greg followed them through the waterfall with a portable generator. Once in the cave, they put all their might into forcing the rock door open another two feet so they could get the equipment into the passageway.

"Where's Remi?" Sam demanded.

Leonid scowled, perplexed. "I asked her to remain here until I returned. She must have gone on alone to investigate the mysterious light."

Sam fixed Leonid with murderous eyes. "Mysterious light? You never said anything about a light."

"At the far reaches of the tunnel, a glint shows itself every few minutes. I thought it was nothing . . ."

Sam turned to where Rob and Greg stood by the stone door. "We're going to see where this leads. Remi's somewhere in there and we're going to find her."

Sam led the way, beams from the hand lights swinging in arcs and probing through the blackness as they carried the equipment farther into the cave system.

Sam stopped after fifty paces and shouted Remi's name. His voice rebounded off the rock walls and returned as an echo. Hearing no response, he continued another fifty paces and repeated his cry, again with no answer. His flashlight was dimming but he pushed on, not wanting to wait for the others to catch up, his fear that something had gone horribly wrong for Remi growing with every step. After the sixth shout, Sam's voice cracked and he felt the beginning pangs of hoarseness. He cleared his throat and was about to call out again when he heard Remi's voice, faint, from deep in the earth.

"Sam? . . . Sam!"

"Remi!" Sam cried, abandoning caution as he began running through the gloom, his light now so faint that he could barely make out the tunnel's floor.

"Sam!" Remi's voice grew louder as he neared, but he still couldn't see her even though she now sounded as though he were practically on top of her. The empty tunnel stretched endlessly before him.

"I can't see your flashlight," he exclaimed in frustration.

"The batteries gave out," she said. "Shine yours on yourself."

Sam aimed the meager beam at his face and, before he knew it, Remi had her arms around his neck in a tight grip.

"About time you showed up," she said after a long kiss.

"Why didn't you wait at the entrance?" he asked. "Where Leonid left you?"

"I knew you'd be along eventually, so I went exploring."

Sam suppressed a grin and gave her a tight hug. "Please refrain from doing that ever again."

Leonid approached them and cleared his throat, the others behind him with the equipment. "I'm glad to see you're in one piece. Did you find anything interesting?" he asked.

Remi nodded. "Fifty feet beyond us, the tunnel becomes man-made, with a smooth bore and an arched ceiling. It seems to glow." She paused and looked at Sam. "That was all I could make out before my batteries died."

Sam stepped toward the Russian. "I'll trade with you, Leonid. Your light seems to still have some juice left."

Leonid nodded and handed his flashlight over. Sam probed the shaft with its beam and a bright reflection returned—a flickering glimmer.

"There's the answer to your mysterious light," said Leonid.

"It doesn't tell us how it manifests itself," Remi said. "But there's one way to find out." She snatched the flashlight from Sam and darted farther into the tunnel.

"Remi," Sam called, but she was already around a bend in the passage and out of sight. He exhaled in frustration and gave Leonid a dark look and then followed Remi deeper into the unknown.

The tunnel stretched downward in a gradual slope. Sam and Leonid followed Remi down the passage until the floor leveled and the walls' texture changed.

"She's right. It does look as if this part was worked by human hands," Sam said.

Leonid ran his hand over the surface as Lazlo's hurried footsteps sounded behind them. "It's almost like it was polished," the Russian whispered.

Lazlo joined them and squinted at the wall. "Quite remarkable," he murmured. "Never seen anything like it."

Remi's flashlight beam had faded into the darkness and they could no longer see its glow. Sam was about to go after her when she suddenly returned at a run, out of breath, the color drained from her face.

"What is it, Remi? What did you find?"

"Oh, Sam," she said, her voice tight. "The whole chamber is filled with dead people."

CHAPTER 55

Rob and Greg arranged the floodlights and set up the generator at the chamber entrance so they would have sufficient light to explore the interior. Lazlo and Sam helped with the connecting cables while Remi and Leonid held the dimming flashlights for them, the glow now barely sufficient to illuminate more than a few feet. When they'd gotten all the equipment into position, Sam stepped away from the generator and glanced around.

"Ready, boys?" asked Sam.

"Ready," Rob answered. "We've also set up a video camera to record whatever's in here."

"If anything," grunted Leonid.

Sam held up his hand. "Throw the switch."

The floodlights blinked to life, revealing a massive chamber with mirror-polished walls and ceiling, every surface as smooth as glass. The powerful beams refracted from the walls with startling intensity, blinding everyone as they magnified the glare tenfold. Sam shielded his eyes with his arm and the others did the same.

After several long moments, their vision began to adjust and they could make out that the entire chamber was a vast vein of white quartz. They stood in silent awe of the reflective effect, the cavern's faceted walls a natural house of mirrors.

Remi took a few cautious steps toward the nearest surface and gazed at it, her nose only inches away. "Gold," she said softly. "Gold specks and small nuggets within the quartz."

"She's right," acknowledged Leonid. "Gold-bearing quartz is per-haps the most unusual source of natural gold. It's mined in very few locations around the world. It's extremely rare and sought after for making jewelry."

Sam and Remi took a few cautious steps farther into the chamber. A large quartz bench ringed the center of the space, with nearly a hun-dred mummified bodies seated on it in a large circle. Each body leaned against an ornately carved backrest, the skin the color and consistency of leather.

The mummies' torsos were wrapped in what Remi and Leonid rec-ognized as linen. The skulls were bare and tilted slightly forward, with eye sockets staring sightlessly into a central vault set into the floor. It looked to Sam as though they had all died together. There was no sign of violence.

One by one, the group approached the open vault, recessed three feet below the floor, and silently peered down at the mummified couple inside.

Sam, in a whisper, was the first to react. "Good Lord, he's seventeen feet if he's an inch."

"The woman next to him is almost as tall," Remi responded.

Leonid muttered, "Giants—real giants. The legends are true."

"They were worshipped as gods," Remi murmured softly.

"Astonishing," said Lazlo. "They've been amazingly well preserved

by the dry atmosphere deep underground. And look—their facial features are Caucasian. See? Thin lips and narrow noses. Even their hair
and his beard are intact."

"Look at the tattoos on their faces," said Sam. "They're incredible.
Their forehead and cheeks have intricate designs in black and blue. I've
never seen anything quite like it."

The giants had been interred in full dress. The male figure's coat
was crafted from leather trimmed in fur, the lining and tartan pants
woven wool. The female's draped dress and scarf were a royal blue.
Both of their legs were encased in felt boots that came above the knees.

"How old do you think they are?" Leonid asked Sam.

"Two, maybe three thousand years? Just a wild guess. DNA would
give the best estimate."

"So how did they get on an island in the middle of the Pacific Ocean
thousands of years ago?" Remi asked.

"I'll leave that mystery to a qualified anthropologist," answered
Sam.

"Many of the mummies are women," observed Remi, glancing
around the macabre circle. "Their clothing is beautiful." She paused a
moment, eyeing the gold thread of the elaborate embroidery. "Sam,
their jewelry is so ornate. Gemstones, rubies, and emeralds, from the
look of it, all trimmed and inlaid with gold . . ."

Sam laughed. "In their day, precious and semiprecious stones and
gold were probably as common on the island as coal."

Remi stopped in front of another female mummy. Despite the desic-
cation, it was easy to tell she had once been strikingly beautiful. Remi
could only stare in amazement.

"So what do we know about these people?" asked Greg.

"Only what we see," Leonid gave his shoulders a slight shrug. "And
our eyes are the first to see them in thousands of years."

Sam turned his attention back to the giants in the central vault. The
huge man's red hair was long and braided on the sides, the beard was

broad, and the ends of his mustache twisted at the ends. Around the female's head was a gold crown encrusted with semiprecious stones. Unlike other ceremonial burials, the man lacked a spear or other weapons. Small wonder, Sam thought. What man could hope to fight a seventeen-foot-tall giant who probably weighed in excess of eight hundred pounds?

"The giants' immense size would have made it natural for them to be considered deities," Leonid said. "This would also explain the dead around them. They must have been royal nobles, advisers, close friends, wives, and concubines—all those who wished to stay with their gods for continued existence in another world."

They fell silent, staring at the mummies in the vault. Finally, Lazlo spoke in a hushed voice. "We have to keep this secret until the government can be relied upon to preserve, maintain, and build a world-class museum around the entire site."

"Well," said Remi, "with the discovery of the treasure, they now have the funds to tackle a project like that."

"What better place to keep them than right here at their original site?" added Leonid.

"Where they deserve to remain," Sam said in a low voice. "Not only have we discovered a great historic site here today but we've revealed a civilization that was never even suspected to exist. The legends are all true. Gold, gemstones, advanced civilizations . . . and giants."